EVOLUTION

Book One in #BeautyAndTheBell

E. B. Slayer

You are beautiful.

CONTENTS

Please Read

I care about your mental health. Please read Content Awareness before starting Sasha's journey.
eblsayer.com/content

Check my website for music playlist:
ebslayer.com/music/evolution

1. STRANDED

August 15, 2016

Sasha Williams stood at a deserted train station feeling grateful to be alive. She was in the middle of Switzerland surrounded by mountains because she needed to hide from her ex and hopefully restart her life. Maybe moving across the world to teach English was a bit overkill, but she was desperate to get out of Detroit and away from Jackson.

She took another deep breath to settle her nerves then looked at her useless phone. At least the air smelled fresh with a hint of sweetness. The Motor City would always be in her heart, but it had that city stank. Speaking of cities, she hadn't seen one since she left Geneva. Just small towns isolated by mountains splattered with huge green trees.

Her vision blurred from unwanted tears when she stared at the cracked device in her hand. In the rush to escape Detroit, her phone got crushed and half the screen was glitching. The latest email she had seen from the Glockenwald Board of Education stated that someone named Hilda Holte was supposed to pick her up two hours ago.

Sasha sniffed back her tears because she didn't want to ruin her makeup that was hiding a bruised cheek. Grabbing the handle on her heavy suitcase, she pushed from the yellow plastic chair and dragged her luggage toward the lone attendant who appeared to be closing shop. "Excuse me," she hesitated.

"No more trains," the attendant's Swiss accent was thick and exotic. She was busy locking away paperwork and hadn't even glanced at Sasha.

"I'm not waiting for a train. Someone was supposed to meet me here, a Hilda Holte."

The attendant squinted sky blue eyes accented by smoky black eye shadow when she peered at Sasha.

"Can you help me get a taxi?" Sasha asked. "My phone isn't working."

"No taxi. I've got better, ya."

Her heart stopped. The idea of being stranded in a small town in Switzerland constricted her throat.

The attendant slipped a piece of paper her way with perfectly shaped almond nails. "I have note for you."

Sasha snapped up the paper as if it were the holy grail. The note read: *No Hilda Holte for Sasha Williams. Find way to Glockenwald.* "Are you kidding me? I've been here for hours!"

The attendant shrugged.

"How can I get to Glockenwald? How much is a taxi? Can I rent a car? Is there a place for me to stay until tomorrow?" Sasha heard her voice gain an octave with each question. She felt the warning signs of an oncoming panic attack. She turned away from the attendant and took in her surroundings again while she tried to settle her nerves.

The train station was small with an elevated platform next to the tracks. There was an awning that shaded a handful of plastic yellow seats. There were two small buildings, one on each side of a turnstile entrance and exit. One building housed the attendant and a small bathroom. The other building was windowless with a single door. Then there was a small parking lot with a couple of spaces leading to the only road she could see. Past that there were snow covered mountains, green trees, blue sky, and holy fuck she was in trouble.

What was she doing here again? Her stomach twisted painfully, causing her to cross her arms.

"You don't want taxi. Too expensive," the attendant stressed again as if she were talking to a toddler.

The first tear fell. "A bus?" she asked. Her legs threatened to give so Sasha leaned against the wall next to the small window, her fingers digging into her sides. She needed to think and get her bearings. Panic wasn't going to help her.

"Last bus already left," the attendant answered.

She remembered the map she had downloaded on her busted phone. Even if the screen wasn't broken, she had tossed her old SIM card because she didn't want Jackson tracking her.

She heard the attendant talking on her cell. She couldn't understand Swiss German but she was certain she heard her name and Hilda's. Great, now she was probably the focus of local gossip.

The lights turned off in the ticket booth, and the attendant exited then locked the door behind her.

Sasha's heart dropped into her stomach. Not only was the only human she had seen in the last two hours about to leave her, it was getting dark with the sun setting behind the titanic mountains. She watched the older woman walk to the other building, unlock the door, and disappear inside. Panic took hold and Sasha's breathing quickened. This couldn't be happening. She held her phone up to the sky trying to follow the squiggly lines around the cracked glitches on the screen. Thanks to Jackson controlling her money, she had fled with pocket change. She doubted she had enough francs to buy much after she paid rent for her new place.

All that mattered was that she got away.

It took a minute for the attendant's voice to register through Sasha's panic. The woman was rolling what looked like a glorified bicycle out of the building.

"Vespa," the attendant said with a smile. "You take Vespa and I'll get tomorrow."

"I can't ride that thing," Sasha said in disbelief. She looked at her hefty luggage and down to her own thick thighs. "Can that even make it to Glockenwald?"

The attendant shook her head. "Ya, ya. A good ride. Very easy to get to Glocken-VALT."

Wincing at the way the woman corrected her bad Swiss German, Sasha nodded. She had her doubts about the yellow contraption, but she didn't have a choice. She had a great sense of direction. Granted she'd only ever relied on that sense of direction in Metro Detroit.

The attendant handed her a bright yellow helmet. "Safety," the woman said before she turned to lock up the small building.

Swallowing, Sasha stuffed her phone into her purse and squeezed the helmet over her tight coils. She had never been on a Vespa before. It looked like something out of a Saturday morning cartoon from the eighties. The Vespa had a place for her feet and she wondered if her luggage would fit between her thighs. The bright yellow Vespa visibly sagged under the weight after the two women lifted her luggage onto it. "Are you serious?" Sasha repeated to the attendant who smiled at her.

"Is good," the woman nodded eagerly and Sasha's face dropped in horror.

This was a nightmare. Life and the powers above were playing a cruel joke on her. First, she barely made it out of Detroit, and now this. She closed her mouth and clenched her jaw.

It would be completely dark soon. If she didn't leave now, she might as well sleep in the shed. Determined, she swung her leg over her suitcase. She realized she didn't know the attendant's name. "I'm Sasha," she said with a hand over her heart.

The woman smiled. "I'm Giselle. Good luck. Stay safety."

As if on cue, a bell jingled and a man huffing and puffing on a tandem bicycle rolled into the parking lot. He looked to be around Giselle's age with shocking red hair.

Giselle waved to the man and kissed his cheek. "This is husband, Marco," she introduced when they walked over.

Marco offered Sasha a handshake before studying the situation. "*Grüezi.* Should hurry, no?" he suggested with a smirk before he snapped a picture of her with his phone.

A smart retort almost slipped past her lips, but she didn't want to seem ungrateful. Giselle had to get home on a bicycle. Nodding, Sasha turned the key and nothing happened. Giselle flipped a switch, squeezed the brake then pressed the power button. The yellow contraption made a pathetic skittering sound. Giselle flipped another switch and the single headlight turned on. It wasn't that complicated, but Sasha was nervous. Rotate the handle to go and squeeze or put out a foot to stop. After a couple of revs, she shimmied her feet next to her suitcase and was puttering along the paved road, leaving the little train station and her sanity behind her.

2. BRIGHT & YELLOW

She had barely been on the road for five minutes before regret bloomed. Thankfully, there was only one way to go. Whenever she came to a fork, she followed the signs to Glockenwald.

After a half hour of forest, mountains, and fear, Sasha noticed there had been fewer signs of human existence. Every now and then she saw an obscure light in the distance, and at one point a car had passed her. But otherwise, she was alone on the deserted road. At this point, anything was better than being in Detroit.

The Vespa suddenly made a sickening crunch followed by a loud popping noise, and lurched. Frightened by the thwomping and bumping, Sasha gripped the brake. The sudden stop caused her body to keep going, and her stomach hit the handlebars.

The pain in her abdomen made it difficult to breathe, especially compounded with the panic that threatened to drown her. After turning off the engine, she dismounted from the Vespa and yanked the helmet off. Her luggage tipped over and would have busted open if not for the neon suitcase travel belt.

The front tire of the Vespa had a flat. Something

was caught in the rim and had shredded the sidewall of the tire. She wasn't going anywhere. She half rolled, half dragged the Vespa closer to the side of the road.

Tears burned her eyes. She was stranded in a foreign country with a busted Vespa. To make matters worse, she was on a curve. People wouldn't see her until they were about to pass her. And if they blinked, they might miss her altogether.

She pulled her phone out of her crossover bag and lifted the useless device up to the darkening sky. She could see stars. The sun had set and the sky was dark blue fading into a purple galaxy.

Her stomach was a bundle of knots. This was it. The headline would read: "Bones of a Black woman found in Switzerland holding a broken Samsung and straddling a yellow Vespa."

She turned on the hazard lights, grateful this thing had them, and lifted the seat to see if there were any spare parts.

The haunting sound of a woman's laughter caused her to look up. Sasha searched the dark trees but couldn't see anyone.

"Hello?" she called out and the wind answered her with a rumble.

The forest vibrated with a deep roar. The roaring echoed around her, making her heart beat against her ribs. She wondered if Switzerland had earthquakes.

A full minute passed before Sasha realized what she was hearing. That was a glorious engine.

Even though she couldn't see anyone, she started waving her hands. She had one chance to get this right. She looked at the Vespa, appreciating its bright yellow for the first time. If she could, she would've waved the glorified bicycle in the air.

It was dark enough she could see light filtering through the trees. Someone was definitely coming. She started jumping and even considered getting a shirt out of her luggage to wave. This felt like a life or death situation. Instead she waved the yellow helmet, hoping it would catch the light.

The vehicle passed her so fast she didn't even see it. She just saw blinding light, felt her bones rattle, and then saw darkness.

Fear hissed through her clenched teeth when she turned around to the rumble pulling away from her.

They didn't see her.

Whoever was on that motorcycle was riding so fast they probably didn't even register the yellow streak in the growing darkness.

Anxiety gripped her soul when she heard more eerie laughing echo around her. Her mind went blank, fear tightening her throat. All she could hear was the rush of blood pumping through her ears. She turned to see if another car was coming, but only saw a terrifying abyss.

Through her panic, she realized she could still hear the rumble.

She turned and saw light through the trees coming toward her. She jumped and waved again as the growling grew louder.

"Help," she croaked past her anxiety. She cleared her throat and tried to scream again, "Help!" This time her voice had strength. "Help!" She jumped and waved her arms when the motorcycle approached at a more humane speed.

She lifted her hand to her face when the single

headlight blinded her. She could see the rider put out the kickstand before turning off the engine.

"Thank you," she called out into the sudden silence. She squinted to see past the light because the rider was just sitting there staring at her. Clearing her throat, she tried again, "Hello? Thank you for stopping."

After another beat, a large form disembarked and pulled off his helmet.

"Are you okay?" His voice was thick with an accent. After being subjected to the loud rumble of the motorcycle, her ears had issues hearing his baritone.

"I have a flat," she gestured toward the yellow vehicle of death.

"Ah. I barely saw you," he explained when he approached, pulling off his gloves.

Sasha's voice was gone. This man was a beast in his black leather jacket and blue jeans. He was about six feet of muscle, dwarfing her five feet-three-inch curvy frame. He had a full beard that reached his collar, the thick hair was the color of aged bourbon. It was too dark to discern the color of his eyes but she figured they were the typical blue for this region. She could see his high cheekbones and the cut of his jaw with the headlight filtering through his whiskers.

Sasha swallowed. She chastised herself for trying to smooth her frizzy edges. Even though she was an equal-opportunity lover and didn't care about ethnicity, she wasn't in Switzerland for entanglements. She was there to hide.

"Get it together, Sasha," she muttered to herself.

"Get what together?" He crouched to look at the tire.

"Thank you for stopping. Can you call a taxi?" she

asked.

"No taxi," he shook his head.

What was wrong with this place?

"I need one," she stressed.

He stood to face her and she found herself stepping back when she looked up at him. Now that he faced his motorcycle, she could see a crook in his nose. His beard looked even wilder. Was he a gorgeous lumberjack? She swallowed her drool.

His eyes were wide as if he were looking at a ghost while he stared at her; his golden brown irises were mesmerizing. Then his eyes narrowed and he shook his head. "No taxi," he repeated. "Where are you going?"

"To Glockenwald. I don't mind waiting for a taxi." She gestured behind him. "Should be just down the road."

"I know it. I can take you," he said then proceeded to remove the key from the Vespa.

"Oh, no," she gestured to her luggage. "I don't mind waiting."

He looked at her confused. "I said no taxi," he stressed as if she were a child. His arms went up and he gestured around them. "There are wolves out here. I can't leave you."

As if the wolf was waiting to be introduced, a howl echoed through the forest. She darted a glance over her shoulder and the air left her lungs.

"And," his voice was closer to her.

Sasha's head whipped around. Had she taken a step toward him? She could feel the heat radiating from his wide, leather clad chest. She swallowed her fear when she looked up. "And?"

She flinched when a rough thumb rubbed her

cheek.

His touch was electrifying. "You've been crying," he stated, his voice a soft whisper.

Reality hurtled her common sense back to earth and she jerked herself away, tripping where the pavement met tangled nature. She wiped at her face, embarrassed. "I've had a rough day." She'd had a rough life. But he didn't need to know. "Why can't you call me a taxi? I have luggage."

He lifted her luggage as if it weighed half a pound and closed the clasps that had busted open. He placed the heavy-duty bag on the wild grass and then lifted the Vespa with a grunt.

Her jaw unhinged in utter shock.

Must be a lumberjack.

He moved the Vespa off the road, then placed her luggage behind it.

Scoffing at his audacity, she became desperate. "I can't leave that." She struggled to drag her bag to the road. "I don't mind waiting for—"

"There is no fucking taxi," he grabbed her bag and replaced it. "Listen, no taxi out here. Do you understand me?" His handsome face was contorted with confusion.

Her heart dropped. "Yes, you don't have to be rude. I'm sorry. I just...." she looked around them. The sky was almost pitch black because of the new moon. "This is all I have." She swallowed her pride. "If I lose this, all I have are the clothes on my back." She twisted her hands in front of her, trying to hold back the tears she had been avoiding for the past three years. Now was not the time.

He stared at her in silence. Then he sighed and his hands went out in a shrug, "I will come back tonight and get your bag. After I take you to Glockenvalt."

She breathed a sigh of relief. "Okay, thank you."

He gestured towards the motorcycle. "Let's go. It's cold."

"Okay." She wasn't going to argue. She had no one else. This bearded stranger on a motorcycle in the middle of nowhere Switzerland was her only chance to survive the wolves. "I'm Sasha," she extended a shaking hand.

He had already turned away from her and was walking to his motorcycle. "Have you been on a motorcycle before?" he asked when he handed her the yellow helmet.

She pointed to the Vespa. "Does that count?"

A genuine chuckle rumbled through his massive chest. "*Nai.*"

They both put on helmets and she secured her purse over her shoulder. She had never been on a motorcycle before. They were never on her radar and frankly, she was afraid of them.

He straddled the motorcycle and then held out his hand to help her climb behind him on the rear seat. His palm was warm and rough against her fingers.

"All you have to do is hold on to me," he explained in his lyrical English.

"Um, okay." She wasn't ready for that.

"Never put your leg or foot on the chrome," he pointed to a long, chrome exhaust pipe. "It will burn you."

"Got it," she said through clenched teeth. She was still wrapping her head around a stranger being between her thighs. Why did he feel so good? What the fuck was she doing? She was trusting this man blindly because it was either him or the wolves.

"Are you cold?"

His question caught her off guard. She stared at the back of his leather jacket. "I'm alright." She had on a long sleeved shirt and jeans. She hadn't expected the weather to be so cool in August.

"You're shivering," a warm hand grabbed her thigh. He might as well have branded her.

She flinched in response and he removed his massive hand.

"I'm sorry. I can feel your body shake."

The adrenaline had worn off. She was trembling. "I am cold," she admitted.

"Do you have a coat in your luggage?" He turned to look over his shoulder at her, his eyes searching hers.

She didn't have many clothes in there. She shook her head no.

He shrugged out of his leather jacket to reveal a dark, long sleeved flannel button down that had to be a size too small. This man probably didn't have an ounce of fat on him. Every movement he made, no matter how minuscule, caused his muscles to flex and impress.

She hated that her panties were impressed.

Confused by her lust, she put her arms into his coat. His aroma whooshed into her face when she zipped up. Pine, sandalwood and vanilla caused her eyes to roll. Even though she was thick and curvaceous, she had plenty of wiggle room in the supple leather.

She opened her eyes to see that he was watching her again. When had she closed her eyes?

"Ready?" he asked. He pulled on his gloves.

She nodded.

"Just hold on and lean with me into curves," he

insisted.

She nodded again feeling like a bobblehead. He righted the motorcycle, flipped a switch and the beast roared, prompting her to grab onto his hard rippled middle for dear life.

She felt his hand pat hers twice and then they were off.

_ᴧᴧ_

Why were motorcycles only for men? It was basically a powerful vibrator between her legs. Due to the thrumming, his heat, his scent, and the emotionally charged day, Sasha orgasmed.

She really didn't have a choice. What was she supposed to do? Ask him to pull over because everything felt too good?

Her thighs clenched and a groan escaped her lips. She hoped the roar was louder than her. This was embarrassing. And intimate.

There was something about the constant oscillations and the lumberjack. Well, she was assuming he was a lumberjack. She didn't even know this man's name, but her tits were pressed against his warm back, he was between her thighs, and she needed a stress reliever.

Before she was even able to finish coming down, a second orgasm ripped through her. This one was definitely louder than the previous and she couldn't control her body. With her head against his back, her fingers digging into his abs, her thighs clenched him again. And did she just dry hump him?

Through the blissful fog, she became aware that a

gloved hand was squeezing her knee.

He was probably trying to see if she was okay.

But when he slowed down, the lowered rumble of the engine deepened the vibrations and a third climax slashed through her. With her head thrown back, she yanked on fistfuls of his shirt, her groan echoing around them. She was sure he and the wolves within five miles heard that one.

He grabbed her knee again and pulled her closer to him. Her body was still acting of its own accord, squeezing him while tremors undulated through her core. His gloved hand trailed from her knee to her thigh and she almost lost her mind again because her nerves had short circuited from his caress.

The lumberjack knew she was orgasming.

His back was straighter than before and she was thankful to have the support. His hand left her thigh and rubbed her right hand which was still digging into his stomach because she was afraid she'd fall. When she started to come down from the earth shattering bliss, he squeezed her thigh gently before he patted her hand twice. "Don't let go!" he shouted.

Sasha gave a weak nod against his back. These orgasms were exhausting her after the day she had.

She wanted to berate herself. She just juiced this man's motorcycle. The horror of him acknowledging her orgasm through the leg caress was palpable. If she was honest with herself, wolves weren't the worst way to die. At least she had three amazing orgasms before her untimely end. She could see the headline now: "Woman jumped off motorcycle after third orgasm. Fed herself to wolves." She was fine with that.

Darkness enveloped them. Sasha was grateful he

happened upon her because she couldn't imagine riding a Vespa through this. Since the motorcycle was much faster, they reached the village within half an hour.

Glockenwald was nestled in a small valley between titanic snow capped mountains. All she could see was the vast blackness dotted with stars. Lights spotted the valley, but it was too dark to really appreciate her new home. Which was for the best, she was already emotionally drained.

He slowed before pulling up to a single gas pump.

Sasha missed his massive back once he got off to get gas. She barely had the energy to hold herself up.

While he filled the tank, he nodded to her. "Where to? We're here."

She swallowed, trying to avoid his eyes and looking in his general direction. She was grateful he hadn't mentioned her multiple indiscretions. "I'm the new English teacher. I was supposed to be picked up by Hilda Holte, who was supposed to get me situated."

"Ah, Hilda. I know her. Hold on." He finished pumping and pulled out a cell phone from a leather bag next to her thigh.

Sasha noted that he was careful not to touch her. He swiped a few times before putting his phone to his ear. "Hilda?" He spoke in Swiss German that she couldn't follow.

How many more times was she going to second guess why she ran to the Swiss Alps. She didn't know the language, she wasn't adventurous. This was just her way of escaping.

Surviving.

He handed her his phone and she placed it to her ear. "Hello?"

"Sasha!" a thick-accented female voice exclaimed "I try to reach you all day. I'm glad you are alright. I'll meet you soon, okay?"

"Oh, okay," she just didn't have the energy for a full conversation. She ended the call. While the lumberjack pulled on his gloves, Sasha touched his arm. "I'm sorry," she found herself saying.

When his eyes met hers, there was a moment where they both just stared before confusion was written all over his face. "What?" he asked.

"I don't even know your name."

"Ah, I'm Rickart. In English you say Richard. But a C-H in German is a hard K sound, and D sounds like T."

She stared at him with wide eyes. Her body was still vibrating and his name sounded hot.

"Just call me Ricky," he insisted after her prolonged silence.

She held out her hand. "Nice to meet you, Ricky. I'm Sasha, and thank you for helping me."

He stared at her for a hot minute before giving her hand a single curt shake.

Humiliation tightened her chest. Sasha was positive that he was thinking of her orgasms and didn't even want to touch her. He mounted in front of her and started his motorcycle.

She tried to scoot away from his back when they rumbled away from the gas pump and down a dark country road.

Not even thirty seconds later, they stopped in front of a small, single-story duplex next to a field of darkness.

Ricky turned off the engine and they were bathed in starlight and an eerie glow from a neighbor's porch light. Ricky got off and held out a hand to help her. Even though the engine was off, her legs and core still quivered. Her shoes touched the ground and her knees would have followed if gloved hands hadn't caught her.

"I'm sorry," she moaned, the inky abyss around them twisting and turning.

"Are you okay?" Ricky asked her.

"I'm exhausted," she mumbled. It had been twenty-four hours since she last ate anything. She was dehydrated and starving.

A door opened behind them. "Sasha!" a woman called.

Ricky responded in Swiss German.

A tall, blond woman in her sixties approached them. "I'm Hilda. I'm sorry I didn't get you. I had a family emergency."

Sasha was surprised by the long, firm hug. She was sure she smelled ripe after traveling for almost three days. She licked her dry lips and tried to hug back.

"Oh, you're shaking," Hilda held her at arms length, her blue eyes searching Sasha's face in the low light. "Let's get you inside."

With Ricky's help, she followed Hilda to the apartment with a wooden number three below the porch light. The door was unlocked and they entered a small, outdated space. There was an efficiency kitchen to the left with a compact fridge, a three-burner stove, and a table for two. A contraption that looked like a fat-bellied goblin was in the corner. Straight ahead there were three doors and to the right was a small living room with a couch, a coffee table, and an armchair.

Sasha headed for the couch, thankful to be on

something without wheels or vibration. "Thank you."

Ricky spoke with Hilda as they stepped outside, leaving her alone.

This was it. This was her life now in this small apartment in Switzerland where no one knew her and she could hide.

The door to the apartment opened and Hilda entered alone. "Ricky will go get your things."

Sasha opened her eyes. She was exhausted and surprised that she was horizontal. "Okay."

There was noise in the kitchen before Hilda placed a cup of liquid on the coffee table. "Drink this. Relax and sleep. I'll lock up and bring breakfast tomorrow, ya?"

Sasha pushed herself into a sitting position and drank the sweet liquor in one gulp. Then she allowed Hilda to lead her to the bed where she fell asleep, wrapped inside the leather jacket.

3. THE SANDWICH

August 16

C hoking on a scream, Sasha opened her eyes the next morning. With her heart pounding, she stared at the unfamiliar cream wall with a wooden dresser and silver lamp on top. Bright sunlight filtered through a window to the left of the dresser where her suitcase was located.

Last night came rushing back when she heard laughter and a familiar baritone.

Sasha sat up so fast her head throbbed. Not only was she in Switzerland, she was still drowning in a delicious smelling leather jacket which she ripped off and threw to the floor as if it were filled with snakes. After more laughter exploded through the thin walls, she stomped on the soft leather once out of spite and to make sure that last night stayed dead.

She was positive he was telling everyone how she creamed his motorcycle. And what were they doing in her apartment?

She couldn't even swallow, she was so upset. She picked up the leather she killed and crossed the tiny

22 E. B. SLAYER

bedroom and yanked the door open.

In the small living room, Hilda and Ricky were wiping tears from their faces as they cackled around their Swiss German words. They didn't even notice her because they were doubled over laughing so hard.

Sasha's stomach clenched. She hadn't even been there for twenty-four hours and was already the laughing stock of the town.

This was her life.

She cleared her throat to give herself something to do. Both of them sat upright and looked in her direction.

"Ooooh," Hilda crossed the tiny room. "Sasha, did we wake you? Sorry. Ricky is funny." Smiling and chuckling, the woman wrapped her arms around her in a greeting Sasha didn't want. "I came back to check on you. How are you feeling?" Hilda asked, her blue eyes roaming Sasha's tear stained face.

"Fine." Sasha forced herself to swallow. "What's so funny?"

"Oh, it's nothing, just memories." Hilda waved the air when she went towards the kitchen table and grabbed her purse. "There's food in the fridge. I need to go to the office, but tonight is your welcome party. So I'll be back to pick you up before five. Everyone is excited to meet the new English teacher."

Before Sasha could say two words Hilda was out the door.

Looking down at her feet, Sasha thrusted the jacket towards Ricky. "Thanks again for yesterday."

"No problem," he took his jacket and stood to his full height. "I'm glad you're okay." He was wearing a cream-colored long-sleeve jersey shirt that made his skin appear tan. His beard was dark and combed.

Yawning, he raised his arms as he stretched, his shirt lifting to reveal soft, dark hair over a taut stomach framed by a red and white plaid waistband, and dark blue jeans.

Sasha gulped when she imagined running her fingers over those bumpy abs.

He stopped mid-stretch and glanced at her.

Was her gulp that loud?

He pulled down his shirt and folded his jacket over his arm. "I should go. I'm sure you want to be alone."

She reached out a hand but didn't touch him. "Wait, can we talk about something first?"

He hesitated, "About?"

She twisted her hands as she battled her nerves. She wasn't sure where to look. But she had to stand up for herself. She was tired of letting people walk all over her and use her for their entertainment. She gazed into his whiskey eyes, determined. She balled her fists at her thighs before crossing her arms. "Last night."

He arched a bourbon eyebrow. "Ya?"

"Could you—will you please not tell everyone wha —what happened between us?" She gestured between them, her hand shaking with nerves.

He folded his arms across his chest, his muscles flexing. "I don't understand."

"Look, I'm sorry, okay. I couldn't control it. My first time on a motorcycle and I didn't know that would happen."

"You got here, okay, *nai?*" His eyes roamed her body as if looking for an injury.

"I'm talking about the orgasms."

He gasped, his nostrils flared, and his face flushed a deep pink. "Ah, that."

Sasha swallowed. She knew if she stopped now she wouldn't get to the root of her worries. "I just don't want people laughing at me. Can you keep that between us?"

His eyes widened. "Laugh at you? That was sexy, no?" His tongue flitted across his bottom lip.

She sighed before she could stop herself. What the fuck was wrong with her? After her ex Jackson, she had sworn off men for a while. She wanted to avoid them at all costs. But this man was already testing her resolve. "Yes. It was hot, but that's not the point. I don't want people to know. I don't want Hilda laughing at me."

His eyes lit with understanding. "I didn't tell Hilda. I didn't tell anyone. I won't."

The tension in her shoulders released with a sigh. "Oh, thank god. I was sure you were both laughing at me." Her legs started to shake so she hobbled over to the dark leather couch where she sat and leaned her head back.

"Are you okay?" his baritone reminded her of last night.

She released a deep breath. "No, I'm not okay. I haven't eaten in a while. I need to shower. I'm still exhausted."

She heard his coat fall next to her. "Go shower. I'll make you a sandwich and coffee."

"I don't drink coffee. But a sandwich would be amazing."

"Tea?"

"Water is fine." She lifted her head to see him in her kitchen. His size made her three-burner stove comical. Was everything going to seem small around him? Her eyes followed the slope of his shoulders into the V of his hips and the dark jeans over a tight ass. She may have sworn off men, but she decided looking was okay.

She stood and excused herself to her room. She closed the door behind her. There was something about him that made her ache with an unfamiliar desire. The mere idea of him in the next room sent heat straight to her happy place. But there was fear too. He was still a man and all of the men in her life had hurt her. She rushed to her suitcase and pulled off the straps and snapped it open. Items were tousled but nothing was missing.

Since Hilda mentioned a welcome party, Sasha pulled out black slacks and her only nice top, which was soft and pink cashmere sweater.

The bathroom was small and efficient like the kitchen. They had provided a set of towels and some soap and shampoo. She was grateful to be able to take a hot shower after almost 36 hours of running for her life.

After her shower and brushing her tight curls into a controlled Afro bun, she quietly opened the bathroom door a crack and tried to see where he was. With her apartment being so small, she couldn't hide. After poking her head out the door, she saw him sitting at the table with his back to her bedroom. "Your sandwich is done," he called over his shoulder.

"Thanks, I'll be right out." She made record time with her cocoa butter and a dab of pheromones. She used makeup to hide the ugly bruise on her cheek, then rubbed vaseline on her lips before she entered her tiny living room feeling refreshed and starving.

She walked past him to the other side of the table. "I appreciate this."

He nodded and inhaled a deep breath. "No

problem," he tapped his fingers on the table.

"Did you make one for yourself?" She lifted the multigrain bread to see mustard, lettuce, tomato, and thick slices of white meat. "Chicken?"

"Turkey. I ate before." He dragged in another deep breath and crossed his arms. He studied her with curious whiskey eyes.

She smiled. "Ah. This looks delicious." She shoved the sandwich into her mouth and took a generous bite. She was too hungry to be ladylike and shit. "Mmmm," she groaned when the flavors danced across her parched tongue. The spicy mustard was perfect and the juicy tomato was savory. She closed her eyes and chewed. "Mmmm," she swallowed enough to talk behind her hand. "Ricky this is amazing," she smiled and looked at him but he seemed uncomfortable.

She put her sandwich down, alarmed and drank some water. She patted her mouth with a napkin to make sure she didn't have juices on her chin. "What's wrong?"

"It's just a sandwich," he said with a breathless voice, his eyes darting to her lips.

She was shocked into silence. This wasn't the first time he seemed to think something was wrong with her. Was he uncomfortable because she was a Black woman?

"You know what, I have a feeling I'm keeping you. I appreciate you getting my luggage and making me this sandwich though."

She retrieved his jacket from the couch and handed the soft leather to him.

"Right," he stood and accepted his jacket. "Take care." He filled her doorway and bright sunlight filtered

EVOLUTION 27

around him. She could see his shiny black motorcycle outside. It was an impressive machine with chrome and vibrations. She crossed her arms to hide her taut nipples.

She watched when he shrugged on his jacket in one smooth movement, then put on his helmet. When his bike roared to life she was reminded of last night. He saluted her and she waved before he rumbled up the hill towards Main Street. She closed and locked the door. She could still smell him.

4. INTRICATE

When Sasha sat at her small kitchen table, she was able to take in her new life. The apartment was small, but it was enough. She was thankful she had an actual bedroom and not a studio. The floor was dark wood with a beige area rug under the oval wooden coffee table. The mahogany brown leather loveseat was against the cream wall. Past the couch was a small sliding door that led onto a small stone porch. She could see a green field with some planted crop she couldn't identify. Past that was a breathtaking view of snow-capped mountains and deep blue sky.

Next to the couch was a small side table with a lamp. Across from the couch was a wooden armchair with cream leather cushions. There wasn't a TV or any wall decorations. She already had ideas for adding her own touch.

After she devoured the made-by-lumberjack sandwich, she went to her room to unpack her old life.

A month ago she was squinting at her phone through a swollen eye when she applied for this job. She had nothing to lose. She filled out the application, sent her resume with a long email almost begging for the opportunity. It was her last lifeline. When they sent a reply for a voice call, she locked herself in her bathroom while Jackson slept off his booze-induced rage.

With her earbuds in, she interviewed with a man named Eric who asked her how soon she could be there. She said if he was paying, she would leave the next day. He laughed. She wasn't joking.

The next day, Eric emailed an offer and she secretly packed what she could fit into a single suitcase and made arrangements to leave Jackson in order to survive. So here she was in a small one-bedroom apartment in Switzerland, unpacking all that she owned and rejoicing.

There was a knock on her front door that brought her out of her reverie.

"Giselle?"

"Yes, Sasha, hello." Giselle smiled with sparkling blue eyes, crinkled from a life full of laughter. Giselle was wearing dark fitted jeans with hiking boots and a pink plaid shirt. Was plaid all the rave here? "I see you made it home!" Giselle surprised her with a hug. "I just saw Hilda," she pointed a thumb behind her.

Sasha looked up the hill and saw an impressive stone building. "I did, thank you. I'm sorry about your tire."

Giselle looked to her right and Sasha stepped out to see the yellow death machine parked next to the stone wall of her apartment. "It looks alright, no?" Giselle asked.

The tire had been replaced. "Oh, yeah. Thanks again for lending it to me."

"No problem. I'll see you tonight, ya?" The key was in the ignition so Giselle used it to unlock the seat and take out the yellow helmet which she pulled over her blond hair.

"Tonight?" Sasha asked.

"Ya, at velcome party, ya? My husband come, too."

"Oh, right. Be careful on that thing." Sasha wondered if it was really mountain worthy. There should be laws against riding those glorified bicycles.

Giselle tapped her helmet with her manicured nails and smiled, "Safety." She turned the key, pushed the button and puttered up the hill to the paved road. Sasha hoped she would never have to ride that thing again. In fact, she was going to stick to four-wheeled vehicles from now on.

After unpacking a couple of hours later, Sasha stood next to her sliding door wondering if she would wake up from this dream.

From her window she could see part of the main road, the end of a row of houses and apartments which led into an expansive valley of green farms framed by mountains. Climbing up the mountain was a ski lift that looked like a zipper against the green and white landscape. This was so different from Detroit. Even though Michigan had beautiful scenery and nature, there weren't mountains like these. They were majestic.

A knock on her door ripped her away and she went to answer. Hilda stood there with a smile on her thin pink lips. Her blue eyes twinkled before she pulled Sasha into a hug and invited herself in. Her straight blond hair was cropped at her chin showing off her long, elegant neck.

She preferred Ricky's dark hair and whiskey eyes. Her insides coiled when she thought of him and she pushed the thoughts away when Hilda dropped a stack of papers on the small table.

"I hope you feel rested," Hilda said when she gestured to the seat across from her and sat down. "I am sorry about yesterday," she shook her head with a frown. "But you made it safely." She opened a thick folder. "Before the party, we have paperwork." She started signing and handing paper after paper to Sasha. The legalese required mental strength. "Do I have to sign all of this now?" Sasha asked.

"Of course. You want to get paid, no?"

Sasha learned the hard way to read everything she signed. She was still paying off debt Jackson acquired in her name. She stared at the one inch stack and felt her stamina drain from her. After thirty minutes of Sasha signing her life away, Hilda finally closed the folder. "Welcome to Glockenvalt Board of Education. I am so happy to have you here with us, Sasha."

"Thanks. I'm excited to be here." Relieved was more like it. Even with the nightmare, last night was the first night in years she had slept with both eyes closed.

Hilda packed the paperwork and then checked her silver watch with a diamond studded face. Sasha didn't know people still wore actual watches. "We're late for the party," Hilda commented. "Are you ready to go?"

"Give me five," Sasha rushed to the bathroom and checked her natural hair and makeup. She applied more Vaseline to her lips, then shimmied into her flats and grabbed her crossover purse.

The air was crisp for August. Maybe Sasha should have packed heavier clothes. She packed business casual with the intent to shop once she got situated. But when she observed people walking around and waving, she realized they may not have anything in her size. These people were poles: tall and slim. Her double Ds and curves wouldn't fit in much that they offered here.

Hilda pointed around them naming the local sights. Glockenwald was a small town with two paved roads and a couple of dirt side roads. Her apartment was a five minute walk uphill to Main Street where there was the impressive two-story town hall. Hilda also pointed out the library, the steepled church, the school where she would work, the only café, the general store, and a few more small shops. There was a small inn next to town hall and a lodge across the valley that opened for the ski season.

One of the paved roads sloped up the side of the mountain and disappeared around a bend. Her apartment was near the outer edge of the small town where the valley sprawled out dotted with tiny farms. There were mountains all around them which made for picturesque views no matter which way she looked. She could see four different ski lifts, one in each direction. One was right behind the town hall. She liked being nestled in the mountains. They made her feel safer.

The town hall was a stone building framed by two stone pillars. It reminded her of an impressive giant mansion you would see in the middle of the woods. Walking in, there were two wooden staircases, one to the left and one to the right, that went up to the second floor. The first floor looked like a massive cabin with horizontal-log walls and wood flooring. There were desks arranged behind a dark granite service counter with one of those annoying handbells.

They headed upstairs where voices and music could be heard. When they reached the top of the stairs, a sea of various shades of blond heads and blue and green eyes turned to face them at once.

Voices and glasses raised with a smattering of 'Heys' that ricocheted off the log walls.

Hilda said something in Swiss German and a unified, "Velcome, Sasha!" rang in her ears.

Gulping, Sasha smiled and uttered, "Thanks."

She didn't do well in crowds. There was so much noise she wasn't sure if even Hilda heard her. Hilda entwined her thin arm with Sasha's and led her around the room.

She met her final interviewer Eric, who happened to be the mayor. In person he was a tall man with steel eyes and stark white hair that reminded her of Ted Danson. As she made her way around the room, food and drink were shoved into her hands which she graciously accepted. The drink turned out to be champagne and she gulped the liquid courage. After the flute was empty, someone replaced it before she could even consider if she wanted a fresh one.

With Hilda at her side, they made rounds. So many faces and names, she could never hope to remember them. By the time she was on a third glass, a rumble vibrated through the open door downstairs and the voices dropped in unison. She could hear a few muttered 'Ricky's' and many eyes flicked toward her while people whispered behind their hands.

She could feel the vibrations in her core and quickly downed her third glass. There wasn't enough alcohol in all of Europe to settle her nerves.

Within moments Ricky climbed to the top of the stairs and entered the large room. He had changed to a stark white dress shirt, under his black leather jacket with dark blue jeans. Everyone raised their glasses and called his name when he smiled and started greeting people.

Who was Ricky? She assumed he was a lumberjack. It was a silly assumption, but it fit her fantasy. Not that she needed a fantasy right now. The way he made rounds and greeted others made him look like a local celebrity. People were even taking pictures with him.

She tried to keep her gaze on her drink, but he was like a magnet and her eyes kept darting to him. His voice was a deep undercurrent in the crowded room, her ears picking up his location no matter where he stood. A couple of times he even nodded at her with a hesitant turn of his lips which was either a grimace or a failed attempt to smile.

With her fourth magical glass of champagne, Sasha allowed herself to be guided around the room from group to group. Even though it became clear she was the only chocolate drop in the rural town, they were nice enough that she didn't feel like an exhibit.

She wasn't sure how long Hilda had dragged her around, but Sasha was jet lagged and tipsy. People were dancing a type of jig to music she couldn't identify. She stood off to the side and watched, missing the club scene in Detroit where people could catch the beat.

She felt the electricity of him when he approached her.

"Do you need more drink?" His baritone cut through the noise.

She turned to face him, looking up since he towered over her. "I'm okay, thanks." She attempted to smile but it faltered when she remembered that afternoon. He may have helped her, but he obviously couldn't stand her. This was a public hello so everyone could witness him greet the foreigner. She placed her empty glass on the table near them.

His smile faltered too, but he forced on. "How do you like Glockenvalt?"

She pasted on a fake smile she gave creepers. "I haven't seen much, but it's alright."

"Rural compared to America, ya?"

She swallowed when she got a whiff of him. Why did he smell so good? Who the hell smells like vanilla and sandalwood? "Um, no. America is mostly empty countryside." She broke eye contact and her gaze traveled down his chest and settled on his shiny belt buckle. Was that a wolf? The long canines caught the light. In her drunken stupor she squinted and leaned forward to examine the intricate engraving.

"Is something wrong with my crotch?" his voice was a whisper between them.

Her eyes snapped up, wide with embarrassment. She covered her mouth in horror and glanced around them. Sure enough, a couple of people were whispering behind their hands and holding up their phones.

"I'm sorry," she hugged herself before she looked up into his whiskey eyes. "I was looking at your belt buckle. Is that a wolf?"

Ricky's expression was a mix of emotions she couldn't decipher. "Ya." He visibly hesitated. "Did you —" his voice lowered, his accent thicker, "—vant a closer look?"

Sasha took a step back, "No." Hands up in surrender, she said, "It just looked intricate. I'm sorry. This is embarrassing." She folded her arms again. She felt tipsy and tired. She had to get away from him before she completely unraveled.

Hilda had stepped to the side to give them privacy so Sasha approached her. "I think I'm going to go home."

"Already?" Hilda checked her diamond-encrusted watch.

"Jet lag." It was the only excuse that didn't require any explanation.

"Ah, of course. Let me walk you." Hilda placed her glass down on a side table near a window.

"No, that's okay. I can find my way back," Sasha insisted before she stepped towards the stairs.

Hilda stopped her, her bright blue eyes laced with concern. "Are you sure?"

"Absolutely, it's just down the hill, number three." She hugged Hilda since that seemed to be the custom here. She thanked people near her and side-stepped Ricky who happened to be close enough to cause goosebumps. It was time she made her quick exit.

She took the steps too fast, tripping and stumbling down half of them in her haste and drunkenness. Thankfully no one witnessed her embarrassment. When she got outside, the dark night and fresh air embraced her. She exhaled in relief and took several deep breaths, allowing the anxiety to melt away. She really did not like crowds, especially in tight spaces. The road that led down the hill was right in front of her, but parked directly under the single street light was Ricky's motorcycle.

Without her permission, her feet took her to the shimmering chrome like a moth to a flame. Her hand also rebelled and touched the soft leather seat. It was a beautiful piece of machinery: soft shiny curves and bright chrome accents. It was sexy as hell. Although she would never ride one again, she had a new appreciation for Harleys.

"Did you want a ride?"

Her breath caught when she turned around, feeling guilty.

Ricky stood near the street light, his eyes twinkling. He had swagger and confidence in the way he leaned against the lamp post.

She folded her arms when a breeze blew through her sweater. "You caught me," she attempted to smile. "I was just looking. Remembering," she admitted.

His eyes smoldered and his jaw clenched causing his beard to twitch. "Oh?"

Her heart lurched. "I should go. Have a good night." She turned and almost walked into his motorcycle. She skirted the vibrating chrome and walked towards her apartment with brisk steps.

"I'll walk you," he caught up, his scent enveloping her.

"You don't have to. I'll find my way." She attempted to walk faster.

His long stride caught up to hers with little effort. His leather boots crunching on the road while he walked beside her. "I want to. Safety."

Years of growing up in a society that supported rape culture had bred her to fear his intentions. This couldn't end well. Yes, he had been nice to her the day before, he had even saved her. But did that mean he expected something? Who else knew he was walking her home? She had been a victim too many times before and her hackles began to rise. But she wasn't going to argue. He was a large man and could lift her like that damned Vespa.

They walked in silence while she stewed on exit

strategies.

The short walk ended at her door. He stood a few feet behind her, hands stuffed into his pockets.

She was relieved he kept his distance. "Thanks for walking me home."

"Anytime. Have a good night." He waited.

She waited.

She realized he was waiting for her to go inside. She fished into her purse and pulled out her key. Once her door was open and she was inside, he saluted her before walking back toward town hall. She closed and locked her door, her heart pounding. But not because she was terrified of him.

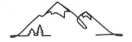

5. PRICELESS

August 17

The next day, Hilda arrived bright and early. Too early and too chipper for Sasha's taste. They climbed into a white BMW and drove to Geneva where Hilda filed necessary paperwork. Sasha opened a bank account, and bought a super cheap used phone. After they ate lunch, Sasha signed up for internet service. Then she requested time to go shopping because she needed to buy hiking boots since she noticed everyone wearing them in Glockenwald. She also needed a heavier jacket and some sweaters.

By the time they rolled back into Glockenwald, Sasha had spent most of her money. But she had a phone and the internet would be working the next day. She didn't need much else.

_ᴧᴧ_

Hilda left her with a thick welcome folder that detailed her job description, duties and schedule. Besides the English development of the local children, she was required to offer adult English conversation enrichment once a week. Being in a rural area, the class sizes would be small. Even so, she had a busy schedule. The board of education was gracious enough to give her a week to adjust before they expected her to start teaching.

Sasha sat at her mini table with water and a sandwich. She frowned at her sandwich after the first bite because it didn't taste as good as the one Ricky had made for her even though she had used the same ingredients.

In the welcome folder was information about Glockenwald. It detailed how she could wash clothes and pay bills. There was a map which showed Hilda's house, the police, access to ski lifts, and the only petrol pump.

Her eyes fluttered when she remembered Ricky standing under the LED light pumping gas. Dear god, he was a fine specimen.

Shaking the thoughts from her head, Sasha shuffled the rest of the paperwork into the folder. Her eyes were getting crossed from all the reading. All that mattered was that she was safely nestled in the mountains.

She had deleted all of her social media accounts and had changed her email address so he couldn't track her. She hadn't even risked saying goodbye to Betty, her last foster mom. Sasha didn't know her real parents. She was orphaned as a baby. Her relationship with Jackson had driven a wedge between her and Betty. This was her chance to start all the way over. No one knew her here. She had a credit card and student loan to pay off, but besides those debts which she could pay online, she had nothing else stateside but heartache and abuse.

Sasha shook her head again. She pushed thoughts of her old life away, then finished the dry-not-made-by-lumberjack sandwich. Once everything was cleaned up, she decided to go for a walk.

The sun hung low in the west and the air was chilled. Sasha reminded herself to wash her clothes soon.

She walked along the dirt road which was lined with small houses and duplexes. People were coming home from work and waved to her. That was nice. At least they were attempting to be friendly. She headed toward the town center. The only café was busy. Apparently there was a restaurant at the lodge, and the inn had lunch and dinner service, but she couldn't afford those right now. Looking through the large café windows, she could see several people were in line for fresh bread or coffee.

Past the café was a little flower stand which had closed for the day. The red and white checkered awning had been pulled in and strapped down. A few tubs of sad looking flowers stood outside. She saw several people take a flower or two and leave change in a locked green box with a slit.

"They're free."

Sasha whipped around to see Ricky standing behind her.

He waved with a small smile. His beard looked tamed, hiding his neck and the collar of his blue plaid shirt.

She lowered her hand that had been over her heart. "You scared me."

"Sorry," he looked at his boots and then gestured to the flowers. "These are free. They're the old ones that didn't sell, but people leave money anyway."

She looked at the buckets that had a couple of flowers left. "Ah, okay." She had never bought flowers before. She had never received flowers before. "They're still beautiful," she whispered.

He stepped next to her and looked through the leftovers. "Here, this one is nice." He handed her the most exquisite flower she had ever seen. Its tiny petals were a buttery orange that transitioned to dark pink with hints of violet towards the center.

"What is it?" She sniffed the flower while she waited. She didn't expect the earthy aroma with herbal undertones.

"We call it *chrysantheme.*"

"A chrysanthemum?" She looked up, confused.

"That's right," he smiled.

Sasha felt silly and stupid. What kind of life had she led where she didn't even know what a chrysanthemum looked like? Sadness washed over her. "It's beautiful," she whispered, her voice thick with emotion.

"Are you okay?" He shoved his hands in his jacket pockets. The sun had set behind the mountains and a chill had settled over the valley.

"Yeah, thank you for this. How much should I pay?" She gestured towards the green locked box.

He shrugged and pulled change out of his pocket. "Let me. It's free."

To her, the flower was priceless.

His coins jingled into the box. "Where are you going? I saw you walk by the café. They have great coffee."

"I don't drink coffee," she whispered, staring at the

purple center of the flower.

"Right."

She shivered when a breeze blew through her shirt.

"I'm actually headed home. I need to remember my coat from now on," she said to herself. "Thank you for this," she lifted the chrysanthemum, unable to look away from the delicate petals. "Have a good night."

She didn't wait for him to respond. She was cold and on the verge of a breakdown.

She hadn't gotten two feet when she felt warmth on her shoulders with the familiar aroma of pine, sandalwood and vanilla.

"Wear this. I'll walk you home," he fell in step with her.

She didn't even have the mental fortitude to argue.

They walked in an awkward silence towards her apartment. She tried to keep her head down, wiping at tears. Thankfully he walked with his hands in his pockets and his gaze seemed to be everywhere but on her.

After she unlocked her door, she returned his jacket for the second time in less than a week.

"Thanks," she sniffed.

He looked uncomfortable when he shrugged into the supple leather. "Anytime."

"Have a goodnight," she turned to go inside when she felt his warm hand on her shoulder. She flinched away.

"Wait," he asked, dropping his hand. "Please?"

She stopped, but didn't turn around. Years and years of being strong and not shedding a tear were unraveling. She sniffed. "What?" she whispered.

"Did I upset you?" he sounded worried. "Do you

hate flowers? I just don't understand why the tears?"

She shook her head. If she was strong enough she would have forced a smile. She swallowed several times trying to form words. "I've just had a long day," she said finally. "Thanks again," she headed inside before he could say more. The sob ripped through her when she slid to the floor with her back against the door.

So many emotions had bubbled to the surface. She was a thirty-one year old woman who had just received her first flower. She was a thirty-one year old woman who had left everyone behind so she could find her self-worth. And for the first time in her life, she allowed herself to cry for her broken soul.

6. WHO DID IT?

August 18

The afternoon light filtered into Sasha's bedroom. Her eyes were swollen and encrusted from hours of crying into the night until exhaustion dragged her to a deep dreamless sleep. She picked at her lashes, trying to unstick them. When she sat up, she saw the chrysanthemum on her nightstand. Its petals were tinged brown because she had neglected to put it in water.

Cursing her forgetfulness she went to the kitchenette to fill a glass. She wondered if she could save the precious gift.

After placing the chrysanthemum in the middle of her tiny table, she peeled off yesterday's clothes and climbed into a cold shower. She was too tired to wait for the water to heat up. The cool cascade felt good on her swollen lids. After she was cocoa buttered and her hair was pulled back into a curly Afro puff, she gathered her laundry.

It was a short walk to town hall. There were a couple of people in the office who waved to her. "Where can I do laundry?" she asked a woman who wore a thick purple sweater over jeans. Sasha wished she had brought more jeans. She was going to freeze in her dress pants once winter arrived.

"Ah, Sasha," Hilda had exited a back office and approached the granite counter. "Laundry?"

They hugged. "Yes, the packet mentioned that I could wash clothes here."

Hilda entwined arms and led her to a door under the set of stairs to the left. "Yes, of course. You should consider getting your own so you don't have to come here. These machines are so old." She opened the door to reveal a stacked washer and dryer from the nineties. Sasha hoped they still worked.

She loaded her new and old clothes, which barely made an entire load, then used the detergent provided. She was thankful the machines weren't coin operated, so she could do laundry for free.

"I wanted to thank you for fixing the tire," she said to Hilda after they made sure the washer still worked.

"Tire? What do you mean?"

"The Vespa. Didn't you fix the front tire?"

Hilda tilted her head, her straight hair looked like a blond curtain above her long neck. "I don't know what you're talking about."

Sasha shook her head. "Never mind." Only one person could have fixed the busted tire. "Am I able to get the lesson plans early?"

Hilda smiled and entwined arms again. "Of course! The kids should be at recess," she checked her wrist diamonds. "Come, you should meet them."

Hilda loved talking about her family. She had a son who lived in France. Her husband, Franc, had recently retired. He spent his time gardening and collecting rare wines.

"You should come to dinner," Hilda offered when they were returning with the lesson plans.

Sasha smiled, "I don't want to intrude."

"You're not intruding. I'm inviting you. It's hard, ya? Moving to a new country with new languages? I'll cook lamb."

Lamb? As in next to sweet Black Baby Jesus on Easter Sunday lamb? As in Mary had a little lamb?

"Um, I really don't want to bother you," Sasha insisted.

"It's no bother, and you can meet Franc. Let him tell you about gardening while I get some peace and quiet." They entered town hall and Sasha could hear her clothes spinning beneath the stairs.

"Ah, okay, sure," Sasha gave in.

"Wonderful. I'll hold on to the files while you check your clothes." Hilda walked behind the service counter leaving Sasha by the stairs.

While she waited for the final spin cycle, Sasha busied herself with admiring the entrance to town hall. The floors were a dark wood with a gold scroll inlay she hadn't noticed a couple of nights ago. The wood walls and banister to the stairs looked rustic and well oiled. She could see the craftsmanship in every plank.

Once she transferred her clothes to the dryer, she retrieved the files and made her way to her apartment. No point sitting and waiting in town hall feeling awkward. This gave her more time to be nosy. The café looked slow so she poked inside to see the menu.

The woman behind the counter said something to her and Sasha felt intimidated. Why did Swiss German sound harsh sometimes? She felt chastised. She shook her head and left. Maybe after she learned some phrases she could try again with more confidence.

If she had had more time, she would have at least tried to learn a couple of words. But a month ago she wasn't in the situation to 'take her time'. Her life had been hanging by a frayed thread. It was a hop, skip, and a leap of faith that landed her in Glockenwald.

The flower shop was open and she admired the offerings. She zeroed in on the chrysanthemums, the same color as the one Ricky had 'bought' her last night. She wanted to learn about them. Maybe talking to Franc about gardening while eating baa baa black sheep wasn't a bad idea.

_ᴧᴧ_

A couple of hours later, Sasha sat at the intimate dining table at the Holte's residence. Hilda had invited others so the evening morphed into an intimate dinner party with lots of wine and casual conversation. She had tried a small bite so as not to be rude, but lamb really wasn't her jam. The roasted potatoes and carrots were delicious, so she had seconds of those.

The people Hilda had invited were around Sasha's age and had lived in America before. Sasha appreciated the effort Hilda made to help her feel welcomed. So far everyone was kind and made of model material; tall, lanky, pale walkers compared to her below average height, double Ds, and cocoa-buttered curvy hips.

Most of the men had a bit of muscle and they all had beards. Beards, flannel, and hiking boots. She was learning that plaid was still an international favorite.

"So Sasha," she was sitting between a young couple who owned a beet farm, Claud and Serena, and an investment banker, Pietre, who had his arm draped on the back of her chair. The couple had just married and recently inherited the farm. It was obvious that Claud and Serena were still in their honeymoon stage. Serena leaned close to her with a wink and a nudge when she whisper-shouted, "Do you have a man in the states?" Sasha couldn't stop her flinch. "No, not at all." She tried to smile, to downplay her heart trying to burst through her rib cage. "I'm single."

She felt fingertips brush her shoulder and she readjusted so they couldn't touch her.

"So is Pietre," Serena said with a waggle of her pristine eyebrows before she winked.

Sasha gulped and side-eyed the investment banker, Pietre. Like all of the people here, he was decent looking, but the fact that he was stroking her shoulder made her skin crawl. "Ahhh," she tried not to gag when he grinned at her. She drained her wine glass. "I need a refill," she mumbled before she made her escape to the kitchen where Hilda was stacking rinsed dishes.

"Thanks for the invite," Sasha said to Hilda while she refilled her glass from a bottle of wine she couldn't pronounce. "It's nice meeting people who have stayed overseas."

"Pietre is from Geneva," Hilda smiled, rinsing soap off a dish before stacking it. "His uncle, Liam, lives here."

Sasha put down her wine. "Let me help," she offered when she picked up a white towel.

"Oh, no. Maybe next time."

"I insist." They worked in tandem, rinse and dry.

Hilda cleared her throat, "Do you like Pietre? He's nice, no?"

Really? The entire point of escaping to the kitchen was to get away from that conversation.

"Ugh, he's nice, I guess."

Hilda handed her a dish to dry. "He has money."

Sasha shrugged. "I'm not really in the market," she insisted.

"The market?" Hilda asked, confused. "What? You need groceries?"

"I'm not interested in dating," Sasha clarified.

Hilda shrugged and handed her a pot. "Who needs to date to have sex?"

The pot slipped from Sasha's fingers and clanked to the floor. Thank goodness it was metal and not a plate or glass. "Sorry," Sasha mumbled. She retrieved the pot and inspected for dents.

There were calls from the other room asking if things were okay and Hilda yelled over her shoulder, "We're fine!" Then she eyed Sasha. "Are you okay?"

Sasha dragged in a shaky breath. "I've had a rough past with men," she whispered, concentrating on drying the pot. Admitting her demons out loud was petrifying.

"Ah." Hilda handed her a metal lid. "There's no rush. With the right lover, sex is a beautiful thing."

"I'm done with men," Sasha declared.

"Women are fantastic lovers too," Hilda lifted a glass of wine with soapy hands. She eyed Sasha while she drank. Then she shrugged and rinsed the glistening suds off her long fingers. "I'll finish tomorrow. Come, let's make friends."

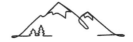

7. THANK YOU

August 21

The week went by in a jet lagged blur. Once the internet was installed, Sasha was reconnected to the digital world. It was the hardest thing for her to endure. Being online, but not being on social media, was a necessary torture. She had to move forward, and to move forward she had cut all ties.

Serena had invited her for lunch at the café on Saturday. She hadn't had a girls lunch date in years. Jackson didn't allow her to go anywhere without him. She was allowed to go to work, then immediately home. She couldn't even pump gas without him present.

Even sitting outside, surrounded by mountains and cotton ball clouds, Sasha felt guilty and the tension hindered her from enjoying her lunch date. She kept telling herself that Jackson didn't know where she was. And even if he did, there was no way he was coming to get her.

"You seem distracted?" Serena asked when she gestured to the half-eaten sandwich on Sasha's plate.

Sighing, Sasha apologized. "I'm adjusting," she

said, which was the truth. "Things are much different in Michigan. More people, more buildings, no mountains," she gestured to the view. From where she was sitting, she could almost see the entire valley. She even found her apartment.

"Did you want to visit the city? We can take a weekend trip to Geneva, Zurich, or even Milan before the snow."

Sasha didn't have money for traveling. She had spent her last franc on this meal. "Why can't we go after the snow?"

Serena raised an eyebrow. "How do you say—too much snow? The mountains become dangerous, ya."

"Wait, you get snowed in here?"

"Is that how you say it? Snowed in?" Serena shrugged and sipped her espresso.

Why hadn't Sasha done more research? Michigan got its share of snow, but she could still drive and get around. She observed the valley below them and the snow capped mountains no longer looked majestic. Their jagged peaks were bad omens. "When does the snow start?"

"Soon. October or September."

"What?" September was two weeks away. These people were crazy. How could anyone live here? "What do you do for food?"

"We have town storage for beets, grains, dried fish and meats. The café and the lodge will always be open if you don't want to cook," Serena said before taking a bite of her croissant.

Sasha unlocked her phone and set a reminder to ask Hilda when she was getting paid. Maybe she could learn how to bake bread or something.

Serena was unaware of her distress and kept talking. "Thanksgiving is in two weeks. We'll harvest the fields and everyone helps make butter, store beets, and chop wood. You should come. We make a big party out of the weekend. Lots of kirsch."

"Kirsch?"

"A delicious cherry brandy. You want to take that home?"

Sasha looked at her sandwich. She wondered if they expected her to churn butter in her hiking boots. She wasn't about that life. "Yeah," she couldn't waste food since she didn't have money.

They walked together to Sasha's apartment. Serena and Claud lived on a farm further down the dirt road that was about a fifteen minute walk away. Serena invited her for dinner next week before a quick hug and then heading home.

While Sasha unlocked her door she heard an eerie laugh behind her. She glanced around but the street was empty except for Serena walking home with her eyes on her phone. Then she heard the familiar low rumble approaching from the mountains. She knew it was Ricky. She hadn't seen him since he gave her the chrysanthemum. She hesitated because she wanted to thank him for replacing the tire on the Vespa. At the same time, she wanted to avoid him and all men.

The sooner she got this over with, the sooner she could forget the lumberjack. She entered her apartment and placed the half-eaten sandwich next to the small wedge of cheese in her bare fridge. She wished she could go grocery shopping.

Being poor was nothing new to her.

She went to the bathroom and checked her edges

and makeup before reapplying vaseline to her thick lips. "You can do this," she said to her reflection while admiring her high cheekbones.

A few minutes later she was walking toward town hall. Every time she had seen Ricky's motorcycle, it had been parked there.

Sure enough, he was outside talking to the mayor with his helmet tucked under his arm.

"Hello, Sasha," Eric greeted her and shook her hand.

"Hey, Eric. How are you?" She smiled and gave a small wave to Ricky. No point in touching the man.

"I'm great. How do you say—trying to organize with Herr Bell. I'm surprised he's here."

At least she knew 'Herr' meant Mister. "I'm sorry to interrupt."

She wandered towards his motorcycle while the men continued their conversation.

Why was she drawn to the metallic beast? Those had been amazing orgasms. The chrome and black paint were so shiny she could see the sky and mountains reflected on the perfect finish. The Harley Davidson logo with wings decorated the gas tank. She wanted to know more about his motorcycle. What made it vibrate like that? Would other motorcycles do the same thing to her? She traced the seat again, feeling his lingering warmth. She reached for the chrome when a warm hand clamped on her shoulder, startling her.

"Don't touch the chrome. It's hot. It'll burn you."

She inhaled his comforting scent and took a step back. "Right. I shouldn't be touching anything." She hugged herself, trying to keep her erratic heart from leaping out of her chest.

"I don't mind," he hung his helmet on the handle bar. "Safety."

Sasha lowered her arms and forced herself to meet his curious gaze. She had gone years without really looking at men. If she didn't make eye contact, they were less likely to notice her. Less likely to hurt her.

Sometimes.

"How are you?" she tried to keep the tremor out of her voice.

"Fine. You? Did you buy a jacket?" He looked down at her. She studied his crooked nose, which leaned a fraction to the right. She wondered if he had broken it in a fight. She could imagine him fighting bears. Or wolves. Didn't lumberjacks do that? Fight woodland creatures and split trees in half?

"A jacket? Yes, why?"

He crossed his arms. "You're always trembling when I see you. It's cold here, ya? Colder than the States."

She averted her gaze, embarrassed. She wasn't trembling from the cold.

Time to end this.

She just needed to thank him, then she wouldn't have to talk to him again if she was careful. She swallowed and looked up into his whiskey eyes. "I ugh— I wanted to thank you for fixing the tire on the Vespa."

"Ah."

"How much do I owe you?"

"No problem." He uncrossed his arms and shuffled from one leg to the other. "Don't worry."

"Okay. Well, thank you. That's all I wanted to say."

He nodded and shrugged, "Not a big deal."

It was to her. "I see. Well, sorry to bother you."

"No bother." He smiled at her and then waved to someone behind her.

That was her cue. "Okay, well take care."

His hand reached for her, but didn't touch her. "Do you want to eat?"

"I'm sorry?" She was so hell bent on walking away she didn't understand his melodic words.

"Are you hungry? Do you want to eat?" He gestured to the café she left not even twenty minutes ago. This is what happens when you live in a small town; not a lot of options.

"Um," she thought of her empty fridge and half-eaten sandwich. Then she remembered her empty wallet. "I can't," she shrugged.

"Why not?" He lifted an eyebrow and the wind ruffled the top of his bourbon hair. Why was the hair on his head shorter than his beard?

She wanted to say that she didn't have money because she lived with someone who controlled everything she did and only gave her a small allowance, so she had to hide pennies. She had just used her last penny. Instead she took in a shaky breath and blinked away her anxiety. "I just ate lunch there," she exhaled.

"Ah, I see."

She nodded, a tight smile on her lips, "I should go."

"I want an espresso. With you."

"I don't—"

"Drink coffee. Yes, I remember. I just…." he looked around as if he was searching for words. "I just want to talk. I can drink espresso, you can drink water. We can talk, no? Like friends?" He looked hopeful.

She blinked in the silence that followed. She never had male friends. She didn't have girlfriends. But she did come here to start over. But she orgasmed on his motorcycle.

Three.

Fucking.

Times.

She shook her head and looked at her feet. "Um," she didn't know what to say. Her emotions and her body were at odds with each other. She looked up into his eyes, they sparkled while he watched her. "I'm not sure," she admitted, chewing on her lower lip.

"Ah, okayyy," he looked around trying to figure out what to say next. "We can skip espresso and just walk?"

She swallowed and her eyes trailed down his body. He was wearing his smell-good leather jacket, a green shirt, and black jeans over his leather boots. She could see a shiny oval belt buckle and wondered if it was the wolf. She clenched her jaw and fisted her hands before hugging herself. "Okay, you can get espresso and a walk would be nice."

His face split with a handsome smile, "Great." He gestured toward the café and she walked alongside him.

What the hell was she doing?

8. THE WALK

They walked aimlessly around Main Street before taking a dirt road toward the valley. They walked in silence for a while, listening to rural life around them. Kids were outside playing and their shrieks of excitement echoed between the mountains. Could they cause an avalanche?

With one hand in his pocket, Ricky sipped from his steaming to-go cup. She couldn't stop glancing at him. His profile was handsome against the blue sky. Mesmerizing.

"Where did you go to university?" he asked after two kids ran past them and towards a nearby farm.

Sasha had been deep in thought. Mostly wondering why she was there. With him. "I went to Wayne State."

"I don't know it," he shrugged when he smiled at her. "I did two years at Harvard," his hand slipped out of his pocket. He was a hand talker. And he was a lumberjack who studied at Harvard.

His smile made her heart beat faster which made her hesitate. Sasha reminded herself that he was just attempting to connect and maybe it was time she connected to nontoxic people.

Plus, his smile was contagious.

"That's nice," she tried not to sound jealous. She had wanted to apply to Stanford but couldn't even afford the application, let alone move across the country. It was either a community college or Wayne State for her. "Is that where you learned English?"

"I've always studied English. It's part of the educational system here," he looked at her and gave a small smile.

His English far exceeded her non-existent Swiss German.

They fell back into silence while they walked. She had to take two steps to his one.

"Where did you learn to ride a motorcycle?" The question erupted from her.

"I love vehicles," he looked up at the mountains, his face glowing when he smiled. "I love engines. How they work. I love to drive, ya?"

"Lots of cars where I'm from. There's an auto show once a year in Detroit. It's massive."

"Ah, yes. I've been there. The cars are—" he stopped short when he saw her face. "Is something wrong?"

Talking about college and Detroit reminded her that she was in another freaking country. She had left everything and everyone she knew because of one man. And here she was surrounded by mountains talking to a lumberjack. She had loved Detroit, but hated Jackson.

"I kind of rushed coming here. I'm still in shock," she admitted before she hugged herself.

"You're shaking," his warm hand patted her shoulder causing her to flinch so he pulled away, a frown on his lips. "It's different here," he offered with a sad smile.

She nodded, unable to articulate words.

"Here, hold my espresso?"

There wasn't much left in his cup, but the thick paper still felt warm in her hands. He unzipped his jacket and she found herself taking a step back. "No, I'm okay, let's walk back." She turned toward town. The buildings looked like dots along the mountainside. She had been so caught up in being with him, she hadn't noticed how far they had strolled.

"It will get cold soon," he stated before he draped his jacket around her shoulders anyway. The mountains bathed the valley in shadows early in the day. He retrieved his cup and she pulled his jacket closer to her; the sandalwood and vanilla was comforting.

"Okay, let's hurry back," she suggested.

He fell in step next to her and they walked in silence, the shadow of the mountain beginning to stretch around them. She could see the edge of the town and her apartment building.

"Do I make you sad?" his voice was so low she wasn't sure she had heard him.

"I'm sorry?"

He cleared his throat. "Do I make you sad?"

"Um," she looked up at his handsome bearded face, confused. "Why do you ask that?"

"Every time I see you, you're sad and crying."

Her heart dropped. He was right. She was putting out major somber vibes because she was in fact depressed. "It's not your fault."

"But you're sad, no?"

"I am."

"I'm sorry," his shoulders dropped a little.

"Me, too."

They fell silent and continued with unspoken words hanging between them. She appreciated that he didn't pry further. Why Sasha had even said anything to him was a surprise to her. Maybe she was already turning over a new leaf.

When they got to her apartment, he stood several feet behind her while she unlocked the door.

"Can I use your restroom?" he asked when he crushed the to-go cup with one hand.

"Of course," she let him in and closed the door behind her. She draped his jacket on the chair, and the chill in her apartment made her shiver. She could hear him handling his business and felt on edge knowing he was in her apartment. She sat down at the table and crossed her arms while she waited.

"Thanks," he muttered after he joined her in the kitchen, his eyes taking in the small space. He walked to her sliding door and looked out over the valley, leaning his shoulder against the frame. "It's a nice view," he stuffed his hands in his jeans.

Yes, her view was nice too. He stood there, appearing to be comfortable in her space. She wondered what he was contemplating when he gazed at the field of beets. She felt nervous when she became aware of their aloneness and dragged in a shaky breath.

His gaze whipped in her direction and he straightened when he saw her face. "I'm sorry. I'm rude, ya?" He shook his head, his skin flushed with embarrassment.

She trembled when he approached. Apprehension and flashbacks caused her to flinch when he quickly grabbed for his jacket on the back of her chair.

He stilled.

She gulped. Her mind was still in Detroit, beaten and bruised.

He crouched next to her, his face level with hers and he searched her eyes, worried. "You're scared," he whispered.

She sucked in a shaky breath. She couldn't speak. It was always safer not to talk.

He started to reach for her and she flinched again causing his hand to pause. But then he continued, wiping a tear from her cheek with his thumb.

She hadn't realized she was crying.

He continued to search her ebony depths even though her eyes had glazed over in defense. "Someone hurt you," he whispered.

She nodded. That was all she could manage because her entire body was trembling.

Air left his lungs. She could see the disgust on his face. He stood to his full height. "I'm sorry. I will go," his voice cut the silence and slashed around her. He slowly removed his jacket from her chair. "Thanks for the walk," he opened her door and stepped out, leaving her alone with her tears.

9. LUMBERJACK

September 3

Wasa hen work officially started for Sasha her days began to meld together. Every morning she bundled into her coat and walked up the steep incline to the school. Her younger students were eager and always excited to see her, the older ones were bored and uninterested after the novelty of her newness wore off. She didn't hold their lack of interest against them because she remembered the monotony of school too.

She hadn't seen Ricky or heard the rumble of his Harley so she figured he was driving a regular car in the cooler weather while doing Harvard lumberjack things around town. Which was for the best because just being in his presence made her reconsider her no-men rule even though she didn't know much about him. She reminded herself she wasn't in Switzerland to get to know anyone, she was there to work on herself.

With no money she was forced to accept every meal invitation to survive. She was too embarrassed to ask Hilda for an advance. Instead she sat around tables with welcoming people and ate delicious home cooked meals. Then she would get seconds and move the food around her plate and pretend to nibble. When they went to clear the table she'd ask to take the leftovers home so the food didn't go to waste. It was the only way she could keep from starving.

As Swiss Thanksgiving approached large machines were brought into the valley. She could see their imposing silhouettes against the mountainside like giant yellow praying mantises. Loud hammering and machinery kept her up at night and she wondered what she should be doing to prepare for the snow.

Wednesday night Sasha snuggled in her bed underneath two blankets and her sweats. The temperature dropped so dramatically after the sun set she usually ended up shivering in her bed with the door closed to try and trap her body heat in the small room.

The banging from outside kept scaring her. The logic part of her brain knew that they were prepping for tomorrow, but the skittish part of her kept clenching the blanket so hard her fingers hurt.

Since she had to get up in a few hours to help with the harvest, she closed her laptop and set it on the floor next to her bed then tried to get some sleep. She put in earbuds and listened to Jill Scott in a poor attempt to drown out the noise.

_ﻼ_

A door slammed and the rattling windows answered.

"Sasha!" a deep menacing voice shouted her name.

"Why is there gas in the motherfuckin' Jeep?"

Drawing in a sharp breath, Sasha sat up in bed, trying

to figure out where she was. Her heart thundered against her ribs with every step he took. Throwing off the covers, she ran to the bathroom. The small space was usually safe. She closed and locked the door before turning on the faucet.

The banging behind her made her flinch. She could see the door shake in the reflection of the mirror because he pounded on the wood like he wanted to knock it off the hinges.

"Sasha!" Jackson yelled again. "Open this damn door."

Splashing water on her face, she tried to ignore her shaking hands. "I'm just washing my face," she lied. "What happened, baby?"

"You put gas in the damn car?"

She blinked at her reflection in the spotless mirror. "The light was on," she explained to herself, looking into her own dark eyes that were so wide they were mostly white.

"What the fuck did I tell you about gettin' gas?"

Holding her breath, she lied some more. "I'm sorry, what? I'm washing my face."

He hit the door so hard she was surprised it didn't break in half. "Bitch! Don't fuck with me! You know your ho ass ain't supposed to make stops. Who da fuck did you talk to?"

Closing her eyes, Sasha covered her ears to muffle his screaming. She slid to the floor and leaned against the wall across from the toilet. There was no point in explaining to him that she wouldn't have made it to work. There was no point in telling him she hadn't spoken to anyone but the attendant. He wouldn't believe her.

"Open this damn door!" he screamed. "You no good bitch."

Maybe he would tire himself out and drink himself to sleep. Maybe the door will hold this time.

He kept banging on the door. Each fist pound against the wood foreshadowed what he was about to do to her.

Maybe it was her fault. Maybe she should have called out from work and went back home, and let him put gas in the car. But that would have angered him too. Everything she did or didn't do angered him.

The door rattled the rhythm of his fists.

She tried to slip away, deep into the numb recesses of her mind where there was no pain and no Jackson. Where she was safe.

Why won't he stop?

Why won't he just leave her alone?

⚮

Sasha sat up with a gasp, the blankets were tangled around her legs and her heart was beating in her throat. Her room was pitch black and Jackson's face flashed before her eyes when banging echoed from the next room. She knew Jackson couldn't be knocking on her door, but her subconscious screamed at her to hide.

"I'm in Switzerland," Sasha reminded herself before she reached for her phone to check the time. Large white letters announced that it was almost five in the morning.

Wrapping the blanket around her, she slipped out of bed and scurried across the wood floor that was cold under her bare feet. She had to stand on her tiptoes to reach the peep hole. Sighing in relief, Sasha opened the door and let Hilda in.

"Morning! It's time to harvest, ya?"

No one should be this chipper before sunrise. This woman had to be bionic with artificial intelligence.

Blue eyes observed her face. "Are you okay? Did I frighten you?" Hilda asked.

"I'm okay," Sasha faked a yawn so she could fix whatever emotions were written across her face. "I just woke up." She rubbed her eyes and headed back to her room. She had forgotten to set her alarm for the harvest.

"I'll wait for you here," Hilda called when she sat at the small kitchen table.

Dear lord, the pressure to function was unreal. Pushing the nightmare and Jackson out of her mind, Sasha got ready.

Fifteen minutes later, Sasha followed Hilda to the fields. Hilda was in charge of a section of beets. For the first time in Sasha's adult life, she was pulling plants from the ground. It was exhausting work that pushed the nightmare of away. Thankfully, after she pulled a few and posed for pictures that would go in the town's newsletter, the machines took over. There were only a couple of self-propelled harvesters for the farms to share. The valley was alive with the hum of engines, soft voices, and the stench of earth mixed with sweat before the sun had even risen.

The beets were driven to a small building where they were washed and sorted. Some were taken to another building where they were chopped and boiled, while others were packaged to be shipped to markets.

Sasha was put in charge of a pot so large it could hold the lumberjack. The ladle's handle was at least her height. She stirred occasionally to keep beets from sticking to the bottom. She figured this was the least fuck-up-able job they could give her.

When the sun rose, everyone dropped what they

were doing and shared cold-cut sandwiches and coffee. There wasn't water so Sasha choked down the bitter liquid.

"It's exhausting, no?" Serena plopped down next to her on a wooden bench and bumped elbows.

"It's different," Sasha said with a smile, attempting to avoid saying anything rude. She was glad to have received food for the work.

"The snow will be here soon," Serena guessed when she looked up to the sky and smiled. "Do you ski?"

"Um, no." She had never skied in her life.

"Ah, it's fun."

Sasha nodded and glanced at the ski lifts. The only thing she had seen these people do for fun was drink wine and that jig.

"How are your beets?" Sasha asked her.

Serena pointed to the cut-and-boil house. "Already in," she smiled. "It's a good year," she said when she sat a little straighter.

It must be nice to have something to be proud of. Sasha felt inadequate sitting next to the blond-country-bumpkin bombshell with her farm and her beets. She savored the last bites of her sandwich, her stomach thankful to have food. Soon she returned to work with everyone else.

If she still had social media she would have posted the rows and rows of canned beets. By the time dinner had rolled around, Sasha was exhausted. Her headline would read: "Black woman dies of exhaustion on beet farm in Switzerland. Body left for wolves."

Rural life was back breaking work. She hurt in places she didn't know had muscles. But at least she got to see the process and be a part of something positive.

There was a massive break for dinner and everyone congregated in town hall. Sasha found her feet had refused to move when she saw the shiny Harley of Orgasms parked outside. She hadn't even noticed him since she'd been so busy stirring beets and trying not to fall into the pot. She considered going home, but her selfish stomach ached for more sustenance so she dragged herself inside and upstairs. Long tables had been set with platters of stewed meats, roasted root vegetables, and piles of soft bread rolls. Everyone invited Sasha to sit next to them. She took a seat near the stairs at the end of a table so she could make a quick exit if necessary.

The meat was lamb and she didn't care. She spooned the gamey chunks onto her plate and used a roll to make a sandwich, dipping the bread in the gravy. After stuffing her face and remembering that it was rude to ignore people, Sasha tried to converse with the family who had invited her to sit with them. They had a potato crop this year and talked about making vodka. Now, that was a process she would love to see.

When people started going back to the fields, Sasha wondered if she could get out of stirring the beets if she volunteered in the kitchen.

"Can I help clean up here?" she offered Hilda.

"If you want. You like dishes, ya?"

Dishes beat being outside with dust and machinery or standing above a pot that was big enough to boil her alive. She nodded.

"Sure. Ask Lilith if she needs help," Hilda pointed to an older woman wearing a red scarf over her white hair who was stacking dishes.

Thankfully, Lilith accepted her help.

While people filtered out, Sasha collected dishes and carried them through the double-swinging doors to a huge stainless steel industrial kitchen. When she went back to the hall to gather more serving platters a group of men had trudged up the stairs looking tired and covered in wood chips and dirt. Her breath caught when she realized Ricky was amongst them.

"Hello," Sasha greeted the men.

They offered greetings and sat at a table.

"Food?" an older man with stark-white hair asked.

"Of course," Sasha retreated to the kitchen where she checked the pots on the stove and helped Lilith prepare fresh platters of food.

She smiled at Ricky when she placed warm rolls on the table. Her heart skipped a beat when he smiled back. Nervously licking her lips she said, "I haven't seen you all day."

His large dust-covered hand reached for a roll. "We were up the mountain, cutting a tree."

He was a lumberjack. That was hot.

After a beat she realized she was staring at him with her mouth hanging open while he shoveled food like a starving man. When his gaze narrowed at her, she closed her lips and nodded before escaping to the kitchen to rinse dishes. She left serving the men to Lilith.

Once the sink had been emptied and all the counters were wiped down, Sasha helped Lilith plan meals for the next day. They separated potatoes as large as her head and checked pantry items.

After some time, the swinging doors opened when Ricky entered carrying a pile of dirty dishes.

Lilith went out to collect the rest leaving her and

Ricky alone.

Sasha tried to avoid looking at him. She leaned against the sink where she and Lilith had been rinsing potatoes. "Why were you cutting down a tree?" she asked to fill the silence.

He shrugged. "Mostly tradition. But also for heat." He placed the dishes on the counter and turned to face her, gripping the edge of the sink while he leaned against the stainless steel. He was covered in dirt and wood dust. His blue and black flannel shirt had been rolled up to his elbows. Even the muscles in his forearms were corded and defined.

Someone in the hall must have made a joke because muted laughter erupted behind them.

"Okay." She turned on the water and grabbed the first bowl to rinse. She could feel him staring down at her and his scrutiny made her nervous.

"I'm sorry," he whispered just above the noisy laughter.

She looked up confused, meeting his angry whiskey gaze. "What?" Remembering not to make eye contact when alone with a man, she quickly averted her attention back to the sink.

"I'm sorry someone hurt you," he flexed a hand. She could see the dirt encrusted under his nails before he made a fist.

Her heart pounded and a high pitched buzz sounded in her ears. "Okay." She wasn't sure how to respond because of his anger. She focused on the soap bubbles and the bowl in her hand, holding her breath.

He took a step toward her, the fear that had taken hold caused her to flinch. His large hand gripped the sink next to her elbow. She could feel his heat, and a strong smell of pine and sweat infused the air around them.

She inhaled deeply and closed her eyes, waiting for the punishment to start.

The doors behind them swung open and Lilith entered the kitchen, the sounds of laughter ricocheting off the steel appliances. She spoke to Ricky and he moved away, chuckling before leaving the room. Sasha glanced at the dirty handprint he had left behind.

This was a situation she didn't want to be in. Without a franc to her name, she had to figure out how to live safely in Glockenwald. The way he had gripped the sink until his knuckles turned white scared her.

When Sasha left town hall, the sun had completely set and the sky was glittering with stars. Some people were still in the fields, but most had called it a night and turned in. She saw that the Vibrator on Wheels was still parked under the streetlight, so she hugged herself and avoided the dangerous machine. When she got to her apartment she could see the field adjacent to her place had been harvested. The freshly turned soil was dark and the earthy aroma had saturated the usual sweet smelling air.

In the field, men were unloading the largest tree trunk she had ever seen in her life. No wonder the loggers had been away all day. They worked under the night sky using a portable LED light that had been tied to a crane. She could hear the men shouting directions to each other while they worked with ropes and pulleys, their axes and chainsaws echoing between the mountains.

Sasha approached her door and stepped on something because she was busy searching for a certain lumberjack.

Soft petals caressed her fingertips when she reached for the object. She picked up the partially crushed chrysanthemum then a smile pulled at the corner of her lips.

10. BEFORE THE SNOW

September 4

The sound of chainsaws and axes dragged her out of bed before the sun had risen. These people didn't know how to Thanksgiving. This was work. She dressed in jeans, a long shirt and hiking boots. Hilda had convinced her to leave her purse and belongings at home because they would just get in the way.

When she stepped outside into the frigid air, she could see men working on the massive tree trunk in the field next to her. She found Ricky's silhouette this time. His impressive frame swung an ax in one smooth mesmerizing movement.

Her core heated.

Sexy lumberjack.

She shook her head and swallowed her drool. At least admiring him from a distance was safe. She made her way to town hall to see if Lilith wanted her help cooking.

While Sasha peeled potatoes and chopped onions, she kept debating with herself. Was Ricky off limits?

She wasn't there to have entanglements, but she was obviously attracted to him, or at least attracted to his motorcycle.

That must be it.

She wasn't attracted to the man, she wanted the vibrating chrome. Besides, she didn't know if he was taken. He didn't wear a ring, but that didn't mean anything these days. He could still have five baby mamas in nearby rural towns. Tall, blonde, and blue-eyed baby mamas. She took her frustration out on the potato in her hand and slammed it on the steel prep surface.

Lilith eyed her but went back to chopping and humming folk songs Sasha didn't know.

Sasha liked being alone in company because she wasn't harassed about the States or her past. The only downside was she kept thinking about a certain lumberjack.

Once the root veggies were chopped and herbed, they were set aside. She helped Lilith assemble and deliver sandwiches and coffee in a little truck. Sasha was amazed to see how different the valley looked with all the fields harvested and turned. She could see why it required all able bodies.

_ᴧᴧ_

After two more days of harvesting, Sasha wondered if limbs just fell off. She was positive she couldn't wash another dish or can another beet or look at another butter churner for the next decade without horrible flashbacks. Every day had been nonstop work, short meal breaks, and exhausted, dreamless sleep.

Thankfully the last day of the harvest was cleanup. The farming equipment was disassembled and hooked up to trailers and hauled away to other towns for their torturefest. They swept up the detritus and debris from the lumber and packed the canned food into insulated sheds near town hall.

And then there was the Thanksgiving party at the school. Everyone congregated at tables and benches that were set up around a huge bonfire on the athletics field. The tables were laden with food and alcohol, and the benches were overcrowded with sweat drenched bodies.

Since Sasha got anxiety in crowds she considered calling it a night and disappearing into her apartment. But before she could escape, Hilda entwined arms and thanked her for her help and led Sasha to a table piled high with mashed potatoes she had helped prep. She was plopped down next to none other than Ricky.

He gazed at her with a small smile, his beard was extra ragged with wood dust after days of swinging his ax. Before they could greet each other, Serena and Claud slid in across from them, grinning.

"How was your first harvest?" Serena asked before she reached for a dinner roll and ripped off a soft piece.

"Exhausting. I could use a massage after that," Sasha groaned and rolled her shoulders.

More people slid onto the bench around them, forcing her side to touch Ricky's. If it weren't for him, she might have had an anxiety attack squished between two people. But his body felt like an inferno and the heat was soothing.

Her mind wandered to their ride through the mountains and she had a hard time focusing on Claud's words.

"Next we distribute wood and food and prepare for snow," Claud smiled at his wife.

"How should I prep?" Sasha asked them, glancing at everyone but Ricky. She could feel him bouncing his other leg. She tried to ignore the constant movement and bit into a piece of tender lamb.

"Get warm clothes—" Serena suggested with bright eyes.

"Or a warm body," Claud interjected before he leaned over and kissed Serena on the cheek.

"I guess I have shopping to do," Sasha said to herself.

Serena perked up. "We should go to Geneva. You should buy skis or a snowboard."

Both sounded expensive. "Maybe. I do need some snow pants and boots."

"I bet Pietre would love to take you skiing," Serena waggled her eyebrows.

Sasha's stomach bottomed out. She had completely forgotten about the investment banker.

"Pietre who?" Ricky's eyes were wide with alarm.

"Furrer," Serena answered when she stabbed at her chunks of lamb and her eyes twinkled playfully. "He's Liam's nephew. You know him," she waved her hand dismissively at Ricky who had turned into granite when he stopped moving.

Sasha gazed up into whiskey eyes and shook her head. "He's no one. I'm not interested," she insisted before scooping up some garlicky mashed potatoes.

Serena was in her element. "Oh come on! He can't stop asking about you."

Sasha groaned and tried not to gag on the potatoes.

Claud leaned forward, his shoulders bumping into Serena. "And you're both young, single, and beautiful, ya? Why not enjoy each other?"

These people and their matchmaking.

Sasha shook her head before she gulped down wine to wash down the potatoes.

"Ricky is single too," Serena offered up with a snicker.

Sasha inhaled wine, choked on wine, spewed wine, and wished for a quick death.

The faces across from her split into smiles so wide she hoped they were painful.

"Wait," Claud was leaning forward on his elbows. "You like Ricky?" he asked, pointing his chin at the man who had become still again.

"Holy shit," Serena whispered, her eyes bouncing between them.

Sasha continued to cough and avoided looking at the sexy beast next to her. She didn't want to see his reaction and she was coughing too hard to speak.

Hilda came out of nowhere and patted her back. "Lift arms," she commanded and Sasha obeyed. Her coughing receded and she was able to drag in a wine-flavored breath. One more good cough and she almost felt normal.

Claud had the stupidest grin on his face when he continued to lean on the table. "That's too bad, Sasha. Ricky's parents would never approve."

Sasha clenched her jaw when she saw Serena nod in agreement. She glared up at Ricky, "Why not? Because I'm Black?"

He glared down at her, his face was flushed with embarrassment. "No, because you're American." He started to stand up and she stood up as well.

"No, please. I'm the outsider here. Have a good night." The table was hushed when she downed the rest of her wine. She saw Serena hit Claud's arm before she maneuvered from between the bodies and walked towards the road.

Because she was American. The audacity.

It was still early in the evening. The sun had sunk behind the mountains, leaving the sky a brilliant gradient of blues dotted with a few twinkling stars. Sasha hugged herself while she walked past the library towards the road that led to her apartment.

She wasn't upset. She was disappointed. She had argued with herself about Ricky, and now it didn't matter. No wonder he looked at her with discomfort sometimes. She was American.

She heard footsteps on the pavement behind her, making the back of her neck tingle.

"Sasha?"

"Good night, Ricky."

"Wait, please?"

They were in front of town hall when he stepped in front of her. She stopped and looked down at her feet, unsure of why she waited. The chatter from the party carried on the wind and it sounded like someone started playing a guitar. She had probably left just in time if they were going to start dancing.

"My parents can be overbearing," he said when he leaned from one leg to the other.

She rolled her eyes at his boots. "It's none of my business. Besides, if you need your parent's approval, then you're too young for me." She shrugged and tried to side-step to go around him but he moved in front of

her.

"It's not age. I'm thirty-five. They want lineage, prestige."

Sasha looked up, confused. "Okay," she threw her hands up. "None of that matters. Nothing has ever happened between us and nothing will." She crossed her arms again and started to walk around him.

This time his hand reached out and grabbed her arm, causing her to flinch.

He let go. "Sorry," he whispered. "Sasha, I like you," he said into the growing darkness. "Ever since I found you that night I...." he trailed off and stared at her feet, his body rigid. "I haven't been able to stop thinking about you." His intense gaze met hers. "I want to know you better."

She swallowed her disbelief. She hadn't seen much of him in weeks. They only had a couple of conversations. But she would be lying if she denied the electricity she felt whenever he was nearby. She had been curious about him from the moment he found her stranded.

"Well, I'm sure you'll find someone else to occupy your thoughts," she said, ignoring that her body hummed in protest. She started to walk away.

He didn't grab her but he did fall in step beside her. "The snow is coming," he said, gesturing to the darkening sky. "Will you ride me?"

She stopped and looked up at him. What was he playing at? "What did you just say?"

His face flushed in the dying sunlight. "Come ride the motorcycle with me."

Her heart skipped a beat before pounding hard against her sternum. She swallowed and stared at him.

How often had she imagined riding on that glorious machine? Too often. "I shouldn't."

"You should. One last ride, before the snow," he suggested with an intense gaze.

She ground her teeth when desire curled in her belly. She took in a shaky breath and let her arms drop to her side.

She was at a crossroads. There was no way they could become serious. Maybe this was exactly what she needed.

She turned towards his motorcycle and licked her lips. She'd be creaming that, not him.

Was it wrong to use a man for his machine?

No.

No, it was not.

"Okay," she gave in.

He reached for her hand and she hesitantly accepted, allowing him to lead her to his Harley.

Holy shit she was going to do this. And half the town was going to witness her riding off with him.

He handed her his helmet and fished out yellow glasses from the leather sack on the side. Within minutes she was behind him on his Harley and they were roaring out of Glockenwald.

11. DELICIOUS

They rode in silence surrounded by mountains and a sea of twinkling stars.

Sasha was so tense she couldn't even enjoy the ride. At some point, he pulled over to the side of the road, darkness enveloped them and her heart hammered again. This could either be fatal or the best night of her life. The motorcycle angled and he twisted to look at her.

"Tell me how you like it?" His voice was thick with desire and her thick thighs squeezed him when she trembled.

"What?" she whispered.

His right hand touched her knee. "Is this okay?"

Electricity pulsated from his hand through her body. She nodded and gulped.

"Do you want me to go fast or slow?"

"Oh god. Um, slow I guess." She heard him swallow and she hissed in response.

"Can I touch you more?"

Licking her lips, she considered his request. He wouldn't risk his life to hurt her. Her heart thumped painfully when she realized she did want his touch.

"Yes," she gripped his jacket and shimmied behind him. He stroked her hand with his and righted the Vibrator on Wheels. "Relax," he said over his shoulder. "Enjoy it." His hand returned to the handle bar then he revved the engine.

Her core immediately jolted from the strong oscillations. She gasped and gripped him tighter. She kept replaying his words in her mind: Relax, enjoy it.

He eased back onto the road shifting slow and easy through the gears. When the engine was in a lower gear, she gasped, "Right there, keep it there." With her head thrown back she climaxed for the first time that night, his hand caressing her thigh when she trembled against his back.

"That's hot, Sasha. So sexy." His accent was almost enough to send her over again.

When she came down, she rested her head against his back.

"More?" he asked.

She might as well. She won't be getting this treatment again for who knows how long. "Yes, please."

He revved for her up and down the same stretch of road until she was exhausted and begged for him to take her home. By the time they rolled back into the village, the bonfire had been put out and everything had been cleaned up.

How long had they been gone? She didn't even have her phone on her. He pulled up to her apartment and turned off the engine. The sudden silence made her antsy. He helped her get down and her legs felt like jelly. She was trembling from her tight curls to her pinky toe.

"Are you okay?"

She had no words. She just juiced his motorcycle

again. This time on purpose. "I'm a bit embarrassed."

"Why?" He helped her to her door, his whiskey eyes following her every move.

"I'm sure you give all the women joy rides."

"Joy rides?" He knit his eyebrows and then leaned towards her. "You're the first to orgasm," he whispered in her ear. Then he stood back and waited for her to unlock the door. "I haven't had many women on my Harley," he shrugged.

She peered at him, her insides coiling again. Why was he so sexy? She had never found bearded men attractive, but this man.... She shook her head and took in a ragged breath. She unlocked her door and stepped inside.

"Can I use your restroom?" he asked before he tapped the helmet still on her head.

"Of course," she stepped back so he could enter. When he closed the door to the bathroom, she took off his helmet and placed it on the table before peeling off her jacket. She was exhausted from four days of harvesting.

After all of that vibrating bliss, she had enough energy to lean against her front door and wait.

When he exited the bathroom she pried open her tired eyes and gulped. His beard was extra ragged after the ride, and it increased his hot factor. He watched her watch him, the desire in his eyes chasing away the exhaustion in her bones.

She bit her lip because she wanted him.

He leaned against the door frame of the bathroom, then he glanced into her bedroom. "I can stay," he offered when his eyes met hers again. "If you want."

She gasped. She did want.

"Or I can go," he walked to the small table and touched the two dry chrysanthemums before picking up his helmet.

She watched him. Maybe they were attracted to each other because it was forbidden.

Forbidden always tasted delicious.

She licked her lower lip when he stepped towards her, helmet dangling from one hand. He lifted his other hand and placed it above her head before leaning so close she could feel his heat. Unfortunately, their bodies didn't touch.

"I want to stay," he whispered. "I want you to want me," he murmured into the space between them.

"I do want you," she admitted before meeting his hooded gaze. She could smell the fresh pine mixed with sweat.

"But?" he searched her eyes while he waited.

Her body was humming from the motorcycle ride. A sudden desperation to feel him everywhere made her feel intoxicated. "I don't know."

His hand lowered and she heard the deadbolt slide into place.

Holy shit.

This was about to happen.

She was nervous because he might flip the script.

He dropped his helmet next to the door and went to touch her face. She flinched and his hand paused in midair.

"I won't hurt you," he whispered. "Whoever hurt you is a coward." He lowered his hand to his side. "Why don't you touch me first?"

She sighed when she unzipped his leather jacket. She untucked the black and gray plaid shirt that was dust and wood-chip covered. He shrugged out of his jacket, letting it fall to the floor behind his feet.

She ran her fingers under his shirt along his warm abs with soft hair. She had been wanting to touch these since August.

He groaned and fisted his hands which made her pause. "Don't stop," he urged.

She unbuttoned his shirt from the bottom, working her way up to reveal a white, sweat drenched undershirt. "Take this off," she pleaded.

A shrug and tug later, he was shirtless in front of her. His chest was hard with soft dark curly hair covering his pecs and leading to his happy place.

The bulge in his pants was impressive.

Her fingers ran across the wolf belt buckle. "I'm not sure how to take this off," she whispered when she traced the wolf's canines.

One swift yank from him and the silver buckle swung to the side revealing the rest of his belt.

"Fancy." Her fingers made quick work of unbuttoning his pants and then she froze. They hadn't crossed the line yet.

He seemed to notice the change in her demeanor and dragged in a deep breath. "When you're ready. If not now, it's okay. Don't push it."

This man had already given her several orgasms and he hadn't asked to put the tip in, which was new territory for her.

She exhaled again, her eyes trailing up and down his torso. She wanted him. She wanted to please him. Even if he was forbidden. "Go shower," she whispered.

He raised an eyebrow. "Shower?"

"Yes. You should rinse off the wood dust."

"Only if you come with me."

Sasha's eyes were wide with surprise. Her ex liked to beat her in the shower. Jackson would beat her everywhere. She shook her head, "I can't."

"Okay. Are you going to take one too? Maybe you should shower first?" he offered.

She shook her head and skirted around him, tripping over his jacket when she headed to the bathroom. She started the shower and grabbed a clean towel for him. "Here."

He didn't say anything, just nodded and stepped into the small room.

Sasha rushed into her bedroom and fisted her hair. What the hell was she doing? That hot specimen of man was in there wet and glistening. She bit her lip so hard she tasted iron.

At some point she was going to have to reclaim her life.

She pulled off her clothes then silently slipped into the steaming room. When she stepped in behind him, his head was under the water and he was washing the shampoo out of his beard. She touched his back and he tensed.

Dear lordt he was ripped. Jacked to perfection.

He turned to look at her, his eyes roaming her naked curves with appreciation. Her eyes roamed him freely too. His body was a symphony of defined peaks, valleys, and plains. Taking in every millimeter, her eyes grew wider when she saw below his belly button and noted that he had a curve. She drooled.

He went from half-mast to full armed canon within seconds.

She reached around him for her soap and wash

cloth, then started to rinse herself while he watched. This was the most erotic thing she had ever experienced. He didn't touch her, but he stroked himself while he observed her every touch and caress.

When she couldn't clean herself anymore and the shower had started to get cold, she turned off the water and handed him his towel before she stepped out with hers. No words were exchanged when he followed her into the bedroom with his pants dangling from one hand while he held his towel closed with the other.

She took her time drying off, watching him watch her. She wasn't sure if she could take any more. She just hoped he would be worth the wait. She draped her towel on the door handle and approached him again. She ran her fingers through his bourbon chest hair.

His skin was clammy from the long shower. He sighed and made a fist before closing his eyes.

"I want to touch you," he murmured. That's why he kept clenching his fists, he was holding back.

"Where?" she asked.

He opened his eyes and captured hers. "Everywhere," his baritone vibrated between them.

She pushed him towards the bed. "Lie down."

His large frame took up most of her full-sized bed, his feet dangling off the edge.

"Hands behind your head," she demanded.

He complied.

"Don't touch me."

He groaned his disappointment but nodded. She touched his knee and ran her hand up his thigh. His skin was blazing again and she felt the need to curl up and press against him.

She could feel whiskey eyes watching her every

move. When she ran her hands up his thigh, to his hip, she could see his arousal jump in response.

She positioned next to him, relaxing her head on his shoulder and her leg on his thigh. Then she ran her fingers through his beard, down his pecs and over his bumpy abs. She flicked at his nipple with her tongue while she ran her fingers through his chest hair.

He squirmed but didn't move to touch her. His control was such a turn on.

Sasha sucked his nipple and gently ran her teeth over the puckered skin. Then she trailed her tongue down his side, nipping each time she had to readjust her body so she could keep going. She nibbled at his waist, causing him to gasp. She nibbled along his thigh to his knee while her hand stroked the other thigh. She made sure her ample breasts never lost contact with his skin.

"Sasha," he murmured. "You drive me crazy."

She didn't respond. Instead, she grabbed him for the first time. They both groaned. She loved the feel of his granite silk in her hand and with each firm pump she could see his entire body tense and relax.

"Oh, Sasha," her name danced across his lips and he closed his eyes.

She leaned forward and licked from his throbbing base to the swollen tip before taking him into her mouth.

His legs trembled beneath her. She had built enough tension that he was on the edge.

"Wait," he propped himself up when she sucked him down to the hilt. He filled her mouth sliding into her throat. "Stop."

She pulled away, "I'm sorry." She wiped the drool from her lips.

"Not sorry. I just—I want you to go first."

She was surprised. "Oh. I already came many times tonight." She caressed him with gentle strokes.

"But because of the Harley, not because of me," he bit his lip, concerned. "Let me do you first."

She was kneeling between his legs, not sure what to do next. "You don't have to."

"I vant to," his eyes glazed over with desire. "I need to. Please?"

She bit her lip with indecision. "Oh, okay." She wasn't sure if she could orgasm again. She released him and backed away.

He rolled off the bed. "Will you lie down?"

She nodded and they traded positions, her body trembling from anticipation mixed with fear. Feeling exposed and vulnerable, she grabbed the blanket to help anchor her emotions.

"I won't hurt you," he whispered before he kneeled between her legs. He hovered his hand above her fist, "Place me."

"What?" she asked, confused.

"Where can I touch with this hand?"

She touched his palm and then moved his hand to her hip.

He swallowed. "And this one?"

She moved his other hand to her thigh.

"Use me," his voice was just above a sigh. "Move my hands where you want them. Use me."

Her heart pounded. He was giving her control over his body. She placed her shaking hands on his and guided them around her hips and stomach. She was beginning to relax and enjoy his touch. His hands were hot and rough with calluses, and his rough heat sent sparks to her core.

"Vhere can I kiss you?" His Swiss accent thickened with desire.

She guided a rough hand up her abdomen to her breast. "Here," she replied.

Bracing himself above her with his free hand, he lowered his lips to her dark brown pebbled skin and moaned when he sucked a nipple into his mouth, his tongue branding her with each flick and caress. When he pulled away, the cold made her shiver.

"Vhere else?" he inquired.

She guided his hand to her collar bone. "Here."

His beard tickled her before his kiss feathered over her sensitive skin, licking the outline above her breasts.

She moved his hand higher up her neck, to her chin, until finally she brushed his fingertips over her lips. "He—" she didn't get a chance to finish before his mouth crashed into hers.

His tongue slid across her lips before invading her mouth with the urgency of a starving man. Their first kiss threatened to devour her soul and body. His fingers entwined with hers and she felt the weight of him press her deeper into the mattress. His soft beard felt damp, tickling her chin and neck when he moaned.

She drank him in, her legs wrapping around him on their own and her hips moving against him with a carnal need. He propped himself up on one elbow while his free hand began to trail down her chin to her breast. She ran her fingers along his bicep up to his shoulders, her hips grinding against his stomach while they enjoyed the long kiss.

After a gentle twist of her nipple, his hand trailed to her hips where he squeezed her thick curves.

He pulled away from the kiss. "Sasha," he gasped against her lips. "Can I touch more?"

Her brain wasn't functioning properly. "What?" She searched his eyes confused.

His lips skimmed hers and he rained kisses along her jaw and down her neck. He licked the line of her collar bone to the center of her body before he kissed between her breasts, squeezing each one and caressing with his tongue.

She arched into him when he kissed her hips.

"Can I lick your pussy?"

She groaned. He had been gentle, letting her approve of every place he touched. She had never been shown such consideration in bed. It was new and a turn on. She sighed, nodding, "Yes."

His breath was hot on her apex. He pushed her legs apart and licked her with firm strokes. His beard tickled her thighs, adding texture to the heat of his velvet ministrations. She whimpered when he circled her slit and sucked her swollen clit into his mouth.

Her breath hitched. "Careful," she whispered. "That almost hurts."

He grunted and lightened his flicks. He was gentle and firm with every movement. "You taste delicious. Can I touch here too?" he asked before he licked her once more.

She gulped, her breath shallow, "Yeah."

He worked her slow, taking his time. When she gasped he repeated, when she tensed, he backed away and worshiped elsewhere. When he slid his thick fingers into her core, it took everything in her not to grind against him for more. He curled his fingers and stroked until she squeezed his head between her thick thighs. He muttered something in a language she didn't understand and then rubbed her G-spot until she came around his fingers with a guttural moan and his name on her lips.

When her tremors had calmed, he stretched next to her, stroking himself while he waited.

Her mouth was dry from all the gasping. She wrapped her arms around him and pulled him close. "That was amazing," she whispered against his glistening lips. Her scent was on his beard.

"Good." He kissed her chin and grabbed her hip. "Do you vant more?"

She smiled. He was a generous lover. "It's your turn," she dragged her fingers through his rough beard.

He rested his head in the crook of her neck, "Okay."

"What do you want to do?" she asked.

A growl vibrated in his chest. "Whatever you want. I vant all of you."

"I want to ride you."

"Mmm," he groaned before he rolled off the bed, taking his heat with him. He picked up his jeans and took out his wallet. Seconds later he rolled on a condom and stood next to the bed. "Are you ready?" he asked with hooded eyes.

The visual of him stroking himself drove her insane. "Come here." She scooted and made room for him after she patted the bed. He laid on his back and rested his head on his hands.

She straddled his waist, her hands on his chest. "Grab my hips," she directed, his hands obeyed, searing her sweaty flesh and digging into her thick curves. She guided him in, feeling him throb between her fingers. When she slowly lowered onto his curve, they both hissed in pleasure.

He stretched her in every direction. She waited for her body to adjust before she began to rock them to oblivion.

For the first time since arriving in Switzerland, the language didn't sound harsh to her. A melody of words graced his lips when he reverted to his mother tongue. Whether he was cussing her out or praying for salvation didn't matter; his baritone was music to her soul, fracturing her defenses.

She closed her eyes, lost in the pleasure of him, her gasps getting louder and less controlled.

"Harder," he begged before his thumb thrummed against her bundle of nerves, shocking her.

She moaned and clenched around him. "What are you doing?" She looked into his hooded gaze, her nerve endings short circuiting.

"Come vith me," he sounded drunk and he gasped for air with each pump of his hips as he moved under her in tandem to her rocking.

When his fingers gently twisted her nipple, she grabbed his hand with both of hers. She could feel a delicious heat spreading through her as she rode him faster and harder. Her eyes started twitching seconds before her body splintered and the world went dark.

Sasha listened to his breathing and strong heartbeat. She didn't know how long she had been passed out on him with their legs entwined. Her eyes were closed and her brain was still rebooting. He had pulled out and was dragging his fingers up and down the valley of her back with long strokes. She wasn't even sure if he had finished. But she couldn't talk yet, so she let her mind wander through the shock of what just happened.

She screwed the lumberjack.

She just had the best sex of her life.

How many times had she had sex and never even orgasmed? It might be faster to count the few times she was left satisfied. Men were either selfish or they enjoyed slapping her around.

But tonight was different.

Ricky Bell was different.

She had creamed herself so many times today that her body vibrated continuously with glorious tremors.

She felt him adjust under her and clear his throat.

"Did you come?" she asked his chest hair, her voice raspy and unfamiliar in her own ears.

"Mmm, you don't remember?"

"I don't."

He chuckled. "I've never felt anyone come like that before."

"You felt my orgasm?" She attempted to lift her head but only saw his beard so she relaxed onto him again.

"I felt every—" he spoke to himself in Swiss German. "I'm not sure how to say...." He grabbed her index finger and squeezed and released it a couple of times. "Kind of like that, maybe?"

"Interesting. I need water," she croaked.

"I'll get some," he readjusted her so she rolled onto the bed when he slid off. He covered her with the blanket and walked his defined ass to the bathroom. She listened to him handle his business while she smiled at her dresser.

He saluted her when he left the bathroom. His body was amazing and she would have to give him permission to walk naked any time he wanted.

He came back with two glasses and handed her one. "You don't have food."

She sat up and pulled the blanket around her. The simple statement reinstated her defenses. "I don't have money." She took the glass and studied the clear liquid so she didn't have to look at him.

"Why not tell me?"

"It's not a big deal," she took a sip of water. She could hear the judgment in his voice.

Silence hung between them until he downed his water and held his hand out for her glass. She gulped it, thankful that he dropped the fact she had been semi-starved.

After he took the glasses to the kitchen, he shrugged into his boxer briefs and jeans. "It's late," he said, buckling his belt, the silver wolf growling at her.

Her heart dropped. Of course he was leaving. This was forbidden. "Right," she had no idea what time it was.

He avoided sitting on her bed with his dirty jeans and kneeled on the floor instead. He searched her ebony eyes as if he were looking for answers. "Can I touch you?"

She nodded and he took her hands in his and kissed her palms.

"I can't stay," he murmured into her right palm, his beard enveloping her fingers.

She swallowed. "I know."

He kissed her palm, soft lips on softer skin. "I want to, I can't."

She cleared her throat. "It's fine."

He searched her face again. "No, it's not."

The words tumbled from her mouth before she could stop them, "We don't have to see each other again. We should stop here. No more motorcycle rides, no more sex."

Annoyance showed in his eyes when they narrowed. "Is that what you want?"

She cleared her throat. "That's what you need." She looked away. "It's late, you should go."

He sighed and squeezed her hands before he stood above her once more. She looked at the wall to avoid seeing his naked chiseled abs. He seemed to be waiting so she closed her eyes.

When her silence continued, he exhaled a deep breath before he left the room and she listened to him pull on his shirt.

Why did she feel so horrible? She knew going into this, they could never be anything but sex. Incredible, mind-resetting sex. Even that was more than she bargained for. She reminded herself to be grateful that he wasn't violent.

She heard his boots approach her room.

"Come lock the door?" he asked.

She nodded. She pulled on a pair of black sweatpants and a black hoodie. Her legs still trembled from the multifaceted orgasms when she joined him in the other room.

He stood at the door waiting for her, his hands stuffed in his pockets.

"I want to see you again," he said when he leaned against her front door.

She studied his face. "Why?"

"Have dinner with me tomorrow?"

"At the café?" She looked out her patio door into

the darkness and noted that without the dark green shadows of the beets, outside was less comforting. "Or the lodge?" She took a few steps closer to him, her past and present warring with each other.

"No, I'll pick you up and take you somewhere. What do you want to eat?"

She chewed on her lip, reminding herself that this couldn't be a date. "A burger would be nice," she said hopefully.

"Ah, American food. Burger and fries?" he asked, with an eyebrow arched in question.

Her mouth watered. If he was paying, she'd eat baa baa stew, but a burger sounded like heaven so she nodded.

"Can I pick you up tomorrow?" he asked, his whiskey eyes watching her.

What was she doing? "Yes," her voice faltered. Her legs had carried her closer than she had intended, the smell of pine and his comforting scent emanating from his leather jacket.

He leaned toward her. "I'll pick you up at four. Can I kiss you?"

Her breath hitched, "Yes."

She could taste herself on his tongue, her honey on his lips drove her wild. She threw her arms around his neck, trying to bring him closer and he responded by grabbing her ass and lifting her up. Her legs wrapped around his waist, the need to feel him again had her rubbing her core against what she assumed was his belt buckle.

With a growl he pivoted, crushing her against the door. The long deep kiss chased away her fear, replacing it with desire. He swallowed and pulled away. "I'm sorry, but I have to go," he lowered her to the ground, his brows knitted and his jeans bulging. "Besides, no more condoms."

She stepped to the side to get out of his way and cleared her throat. "Right, sorry."

He unlocked the door. "It's cold out so don't watch me go." He picked up his helmet and secured it on his head, and then zipped up his leather jacket. "Just lock the door, good night." He kissed her forehead before stepping into the night.

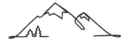

12. THE BURGER

September 7

Can the world agree to get rid of Monday? After the night Sasha had, she was not interested in working. The entire village had witnessed her riding off on the back of Ricky's Harley. They probably heard the motorcycle come back late, and then heard him leave even later. It didn't take a rocket scientist to figure out what happened.

The village was almost back to normal, the empty fields a stark contrast to the lush greenery that painted the valley a few days ago. She went to work where she tried not to bore the kids to tears. Then she hurried home to shower and change for the not date. Next to her door was a pile of wood under a tarp and a box of canned beets.

She had been so deep in her feelings she hadn't noticed that all the neighbors had wood and a box of food waiting by their front doors. Well, that was nice. She dragged in the box and shoved it next to the goblin.

After her shower, Sasha dressed in jeans and her pink cashmere. She used the extra time to clean and straighten up her apartment while blasting music in her earbuds. Music was her safety net, her escape where the world could be blasted into submission with some Ed Sheeran, Beyoncé, or even Metallica. Since her place was small it didn't take long to clean. A notification dinged through her earbuds accompanied by a vibration in her pocket.

Expecting a text from Serena, Sasha was surprised to see that Ricky had messaged her. How did he get her number? How did she get his?

Are you ready?

She replied, *Yes*. She stared like an idiot at his name. He must have input his number. She didn't have a lock on her phone which she would remedy expeditiously.

Two hard knocks jolted her out of her thoughts. She looked at her phone, and saw that it was four o'clock. He must have been outside when he texted her.

When she pulled open her door, he was leaning against the frame holding a basket. His vanilla and sandalwood scent filled the air around her when she stepped back to let him in.

"Hi, I didn't expect you'd be here already," she watched him set the basket on one of the kitchen chairs and shrug out of his leather jacket. He was wearing a light-blue dress shirt and navy blue slacks that had to be tailored judging by the fit. She gulped and closed the door after she looked at his shiny, mahogany brown dress shoes. "Am I underdressed?" she asked.

He was unbuttoning his cuffs and rolling his sleeves up. "What?"

"Do I need to change for dinner?" This wasn't his usual plaid and boots. She looked down at her pink sweater and blue jeans.

He stepped towards her, making her back up to the closed door. "Can I kiss you?"

Sasha gasped her desire, her vagina nodding her head.

He planted both hands on either side of her and lowered his lips to hers. The soft, sensual kiss left her dizzy, then he pulled away and pressed his forehead against Sasha's. He whispered, "You're beautiful."

Ricky returned to the table and began unpacking the basket.

It took her a moment to get her bearings and to remember what she had been asking him. "You're in dress pants," she said when she approached the table.

He glanced at her with confusion and then looked down at his shirt and slacks. "I wore this to work."

So he was a lumberjack who wore tailored clothes.

He placed jars in the small fridge and on the counter.

"What's all this?" she asked when she looked into the basket.

"Food."

She gestured towards the beets on the floor. "I have food now."

"Here's more." He placed bread and tomatoes on the counter and something wrapped with butcher paper in the fridge.

"Um, thanks?" She didn't want to seem ungrateful, the gesture just made her feel weird. Did he expect more from her now?

"Snow is coming," he gestured towards the empty fields outside of her sliding door. "Time to prepare."

She nodded but didn't say anything. She was hungry. Her first pay day was Friday so she wasn't going to turn away free food.

Once everything was put away, she was ready to go after she put on her hiking boots. He unrolled his sleeves and shrugged into his leather jacket and gestured to the door, "Ready?"

"Where are we going?" she asked after she locked the door and turned, searching for his Harley.

There was a sleek, dark blue sports car parked to the left of her apartment building. He jingled his keys and sleek, cat-eye headlights blinked halogen prestige. He walked to the passenger side and held open the door for her.

Her eyes widened in surprise. "Where's the Harley?"

"In storage."

She stared at the red oval emblem stamped with 'BUGATTI' on the grill. Her feet hesitated and she tripped over air when she approached. Maybe he wasn't a lumberjack. She slid into the bucket seat and he closed the door. After she buckled herself in, she couldn't stop her eyes from roaming the lux interior.

Everywhere she looked was blue leather or shiny chrome. He slid in next to her and readjusted since it was a snug fit for his massive frame.

There was a center console that separated them, she guessed for safety reasons, but it felt impersonal.

While he buckled in, she looked up through the double-moonroof to the deepening blue of the sky.

"Ready?" he asked with his hands on the wheel.

She nodded. Her mind was still trying to wrap itself around this situation. She had never been in a Bugatti before. This was the type of vehicle in rap videos with lucious, twerking booties. Not something real people actually drove.

He pushed a red enamel button labeled 'ENGINE' and the car roared to life as if an angry beast had been awakened. She grabbed the handle on the door, the embroidery felt like melted cocoa butter.

He eased onto the dirt road with a purr. They had to go through the center of town to leave and since it was approaching five in the evening, lots of people were out. Every eye was focused on them; several people were even waving. Ricky smiled and did his customary salute while she scooted lower in her seat and tried to hide her face.

When they finally left town, he shifted and the engine growled in response.

"You're quiet," Ricky said after some time passed.

"You, too." She adjusted higher in the seat and gazed out the window. The car was going too fast for her to actually focus on anything but the road in front.

He sighed. "Long day," he tugged at some whiskers on his beard. "I could only focus on eating a burger with you," he smiled but kept his eyes on the road since the Bugatti was devouring the pavement at an alarming rate.

"Where are we going?"

"Geneva. I know the best place for a burger." He zipped down his jacket and undid the top button.

She had so many questions. She wasn't sure where to start. Maybe this was a rental.

"How many cars do you own?" she inquired.

"Just two cars. This one and a Maserati."

Her heart palpitated and she focused on taking slow breaths to keep her anxiety at bay. She swallowed. "You said you like cars."

"Vehicles," he corrected. "If it has a wheel and can move, I want it." He smiled at her with a glance before focusing on the road again.

Berating herself, she tried to calm down. "That's nice. What other hobbies do you have?"

"Hobbies? Hmmm." He pulled on his beard like before. "I guess the usual? Skiing, fencing, polo, traveling... is that what you mean?" His hand returned to rest on the shiny gear shift.

"Fencing?" She imagined him shirtless swinging a hammer at a white picket fence. She squeezed her legs together to suppress her desire.

"How do you say—en garde?" he made a slashing motion with a flick of his wrist.

"Like Zorro?" she asked, picturing a young Antonio Banderas dressed in black in the classic movie.

"Like that, yeah. What about you?" he glanced toward her, trying to engage while not engaging.

She sighed. Sasha hadn't been allowed to have hobbies. She thought back to when she was in the system and then to when she was adopted. "I like to read," she offered.

"Reading is good. I read too much, but it's all for work. I wish I could read for pleasure."

The way he said pleasure caused electricity to roll through her. "Ah, that's too bad." With each passing second, Sasha felt her world and his world grow more distant. She searched her life for common ground. "When I was at Wayne State, I did a lot of volunteer work."

"Volunteer work?"

"I like to help people."

"Like charity?" he asked.

"Similar. I give them my time. I served at a soup kitchen or helped at-risk kids with homework."

He nodded and unconsciously pulled at his beard again. "I used to do that as a kid. When my mother was alive."

"I'm sorry for your loss."

He gripped the gear shift. "It happens, no? People we love come and go."

"I don't know my real mother."

His eyes darted to her, "I'm sorry."

"I'm an orphan."

He gripped the steering wheel and glanced at her. "I'm sorry to hear that."

"It's okay. It's life." Life was never fair.

The mood had darkened. Sasha shifted against the buttery leather. Even though she couldn't touch him, she could smell him. She took a deep, slow breath to calm her nerves.

"Where do you live in Glockenwald?"

He shook his head. "I live in Geneva."

She tried to wrap her mind around this. Geneva was at least a two and half hour drive. Was he driving that far each time? Why? "Oh, so you have family and friends in Glockenwald?"

"Ah, my—how do you say?" They had reached a fork and he checked for traffic before turning left. "It's my ancestors?"

"Your ancestors?"

"Grandfather?"

"Oh, okay. Your grandparents live there?"

"No, my mom's dad's dad's dad, maybe? I don't have family in Glockenvalt right now."

The cogs in her head were spinning so fast she

couldn't decide what to say next. "I see. So, what do you do?"

He raised an eyebrow while he looked at the road. They were finally on a straight, flat stretch and he pressed on the pedal. The growl vibrated through her when the engine was unleashed in the lower gear.

Being from Detroit, Sasha had an appreciation for cars. The Motor City hosted the Dream Cruise where people from all over the world came to drive and show off their rides. But this wasn't just a car. It was a mythical beast, dripping luxury and raw power.

"What do you mean?" he asked her over the roar.

"What do you do for work?" she asked.

"My work?" He tamed the beast before they entered a bend. He seemed to know these roads intimately. "What do you think I do?" he asked with a small smile that seemed forced.

Realizing that he might be uncomfortable talking about his job, Sasha sighed. "Well, I thought you were a lumberjack."

His eyebrows knitted in surprise. "Why a lumberjack?"

"Well," she thought back to that night he found her stranded. "You're tall and fit, you wear plaid and that wolf buckle, and I saw you swing an ax. You helped chop down the big tree."

He chuckled. "Okay. Well, the belt buckle was a souvenir from the States. As for chopping wood, that's not my job. That is—that's survival."

Of course he wasn't a lumberjack with a Bugatti. That was a nice fantasy while it lasted.

He glanced at her. "You're disappointed."

"No, I'm fine," she lied.

He reached over the center divider and patted her knee. "I'm sorry, I'm no lumberjack. But I'll chop wood for you."

That made her smile. She wanted to do things to his wood. She looked up at the sky above them. The blue was deepening and violet streaked behind orange clouds.

He changed the topic from work and they continued talking about likes and dislikes until they entered the outskirts of Geneva. He took side streets and alleyways, somehow avoiding the evening traffic. When he pulled up next to a dumpster in a dark alley, Sasha wondered if he was lost.

There was a light over a nondescript door which he opened and gestured for her to go first.

They entered a busy kitchen with people cooking and shouting orders to each other while steam wafted up to the ceiling. A man who wasn't much older than her approached them, wiping his hands on his apron and speaking French.

"*Monsieur Bell, bienvenue!*" he half hugged Ricky and then turned to Sasha, "*Madame,*" he kissed her hand.

How many languages did Sasha need to learn? She smiled and waited while the men conversed in French.

"Sasha, this is my dear friend Chef Louis. He will make you the best burger ever."

She was hungry. "Nice to meet you. I can't wait for dinner."

Chef Louis led them through the swinging doors where an elegant dining room with low light and sparkling crystals greeted them.

Sasha was not dressed for this.

This was the type of restaurant that required tuxes, diamonds, and trust funds.

Thankfully, Chef Louis led them to the right through an arched walkway where there was a smaller dining area that was empty. There was a wall of mirrors across from a wall of windows, but the cream silk curtains had been drawn, allowing the soft glow of the streetlights through.

A single table set for two was lit with a single candle and a fancy, gold ice bucket with a bottle of champagne.

Chef Louis pulled out the chair for her. *"Madame,"* he helped her scoot in. "So, you will 'ave burgers zis evening?"

"Yes, please." Sasha's stomach was twisting from all of the smells in the kitchen.

After pouring their champagne, Chef Louis disappeared, leaving them alone.

Ricky had taken off his jacket and slouched slightly in the chair, massaging his neck and stretching his muscles. Then he straightened and picked up his flute. "Shall we toast?"

"Sure. To what?"

"Burgers and fries?"

She smiled. "I'll toast to that. So where are we?" She sipped her champagne which was sweet and bubbly.

"This is Chef Louis' restaurant, La Petite Celeste. He has two Michelin stars," Ricky held up two fingers and then poured her more champagne before moving the ice bucket to the floor.

"It looks fancy and expensive."

Ricky shrugged. "We are friends. I never pay," he smiled.

"That's nice." She looked down at the plates in front her. Fine china with a gold line around the edges, silver cutlery she could see her reflection in, and crystal goblets that required shades.

"What's wrong?" Ricky was studying her.

She sighed, "This is a lot."

"A lot?"

"It's overwhelming, and I'm not this," she gestured at the stack of plates in front of her.

"Ah," he placed his flute on the table and pushed out of his chair. He stacked the plates, gathered all but one knife and fork and placed them on the empty table next to them. "Is that better?"

She sighed a breath of relief. "Actually, yes," she smiled at him. "Thank you."

He topped off her champagne. "Don't push it, yeah? Just be you."

"It's hard to be me when I'm not enough," she murmured before taking a sip.

"Who said you're not enough? What do you mean?"

She didn't want to rehash her lack of lineage and prestige. Her mind and emotions were working against her.

Thankfully, Chef Louis arrived with their food. He replaced their bottle of champagne and took the extra dishes away.

The burger smelled amazing. It looked like something out of a food magazine with melted cheese, grilled onions and mushrooms, crisp lettuce and juicy tomato. The meat patty was thick and oozed sparkling juice.

She drooled. She picked up the sustenance from

heaven and squeezed the bun so she could shove it into her mouth. Her first bite was probably the unsexiest thing she could have done in front of the sexiest man she knew. She groaned when the savory and earthy flavors partied on her tongue.

"You like that?" Ricky's voice was husky and his eyes hooded when he sat back and watched her.

Her core heated in response. She nodded, "Yeah, this is delicious." She picked up a long, seasoned steak fry which was still too hot to touch but she didn't care. She could see the herbs and garlic and maybe specks of black pepper, but she wasn't sure. The crunchy potato was crisp when she took a bite, the inside was fluffy while she blew around the fry to cool it as she chewed. She could taste garlic, salt and something earthy.

"Why does this taste so good?" she asked him.

"There's black truffle," Ricky wiped his mouth while he chewed.

Sasha picked up her napkin to wipe her chin. She wasn't familiar with truffles so she just nodded. She had a vague recollection of it being a mystery ingredient on a cooking show.

While they ate, he talked about things to do in Geneva, possible tourist places if she was interested. When Chef Louis came to take their plates away, Sasha asked if she could take the leftovers home.

The disapproval on Chef's face hinted that this was not the place where people took food home.

"I'll take care of it," Ricky patted her hand and went to the kitchen before Chef Louis tossed her burger.

Folding her arms, Sasha stared around the empty room. She could imagine the scandal if she sat in the main dining area with her natural hair, jeans, and hiking boots. Those high-society people would lose their damn minds. The thought made her smile. There was noise outside the doorway, but she wasn't nosy enough to go check. Suddenly a woman dressed to the nines in a satin pink dress that cinched at her thin waist with a sweetheart neckline tapped into the room on diamond encrusted stilettos. She had diamonds dripping from her neck and ears.

"*Où est Monsieur Bell?*" the woman asked.

"I'm sorry, I don't understand."

"Ah, of course. An American," she spat the words like they were poison. "Where iz Mr. Bell?" the woman enunciated as if she were talking to someone with half a brain cell.

Sasha shrugged. She wasn't the man's keeper.

"You're... eating wiz him, no?" There was an accusation in that question.

Sasha nodded.

Ricky appeared next to the bitch in diamond heels. "Bernadette?"

Sasha saw the recognition between them, the way bitch-on-heels readjusted her attitude made her wonder what their relationship entailed. They talked in French while Bern-whatever used her slender fingers to button his top button and rub her hands all over his chest.

Sasha wished she spoke French. It sounded like they were word fucking each other even though Ricky appeared to be uncomfortable and kept glancing towards Sasha. Whether it was a lovers quarrel or setting up for a future booty call, it was quite clear to her that she would never equate to Bernitwat. Unable to stop her anger from rolling in, Sasha tried to ignore them. The last thing she needed was a headline: "Detroit woman attacks hussy in Geneva over lumberjack."

She fingered the stem of her flute while she waited for them to finish their conversation. Even though they probably talked for less than two minutes, it felt like hours before Bernabitch stomped off on her diamond stilettos and Ricky joined her at the table.

He placed a foil packet in front of her. "Sorry about that," he sat across from her and undid his top button, again.

Sasha shrugged before she sipped her champagne.

Whiskey eyes studied her. "You're angry."

"I'm fine," she lied.

He ran both hands through his hair and exhaled a frustrated sigh. "This is why I wanted to eat in here. I know too many people."

That wasn't a know-too-many-people woman. "Okay. Who you screw is your business."

His eyes narrowed. "I've never touched her."

Sasha sighed. "Whatever." She finished her champagne. "Are you ready to go?" She was already dreading the long drive back.

"Can I have espresso first?"

"Do whatever you want." She hugged herself for comfort.

His jaw clenched, and he tapped the table. Then he got up, "I'll be right back." He left her alone again.

_ɅＬ_

After his espresso, they drove back in silence. He attempted conversation but due to her one word responses, he gave up. Sasha's mind had entered the rabbit hole of letting go of a man who wasn't even hers to begin with. Maybe she wanted to keep him because of how he treated her; because she felt safe around him.

When they arrived in Glockenwald a couple of hours later, all of the shops were closed and the streets were deserted. He parked as close to her building as he could without being in the field and walked her to her door.

"Thanks for the burger," she offered once she was standing in her doorway. She couldn't read his expression.

He shoved his hands into pockets, making his slacks look even tighter. "Of course."

"Are you okay to get back to Geneva?"

He shrugged. "Maybe. I'll go slow," he gave her a sad smile. "Can I use your restroom?"

She gestured for him to enter and she closed the door behind him. While she waited she took off her shoes and stowed her leftovers.

When he came out he looked exhausted.

"You can sleep here," she offered.

He raised an eyebrow. "I shouldn't."

"You also shouldn't be driving this late." Even if she was aggravated with him, she didn't want him running off the road in his beast. They'd never find him in those mountains. "You can sleep for a couple of hours and then go," she suggested.

He cleared his throat when he looked at her. "That is smart."

She gestured for him to follow her and she led him to her room. She tried to push thoughts of last night away. "You sleep here, I'll sleep on the couch."

"You don't want to share with me?"

"Not tonight."

"Because of Bernadette?" He stepped closer, towering over her.

She looked at his chest, not ready to meet his gaze.

"I swear I have never touched her."

"Well, she wants to fuck you," she couldn't keep the bitterness out of her voice.

"And I want to fuck you," he declared. "Again."

A gasp escaped her lips before she dared to look up.

"We shouldn't."

"Okay," he inched closer and dragged in a deep breath. "I'll sleep a couple of hours and then drive home."

"Good idea."

He unzipped his slacks and lowered them revealing black boxer briefs and a semi-hard print.

Then he unbuttoned his shirt and folded it in half along with the slacks. He kept on his undershirt and deep blue dress socks with green cactuses wearing sunglasses. He carried his clothes to the kitchen, and she heard him lock the front door.

She hadn't moved, ideas of what could happen next left her immobile.

When he returned, he pulled back her blankets and slid into bed. "Are you joining me?" he asked.

She already needed fresh undies. She swallowed and undressed while he watched. Then she slid in next to him in her undergarments.

He was warm. The kind of warm that made you feel safe and cozy, like fresh chocolate chip cookies with warm milk. She shimmied until she was comfortable. He put his arm around her and turned off the light.

"I enjoyed dinner," he mumbled. "Except for

interruption." The interruption in heels.

"That burger was delicious, thank you." She ran her fingers through his whiskers.

"Can I take you out again?" his baritone vibrated through his chest.

"I guess."

His body tensed. "Don't push it. Only if you want."

"I do want," she admitted.

He hummed in agreement and then his breathing deepened.

What did she want?

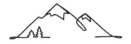

13. SURPRISE VISIT

September 18

When Sasha's alarm buzzed the next morning, Ricky was gone. She had no idea when he had left or how her door ended up locked.

She opened the chat on her phone and messaged him. *Did you get home safely?*

Of course.

Well, at least she knew he hadn't run off the road.

The rest of the week she had to keep pushing Ricky from her mind. She liked him. He was kind, generous, and handsome with his thick beard. He was the only man who had ever treated her with respect behind closed doors. A small part of her wondered when he'd flip the script, but until then she wanted to get to know him. She wished he didn't live hours away in Geneva.

She thought about searching for his name online because he still hadn't told her what he did for a living, but she hesitated. She knew he wasn't a lumberjack, but he was so sexy as one. She didn't feel inadequate if he was a lumberjack. Whoever drove the Bugatti and went to Michelin star restaurants wasn't someone she would normally meet. The lumberjack was more her speed. He was attainable.

There was radio silence from Ricky the next week, which Sasha tried to ignore because she didn't message him either. Instead, Serena treated her to lunch every day which was nice. Having a friend to chat with helped her adjust to her new life.

Friday after work she rushed home, plugged in her phone, then showered before walking to Serena and Claud's farmhouse for dinner. She froze just outside their door when she heard a wolf's howl echo through the alps. It sounded far away, but she was still eager to get inside.

They enjoyed a dinner of a hearty meat pie with minced beef and pork, and a salad.

"We should go to Geneva tomorrow." Serena had stretched out her long, shapely legs over Claud's lap while she nursed a big glass of wine.

Serena had been working Sasha over going to Geneva for weeks. Sasha finally had money in the bank. "I can go tomorrow."

"We can spend the day there. We go early and have lunch. Shop. Have fondue then come back," Claud suggested.

"Sounds good," Sasha agreed.

"I can ask Pietre to join us for fondue," Serena winked at her.

Sasha's anxiety kicked into high gear. "Ugh, no thanks."

"Why not? He still asks about you," Serena pressed.

Sasha shook her head, "I'm good."

Serena nodded and gulped the rest of her wine. "We walk you home, ya? Tomorrow will be a fun day."

Sasha found her purse and checked for her keys and phone. She realized she must have left her phone plugged in on her nightstand. She reminded herself to set an alarm for tomorrow.

She walked between Claud and Serena along the dirt road, arms entwined while they belted a Swiss folk song. When they got to the hopping and the skipping it took every ounce of concentration and watching her feet to keep from tripping all three of them.

The anticipation of shopping put Serena in a really good mood.

When Claud and Serena stopped short, the song deflating in their throats, Sasha looked up to see her lumberjack leaning against his sleek Bugatti.

Serena lowered her arms. "You have date with Ricky?" she whispered.

Sasha shook her head, confused. "No, I don't."

"Well," Claud withdrew his arm. "He waits for you, no?" He lifted a hand and waved, "Hey, Ricky! *Grüezi!*"

Ricky saluted silently before slipping his hand back into his pocket.

Sasha bit her lip. She hadn't heard from him for two weeks and he just showed up like this? This screamed booty call. "I'll see you tomorrow." She walked towards Ricky who was putting off somber vibes.

"We pick you up at nine sharp!" Serena shouted for the entire valley to hear when she waved before dancing away arm-in-arm with Claud.

"Hey Ricky, what're you doing here?" Sasha asked when she was a few feet away from him.

He looked tired, his eyes red. "Can we talk?"

She could still hear Serena and Claud belting folk songs. "Sure," she unlocked her door and he followed her inside.

Sasha was nervous. She didn't expect to see him and she was wearing granny panties. He was in a full black suit. He kicked off his shiny shoes and sat on her couch with a frustrated sigh while he loosened his goldenrod tie and unbuttoned the top button of his white shirt.

She had seen this on a GQ cover once. Maybe he was a model. Modeling was hard work and would put him in the company of beautiful women. He ran both hands through his hair before he stretched his neck and her apex became moist. She didn't move from the door.

He finally looked at her. "I called. No answer."

"I forgot my phone. Sorry." She kicked off her hiking boots. "How are you?"

"Exhausted. I need a damn break."

Wondering if this was when the bad started, she pressed her back against the door, nodding and watching his knee bounce with nervous energy. "Did something happen?" she asked.

His jaw clenched. "I think in America they say 'hostile takeover'?"

"Yes. The lumberjack business?"

His smile was genuine. "Something like that."

Pressing her hands against the door, she slowly exhaled, unsure of what to do next.

He crossed an ankle over his knee then he opened two more buttons. "I wanted to see you."

Her heart flipped in her chest. "Okay."

He shifted his foot back to the ground and cracked his knuckles before he leaned forward. "I missed you." Why did every movement seem as though he was working the camera?

Licking her lips, she wanted to agree that she missed him too. "Well, you're here now."

He stood and after three long strides he was in front of her, his eyes searching hers. "Can I touch you?"

So this was a booty call. She wanted him too. She ached for him. "I haven't heard from you in a while," she heard herself say.

"I know. I'm sorry," he looked disappointed. "I was out of town for work. I'll do better."

"You can have anyone you want." Why was she reminding him of this again?

Confusion crossed his face. "What do you mean?"

She crossed her arms so she wouldn't touch him. He seemed to recognize her discomfort and stepped back, shoving his hands into his pockets.

"I mean," she looked down at her feet before confronting him again. "There are plenty of women you can fuck in Geneva."

His beard twitched, "Yes. Lots of women."

"So why are you here?" Sasha was screaming internally. She didn't want anything serious. Maybe she could be his side chick. But the part of her that had experienced his gentle caresses wanted more.

"I can't stop thinking about you," he admitted before his stance changed and he crossed his arms too.

She shook her head. "So you just want sex? To make me orgasm on your Harley?"

He glared at her. "No," his jaw clenched and he dragged in a breath. He closed his eyes then dragged in a second breath before he gazed at her again. "I like being around you."

"Why?"

He shrugged. "I can't explain, I just do."

Sasha reminded herself that she was in a different culture with different people. She remembered Hilda suggesting she find a lover and enjoy herself, because that's what normal people do. Sex could be a pleasure filled experience with the right person.

She dropped her hands and sighed.

He relaxed too. "I just want to talk. Don't push it."

She nodded and gestured to the kitchen table and they both sat.

He talked about his week in vague terms. He kept mentioning an attempted hostile takeover and she figured he had endured a bad business deal. When he asked about her work, there wasn't much to say besides trying to find better engaging materials for the children.

"What happens at nine tomorrow?" he asked suddenly.

"I'm going to Geneva with Serena and Claud."

He leaned back in the chair. "Can I meet you there?"

"Um," she tapped the table. "I don't know what Serena has planned besides shopping and fondue. But sure?"

He stretched. "Fondue is good." His eyes darted around her place. "You need espresso maker."

"I don't drink coffee."

"For me. So I can drink and drive, ya?" he yawned.

"Wow, okay." The audacity. "But it'll snow soon, right? You won't be coming here."

"Yes, I'll drive through snow for you."

She gulped. The way people had been talking, the winters sounded harsh. "Please don't," her imagination ran him over a snowbank and into a tree.

He tensed. "You don't want to see me?"

"I do," she admitted. "I want you safe."

"I'm always safe."

Men. This is why they don't live as long.

She hugged herself. "Okay."

He stood up, stretched and yawned again. "It's late. I'll see you tomorrow, ya? In Geneva?"

"Yeah, I guess. Are you good to drive?" She stood, worried about him driving a couple of hours when he already looked exhausted.

"Always." He was in his leather jacket and had slipped into his shiny black shoes. He turned to her. "Can I kiss you?"

"Yes."

She exhaled when he enveloped her in his soft leather and vanilla sandalwood scent. He kissed her as if she were his oxygen, causing her to moan in response. He gifted her with a growl before pulling away. "Your lips are sexy," he murmured. Then he hugged her close, relaxing his warm physique against hers in a way that comforted her.

When he let go, her body protested.

"Tomorrow?" he asked again before he unlocked her door.

Her throat felt thick. "Yes. Text me when you get home?"

"Mmm," he kissed her forehead then left.

Whew chile, why did she just let that man walk away?

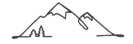

14. I'M GOOD

September 19

Sasha woke up suddenly from a nightmare. She reminded herself that she was in Switzerland when she grabbed her phone and stared at Ricky's text.

I'm home.

The message was sent less than two hours after he left and that shook her. How fast was this man speeding through those mountains in the dead of night? In Michigan people crashed into deer all the time. There had to be some large animal that would shred that Bugatti. Wouldn't even take much, a large rock or yellow Vespa.

And he was tired on top of it all?

She was buying an espresso whatever-he-needed expeditiously.

Serena and Claud picked her up in their silver BMW. Serena couldn't sit still and bounced in her seat the entire way to Geneva while she talked about the shops and the restaurants.

"I need a coffee maker," Sasha volunteered. "Do you

know where I can get one?"

Serena turned in her seat to look at her. "You don't drink coffee."

"Correct. I still need one. Well, something that makes espressos."

"I know a place." Serena talked about a store with beautiful espresso machines and Sasha wondered if this woman remembered she was on a teacher's salary.

When they arrived in Geneva they enjoyed an early lunch at a French bistro. Then the whirlwind named Serena descended.

Maybe it's because Sasha grew up poor that she didn't quite consider shopping a hobby. When she was younger, she met friends at the mall to walk around and look, not to buy. Serena was hell bent on buying Geneva.

They went clothes shopping where the cheapest thing cost more than her entire wardrobe. With Serena's tall, lanky frame everything looked elegant on her. For Sasha, she couldn't even squeeze into their largest size. So she busied herself with sunglasses, scarves, and hats while Serena tried on clothes in every single store.

Claud was smart and said he had other shopping to do. Sasha wouldn't be surprised if he was sitting at the bistro sipping a beer.

Serena eventually dragged her into a home goods store. They found the espresso makers and Sasha couldn't believe the prices. But she snapped a pic and sent it to Ricky, asking if that's what he wanted. Half of her monthly salary would be gone. But if the chrome machine kept him safe, it was worth every franc.

He responded immediately. *I'll get one.*

She wasn't going to argue.

After leaving that store, Serena took Sasha to get

skis. Sasha didn't want skis.

"Everyone skis in winter," Serena explained. "It's good sport. Good transportation."

"I'm not trying to break my neck." Sasha stared at the long, slender metal sticks of possible death.

Serena laughed, "You won't. We'll teach you."

Shaking her head, Sasha walked over to the snowsuits and other equipment. This she needed and spent time trying on boots instead. Her phone buzzing in her purse made her check her messages.

Where r u? Ricky asked.

Shopping.

Where's fondue?

I'll ask. She put her phone away and chose a pair of black snow boots that wouldn't break her bank account. Then she looked at the snowsuits. Maybe she had to order something from Amazon. Her short and curvy frame was not about to squeeze into anything on the racks.

When they paid and left, Sasha asked about dinner.

"Ah, Pietre is meeting us for fondue," Serena sang, swinging her fifteen shopping bags.

Sasha's heart dropped. "Wait, what?" She pulled on Serena's arm, bringing her to a stop in the middle of the sidewalk. "What about Pietre?"

"He's meeting us for fondue."

"Oh, hell naw. I said no, Serena." Sasha crossed her arms, pissed.

"You said, 'I'm good'."

Sasha considered walking into oncoming traffic. She did say that. "In America, that means no!"

Serena shook her head confused. "You Americans are so backwards. How could 'I'm good' mean no?"

Sasha took in a deep breath. She wanted to scream. She almost did. She swallowed and blinked back her frustration before crossing her arms. "Can you cancel?"

"Cancel? Why?"

"Tell him we're going back to Glockenwald," Sasha insisted.

"Don't be silly. I'm starving and you're overreacting. Let's go, we're late."

Sasha watched Serena walk away, swinging her bags. She pulled out her phone and stared at Ricky's name. *I can't see u tonight.*

His response was instant. *Y not?*

We're having fondue with that one guy, Pietre. Maybe we can have dinner next week?

Where's fondue?

I don't know. Sorry. Sasha turned off her phone and stashed it in her purse. There was no point entertaining the idea of seeing Ricky. Serena was waiting for her at the crosswalk, and she reluctantly joined her.

_ⅅⅉ_

If Sasha still had social media she would have posted: "Does Switzerland have earthquakes? Volcanoes? Any natural disaster that could take out a fondue restaurant in Geneva? Asking for a friend."

Sasha sat next to Pietre and considered stabbing him with her fondue fork if he touched her thigh again. Dinner had been going okay until the wine hit and Pietre got handsy. Her skin crawled so much she had lost her appetite.

"How do you like Glockenvalt?" Pietre asked before he bit into a piece of cheesy bread and then licked his lips.

"It's okay," Sasha attempted to smile.

He leaned towards her, ignoring her cringe. "I can show you the sights here in Geneva," he whispered when he grabbed her thigh for the umpteenth time.

"I'm g—" Sasha stopped, she wasn't making that mistake again. "No, thanks," she pried his hand off her thigh.

"There's so much to do here," Serena offered, oblivious to Sasha's struggle.

"I'm sure." Sasha scooted away again. Chairs would have been nicer than the booth. She couldn't get any closer to the wall unless she went through it. Was that an option? She checked her phone for the time, forgetting she had turned it off.

"I can show you all of the hot spots here," Pietre reiterated. He was so close she could feel his breath on her neck.

Sasha hugged herself. She had pushed Pietre away several times and he only came on stronger. Now, all she had left was just to go somewhere else in her mind.

"Sasha," a baritone called her name.

Everyone looked up at a huffing Ricky Bell.

"Herr Bell," Pietre greeted him, confused when he inched away from Sasha. "*Was machst du denn hier?*"

Whatever Ricky said next had everyone looking at her with a healthy dose of shame. "Sasha, do you vant to stay here or come vith me?" he asked, his voice laced with anger.

If there wasn't hot cheese on the table, she would have jumped on that bitch to get away.

"I'd like to go with you," she muttered and grabbed her purse.

"I'm sorry, Sasha," Serena said when everyone scooted out of the booth.

Sasha didn't have words. She was still in her hiding place.

"Ready?" Ricky asked her.

She closed her eyes and tried to ground herself.

Ricky stepped closer to her. Sandalwood and vanilla invaded her space, reminding her she was safe.

"Can I touch you?" he whispered so only she could hear.

Her head dipped and she felt his warm calloused hand envelope hers. Her legs moved when he guided her out of the restaurant. Parked on the sidewalk in front of the door was his Harley which she had been too stressed out to hear.

He handed her his helmet and she squeezed it over her hair and fastened it under her chin.

He was stiff and the anger rolled off him in waves when she climbed on behind him, encircling his waist with her trembling arms.

The Harley roared to life and he inched towards rush hour traffic. He revved the engine so loud she yelped. The cars in front of them honked in protest and he revved again in response.

Traffic must have parted for him because he tapped her trembling hands twice before peeling out of there, leaving burned rubber all over the sidewalk and pavement.

15. THE VIEW

Sasha had no idea where they were going or even if they would arrive alive. He weaved between cars and ran a couple of lights. She was waiting to hear the whirp-whirp of the police pulling them over. The world passed by so fast she just closed her eyes and held on.

After some time, he slowed and stopped in front of a locked garage of a tall building. He dug his wallet out of his pants and waved it in front of a red keypad. When the keypad flashed green, he drove into a brightly lit underground garage. He cut the engine once he pulled into a space and kicked out the kickstand. After he dismounted and glowered at her.

Ricky was livid.

So livid he just rode like a maniac through Geneva without a helmet.

Maybe she should have stayed with Pietre.

She heard him swallow, his lips pressed together and his beard twitching due to his clenched jaw.

"I can call a taxi," Sasha blurted. Maybe he needed to be alone.

"No taxi," he growled. He tapped her helmet and

she flinched. Shaking fingers struggled to undo the safety clip, but she managed and handed it to him. He held out a hand to help her get down.

She gasped when she realized he was trembling too. Swallowing, she followed him to an elevator where he touched his wallet to a pad and the chrome doors opened.

The elevator was all mirrors with a camera right above the keypad. He touched his wallet to the red glowing pad which turned green, and then punched in numbers she was too nervous to attempt to remember.

They rode in silence. She kept her gaze on her hiking boots.

The doors opened into a white foyer with a crystal pendant chandelier and cream marble floors. She followed him to the only door, which was white with frosted glass and he punched in a code.

They entered a cream living space with an entire wall of windows with a breathtaking view of Geneva. The room was so large it had three distinct sections: a pair of low armchairs invited guests to enjoy the heat from the marble gas fireplace; a long leather L-shaped couch faced the seamless wall of floor-to-ceiling windows; and a solitary grand piano was angled toward the room in a way that allowed the user to enjoy the multi-million-dollar view. To the left was a step up into a dining area that had a wall of mirrors and where the marble floors continued into the black and cream kitchen which opened to the great room.

Sasha's jaw dropped.

Ricky had left her by the door and had tossed his keys and wallet onto the black granite island. He placed the helmet on one of three sleek, chrome stools and turned to face her.

This was it. She closed her mouth and hugged herself, waiting for the onslaught.

"Are you okay?" he asked.

She wasn't. She stood there unable to move. Waiting.

He sighed and he approached her, hands in his jean pockets. "Did he touch you?"

She squeezed her eyes closed and nodded.

"Did he hurt you?"

Physically? "No," she whispered, wanting to shrink away.

"Can I touch you?" he asked.

She shook her head.

"Can I stand close to you?" he whispered.

She opened one eye enough to peek at him. His face had softened. If he was still angry, he wasn't showing it. She gulped and nodded.

He slowly approached her until he was close enough she could smell him. He didn't attempt to touch her. He just stayed next to her with his hands in his pockets.

The longer they stood there in the silence, the more she relaxed. She inhaled his comforting scent and listened to his slow breathing.

"Thank you," she sighed.

"I'm sorry." He shook his head, a glint of emotion in his eye.

"For what?"

"I took too long." He shook his head again.

"Huh?"

"Geneva has many fondue restaurants," his jaw clenched.

"Okay?" her eyebrows knitted. "What does—wait."
He had searched for her.
"How many restaurants did you go to?"
"Enough."
Her breath hitched and faltered while she tried to wrap her head around what he was saying. This man just zipped around Geneva searching for her, only to find her squeezed into a booth with some creep's hands all over her. She'd be livid too.
"Thanks for finding me."
He grunted in reply.
"I thought the Harley was in storage?" she asked.
"Easier to search with Harley." He shifted his feet shoulder length apart and he pulled his hands out of his pockets. "I'll put it back tomorrow."
Sasha sighed. She looked around what she assumed was a penthouse. The sun was setting, bathing the city in a golden glow. "The view is beautiful," she whispered.
"Yes," he agreed.
She saw out of the corner of her eye that he was looking at her. She backed up and he took a step back too. "I meant the sunset."
He nodded.
She took in another deep breath, trying to calm her nerves. "Where are we?"
"My home."
Of course this was his place. A lumberjack with a Bugatti wouldn't be living in a cabin in the mountains. The chasm between their worlds grew.
"It's nice," she offered, her anxiety gripping her.
He shrugged. "Can I get you a drink?"
"Actually, I'm hungry."

"Hungry? I thought you had fondue?" he nodded towards the city view.

She wrapped her arms around herself. "I couldn't eat."

"Okay. I should have something."

She followed him into his shiny kitchen. Did he even cook? The stainless steel appliances looked brand new. She could see her reflection on the six burner gas stove with red handles that read 'WOLF'.

He pulled open a large cream cabinet door which happened to be the fridge in disguise. "I can make a sandwich. Or we can order food?"

"A sandwich is fine. Can I help?"

He let the fridge close and he rolled up the sleeves of his navy shirt. "You can relax. Do you want wine?" He washed his hands in the stainless steel sink while she leaned against the black granite counter.

"That would be nice. Can I use your bathroom?"

He pointed to a door on the other side of the dining room. She kicked off her shoes near the frosted front door so she wouldn't dirty the pristine marble in the half-bath.

The more she saw the more her brain screamed that she didn't belong there. The half-bath had floor-to-ceiling cream marble tiles and monogrammed hand towels. She could feel heat emanating under her feet.

When she rejoined him in the kitchen, he had poured two glasses of white wine and was slicing a tomato.

She hid behind the wine glass while she watched him assemble their sandwiches, his forearms flexing and his fingers stretching. She sat on one of the chrome barstools. Just as he finished assembling the food, the sun set below the horizon and the city twinkled around them, reflecting off the mirrors. She could see the lights of the evening traffic snake through the streets below. And he had said she had a nice view? She shook her head in disbelief.

"What's wrong?" he asked, slicing a sandwich in half.

"You're rich."

He tensed and stopped mid-slice. "Yes," he studied her.

Her head wouldn't stop shaking back and forth. She tried to tell herself that this didn't make a difference. But it did. The rich played with people like her.

She was being played.

Sasha cleared her throat. "Thanks for getting me but," she set down the glass with a shaking hand, "I don't belong here."

His eyes narrowed, "Why not?"

She pulled her phone out of her purse, her breath quickening. "I'll ask Serena to come get me."

"Do you want to leave? I can take you home." He finished slicing the other sandwich and placed the knife in the sink.

The vibration in her hand caused her to look down. Serena had sent several messages.

Sasha, where r u?

R u ok?! I have ur bags

We can get u?

Call me.

"Serena wants to come get me." Sasha felt like she was going to hyperventilate.

His hands fisted on the counter. "I'll take you

home."

Sasha shook her head and slipped off the barstool. "No, it's best that I go back with them."

Ricky inhaled sharply, "Why?"

"Because this isn't me," she gestured around his penthouse.

"Dammit, Sasha. Can you relax?" He ran a hand through his bourbon hair and his face flushed a deep pink.

She took a step back.

He was frustrated.

So was she.

He shoved his hands into his pockets. "Just—just don't push it, okay? We can eat and then I can take you home. I. Will. Take. You."

She swallowed. "Don't get angry with me."

"I'm not. It's not you. It's this." His hand flew out of his pocket when he gestured to the view of Geneva in frustration.

Sasha flinched when chilled wine splashed across her face after his finger glanced his glass, sending the crystal flying off the counter and shattering against the marble floor.

"I'm sorry," Ricky said before he cursed in Swiss. He had pulled a towel out of a drawer. "Don't move, Sasha." The look of sheer panic on his face was comical.

He didn't know whether to pat her down or not. "Are you hurt?" He handed her the towel.

She shook her head and wiped her face.

Life had jokes.

She chuckled. She left everything she had and everyone she had ever known to come here. And life handed her this? Her laugh grew manic. The first man she fucks in her new life is one she'll never have. She held her side because pain radiated from the laughter and sheer panic.

"Sasha?"

She opened her eyes to see Ricky holding a broom and dustpan.

She laughed harder and doubled over. Rich people do know how to clean! Get the fuck out of here! The only man in her life who treated her with an ounce of respect was completely untouchable.

"What's wrong?" he asked.

She opened her eyes again to see that Ricky looked horrified. She started laughing so hard she couldn't breathe.

"Sasha? What's so funny?"

She sucked in a breath, tears streaming down her face. "I think I'm having a nervous breakdown!" She laughed again, her side and face hurting.

"What? What are you talking about?" he asked while he swept up the sparkling shards.

She attempted to straighten up and take a breath. "I'm sorry," she gasped. "The one man I've ever wanted is the one I can't have," she gestured at him with one hand then wiped tears from her face with the kitchen towel. "If I stop laughing, I might cry," she admitted, horror snaking around her heart and squeezing it to oblivion.

He ran a hand through his hair, the broom paused in mid-sweep. "It's okay to cry."

"No, it's not," she felt the dread take root in the pit of her stomach and her breath hitched.

She should have stuck it out with Pietre.

She rubbed her eyes with her palms before trying

to focus on him through the tears and chuckles. "Oh god," she exclaimed when she threw up a prayer to the god who had abandoned her decades ago.

His jaw tensed as he watched her. "What can I do? I'm here for you."

She covered her face with the towel because she didn't want him to see her ugly cry. She silently screamed into her palms, desiring the release of a real scream. There was an unfamiliar ache in her chest. With her shoulders shuddering, she attempted to ground herself with a much needed deep breath.

She could hear Ricky sweeping up the crystal around her. She could smell him. She'd never forget his vanilla and sandalwood. Never forget his gentle caresses and the way he made her feel.

No, she had to forget. She needed to. She wasn't a high society woman. She wasn't even a high society whore.

She needed to sit down. Her entire body was shaking and her legs threatened to give out. She started to blindly take a step and he stopped her.

"No. You don't have shoes on."

She dared to look at the marble floor. His shadow spanned out around her in many shades of gray. Even his shadow looked prestigious because of the sparkling pendant lights above the kitchen island.

She had to get out of there.

Now.

The manic laughing was replaced with hesitant shallow breaths and a stream of tears. The ache in her chest threatened to consume her.

Ricky cleared his throat. "I don't trust the floor. Can I carry you to the couch?"

She shook her head. She'd rather walk on glass than have him touch her.

"Sasha," he whispered. "Will you look at me?"

She looked at his blurry knees because that was the best she could do.

"Can we talk? Figure this out?"

She closed her eyes. Her head was pounding. "Can I lie down first?"

"Of course," he reached for her. "Let me carry you, ya? I don't trust the floor."

She crossed her arms in an effort to stop shivering. She nodded once and he had to bend to lift her. A gasp escaped her lips and she involuntarily looked up into whiskey eyes when he cradled her close to his chest.

His gaze was softer than she expected.

She wanted to lean into him, to fill her lungs with his comforting scent. It was all too soon when he lowered her to the long, sleek leather couch that faced the floor-to-ceiling view of Geneva guarded by majestic mountains. Even when the world tilted around her, the view was magnificent. The cool, soft leather felt good on her burning cheek when she closed her eyes.

A soft sigh escaped his lips when he squeezed her shoulder before walking away.

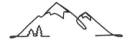

16. CIAO

Sasha opened her eyes to darkness. The memories flooded back and her heart broke all over again. She sniffed and felt movement next to her.

"I'm here," Ricky whispered.

She wasn't on the couch anymore, but felt like she was floating on a cloud. This must be heaven. She remembered dozing off while he cleaned up the champagne and crystal.

She sniffed and wiped her face, she felt sick. Her head throbbed from dehydration and the lack of food.

Every time she breathed, she smelled his sandalwood and vanilla. Every breath hurt. This was a mistake.

"I want to go home," she whispered.

"Of course." A light switched on and she blinked until her eyes adjusted.

They were on a massive bed with the softest comforter she had ever felt. The decor was clean and modern like the rest of the penthouse with white carpets, cream walls and curtains. The bed had a wooden headboard that reminded her of the inside of the town hall in Glockenwald. He was lying next to her, leaning against the headboard.

When she gazed into his eyes she could see his sadness. She swallowed and looked away. He held his hand out and helped her stand. She felt drained of all energy, the room tilting and spinning.

He entwined his fingers with hers and led her to the living room.

He knew.

He knew this would be the last time. They stood next to the door in silence, his eyes trained on their hands.

"Sasha," he started.

"Don't."

His beard twitched when he clenched his jaw, but he remained quiet. He swallowed his words and his emotions. He gripped her hand, as if hoping she wouldn't let go.

She slid into her shoes and put her purse over her shoulder. "Ready?" Her voice cracked, her eyes trained on his feet.

His shadow shook its head. "Sasha, please? Can we talk?"

"Why?" She looked at the handsome man in front of her.

"Please?" his eyes begged her.

Her heart quickened. What was the point? She was an English teacher in a foreign country running away from an abusive ex-boyfriend. She had no delusions about their future. They couldn't be more than fuck buddies. They would never be more. She didn't deserve more.

"Please, Sasha?" desperation laced his voice.

Her throat tightened and she wasn't sure if she

could speak. "Fine," she croaked. She kicked off her shoes and he led her to the long, sleek leather couch she had fallen asleep on. His living room was bigger than her entire apartment.

They sat looking out the window. What time was it? The city was still shrouded in darkness with lights shimmering below them.

He gripped her hand with both of his. He kept starting and stopping as if he were afraid to say the wrong thing. He swallowed several times, his breath even hitched. Eventually he moved to the floor, kneeling next to her with his elbows on the couch cushion while he held her hand.

"Sasha," he swallowed. "I'm sorry."

She turned her gaze from the city below to him. His pain was palpable and his emotion made her eyes burn with fresh tears.

"I'm not trying to hurt you," he continued. He brought his lips close to her hand but didn't kiss her finger tips.

"It's—" she didn't know she had tears left. "I can't do this."

"Why not?"

"Because people like you only play with people like me."

"I didn't tell you because for once, I knew someone wasn't with me because of all of this," he whispered when his eyes glanced to the side. "I feel like our connection is genuine and not because you want something from me. But when you asked about my work, I should have told you." He squeezed her hand. "Sasha, please give me another chance, okay? Let's rest on it?"

Deep down, she knew he was rich ever since he took her for that burger. But a small part of her had wanted her lumberjack to be attainable so she willingly ignored the glaring signs. She couldn't ignore them any longer.

"No." She swiped at the tears on her face with her free hand. They hadn't known each other long. It would be easier to let go, before she was discarded for a European model. Even if they only had one incredible night, their worlds were too far apart.

"Why not?" he spoke to her hand, his beard tickling her finger tips.

"I didn't grow up in this," she gestured around the penthouse with her free hand. "I grew up in foster care before I was adopted—"

"That doesn't matter."

"It does matter, Ricky." Her voice cracked. "I didn't go to Harvard, I couldn't even afford to apply. I'm a nobody."

"Don't say that," he squeezed her hand between his calloused fingers, his eyes meeting hers. "We all have a past. I'm not perfect."

"Not as bad as mine. I was with someone who beat me every day for years," she glared at him.

He gulped, his eyes narrowed while he studied her anger. "I'm sorry. You're a strong woman. You deserve better." He looked at her hand in his. "You deserve the world."

"No one can give me that."

"I can."

She side-eyed him. "Your world isn't me, Ricky." She had seen enough movies and documentaries to know better. "I don't belong in Michelin star restaurants or driving around in Bugatti's."

"Okay. I won't give you my world. I'll give you the world you want. Whatever you want."

"I just want you," she admitted.

Ricky Bell with his Harley Davidson was more than she deserved. He was kind, gentle, and made her feel worthy.

He gazed up at her. "You can have me, Sasha," he whispered.

She shook her head.

Silence rang between them. He continued to gaze at her soft hand in his.

"Give me two months?" he asked finally.

"What?"

"Two months, please? If you don't want me after two months, we can walk away." He searched her face, desperate.

"No."

He sighed in frustration, "Why?"

"Winter is coming. I don't want you driving in those mountains."

"Fuck the snow, Sasha."

"I'm not worth you dead in the alps, Ricky," she retorted.

He growled at her. "I won't be."

That growl vibrated through her. She inhaled sharply, her heart twerking. Her body heated and she looked away, shaking her head.

"I can handle snow," he whispered with less anger in his voice. "I know snow. Even if I have to walk, I'll visit you."

She rolled her eyes. "That's ridiculous."

Anguish crossed his face. "You're being ridiculous.

You refuse me because I'm rich? It's just money. Money comes and goes, ya?"

She exhaled. She closed her eyes and leaned back against the soft leather. Her mind was too exhausted to think.

"Just sixty days," he begged.

"How long will winter last?"

"A long time," his breath was hot on her fingertips. "In Glockenvalt, maybe until April or May."

Worse than Michigan.

She opened her eyes and focused on him. "Maybe after the snow?"

"What? That's a long wait."

She tried to swallow the lump in her throat when she nodded. If he was still interested in her after seven or eight months, then maybe she could try this. Her contract would be up, she wouldn't renew and would go back to the States or somewhere else.

He searched her eyes. "You don't believe me? You don't think I like you?"

She shrugged. "Maybe I'm more like a side chick."

"What's a side chick?"

Holding up her hand, Sasha bent her index finger. "This is the one you love and marry." Then she waggled her thumb. "This is the one you screw and throw away. I'm this one."

"You're not a side chick." He closed his eyes, exasperated. "I will wait seven months, if you want."

"Yes."

"But you might leave next year, no?"

"Yup."

"I can't," he admitted. "You'll just leave me."

He saw right through her plan. She sighed and

regarded him again. This man was begging her to be with him and she couldn't understand why. Had the sex been that good? Well, yes, it was amazing. But he could have any woman he wanted, he probably did have many women. He was tall, handsome, caring, and rich. And it was the rich that terrified her.

Men with money and power used people. They got off on it.

But Ricky....

Sasha bit her lip. "I have three weeks off during Christmas and New Years."

He looked up, hopeful. "Okay. You aren't going back to America?"

She hoped to never go back. "Nope. We can try then."

"For three weeks?" Pain reflected in his whiskey gaze. "That's it?"

"I'll save for a hotel here in Geneva so you don't have to travel to Glockenwald."

He shook his head. "I can go to Glockenvalt."

"No."

He spoke harsh words in Swiss. "Sasha, it's no problem."

"It's a problem, Ricky. I work there. Everyone will know."

He sighed. "I want two months with you." They eyed each other. "After December, I want two months. Maybe three," he looked back to her hand in his. He didn't seem to care that the constant contact had made her fingers sweat.

December was two and half months away. She was sure he would forget about her by then. Two months in the middle of winter meant she wouldn't see him much anyway. "Okay," she agreed.

"*Merci*," he whispered to her sweaty fingers. "*Merci*," he kept repeating.

She smiled. For some reason he was happy, and deep down so was she.

"Can I kiss you?" he searched her face.

"I'd rather not."

He growled, "Okay."

"I should go." She knew the longer she stayed the weaker her resolve would be.

"I need espresso," he sighed. He stood up but didn't let go of her hand. "Come with me?"

She understood his need for closeness. She allowed him to lead her to the kitchen where he worked a fancy espresso maker with one hand. Sasha was sure it took longer than necessary since he refused to let go of her.

"Are you hungry?" he asked. He opened the fridge and took out their sandwiches from earlier. "Might be good, no?"

Sasha was starving so she grabbed one of the plates with her free hand and they walked together to the dining room table. Then back to the kitchen to get his espresso and water for her.

They sat next to each other on black suede chairs and ate in silence. Even though the bread was a little dry, the sandwich still tasted better than any she had ever made. Eating with one hand was awkward, but she wasn't going to pull away from him. This was the only thing she could offer him right now.

When there were crumbs left on their plates, he grabbed his keys and the helmet.

"We should take the car," she suggested. Two plus hours without a helmet wasn't safe.

"This is fine." His voice said it wasn't up for debate.

The ride down in the elevator had been horrific. Her eyes were red and swollen, and her hair stuck out at odd angles. She had to see that reflection repeated a hundred times. He had gotten on his knees and begged her when she looked like that? Maybe he was worth becoming a side chick.

Minutes later she stood next to him and his Harley. He finally released her hand so she could squeeze the helmet over her coils. With his help, she climbed behind him and held on. This is why he insisted on the Harley. He caressed her thigh when he rolled them carefully out of the parking spot. His tense body was hard with frustration. He tapped her hand twice before he pulled out of the garage.

The streets were empty when they roared between dark buildings. He went to a petrol station to fill his tank before taking them into the mountains.

They were alone on the smooth road that snaked along the mountainside. The tall pines whipped by in a nightmarish blur as his Harley snarled at the stars.

She was too busy trying to memorize the feel of him to enjoy the ride. Even still, her body betrayed her once and he caressed her thigh until her tremors stopped.

The ride went by too fast.

Before she knew it, they were cruising past town hall right before he parked next to her apartment.

This was it.

Her chest tightened. She tried to breathe but couldn't.

He helped her off the black and chrome beast.

She handed him the helmet and fished out her

keys. She couldn't speak. Her hands shook so much she couldn't get her key into the lock. After several failed attempts she took a step back and dragged in a breath that threatened to shatter her.

"Let me." His voice was thick with emotion when she handed him her key.

What was she doing?

Why was she pushing this man away?

Because she couldn't fathom that he would want her.

She stepped through her doorway then faced him. He had his hands in his pocket and his shoulders were tense.

"So," he searched her eyes. "December?"

"Yes."

"Can I—" his voice faltered and he broke eye contact. "Can I kiss you, please?"

She needed him to. "Yes."

He leaned toward her and paused, he pulled a hand from his pocket. "Can I touch you?"

She couldn't speak, but nodded.

He wiped away the tears streaming down her face with a rough thumb before his lips touched hers. His lips were soft and tasted of espresso. Maybe she could learn to like coffee. His kiss deepened and his arms wrapped around her when he pulled her closer. He growled, drinking in her soul. The feel of his prickly beard against her sensitive skin was electrifying.

She moaned, desire filling her.

He pulled away too soon. He touched his forehead to hers before he stepped back and readjusted his jeans.

"I'll see you in December," he said when he shoved his hands into his pockets.

"Yes. December."

"*Ciao.*" He saluted her before he returned to his Harley and pulled his helmet over his head.

Her heart threatened to stop. Could she take everything back? Was it too late?

His Harley roared to life. His whiskey eyes found hers before turning to the empty road. He tapped his chest twice before easing away, taking her heart with him.

17. THE WAIT

September 20

Sasha went directly to bed. She didn't have the will to adult. She stared at her wall until sleep claimed her. At some point she went into the kitchen for food and nibbled on chocolate. His scent was everywhere making the ache in her chest deepen.

December couldn't come soon enough.

The soft gray light of dawn filtered through her window when she found her phone at the bottom of her purse to turn off her annoying alarm. A soft gasp pulled from her lips when she saw his name in her notifications. Her heart tap danced against her ribs.

I'm home.

She was glad he had messaged her and sad she was just now seeing said message hours later. Deciding that replying late was better than not at all, she hastily typed in a text, *Great.*

R u okay? His response was immediate. She could picture him sitting in his huge penthouse gazing at the city below while the sunrise painted the sky.

She decided to be honest. *I miss you.*

Her phone vibrated when he called her. Her heart decided to stop while she stared at his name on the wobbly screen because her hand was shaking. Maybe he hadn't meant to call her. "He–hello?"

Ricky sighed on the other end, "Hi."

"Hi." Feeling dizzy, she inhaled sharply. "I'm glad you got home."

"I'd rather be there." He sounded exhausted and hopeful.

Sasha bit her tongue. She knew if she said the words he would be there in two and a half hours.

"Did you eat?" he asked.

"Some chocolate," she whispered. She heard rustling and a grunt.

"That's good," he yawned. "Please eat more. I'll call you later, okay?"

"In December."

He growled his frustration. "This week. Take care, Sasha."

"You too."

She stared at her phone after the call ended. Was this their lifeline?

_ʌʌ_

The weeks dragged on. Sasha finally got around to studying Swiss German via YouTube videos. Learning the basics would make life easier. She spent her evenings with her laptop and a blanket wrapped around her because each day felt colder than the previous. She hadn't seen Ricky, but he did call her to talk.

He would talk about his summers in Glockenwald when he was a kid and pranks he pulled on his parents or on Hilda. Sometimes they wouldn't talk at all. They would sit in silence cherishing what little interaction they had.

She started finding solitary flowers in front of her door after work. There was never a note, but only one person could be leaving them. After researching each flower, she added it to the glass on her table. Eventually she had a bouquet of beautiful flowers in various stages of decay. When one got old, she either dried it on the black goblin in the corner of her kitchen or threw the flower away. The goblin was some ugly cast iron contraption that she covered with a pink table cloth. It was perfect for drying her flowers.

The first snowfall was at the end of September. Sasha woke up and everything was sparkling with thick and fluffy snowflakes that had fallen overnight and were already melting due to the morning sun.

In her excitement she called Ricky, who answered on the first ring. "Hello?"

"It snowed!" she exclaimed.

"Oh? One moment." There were voices in the background and he sounded distracted.

"I'm sorry." Of course he would be at work. "I shouldn't have called." This was the first time they had spoken during work hours.

"Hold on," there was shuffling and then silence. "Sasha?"

"Yeah, I'm sorry I called. I'll let you go."

"Don't. It's no problem. I was just in a meeting." He cleared his throat. "So, there is snow?"

"We can talk later."

"We can talk now. It's raining here."

"Everything is sparkling like diamonds. But the

mountains look so majestic. I've never seen anything like this before," she explained. "I wish you were here. You could sip on an espresso, maybe?" she teased.

He was silent.

Glancing at her screen to make sure the call was still connected, she asked, "Hello?"

"December," his baritone was thick with emotion. She heard a woman's voice call his name. "I need to go back."

"Right, sorry," she apologized.

"Never be sorry." He ended the call.

_ᴧᴧ_

With the snow came the avalanche of tourists from all over the world. Sasha was shocked to see what had become her little hideaway be invaded by throngs of people. She kept her head down and avoided eye contact when she walked to work or to the café to meet Serena for lunch. Then Serena and Claud had the audacity to insist Sasha learn how to ski. One of the families lent her a pair of old skis so she couldn't make up excuses anymore.

When she sat in the ski lift for the first time, she realized she didn't like heights. The view was amazing, but the possible fall to her death had her anxiety in overdrive.

"Look!" Serena patted Sasha's leg, causing more palpitations. "Do you see the wolves?"

Sasha followed the gloved finger to a thin line of minuscule wolves running along a mountainside. If there hadn't been a pristine blanket of white snow, she wouldn't have seen the ant-like wolves running in a pack. "Should we go inside?" Sasha asked, worried.

"No problem," Claud said when he and Serena entwined arms with her, prepping to dismount the ski lift. "They are so far away. Not many wolves here."

While Sasha practiced bending her knees and angling her skis to form a V, she regretted the entire skiing fiasco. Why did people do this? The good part was that the snow was softer than the ground. The bad part was that the snow was softer than the ground. Getting up was a bitch. After her fifth fall, she just laid there, her knees bent with her boots still clipped into the skis while she stared at the darkening sky. This wouldn't be a bad death. The headline would read: "Black American woman found in Swiss alps. Skis still attached to her frozen corpse."

Skiing made her entire body hurt. This is why these people were fit all year long. She was used to munching and hibernating all winter, not sliding down a mountain on metal sticks at break-neck speed.

After the third evening of 'lessons', Sasha decided skiing wasn't for her. She put the skis in her closet and went back to her less painful language lessons on YouTube every evening.

_᠕᠕_

September slid into October. With only a few hours of daylight, huge LED flood lights attached to the ski lifts lit up the slopes. Every afternoon when Sasha trudged home in the snow, she could see dots of people meander down break-neck mountain. Everyone kept inviting her to ski, but she had to draw the line somewhere.

Since the snow kept packing into the valley, town hall became the heart of Glockenwald. They had gatherings every day of the week so people had stuff to do. There was a weekly game night, her adult English conversation practice, ballroom dancing, knitting club, and movie night. She went to everything because that was better than sitting alone in her freezing apartment.

Her English conversation sessions had started with just a couple of people, but as each week progressed, more villagers had shown interest and she had to run two half-hour sessions to accommodate. She utilized YouTube to play short video clips then discussed the differences in cultural nuances and American English pronunciations. One of her first lessons was to discuss the many uses of 'I'm good'.

She enjoyed ballroom dancing the most because there was something elegant about gliding gracefully across the floor. She had only seen dancing like this on TV, but watching couples flow around the hall in person was mesmerizing. Often she had to dance by herself, but that was okay. She had found a new passion that was much safer than skiing.

With October coming to an end, she asked if the town would be interested in a Halloween event. The residents didn't turn down the excuse to party. During school hours, she helped the kids make masks and costumes. Then together they decorated town hall with paper cut outs of pumpkins, bats, and ghosts. Decorating reminded her of being in foster care and helping Betty prep for the holidays. Betty couldn't have kids of her own. She did what she could in fostering at-risk kids like Sasha. Sasha wondered if she could still patch up their relationship.

For the Halloween party, Lilith baked ghost shaped cookies and the kids showed up in their handmade costumes. They danced the night away to Halloween music while munching on cookies and popcorn.

_ᴧᴧ_

November brought a snowstorm of epic proportions. School had been canceled even though the walk wasn't far, the wind was just too cold. Sasha huddled in her room under all her blankets wearing several layers of clothing.

It's so cold. She messaged Ricky. *How do people live here?*

Her phone vibrated in her hand when he called her. She checked the time, he was probably at work. "Hello?" she asked.

"Sasha?"

She could hear talking in the background. "Ricky? Hi. I'm sorry, I figured you would text back whenever." She pulled the blanket over her head in an attempt to cocoon herself.

"Does your stove have fire?"

"I'm not cooking right now," Sasha looked at her bedroom door, confused.

"The fire, Sasha," he seemed frustrated.

Concerned, she got out of bed with her blanket wrapped around her and walked to her tiny kitchen. She checked that her stove and oven were off. "Everything is off, Ricky. I'm confused."

"The black one in the corner."

Her eyes whipped to where she had covered the black contraption with a pink table cloth in order to dry flowers. She lifted up the table cloth. "I'm an idiot." Her place didn't have central heating, but there was an old fashioned fireplace that looked like a goblin on spindly legs putting its head through the wall. She had covered the darn thing back in September and had used it as an extra surface.

"Did you find it?" Ricky asked.

"Yeah, now I have to figure out how to use this thing. Thanks, Ricky. Sorry to bother you."

"Never be sorry."

The process of trying to find dry wood in a blizzard exhausted her. Even though the wood had been stacked near her door, she hadn't touched the stack in months and a lot of the wood was wet and frozen. But after some sacrificial paper and a couple of dried flower petals, Sasha finally had a fire going in her cast-iron goblin stove. She stacked more wood to the side of it so they would dry out and could be used later. At least she had heat; glorious she-would-never-take-for-granted-again heat.

The blizzard continued for three days. This was insane. So much snow had fallen she couldn't even see out her window. She wondered what the mountain roads would be like. Now she understood why everyone freaked out about winter. She half expected white walkers to pass through town on their way south to the wall. At least the snow acted like insulation and helped keep her warm.

Sasha spent her time waltzing around her tiny apartment and practicing her Swiss. Being buried in snow and isolated was still better than what she had experienced in Detroit. As long as the wind didn't blow too hard, she had internet and entertainment.

On the fourth day, the storm had passed and the town dug itself out. There was so much snow they dug stairs and created pathways for walking or skiing on top because that was quicker than digging through snow.

Being so high up was surreal. She could see the roof of her apartment which fed her fear of heights. Since the snow was several feet high, she wondered if anyone would find her if she fell off the path.

She followed the packed maze that others used and made her way to work. Glockenwald became a frosted village, and she realized she loved living there.

_ʌʌ_

As November crept by, Sasha began researching Geneva. She hoped there were other things to do there besides skiing. She realized staying in a hotel for two or three weeks might cost more than she had been able to save.

She texted Ricky to ask where she should stay.

Her phone started ringing.

"What do you mean?" he asked before she could say 'hello'.

"Hi to you, too," she teased.

"Sorry," he said over the background noise. She noted that he was probably still at work.

"I'm trying to find a hotel. I don't want to be too far from you."

"Why do you need one?"

"A place to stay."

He cleared his throat. "Stay with me."

She exhaled and her body reacted to his suggestion.

"Or, I could try and find a place in case things don't work

out."

He was silent so she listened to the conversations in the background. She could understand a couple words. "Why wouldn't this work out?" he asked after the long pause.

She dragged in a sigh. "Can you just text me an area? So I know where to look? I should book something soon."

She could hear him swallow and the background noise receded. "I will find you something," he sounded sad.

"I don't mind looking," she offered. "I just don't know where you live."

"I'll take care of everything," he insisted.

She tapped her fingers on the table. She didn't want this to be an argument. "I just want to have my own space," she explained.

"Okay. I have three bedrooms. You can have space. Don't push it, okay?"

Staying with him would save her money. She chewed on her lip. "I know you're at work. I'll think about it."

They ended the call and she stared through her laptop screen. Three weeks with the lumberjack sleeping in the next room? Or in her room? Or she could sneak into his? Her imagination ran rampant with the possibilities and she had to rein it in so she could focus.

She opened up her period tracker and checked the dates. She knew how squirmy men were with 'woman stuff'. Unfortunately, her monthly was smack in the middle of her vacation. She should get a hotel for that time at least.

Damn body. Ruining her time with the lumberjack.

Thankfully, after she got an IUD a couple of years ago her monthly had been lighter. She had suffered a couple of miscarriages because of the beatings. She decided preventing pregnancy was prudent. She was too broken to raise a child anyway.

Ricky called her the next evening. He mentioned work was busy, and that he had to go to New York. Great. Sexy, Swiss lumberjack in the Big Apple.

"For how long?" she asked.

"A couple of weeks."

"Sounds like a long trip," she sighed. "Does this mean I can't see you in December?"

"I'll be back. I'll pick you up," he assured her.

"Okay."

"I can't talk much in New York."

"Oh. Why not?" Sasha asked.

"Long meetings and time differences."

The real separation was about to begin. She opened up the calendar on her laptop. "When are you leaving?"

"Tomorrow."

Her stomach dropped. "When are you coming back?" She was used to his daily texts and weekly phone calls.

"December 19th."

That was supposed to be the day she was going to Geneva. "Oh, we can move my trip back a couple of days."

"No. I'll fly in and I'll come get you."

She remembered how tired she had been traveling from Detroit to Switzerland. "I can wait a couple days."

"I can't," he whispered. "I'm going to miss you."

"Same." She crossed an arm over her stomach. "Well, I'll be ready."

"Good."

"And I need a hotel," she reminded herself.

"Really, Sasha? I have room."

"It's…" she trailed off wondering how to elaborate. "You know, it's my period—when I bleed."

"I don't care about that. You can stay here," he reassured her.

She sighed. His place was big. With white everywhere. She used a cup, but she would pack extra pads. "Okay, thanks."

They talked while Ricky packed and discussed places he wanted to show her. She was excited about December too.

18. THANKFUL

November 22

T he holidays had always been rough due to excessive alcohol consumption which fueled worse beatings. Jackson always isolated her, no work, no parties with family or friends. She wasn't even allowed to go shopping without him. The loneliness and fear she experienced usually made her dread this time of year.

For once, Sasha looked forward to spending Thanksgiving alone. She would be safe, even though she missed Ricky.

Being an American holiday, she still went to work on Thanksgiving Day. She made turkey handprints with the little kids and the older kids wrote about being thankful in their daily journals. Most of them wrote they were thankful for Friday. Typical teenagers.

On her way home, she passed Hilda who was standing outside the town hall talking with Hans, Sasha's usual dance partner.

Hilda waved her over. "I hear you've been waltzing, ya?" she mused before pulling Sasha into a hug.

Sasha waved to Hans. "It's been fun," she admitted.

"Are you dancing tonight?" Hans asked her. He had also been attending the adult conversation sessions.

"I think I'll try," she offered.

He put one hand to his chest and the other hand out to an invisible partner and moved his feet. "Tonight we could do salsa or tango, ya?" He moved his hips in an exaggerated circle that made her chuckle.

She loved the tango. "That would be nice."

"Okay, see you at six, Sasha!" He walked towards the café with a wave over his shoulder.

"With hips like those, maybe I should tango too, no?" Hilda laughed and did an impersonation of Hans. "Have fun tonight, Sasha."

Sasha walked home. The snow had been well packed by everyone trudging over it. The road and sidewalks were sloshed and muddy but that didn't stop her from dancing the tango the entire way. When she searched for her key in her crossover bag, she saw a flash of yellow in the corner of her eye. Sasha glanced up when she heard the gentle echo of a woman's laughter. The eerie laugh reminded her of the one she heard when Ricky had found her in August. But when she glanced around her, no one was there. Since tourists had packed into Glockenwald, hearing someone laugh or scream was typical. But she felt the hairs on the back of her neck stand up so she rushed inside.

A couple of hours later, Sasha tangoed her way back to town hall. Since not much can be delivered in the winter, one of the ladies in class had made her a flowing dance skirt that fluttered when she twirled. Another had an extra pair of shoes that happened to fit her. She was excited to be spending her Thanksgiving dancing.

When she was almost to town hall, her silver dance shoes dangling from her hands, she saw Hilda exit the building and wave to her. "You came?" Sasha asked when she jogged over. They hugged and hurried inside where it was warmer. "Do you know how to tango?" Sasha asked her.

Hilda was wearing a black suede dress with ruching at the top and a flowy skirt. A black clip with pearls held her blond hair behind her left ear revealing more of her long neck. "I have from time to time," Hilda responded when they climbed the steps.

"I can't wait to see. You look amazing by the way." Sasha wished she had an elegant dress. Or even a basic dance dress would do.

They crested the top of the stairs and Sasha stopped.

"Happy Thanksgiving!" The entire village was packed into the dining hall. The tables had been brought out and they were loaded with food.

Hilda wrapped an arm around her shoulder and squeezed. "You said you weren't going home for the holidays, so we thought we would surprise you with dinner, ya?"

Sasha's chest tightened with anxiety, her ears felt as if someone had stuffed them with cotton. She shook her head and backed up, her feet taking her to the edge of the stairs. "I'm sorry." She ran back down the stairs with Hilda at her heels.

"Sasha, what's wrong?" Hilda caught up to her just outside the main door and grabbed her hand.

Fear had taken hold of her. The logical part of Sasha's brain knew that Jackson wasn't there. But the beaten part of her brain knew there would be consequences for her being around so many people and her fight or flight response kicked in. With tears streaming down her face, she shook her head at Hilda. "I'm sorry," she gasped. "But I can't—Thanksgiving—" Anxiety choked off the rest of her words.

With wide blue eyes, Hilda waved the others back inside. "You're okay," she insisted when she gripped Sasha's hand to help anchor her. "Do you want to talk about it?"

Sasha wiped at her tears with her free hand. "He would beat me so bad, I'd pass out for hours." Covering her face, she couldn't hold back the sob anymore.

"Oh no. Sasha," Hilda pulled her into a hug. "We didn't know. We just wanted to give you a special dinner. Come on," Hilda guided her back to her apartment. When they got there, Hilda fed the goblin and they sat together on the couch while Sasha recounted what happened to her for three years. Although the excruciating process caused both women to sob, it had also been cathartic.

Franc brought food for them and a poster the village had decorated with a bunch of turkey handprints and names under each one. Big colorful words, 'We Are Thankful For You' were written across the top.

"I feel awful," Sasha told Hilda while the two women ate at her small kitchen table. "I just walked out on everyone."

"No worries," Hilda waved off her concern with a sniff. Her blue eyes were red and swollen. "I didn't know about the abuse. I promise you, no more surprise parties."

"Thanks. I guess I have a lot of apologizing to do," Sasha said when she eyed the poster propped against the couch.

Hilda shrugged. "Don't apologize for being you. They'll understand. Everyone adores you." She tapped at her plate with her fork before grabbing Sasha's hand and giving a comforting squeeze. "I hope I'm not overstepping, but you have access to therapy. I can help you make an appointment."

Sasha nodded. Running to Glockenwald had saved her in more ways than she could count. Her broken soul was beginning to mend. "I'd love that."

19. LINEAGE

December 13

Decemeber rolled in with more snow and blistering winds. The altitude was no joke. After the Thanksgiving fiasco, Sasha made more of an effort to get to know people. She stopped by the café alone and tested her language skills, she accepted dinner invitations, and never missed an event at town hall.

The 'We Are Thankful' poster precariously hung above her couch because she was too short to hang it higher. But when she came home everyday, the handprints reminded her that she was thankful for them too.

The week before her vacation, she joined in decorating town hall. She had finished helping Hilda hang lights on the tree in the corner. They had more lights to detangle for the banisters.

"What will you do for Christmas?" Hilda asked while they each pulled at different cords.

"I'm going to Geneva."

"Oh, that's nice, ya? You should travel more, no? Go

to Paris, Zurich, and Amsterdam."

She hadn't been anywhere since Geneva. "Yeah, I should."

"Enjoy yourself," Hilda yanked on the twisted cables and cursed. "I don't know why, every year this shit happens." She dropped her end of the tangled lights and dragged another box out of the storage closet that was under the stairs. "What about New Years?"

"I think we'll still be in Geneva," Sasha answered when she picked up the end Hilda had dropped.

Hilda didn't miss a beat. "We? Who are you going with?"

Sasha looped the cord around her fingers. "A friend."

Hilda faced her, hands on her slender hips. "A male friend?" she asked with a smile gracing her face. "Tell me who, I'm curious."

Sasha shook her head. "I shouldn't."

Hilda went back to the box. "I know who you know. The only single men I know who spend time in Geneva are Pietre and Rickart." She pulled out a red bow bigger than Sasha's head.

"I haven't really spoken to Pietre," Sasha admitted and then gasped. Well, if Ricky was going to pick her up, everyone was going to see them together anyway.

Hilda nodded at the bow. "I grew up with Ricky's mother. Wonderful woman. Tragic what happened to her."

"What happened?"

"Not my story to tell," Hilda pulled out another red bow and turned to Sasha again. "But if it's Ricky you're seeing, just be careful."

"Why? He's a nice guy."

"He's nice, ya? He isn't the problem. His family however...." Hilda placed the bows on a bench. She walked to the hidden closet under the stairs and disappeared inside. "Come here," she called.

Sasha dropped the tangled lights and joined her.

Hilda had dragged out a large dusty box. Inside were old pictures and albums yellowed with age. "These used to hang in here. When Marie died, Tobias wanted them destroyed. I hid them here."

Hilda pulled out a framed black and white photo and pointed to a group of men with beards. "This is Leon Glocke. He founded Glockenvalt. He built Town Hall. Glocke is German for Bell."

Sasha swallowed. She stared at the black and white photo trying to find a resemblance. Her heart started to pound. Bell was Glocke, which was in Glockenwald. Holy shit. This is why everyone knew Ricky. He was Glockenwald.

Hilda took out a black photo album. She flipped pages and found a black and white photo of town hall when it was just a wooden frame. Leon Glocke stood in front of the structure looking somber.

Then Hilda flipped a few more pages and pointed to Leon Glocke with a boy. "Rickart Glocke, great grandfather." Sasha attempted to read the faded fine scripted ink in the yellowed border of the photo. These pictures were more than a hundred years old.

Hilda kept going, "Rickart Bell. When world trade started to ramp up, Rickart changed the family name to Bell to appeal to Westerners."

Time had fast forwarded and Richard Bell now had a son. In this one, the boy was smiling with his arms crossed. She recognized that smile. Sasha's heart double dutched hard against her chest.

Hilda closed the album and pried out another one that didn't look as fragile. She carefully turned a couple of pages. "Marie Bell and her father."

This was in color, but still faded with age. A young girl smiling up at her dad in front of town hall. She had on a yellow dress with black shoes and frilly socks.

Sasha blinked when Hilda turned more pages. She seemed to be searching for certain pictures and Sasha wanted to scream at her to stop. She needed more time with each photo.

The pages stopped turning and Hilda pointed to a photo of herself and another teenage girl with golden curls and piercing blue eyes. Marie Bell was in blue jean shorts and a yellow hat smiling up at the camera while holding up clumps of dark earth.

"She was my best friend," Hilda said, her voice thick with emotion. "Until she left. Then she changed." Hilda sniffed and turned the pages again.

"This is Ricky," Hilda pointed a long finger at a fat toddler boy with dark curls dressed in dark blue overalls, and a striped red and white shirt; carrying a beet. She had trouble picturing Ricky without a beard.

"His baby brother, Finn," Hilda pointed to a baby boy with blond hair and blue eyes digging his hand into the dirt and looking up smiling. "Marie and Sofia, Ricky's sister. They were twins, Sofia and Finn."

Sasha was speechless. She stared at Marie Bell holding a chubby baby girl with a red bow in her blond curls. "I didn't know he had siblings," she said to herself.

"He doesn't," Hilda snapped the book closed and Sasha looked up confused. The emotion on Hilda's face stopped her heart. "They all died," she sniffed and put the album back in the box.

Sasha's heart broke. "What happened?" she asked.

"Tragic accident," Hilda shook her head and wiped at her eyes. She pushed the box back into the closet. She sniffed back her tears. "Anyway, Ricky is amazing. It's his family I don't like."

Sasha half wondered if she should do an internet search to find out what happened. But she preferred to hear from the source. She hugged herself. She had seen so much history in a matter of minutes.

"I haven't met them," Sasha said more to herself. "We aren't really dating. Just friends."

Hilda picked up the bows and regarded her. "That's too bad," she said finally. "Marie would've liked you."

_ʌ_

True to her word, Hilda helped Sasha get an appointment with a therapist. Hilda was kind enough to drive her to Frutigen because Sasha still wasn't comfortable navigating the mountain roads or using public transportation. Since Sasha had never been to a therapist before she wasn't sure what to expect. Nervousness made her stomach twist and clench, and sweat dampened her forehead when she waited to be called while seated in the modern lounge.

The waiting room was small with three blue plastic chairs facing a glass coffee table covered in old magazines. There was a plastic plant in the corner that needed to be dusted and generic looking pictures of a desert. The receptionist sat at her desk typing quietly and ignoring that Sasha was there.

When the door opened suddenly, Sasha almost

jumped out of her skin. A young man eyed her curiously before escaping through the main door.

A woman in a black pencil skirt and powder-blue blouse stood in the doorway looking at her watch with a sigh. "Sasha Villiams?" she asked when she caught Sasha's nervous gaze.

"Yeah," nodding and standing up, Sasha gripped the strap of her purse for dear life.

"Come in," the woman encouraged her. "I'm Ana Meier, nice to meet you."

Keeping the handshake brief because her palms were clammy, Sasha nodded. "Nice to meet you too. Thanks for seeing me on short notice."

"Of course, have a seat vherever you like."

There were three possible seats. The couch was a definite no because she didn't want to lie down. There was an armchair that looked semi-comfortable and then there was an office chair on wheels. Feeling frozen, Sasha just stared.

"Anyvhere you like," Meier said again.

Forced to choose, Sasha sat in the armchair and continued to grip her purse.

Dr. Meier sat in the office chair and grabbed a notepad from her desk. After a brief introduction, Meier asked, "So, tell me, vhy are you here?"

That was a loaded question that could take months to answer. Licking her lips to buy time, Sasha then cleared her throat. "Um. I had a rough past."

"Vhat do you mean by rough?"

Swallowing her shame, Sasha stared at the floor. "I dated someone who was abusive." She inhaled a shaky breath, trying to find courage to speak through her anxiety.

"I'm sorry to hear that," Meier said. She crossed her thin legs and tapped her pen lightly against her pad of paper. "Did you vant to address your past?"

Closing her eyes, Sasha wondered if she could talk about it. "Not really. I'm having trouble relating to people right now," she explained. "I have anxiety attacks in large groups. I can't stand to be around men." Ricky's bearded face flashed before her eyes. "Most men," she corrected.

Ana was scribbling on her pad and nodding. "Vell, a lot of our anxiety stems from past trauma. In understanding our trauma, ve can move forward in our current relationships."

That sounded reasonable so Sasha nodded.

"Hilda Holte told me you are from America. Is that correct?"

"That's right."

"And how have you been adjusting?"

Heaving a sigh, Sasha shrugged. "It's different."

Meier tapped on her pad and her foot wiggled slightly. "That's to be expected. Vhat have you been doing to cope vith the change?"

"Not much. I just kind of freeze up before I go somewhere else in my head," Sasha admitted.

"That's not a healthy vay to deal vith your anxiety."

"I figured," Sasha frowned. "That's why I'm here, trying to address it."

Nodding, Meier smiled at Sasha with keen green eyes. "Tell me about yourself. Your family? Friends?" She leaned toward her desk and picked up the form Sasha had filled out earlier. "It says here you vent to college?"

Feeling overwhelmed, Sasha nodded. "There isn't much to tell. I don't have any family and I don't really have friends."

Green eyes narrowed before the sound of the pen scratching across the paper made Sasha wince.

Clearing her throat, Sasha tried to push on. "But yes, I did go to college. I studied English and journalism."

Once the pen stopped moving, Dr. Meier glanced at the form again. "You've been in Glockenvalt since August. Vhy do you think you have difficulty making friends?"

"Because I just want to hide."

"Hide? Please explain."

Crossing her arms, Sasha tried to hug herself. She wanted to melt into the armchair and disappear. She dragged in a deep breath, looking everywhere but at the woman who was observing her every tick. "I wasn't allowed to have friends," she answered finally. "My ex, Jackson, he controlled who I spoke to, where I went, and if I had money."

The interest on the other woman's face as Sasha retold some of her trauma made her wonder if she should forget about therapy. The session didn't feel cathartic like when she had cried on Hilda's shoulder. This felt like she was ripping her soul apart while someone watched through a microscope.

20. DECEMBER

December 18

The night before Ricky was supposed to pick her up, Sasha was in the zone. She cleaned her apartment; painted her toes a dark red with the only bottle of polish she had; washed her hair and twisted her tight curls into Bantu knots; shaved her legs and underarms; trimmed around her lady-bits; and slathered her body with cocoa butter.

She packed most of the clothes she owned because she didn't have much. She noticed she had lost some weight over the last couple of months thanks to trudging through the snow and dancing. Maybe she could go shopping now. She still had her curves, they were just slimmer, and a little more defined. Her booty even looked bigger.

After the chores were done, she sat at the tiny kitchen table, enjoying the heat that radiated from the goblin while she ate canned beets and stared at her phone. He hadn't messaged her since last month.

Her anxiety was kicked into high gear. New York had beautiful women from all over the world. And he could have any woman he wanted. She bit her lip and dropped her fork back into the jar. He had sent her a text before he had left for New York and she couldn't stop staring at the eight letters.

December.

She put her phone down and opened her laptop to double-check that she had paid her bills. Then she searched for things to do in Geneva for Christmas. There was a parade where everyone wore bells which could be interesting. She wanted to go shopping for a dress and shoes she could tango in. Maybe she could find a ballroom class to attend.

She loved ballroom dancing. Gliding around the floor made her feel in control and powerful. Hans was usually her partner and he was amazing. He was in his sixties and had been studying ballroom for a long time. He would bow to her, ask her to dance, and then whisk her away. Sitting at her table, she wondered if Ricky knew how to dance.

She wrote down some store names and addresses and then searched Geneva for New Year's events. There were many parties that required registering on guest lists which were already closed. Sighing, Sasha closed the laptop and picked up her phone. She wanted to text him. She couldn't stop staring at his *December.* She didn't even know if he had returned yet. What if his flight had been delayed? She bit her lip while she texted the only thing she could think of.

It's December.

Sasha tossed and turned all night. Her nerves had kicked into overdrive and she was second guessing her life.

The next morning she turned off her D-day alarm

before she bounced out of bed. She dressed in her loose-fitting jeans and pink cashmere sweater. They looked frumpy on her without a belt.

After making her bed and checking her luggage for the third time, she paced around her tiny apartment not knowing what else to do. She was so high strung she was trembling.

She checked her phone to make sure the volume was up so she wouldn't miss his text. She checked her Bantu knots and couldn't decide if she should leave a scarf on them or not. What time was it? Apparently it wasn't the time he was supposed to be there.

Sasha opened her laptop and found her favorite tango song. "Mil Millones" by Gotan Project filled her apartment and she pushed her coffee table in front of her bedroom so she could dance. Time to calm her nerves.

While she listened to the sound of the train at the beginning of the song, she took in a deep breath and then lifted her arms to her invisible partner. With her knees bent together, she moved around when the beat started. She closed her eyes and envisioned a dance floor.

Back, back, back, twist, back, back—she bumped into her front door. Sometimes her tiny place was frustrating. This time she kept her eyes open while she walked through the steps.

She danced through her complete tango playlist and still no Ricky.

The idea that he might not show played across her mind. She plopped into a kitchen chair and checked her phone.

Nothing.

She told herself he would have a reason. He wouldn't just not show up.

Unless he met someone in New York.

She panicked. Could he have driven off the road? She had no idea how the mountain roads were. The what if's started to eat at her. And she couldn't just text him and distract him.

She sat at her table and searched the weather conditions. Yesterday had been clear and today should be too. That didn't mean the roads were safe.

Just as her mind reached peak carnage and mangle there were two hard knocks on her door. To say she flew to the door knob was an understatement. Her chair had tipped over, hitting the goblin before sliding onto its back. She unlocked and threw open her door and stared at a Henry Cavill doppelgänger.

First Ted Danson and now Superman?

"Sasha," whiskey eyes drank her in.

"Ricky?"

He was clean shaven revealing his strong jaw and dimpled chin. She thought he was handsome with the beard and she wondered how this man was single without.

"Can I come in?" he asked before he shoved his hands into his pockets.

He was definitely her Ricky.

"Yes, of course. You shaved."

He stroked his strong chin. "Yeah, I miss my beard. Stupid American business." He walked past her, his black long sleeve shirt was stretched tight across his chest and he wore dark designer blue jeans.

He smelled like sandalwood heaven.

She gulped her drool. "You look different," she

heard herself saying.

"Am I bad?" he asked.

He was incredibly hot. Okay, so he wasn't Henry Cavill. His nose was still crooked and his eyes weren't blue. But the definition of his jaw and cheekbones were similar.

"No, not bad." At all. Good enough to leave her fumbling and speechless.

"Can I use your restroom?" he asked.

"Yeah, sure."

Her coffee table blocked the bathroom door. "What's this?"

"Oh, I was dancing. Sorry." She was flustered. She had been expecting her lumberjack for months and instead got a hot Superman.

"Dancing?" He lifted her table and placed it in front of the couch. "With who?"

"By myself, silly."

He nodded before he closed the door behind him.

As soon as the door clicked, she quietly danced in place and did a celebratory jump and mouse like squeal.

Ricky had arrived, bitches!

She picked up the fallen chair and closed her laptop. She couldn't stop dancing, twerking in her excitement. She had already dragged everything to the front door. So she just had to put on her jacket, shoes, and purse. She hadn't planned on taking her laptop but wondered if she should.

He came out of the bathroom and leaned against the wall next to the couch. "Are you ready?"

"Just about." The anxiety she felt before was chased away by the pure excitement flowing through her now.

"They're unloading the truck. We should wait a

little bit." He crossed his arms, his muscles flexing against the thick fabric of his shirt.

"That's okay."

He sat at her table. "It won't be long." He looked at her laptop. "Do you—" he hesitated. "Do you still want to stay with me?"

"Yes," she nodded and leaned against the door.

He sighed a breath of relief. "You didn't hug me so, I thought maybe—maybe you changed your mind."

No wonder he was acting standoffish. She had barely said hello since she had been stunned into silence with how handsome he was without a beard.

She crossed the room and straddled him, surprising them both. She caressed his face with both of her hands loving the rough stubble against her palms. She kissed him, licking across his soft lips and rubbing her nose against his.

"I missed you," she whispered.

He groaned, "Can I touch you?"

"Yes."

They kissed again, this time his hands grabbing her ass so hard the pain made her groan. He pulled her close, grinding their pelvises together while they feasted.

When they came up for air, they were both breathless.

He gulped, his lips red from the frantic make out session. "I'm going to help unload. If I don't get up I might bend you over right here."

Her stomach flipped. She would be okay with that even though the table might not survive. She nodded and he helped her stand. When he stood his jeans were straining and he tried to readjust.

"Fuck, Sasha," he unzipped and readjusted again. "You make me so hard."

Her nipples tightened and she hissed her arousal.

He faced the door and started reciting numbers in Swiss German.

"What're you doing?" she asked.

"Counting is boring," he side-glanced at her and bit his lip, then he faced her front door and resumed counting. He cracked his knuckles and stretched his neck. "Is this your stuff?" He pointed to her one and only suitcase which looked big but was mostly empty.

"It is."

"Okay, let's get going."

After locking her front door, she followed him up the road to town hall. There was a sparkling, black Ford F-250 with a crew cab and chained tires that had a couple of boxes in the back. Eric, the mayor, and Hans were unloading the boxes while Hilda watched with her arms crossed.

Hilda waved when they approached. She pulled Sasha into a hug. "Are you off to Geneva?" Hilda asked before glancing at the suitcase that Ricky was stashing in the backseat.

Sasha warmed with embarrassment, "Yeah."

A smile crossed Hilda's lips. "Sounds exciting and fun," she winked. She patted Sasha's shoulder and went to talk to Ricky.

Sasha tried to eavesdrop. From what little Swiss German she could understand they were unloading a shipment of supplies for the town. There would be another shipment in January and while watching her, Ricky promised to bring that too.

Ten minutes later, she was strapped in next to him

and they were leaving.

This was happening. After her nervous breakdown had almost ended things, he waited months for her while she wrapped her head around a rich guy actually wanting to spend time with her. And even though the money still made her nervous, being rich wasn't the worst vice someone could have.

Getting out of the village was slow. He left the truck in low gear while it climbed the steep mountain roads, the chains biting into the ice and snow. They fishtailed a couple of times and he explained that the bed of the truck was lighter now that the boxes had been unloaded.

"You told me you had two cars," Sasha commented. "Wouldn't this make three?"

"I guess I don't see the truck as a car," Ricky shrugged. "Must be semantics, ya?"

"I guess."

"I've got several vehicles. Some are just to look at though. Some are for work, some are for play. This truck is for the mountains and work."

Sasha nodded and glanced out the window at white sparkling snow and thick brown and green trees.

"I'd love to go dancing," Sasha said, listening to the French pop music on the radio.

"I know a couple of nice clubs," he replied. "Big dance floor, good music. Or we can get a private room."

"Not that. Like the waltz."

He glanced at her surprised. "The valtz?"

She hadn't told him about her new hobby. "I've been learning ballroom dancing."

He glanced at her again. "I know a place," he smiled.

She readjusted in her seat and turned the vent blowing hot air towards the window. "I need new clothes."

"You want to go shopping?"

"I need to go. My clothes are too big."

He eyed her again. "You look fine to me."

Men. "Thanks. I'd like to buy a dress and shoes for ballroom dancing. Maybe a nice dress in case I ever go somewhere fancy."

"Do you want to go to a fancy restaurant?" he asked.

"I hadn't thought about that. It's just good to have. Nothing too expensive though, I haven't saved that much money. Maybe we can go to a thrift store," she suggested, watching the snow-kissed trees pass by.

"A thrift store? I'd have to search the web for that," he admitted. Rich people don't need thrift stores.

"How was New York?" she asked.

He shrugged. "It was exhausting. But we may get a good deal on acquiring an electronics company."

She wanted to ask him about Glocke, but she had a feeling it would be over her head. Mergers and acquisitions screamed conglomerates. She still wanted to hang on to the fantasy that he was a lumberjack.

The drive to Geneva took three torturous hours. Ricky hadn't been lying when he said he knew how to drive in the snow. A few times they hit black ice and he navigated the truck with focused composure while she gripped the Oh-Shit handle and screamed inside her heart.

When the road ahead was clear of snow, he stopped the truck and undid the chains. Sasha had never seen this process before. There were fasteners he had to unhook, then he had to drive off the chains before picking them up and putting them in the bed of the truck. They eventually arrived in Geneva and before she knew it she was standing in his penthouse.

"Do you want to pick a room?" he asked when he carried her suitcase toward the bedrooms.

"Sure."

The first door to the right was a guest bedroom with a view similar to the living room. The next door was a full guest bath complete with a tub and rain-head shower.

The second bedroom was an en-suite with a queen bed and a distressed wooden headboard. There was a glass door that led to a snow-covered patio. She passed by a walk-in closet that had a row of garment bags. Past the closet was the full bath.

She figured the third bedroom would be his. "I'll take this one," she said when she ran a hand over the soft buttery comforter.

"You don't want to see the other room?" he asked, setting down her luggage.

"I figured it's yours."

"I'm willing to share," he shoved his hands into his pockets, undressing her with his eyes.

Her stomach gurgled, interrupting the moment.

"Let's eat, ya?" he suggested, heading toward the kitchen and leaving her alone.

She relaxed onto the soft comforter, her arms out when she sank into the memory foam of luxury. Maybe she could get used to this.

After dumping her purse and shoes, and washing her hands and face, Sasha found Ricky in the kitchen sautéing chicken with garlic.

He can cook? She had expected sandwiches.

He had filled two glasses of white wine and left them on the island.

"What are you making?" she asked before picking a glass and sipping the wine.

"Chicken Alfredo."

She watched him cook. There was something mesmerizing about the way he moved those large strong hands which she hoped would be on her soon. He removed the chicken and dumped linguini into a pot of boiling water.

She watched him add the heavy cream and sprinkle some salt and pepper from tiny ceramic bowls. She slipped off the bar stool and entered the kitchen. She was starving and not for food.

"Can I help?"

He looked down at her, "I'll be done soon."

She poured herself more wine. She had waited months, she could wait another hour.

They ate at the island. She sat on one of the chrome barstools while he stood in the kitchen.

"It's delicious," she smiled. The sauce was amazing. The chicken was juicy. She wondered if he would hate her garlic breath.

"Thanks, Alfredo's easy." He shrugged and held his fork against a spoon, spinning it so the noodles spiraled.

So that's how high society eats. The more cutlery involved, the more money they have.

She noticed that he kept stretching his neck and back. This man was exhausted. He probably spent twenty-four hours traveling halfway around the world, and another six or more hours driving through dangerous mountain roads to drop off some boxes and pick her up. He must be on the brink of collapse.

Once the food was consumed he stacked the dishes in the sink.

"I can do the dishes," she offered before she placed her empty wine glass next to his.

"Leave them for the maid."

Of course he had a maid.

Sasha leaned against the counter and watched him stretch. She knew that with the food and wine the itis was about to kick in.

"You look tired," she observed.

"I am," Ricky admitted.

She bit her lip when she considered licking the dimple in his chin. "It's okay if you want to sleep. I can watch TV or something." Maybe she should have brought her laptop.

Ricky stepped closer, his jaw inches from her temple when he gripped the counter next to her hip. She could feel the heat radiating off his body. "Come with me," his baritone rippled through her. He straightened and held out his hand.

She wondered if he could hear her heart threatening to explode. She gulped and placed her hand in his.

He led her through his place, hitting a couple of light switches as they went. The view of Geneva was breathtaking in the dark living room. He led her to his bedroom, the third room she hadn't seen in months. He closed the door with a soft click and then turned a deadbolt. She didn't remember that from last time.

"Do you need a shower first?" she asked.

"I took one after I landed. Do you want one?"

She didn't want to delay this any more. She

couldn't take her eyes off of him. She shook her head. Her body was vibrating with anticipation.

He led her to his massive bed where he sat down then positioned her between his legs.

They stared at each other and held hands, his thumb caressing her knuckles.

Ricky swallowed, "Can I—"

Sasha didn't give him a chance to finish. She crashed into him so hard they fell back against the soft white comforter. She couldn't hold back her desperation to eat him alive.

She pulled off her pink sweater and tossed the cashmere somewhere.

He growled, his eyes roaming her exposed flesh. "Sasha—"

"Touch me. Touch me wherever you want," she couldn't get the words out fast enough. Her mind was drenched with desire from months of the excruciating wait.

His hands gripped her waist and he flipped them. She was on her back and he was kneeling over her tugging off his shirt, revealing his glorious chest with soft bourbon hair. He unbuckled his jeans and kicked them off, his impressive curved penis springing free.

Any self-control she had left, peaced out.

Ricky kissed her with the same desperation she felt. His hand eased behind her and released her bra clasp with a quick pinch.

The lumberjack superman had moves.

Her bra was flying somewhere seconds later. He cupped her heavy breasts in his hand, the rough calluses branding her skin.

She rubbed her pelvis against him. "Ricky," she

gasped. "I need you."

He made a guttural noise, working her jeans and soaked panties off her quivering legs.

"You're trembling," he whispered against a nipple before sucking her puckered flesh into his mouth.

She grabbed his hand and shoved it between her legs "Please touch me," she begged through the ecstasy.

"You're so hot, Sasha," he whispered before he kissed her lips. "And you're so fucking vet," his accent was thick with lust. He pressed a finger into her and sighed. "I can't vait to be inside you."

She arched into his hand, unable to hold back any longer. "Then take me," she begged.

"Not yet. Come for me first," he demanded.

She couldn't stop her hips from gyrating against his hand. He slipped in a second finger and curled into her G-spot in tandem to the pumping. She bucked against him when the orgasm jolted through her.

He kissed her cheek and neck while her tremors subsided. He was worth the wait.

"I need that dick," she begged.

He rolled away and she heard a drawer open. A rip of foil followed and he rolled towards her. "Then let me give it to you." He stroked himself while he kissed the side of her breast. "How do you vant me?" he asked.

She groaned. It was impossible to count the many ways she wanted him. "I want you to use me," she looked into his whiskey eyes as they darkened with desire.

"Are you sure?"

"Yes."

He pulled her further onto the bed and positioned himself between her aching thighs. She felt him press against her entrance when he lowered on top of her. He searched her eyes when he eased in.

"Sasha," he moaned, rocking against her, kissing and biting her lips between gasps. She wrapped her legs around him feeling his perfect ass tense under her calves when he caressed her with his body.

She licked and bit his nipples, then nibbled on his bicep next to her head since he was bracing himself so he wouldn't crush her. Her hands roamed his tense shoulders and back, enjoying the feel of his muscles flexing with every pump of his hips.

He gazed at her with whiskey eyes, panting for air when his speed quickened. Then he stopped and sat back on his knees before bringing her legs together in front of his chest. His warm, soft hair felt good against the back of her calves.

"I'm going to fuck you hard," he promised, his fingers dug into her curvy hips when he slammed into her.

Her entire body screamed for joy. The way he had positioned her legs had tightened her portal of pleasure and he claimed her with quick hard thrusts that threatened to disintegrate her bones.

She had never been so utterly fucked in her life.

"Sa–sha," his voice was strained. He bit her calf, his hips clapping against her thighs. "I'm going to come. Come vith me. Come now." He leaned forward and captured her eyes in his whiskey depths. His full weight bending her legs against her stomach had deepened his thrusts which claimed her soul.

Her body acquiesced to his demand and she unraveled with his deep penetrations. She couldn't hear him orgasm over her strangled scream, but she felt his body tense and jerk against her when he came in two slow pumps.

He collapsed next to her, glistening with sweat. "That vas beautiful." He kissed her jaw before he pushed off the bed with a labored grunt and went into his bathroom.

Sasha stared at the blurry ceiling wondering if her limbs were still attached. Her core hummed and pulsed while her mind floated down from bliss. Were people fucking like that in real life? Sex had always been violent before Richard Bell.

She felt his presence when he entered the room.

"Are you okay," he asked her.

"I think so," she attempted to move. "Do I still have legs?" she asked.

He chuckled. "Can I touch you?"

"Yeah." She felt a warm wet wash cloth slide against her belly and glide between her thighs.

Once he finished cleaning her, he deposited the cloth in the bathroom. He pulled back the comforter and slid between the sheets with a tired sigh. "I need sleep, Sasha," he apologized. "Vill you stay?"

She rolled her aching body toward him and climbed between the soft sheets. "I'd love to." She rested her head on his shoulder and fitted her body to his side. Her fingers ran through his chest hair and he hummed.

He kissed her forehead and covered her hand with his. He was asleep before his third breath.

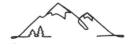

21. SHOPPING

December 20

"**I**'ll always find you!" *Jackson threatened before he slammed her head against the bathroom wall.*

Sasha gasped awake, her heart threatening to split open when she stared around the unfamiliar room and a view of a private patio covered with snow. She was alone in a massive bed and the comforting scent of vanilla and sandalwood reminded her that she was in Geneva with Richard Bell. Relieved, she relaxed and caught her breath. There was no way Jackson was going to find her. After a few moments of gathering herself, she stretched before sitting up, the delicious ache between her thighs reminding her of the night before.

The bedroom door was shut and her clothes from the previous day were draped across the end of the bed. While she got dressed she nosed around his room. It had been difficult to focus on her surroundings when he was destroying her insides.

The bedroom was large with an adjacent office. She wandered around the space touching the different surfaces. There were two wooden nightstands that matched the planked headboard. The tear-drop lamps that hung from the ceiling were made of shiny chrome, adding a modern accent. A small glass bowl held change, next to which was his high-end watch.

In front of the bed was a long, low white dresser below a large wall-mounted TV. Further along the wall she walked through a doorway to the semi-private office with a wall of books and a big wooden desk.

She ran her fingers along some of the books, touching the hard and smooth textures while she read titles about business and corporate law. There was a closed Apple laptop on the desk. She couldn't imagine him typing with his large hands. He was a lumberjack to her, not some rich businessman.

In the corner of the desk under a small lamp was a picture frame. She picked it up and stared at Marie Bell in a yellow bathing suit with her arms wrapped around a boy in blue swimming trunks. They were at the beach and ocean waves crashed around them. They both had their heads back laughing with their eyes closed. Sasha's hands shook when she replaced the frame. It was the only personal photo she had seen thus far.

When she freshened up in his bathroom, she couldn't stop her eyes from roaming. There was a dark stone walk-in shower that didn't have a door. The myriad of shiny fixtures promised a luxurious shower. The jacuzzi tub was big enough for three people to fit comfortably. Sasha could imagine him having several women in there and she had to shake the thoughts away.

She found him in the kitchen slicing a honeydew while a pan sizzled behind him. His chest was bare and he wore dark gray sweatpants that hung low on his hips. She swallowed her drool when she checked out his print and her desire surged again. "Morning."

He looked up, "Good morning, Sasha." He walked around the island and approached her. "Can I kiss you?"

Thankful she had brushed her teeth, she leaned into his kiss, inhaling his scent mixed with sweat. He returned to the sizzling pan and she admired the view of his carved back. "Can I help?"

"I'm almost done. You can get a drink."

She entered the kitchen and opened cabinets until she found the glasses and cups. She filled a glass with water while he dished sausages and scrambled eggs.

While they ate breakfast she admired the distressed wooden table. When she had arrived months ago she was in her feelings and hadn't really appreciated his place. She couldn't see beyond the marble and modern cream everything. But the more she took in she could see reminders of Glockenwald.

"Why are you smiling?" he asked before sipping his espresso.

"Ah, just—the eggs are delicious," she smiled. She picked up a slice of melon and bit into the juicy, sweet fruit.

"I was starving after last night," he chuckled.

"I didn't know you played piano," she nodded to the beautiful white instrument with its understated elegance.

He tilted his head and his gaze shifted to the mirror behind her. An emotion she couldn't quite pin down flashed across his features. "I don't really," he said with a shrug before he returned to his food. He ran a knife just above the skin of the melon and then sliced it into smaller chunks.

She felt self-conscious. Just watching him eat reminded her of the differences in their worlds. She had just shoved the fruit in her face while he ate with a knife and fork. She made a mental note to watch videos about European dining etiquette.

When she watched him chew, butterflies fluttered around her belly. His scruffy jaw flexing and relaxing should be mundane and not turn her on.

She was here. In his place. With him. This had to be a dream. She cleared her throat. "Ricky," she gulped water.

"Ya?"

"Since we are—since we're doing this," she gestured between them, "we should talk about expectations and things."

"What do you mean, expectations?" he asked before his lips closed around the juicy melon on his fork.

She squirmed uncomfortably in her chair. "Have you been tested?"

"Tested?" he asked while he chewed.

"Like for sexual diseases."

"Ah," he gulped some water. "I'm—what do Americans say? I'm clean?"

"That's what we say." Anxiety was eating her insides.

"I test every six months. Besides, I haven't been with anyone for almost a year," he admitted.

She crossed her arms. She found it hard to believe that someone wasn't chasing him and trying to ride that. "How is that even possible?"

He gave her a strange look. "It's very possible. I just

—" he waved his hand in a circle while he considered his next words. "I lost interest, ya?"

A man who fucks like him doesn't just lose interest. Nervous energy flowed through her. She swallowed and tried not to hyperventilate.

He placed his fork on his plate and pushed the food away. "What's wrong, Sasha?" He leaned forward and crossed his arms on the table.

"I haven't been tested in a while." She looked at her plate of eggs, afraid to see his reaction. The last time she was tested was when she got her IUD over two years ago.

"That's no problem."

"It is. I didn't have time. I just needed to get out of there and even being here I haven't been checked." She had only slept with Jackson, he had made sure of that. But even though he came home and drank himself into a drunken rage every night, she wasn't sure where he had been during the day. "I should get tested."

"I'll get you a doctor," he offered, his finger tracing a knot in the wood.

"That's weird," she bounced her leg with nervousness, watching his finger caress the wood.

"Why?" Ricky asked, watching her.

She bit her lip. How long would scheduling appointments here take? "Okay. It's fine."

"You want a doctor?" He sighed and sat back in his chair, one hand silently tapping the table.

"Yes, please."

"I'll take care of everything." He gulped his water.

She couldn't stop her eyes from roaming the length of him. His Adam's apple moved when he drank. She followed the muscles in his tense shoulder to the invisible line down his chest and stomach. She wanted to run her fingers through his stomach hair and follow the trail to the print in his sweatpants.

He set down his glass and mirrored her by crossing his arms.

She bit her lip. "Are we screwing other people?"

His sexy jaw clenched. "I have no desire right now."

She shrugged. "They definitely want to ride you."

"So?"

She drank water, causing the silence to stretch between them. Her thoughts were betraying her, planting seeds of self-doubt because she wasn't the kind of woman who shattered pelvises with this kind of man. Whatever was happening between them seemed too good to be true.

His jaw clenched and he glared at his espresso cup. "Do you vant to sleep with other people?"

Sasha shook her head, "No."

He relaxed. He dragged in a breath and ran a hand through his messy hair. "Look. I believe it's possible to love more than one person. If you want to be with someone, let's just talk about it, okay?"

"Um, okay?" She didn't know how to feel about his statement.

"Anything else?" Tension was radiating off of him.

She dropped her arms. She had gotten through the worst of it. "Are any stores open today?"

Confusion crinkled around his eyes. "For? Shopping?"

She shoved cold eggs in her mouth and nodded. She was sure her quick change in subject matter was sending him spinning.

He dragged in a deep breath and closed his eyes.

"You drive me crazy," he murmured before he gulped down the rest of his espresso.

"Sorry."

"Never be sorry."

"I found some places. But I'm not sure if they're open?"

"For you, everything is open."

_ΛΛ_

After she enjoyed a much needed shower and cocoa butter session, they left to go shopping. His Bugatti snarled between the ornate buildings in Geneva until he pulled into an alley. What was up with this man and alleys? They walked to the front of the building where a huge display window showed mannequins posed in dance positions.

It took everything in her not to squeal.

When they entered Sasha was drawn to the hanging dresses made of beautiful shiny fabrics in many colors. Her fingers ran along the soft, flowing textures.

An older woman approached them. "Monsieur Bell," she welcomed, then started to speak in French.

Sasha sighed to herself. The official language in Geneva was French and she barely knew the basics. And did everyone know Richard Bell?

Ricky gestured towards Sasha.

She cleared her throat. "I'd like to get a dress and shoes," she said, hesitantly.

The woman eyed her. "Shoes first," she said before leading Sasha to the wall displaying all kinds of dance shoes. After trying on several styles, she chose a black satin pair with a diagonal crystal strap. Just a touch of bling with two inch heels.

After strapping into the elegant shoes, they walked back to the dresses. The woman surprised her by grabbing her hips with both hands when she did a quick measure. Then she started pulling dresses for Sasha to try.

Most of them were too sparkly, but she chose a few to try on. After squeezing into a black dress with a flowy skirt, Sasha looked at herself in the mirror. Her boobs were barely contained in the halter. Her heart dropped. Her breasts were too big and she was too short for most of these dresses. The fabric hugged her hips and flowed out at mid-thigh with a slit up her left leg. This dress was perfect for salsa and tango. She slid into the shoes and admired her legs in the mirror.

There was a knock on the door. "Have you tried on a dress yet?" the attendant asked.

Sasha came out with a frown. "It's too low in the back," she said to Ricky who stood by a display looking at bow ties.

His eyes raked over her. "You look beautiful to me."

She shook her head. "It barely fits on top," she tugged on the sides. She pivoted to show him and the attendant her back. "I'm too short." She couldn't wear this to town hall.

The attendant pinched the fabric higher. She walked Sasha to a wall of mirrors where she made adjustments with little clips.

The fit was perfect. The dress was exactly what she had imagined wearing when she danced the tango. "How much?"

The attendant shrugged, "Dress, shoes,

adjustments 700 francs." That was half of her clothing budget.

Sasha bit her lip and nodded. This was what she wanted.

After paying, and getting back into the car, Ricky turned to her, "More shopping?"

She stared at the shoes in her lap and nodded. "Maybe one more place."

While he drove them to the next store, she touched the soft suede soles. She had never owned shoes this beautiful. Too bad they were only for dancing.

They went to a department store where she shopped the discount racks. Everything she tried on was too long for her. But at least they fit her waist, even though her booty was a struggle to get into the largest jeans. She bought two pairs of jeans and three sweaters.

For lunch he took her to an American style diner where she ordered a tuna melt and fries.

"You didn't buy much," he commented when he cut into his hotdog.

She swallowed her mouthful. "I don't have money," she shrugged.

"Why not ask me?"

She pressed her lips together. "I'm good. I'm done with shopping." Because her wallet said so.

"What do you want to do next?"

She drank some of her strawberry milkshake. "Are you up for sightseeing?"

"If I get espresso," he yawned.

Sasha shook her head, disgusted with herself. "I'm an idiot."

He tilted his head. "What do you mean?"

She sighed and sat back against the red vinyl booth,

crossing her arms. "You're jet lagged."

He shook his head. "No problem. I can buy espresso."

"No, let's go home." She felt guilty dragging him around Geneva when he probably just wanted to rest.

"If that's what you want."

She nodded and smiled. She uncrossed her arms then crunched on a fry. She could break in her shoes while he napped.

The ride back was quiet. She took in the architecture of the city and watched people go about their day. When they got back to his place, the breakfast dishes were gone. She dropped her bags in her room and freshened up.

When she found Ricky he was face down on his comforter, sleeping. She climbed in next to him and held his hand.

He opened one sleepy eye. "Mmm, Sasha," he whispered before his eye rolled closed and sleep took him again. If only she could offer him a fraction of what he could offer her, maybe she wouldn't feel so inadequate.

_ѧ_

Sasha jerked awake. Jackson's angry face was fading into the shadows ghosting across the ceiling. She didn't remember closing her eyes. She stretched and propped up on her elbows and gazed outside to see the sun setting behind the mountains.

Ricky had adjusted to his back in his sleep and had one hand behind his head. He was still out because jet lag had taken its toll on him.

Her eyes raked over his body. The bit of exposed skin just above his hip made her bite her lip. Then she saw the bulge in his pants and the game was on. Bless the male's body for self-testing the mechanics. She wasn't going to let this one go to waste.

She pressed her hand against the hard outline that curved towards his hip.

He groaned in his sleep.

She stroked him up and down through the thick fabric wanting flesh-on-flesh.

A gasp escaped his lips. "Sasha," he sighed.

Her core melted. He could have said anyone, but he said her name in his half-asleep state.

She sighed when she climbed on top of him.

He opened his eyes and looked up at her surprised, then he grabbed her waist. He groaned and lifted his hips to grind against her. "You drive me crazy," he murmured, his voice thick with sleep.

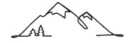

22. THE DANCE

"**D**o you have to work?" she wondered out loud before she sipped white wine. They were eating pizza at the dining table. She looked down at her black sweatpants. After another hot session, they had showered and ordered delivery.

"I always have work," Ricky admitted. "But I told them only to contact me for emergencies," he shrugged.

"I'd love to go to a dance studio. To practice ballroom dancing."

He was in a white shirt and blue jogging pants. She wondered what kind of workouts he did to stay fit. "I know a place," he said, placing his fork on his empty plate. Yes, he ate his pizza with a knife and fork. "Do you want to wait for your dress?"

"Would it be bad if I went in jeans?"

He shrugged. "It's different."

"I should practice," she said to herself. "I should have brought my laptop."

"I can help you practice. Will you dance with me?"

She wasn't going to turn him down. She bounced to the closet where she had stowed her new shoes. She felt bougie slipping expensive shoes on with her sweatpants, but the man requested to dance.

He was rearranging the furniture to clear the dining area when she returned.

"What're we going to dance?" she asked after she helped him move the table and chairs.

He scrolled through iTunes on his phone. "What do you know?" he inquired.

She listed the handful of dances she had practiced.

"The valtz it is." He selected a song and the room filled with violins from unseen speakers. The sound was so crisp, the violin could have been in the room with them. "May I have this dance?" he held out his hand with a bow.

When she accepted he walked her in a small circle as if showing her off. He brought her right hand up to the hold position and she placed her left hand on his shoulder. She could feel the heat of his touch through her hoodie.

She was nervous when she looked up into his whiskey eyes and his jaw clenched before he looked away.

Europeans and their waltzing. He didn't need to practice. His form was impeccable. He guided her through the first two walks before she almost tripped them both.

"I'm sorry," she muttered, embarrassed.

"Never be sorry." He restarted the song. "From the top."

She gulped. "I'm nervous."

"Just let me take you." His eyes were smoldering and he worked his jaw. "Feel my hands on your body."

He looked into her eyes, never breaking contact. The waltz was one of those dances that made people look like they were floating on a cloud. The basic waltz was a simple three step box. But he was taking her through the reverse walks and turns too. She took a deep breath and tried to relax while he guided her across the marble floor. He would give the slightest tug or squeeze so she knew which direction to turn.

After the song ended, he pulled her close. "You're good. Can I have one more dance?"

"Sure." She would never turn down dancing with him.

He reached for his phone on the island and changed the song.

Her heart thudded. A tango? With him? The tango was the sexiest dance she had learned thus far.

He held out his hand and she hesitated. But the music was sensual and she couldn't resist.

"I'm still learning this," she was ready with the excuses.

"No problem," his eyes undressed her. "Just let me guide you."

She took his hand and he pulled her close. Her right hip was pressed against his groin and she could feel him harden. He bent his right leg between hers and his thigh rubbed against her apex.

She might not survive.

He slid his hand lower on her back and she looked away. She could feel his gaze on her when he began to move them around the room.

Her sweatpants felt thin each time his thigh rubbed against her. When she danced with Hans, they usually had a little space between them.

Ricky pushed her into a spin she hadn't expected and she almost stumbled. Her mind had been elsewhere. He pulled her back and dipped her.

"I hate when you don't look at me," he growled before pulling her up.

She wasn't supposed to. During the tango the woman always looked away.

Dancing with him wouldn't have been a tease if she were taller. He was doing everything the correct way. But her shortness coupled with his long legs equated to a distracting stimulation. His hardness against her hip didn't help, causing her to moan more than once.

The song ended but he didn't release her. "I need to be inside you, Sasha."

She pressed against him and he lifted her. Her legs wrapped around his hips and her lips claimed his. "You better blow my back out." She would never get enough of him.

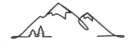

23. THE TREE

December 22

After breakfast the next morning, Ricky took her to the doctor's office. The power of money and prestige. After the blood work, she had to lie on the cold table while the technician swabbed for a pap smear and performed an ultrasound. The doctor was busy so they told her he'd contact her later after he looked at the results.

Office visits always shook her. When she rejoined Ricky in the empty waiting room, he rose to his feet and approached her.

"You okay?" he offered his hand.

"Not really," she admitted when she accepted his hand and they walked outside into the crisp air. Since Geneva was a lower elevation than Glockenwald, the temperature wasn't as frigid.

"Did you still want to see the United Nations?"

"Yeah," she didn't want a doctor's visit to ruin their day.

They spent the rest of the day sightseeing. After the United Nations, they walked to the Red Cross

Museum. When the rain started, he took her to the mall where she window-shopped.

They shared a warm bagel from Bagelstein, watching people who were loaded with shopping bags walk by.

His phone vibrated on the table and she glanced at his screen.

"Is that your motorcycle?" she asked.

He followed her gaze. "No. It's a 1951 Vincent White Shadow. A very rare motorcycle I want to buy." He picked up his phone and swiped his thumb across the screen. "Here are more pictures," he handed her the device.

She swiped to see several pictures of the motorcycle. She called herself being sneaky and pushed the back arrow. A quick scroll showed her they were all vehicles. "No tits?" she asked him.

He raised an eyebrow and held out a hand for his phone. "There are tits?"

She gave it back with a smile. "You don't have naked women on your phone."

"I don't need naked women on my phone. Why look at a picture when I can have the real thing?"

"Touché," she took a sip of her water.

"It's mostly memes and vehicles. When I find something I really want, I set it as my wallpaper for inspiration. The Bugatti was my last one."

"Ah. That's nice. Mine is whatever the phone came with," she shrugged.

He slid his phone into his pocket. "I spend a lot of time on my phone because of work. It's nice to dream a little."

She was staring at her new dream. Something

about him pulled at her. He wasn't just a lumberjack anymore. He was possibilities now.

"Are we—" she wasn't sure if she should ask. "Are we exchanging gifts?"

He was sipping his espresso and looked at her over the rim of his cup. "Gifts?" he repeated before he licked his lips.

"For Christmas."

"Why not?" He looked confused.

"If we are, I need to go shopping," she watched someone with several bags hurry past.

His eyebrows knitted, "For?"

"For you, Ricky." She had hugged herself in her frustration. Getting lost in translation was killer.

"Ah," he eyed her defensive stance. "You are my gift, Sasha."

She narrowed her eyes at him. "That's not what I meant."

He smiled, "I know."

She frowned and looked down at the bagel crumbs in front of her. What could she buy a man who has everything? Who can buy everything? Nothing that was in her budget. The thought depressed her.

She looked up to see his whiskey eyes studying her. "Do you decorate for Christmas?" she inquired. Jackson never allowed her to decorate. She had always wanted to go all out.

"Like a tree?"

"Yeah. Are you going to put one up and decorate your place?"

He shook his head. "I'm not usually home for Christmas," he explained with a shrug.

She exhaled an exasperated sigh. "Okay, never

mind. Forget I asked."

Ricky leaned forward, his elbows on the metal table. "Do you want a Christmas tree?"

She squeezed her legs together and looked at her jeans. "If you don't usually decorate, it's fine."

Clearing his throat, he cleaned up their trash. "Shall we go?"

Ricky drove to a vendor stationed along Lake Geneva that sold Christmas trees. He let her pick one and paid extra for next-day delivery. Then he took her to pick out decorations.

She went a bit overboard because his place was so white. She bought red accent pillows with a white reindeer outline and a red and black plaid throw blanket. Her favorite was the pre-lit garlands with gold berries, acorns, and leaves for the window wall. When they got back to his place, she spent an hour decorating, even fluffing pillows and rearranging them on his couch.

"What do you think?" she asked once she was satisfied with the splashes of holiday cheer.

"Is good," he said with a shrug. Of course he wouldn't be excited over pillows or garlands. He was sitting on the couch, his laptop on his lap.

"Work?" she asked.

"Emails," he clicked, typed then clicked. He was much faster at typing than she would have guessed. His fingers caressed the keyboard with ease.

"Do we have plans for Christmas?" she asked, wondering if she needed to buy a dress.

"What do you want to do?" He closed his laptop and looked at her.

"What can we do? Do you spend the day with

family and friends?"

He stretched and cracked his neck. "Every year there is a charity dinner."

"Oh? Are we going?"

"No. We can do something else." He slid the laptop off to the side and readjusted so he could put his head in her lap.

A charity dinner sounded like a high society event. One where she wouldn't fit in. "A charity dinner sounds nice," she offered when she looked down at him.

He made a face. "So boring. We eat food and sign checks. Then dance and drink wine."

"Dancing sounds nice," she whispered.

He smiled up at her. "Let's dance now," he pushed up and kissed her chin.

24. MUTTER

December 23

The tree arrived while they were eating breakfast the next morning. The delivery men set it up in the corner of the living room next to the piano so its lights could reflect off the mirrored wall in the dining room. Sasha was able to arrange a decorative red skirt before they left to go to a dance studio.

Ricky had arranged for a private lesson with his former instructor. With all of the attention on her she was nervous because his instructor was a former competitive dancer.

Elise had aged gracefully with poise that Sasha envied. Her gray hair was in a severe chignon that showed off a long elegant neck. She floated around them with her own partner Luca when showing the next steps. After the hour-long lesson, they returned home to shower and decorate the tree and hang some more lights along the windows.

Michael Bublé's voice filled the apartment while they cleaned up the boxes and bags. A shadow appeared at his door and the keypad beeped an arrival.

An older woman dressed in a black suede coat, black pants and black stilettos stalked into the condo with a sour look on her botoxed face.

"What is this, Rickart," she demanded in Swiss German when she gestured between the tree and Sasha. She glared at them both with steel blue eyes after she flicked her white, shoulder length hair.

"Sylvie," Ricky muttered between clenched teeth. After inhaling a deep breath, he seemed to relax a little. "This is Sasha," he said in English.

Steel shards of blue disdain aimed at Sasha and it took everything in her not to step back. She stepped forward and held out her hand, "Hi, I'm Sasha."

"Sasha, this is Sylvie," Ricky said through a clenched jaw.

Sylvie crossed her arms ignoring Sasha's hand. She lifted her chin. "I'm his *mutter*," she said in a thick Swiss German accent.

Before Sasha could respond, Ricky started talking so fast in his mother tongue that she struggled to keep up. The two of them had a heated conversation in Swiss German and Sasha tried to listen as best as she could while she continued cleaning. If the woman could ignore her, she could ignore back.

Ricky had called Sylvie out for being rude.

Sylvie asked Ricky where he had been.

He responded that he was busy.

This was almost like a TV drama that required popcorn and wine. But she could tell that Ricky was getting agitated and their voices kept getting louder. Sasha decided to leave them alone.

When she tried to make a quiet exit, Sylvie turned to her. "My son," Sylvie said in English when she slid a side-eye to Ricky before refocusing her daggers on Sasha. "My son has informed me he is too busy for the Christmas Charity Dinner that this family founded." She drummed her impatience on her arm, diamonds glittering on her fingers, wrists, and ears. "His presence is required."

Sasha turned and darted a fervent look at Ricky's back. "Okay."

"I vas just informed that he vill be spending the day vith you. An American." The way Sylvie spat American made Sasha cross her arms in defense.

Ricky stepped between them. "It's my choice, Sylvie. I'm not going," he said in English.

"Yes, you are."

Ricky was tense with anger. "Or vhat?"

The challenge sucked the air out of the room.

Sylvie pointed a manicured nail at Sasha. "I vill get rid of her," she spat before she turned, whipping her white angled bob as she left, slamming the frosted door behind her.

Ricky turned around and approached Sasha. "I'm sorry. Sylvie is demanding."

Sasha took a step back. "Looks like you're busy tomorrow."

He rolled his eyes. "I'm not going."

"Why don't you want to go?" She was afraid to hear his answer.

"I'd rather be with you." He took a step towards her and she backed up.

He wouldn't understand the dread in her stomach. She looked at her feet and then back at him. "Why don't you want me to go?"

"Vhat?" he looked taken aback.

"It's because I'd embarrass you, isn't it?" She swallowed her sadness. She knew better. She knew she wasn't good enough.

"No, Sasha," he held up his hands to stop her. "I just —" he ran a hand through his bourbon hair. "I thought you would hate going."

She shook her head. "So you just don't give me a choice?"

"No, that's not it," he sounded on edge.

She closed her eyes. She turned and walked to her room. She was angry with herself for being upset. The way Sylvie looked at her was how she expected to be treated by high society. She was either a charity project or vermin.

Ricky cursed and followed her. "Don't valk avay, Sasha."

"It's fine," she threw over her shoulder, before she turned to close her door.

"Listen," he blocked the door from closing with his hand. "Please, vill you listen?" his eyes searched hers with desperation.

Fear snaked through her when she crossed her arms and backed away. "What?"

He opened her door but didn't enter the room. "You told me you hate that I'm rich, no?"

She stared at him, blood rushing through her temples.

"This event is just all rich people, Sasha. I thought you vould feel uncomfortable."

She probably would. "Okay."

"Believe me vhen I say, I don't vant to go. I vant to be vhere you are." He held his hand out for her.

She shook her head and backed up, her legs

bumping the bed. "And you let Sylvie threaten me?"

"Screw Sylvie. She can't do shit to you." He clenched his fists and then shoved them into his pockets. "She said that to scare you."

"Well, it worked," she hugged herself and turned away from him.

"I'm sorry. I won't let anything happen to you. Trust me, please?"

She looked down at the yellow comforter. "You should go to the charity dinner."

"Fuck no."

She turned to face him. "Even if you just make a quick appearance."

He rolled his eyes. "Are you coming too?"

She considered going for a hot second. But the idea of being at an event with rich people made her skin crawl. If they were anything like Sylvie that was a hard pass. "I can watch a movie or something. It's just one night."

He started to turn red when he clenched his jaw. "One night I vaited months for," he swallowed his anger, his Swiss accent thickening. "I'd miss the rest of those fucking charity dinners to have a few nights together, Sasha."

Her heart pounded.

"I'm not going vithout you, therefore I'm not going." His tone ended the conversation.

"Fine," she threw her hands up in surrender.

"Fine," he responded before he walked towards the living room.

She sat on her bed in a huff. She knew this was going to be a challenge. If he was ignoring important appearances because of her, people would wonder.

People would talk. People would investigate. She wasn't trying to keep him from his world, she just wasn't interested in joining it. She was trying to stay hidden.

She sat with her arms crossed and stared out her window before relaxing onto her back.

"Sasha," he found her lying in bed staring at the ornate tray ceiling some time later. "I got a call from the doctor."

She dragged in a breath. She wondered where her she had left her cell. "Okay?"

"He said you need to come in again."

"Why? What do I have?" Great. She sat up and waited for the bad news.

"Um..." he searched the room for the words. "Your birth control needs to be removed."

"My IUD?"

He shrugged. "I don't know these things in English."

"What about the test? Am I clean?"

"Ah, yes, that's fine. No virus, ya? Good news. He said your birth control is only for one year. Must remove before damage."

She sighed. She got her IUD over two years ago. She figured it wasn't a big deal. "Okay, when?"

"Now. Let's go."

"Now?" Tomorrow was Christmas Eve. "Why now?"

"Because he leaves for France in the morning. Come on. The longer it's in the more dangerous."

She was stunned into silence.

Ten minutes later they were in his Bugatti driving through the city. When they arrived at the hospital, she was shown into a room where she was prepped.

The doctor informed her that her IUD had moved and was no longer safe. Even with the anesthesia the process was painful. Ricky stayed with her through the removal, holding her hand.

After the procedure, she made a follow up appointment for February and they picked up her new birth control pills. She was informed that there would be spotting and that she should refrain from sex for a couple of days.

By the time they got back to his condo it was almost midnight. She kicked off her shoes and stood near the door in shock. Ricky deposited his phone and wallet on the island. "Do you want water?" He retrieved two glasses and filled them.

Her stomach had bottomed out. "Do you want me to leave?" she found herself asking.

Ricky choked on a mouthful of water. "Vhat?" he croaked before coughing and trying to clear his throat.

"Do you want me to leave?"

"Why? I'm not understanding." He set down his glass and approached her. "What's going on?" His whiskey eyes searched her face. The Christmas lights illuminated his handsome jaw which was clenched with tension.

She hugged herself. "We won't be able to fuck much."

"So?" Whiskey eyes narrowed.

"Isn't that why I'm here?"

The anger that crossed his face made her step back, causing her to bump against the wall. "Really, Sasha?" He ran a hand through his bourbon hair. He swallowed, attempting to talk but couldn't. He turned away from her and walked a few steps before turning back. "I like you," he said before he shoved his hands into his pockets.

"I like you too," she admitted. "I just thought...." she trailed off. What did she think? "I have nothing to offer you but sex."

He narrowed his eyes and shook his head. "I don't understand."

She blinked back tears. "You live here," she gestured around them. "You drive fancy cars, you can buy whatever you want. You can have any woman you want. I can't even screw you."

He kept shaking his head, his eyes closed and his entire body tense. With a heavy sigh, he said, "Relationships are more than sex. I said, 'I like you'."

"But—"

"No but, Sasha. Just stop, please?"

She exhaled and looked down at the marble floor. His feet came into view and she gazed up into his whiskey eyes. He put a hand on either side of her shoulders and braced himself against the wall. His face was inches from hers.

"There is stuff we can do," he whispered. "There are places to go. Food to eat. Whatever you want. As long as we're together, I don't care what we do."

She didn't know how to respond.

"And Sasha," he rested his forearms on the wall, bringing their bodies closer and forcing her chin higher so she could meet his intense eyes. "There are many vays to give pleasure."

She drooled. She had questions.

"Are you hungry?"

She shook her head. "I'm exhausted," she admitted.

"Let me shower you and then let's sleep, okay?"

She nodded and took his hand. He turned off the lights and the Christmas tree blinked against a sparkling Geneva.

In his bathroom, he insisted on undressing her. He praised her with his soft touches and whispered words when he took off her shirt and pulled down her pants.

"Does it hurt?" he asked when he saw the spotting on the pad.

She shook her head. "I think the meds are still working."

He took off his own clothes and turned on the water in the shower. "I'm going to take care of you," he said when he held out his hand for her.

She allowed him to pull her into the glass and slate enclosure with him. The body jets sprayed them from three sides. He soaped up a large loofah and turned her so she faced away from him.

He washed her shoulders, massaging away the tension while he worked his way down her back. "I promise to protect you," he whispered. "As much as I enjoy this beautiful ass," he growled, squeezing juicy flesh before gently scrubbing his way down her trembling thighs. "You're more to me than just sex." After he finished her calves, he pressed his searing hardness against her lower back before he rinsed and applied more soap to the loofah.

She could feel his heart beating against her shoulder when he pulled her against him, then Ricky caressed her neck with the loofah and worked his way down her chest. Feeling his hard plains flush against her back while he touched her was soothing and erotic.

"You feel so good. I love touching you like this," he whispered, his warm breath feathering her ear, his hands gently squeezing her breasts before they moved to her sides.

He took his time cleaning every inch of her, washing off the antiseptic smell of the hospital and infusing the shower with vanilla and sandalwood. After he washed himself, he wrapped her in a warm towel and led her to the bedroom where he dried her. He pulled on a pair of red boxer briefs while she slipped into fresh undies and a pad.

"What do you use everyday that makes you smell so good?" he asked after he finished drying her feet.

"You mean the cocoa butter? It's on the nightstand."

He returned with the two pound jar moments later. He opened it and sniffed, "Yes. Intoxicating. Can I use this on you?"

She tried to stifle a yawn. "Sure."

"Lie down and relax." He pulled back the sheets and she let him position her in the middle of the bed.

He warmed the cocoa butter between his palms and started to massage her. His praises never stopped. Once he finished, he covered her with the blanket, slipped in next to her, and pulled her close.

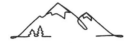

25. I WISH

December 24

Sasha woke up spooning with the lumberjack. For once, she hadn't had any nightmares. Sighing, she relaxed into the large frame that was curled around her, his bicep acting as her pillow, his other arm draped over her naked waist. The skin to skin felt intoxicating. She could feel his soft hair against her bare shoulder when his chest expanded and contracted with every breath.

If only she wasn't so broken, maybe this could've been her future.

She stretched and turned to face him. She was surprised to see he was watching her. "You're awake?"

"Good morning," he stretched, his biceps looking impressive.

"Good morning." She scooted up to kiss his cheek, his scruff tickling her lips. "Are you growing your beard?"

"Of course," he regarded her with a look she didn't understand. "Which do you like better? Beard or no?"

"Hmmm," she ran her fingers along his jaw. "You're

delicious either way."

He growled his desire.

"But my lumberjack has a beard."

Strong arms wrapped around her and he pulled her close then he nuzzled her neck. "Let's eat. You have medicine to take."

While they ate breakfast, he asked, "Do you feel well enough for a dance lesson?"

"It's Christmas Eve," Sasha noted. "Isn't she busy?"

He shrugged. "She texted that she is ready for us. What do you want to do?"

She felt sore, but the meds were doing their part in taking the edge off. And she did like dancing with him. "If it's not a bother for her, I guess we can go."

"No bother. I pay her well."

And there it was.

The power of money.

"Wow," Sasha exhaled. "What if she had plans and you ruined them?"

"Really, Sasha?" He set down his fork and ran a hand through his hair.

"Yes, really. You're Herr Fucking Bell. I have a feeling no one says no to you."

His jaw clenched.

"Did you give her the option to say no?" she asked.

"Of course."

"Fine. Let's go," she took her dishes to the sink and grabbed her shoes. She hoped Elise wouldn't mind her in jeans and a T-shirt.

Elise did mind. She looked at the jeans with disdain, but kept her mouth shut while she clapped out the beat.

Several times, Elise stopped to fix Sasha's posture.

"Shoulders back! Long neck! Tuck your butt!"

"I can't tuck that," Sasha retorted.

"Nor should you," Ricky's eyes were smoldering when he ran a hand down her hips and squeezed her ass.

Elise released an exasperated sigh and threw her hands up in annoyance.

By the time the lesson was over, Sasha was aching from being so tense. "I'm sorry, Elise. The steps are too fast, I'm still learning."

"You'll do better next time," Elise nodded them out of her studio.

Once in the car, Ricky kissed her hand. "You did good, Sasha. How do you feel?" He rubbed his short whiskers over her knuckles.

"Sore."

"You want to go home?"

She shrugged. She stretched and yawned.

"We can do whatever you want," he said, rubbing one of her knuckles into the dip of his chin.

She sighed and looked out the window at people walking by the alley where he had parked. "I wish."

Ricky squeezed her hand and rubbed his scrubby cheek against her fingers. "What do you wish?"

She looked at him. "I wish I was good enough for you to take to fancy dinners, or trips to France or Italy."

He stiffened when his eyes met hers. "Who said you weren't good enough?"

She sighed. "When I said I wanted to go to a dance studio, I meant with other people. I feel like you don't really want to be seen with me."

His eyes narrowed and he stopped nuzzling her hand. "That's not true, Sasha."

"Then why are you always parking in the alley?" she gestured around them.

"To protect car. No scratches."

She bit her lip. Her self-doubt was playing her and she knew it. He had walked around a mall with her and they had gone sightseeing. "I'm sorry. I'm just...." She leaned her head back and closed her eyes.

"So, you want to go to France?"

She shook her head. "No. It's too late for that."

He let go of her hand and pushed the button to start the car. He fished out his phone and swiped. The car speakers rang one and a half times before a man's voice answered with *"Ja, Herr Bell?"* Ricky eased the Bugatti out of the alley while the two men conversed in French.

Twenty-five minutes later they were at a small airport.

Her heart quickened. "What's happening?" she asked him.

"We will have dinner in France," he said when he pulled up to the valet.

Wait, what? She looked at her jeans and black sweater. "Like a baguette?" she called after him but he had exited the car and was walking around to open her door. She took his hand and he helped her out. He didn't let go, even when they were passing through security. They walked onto the tarmac, and approached a private jet that was warming its engines with 'GLOCKE' painted on the side.

The sound of the engines swallowed up her voice. This was happening. He was going to whisk her off to France. The door was secured behind them before they took their seats. Sasha sat next to Ricky and quickly adjusted her seatbelt because the private jet was already taxying the tarmac. The pilot announced to prepare for takeoff. The flight attendant checked that they were belted and asked for their drink order.

Ricky ordered wine and Sasha just nodded.

She was speechless.

Five minutes later, they were lifting off, Geneva disappearing below.

"What kind of fancy dinner did you want?" Ricky asked after the attendant brought them two glasses of red wine and then disappeared behind a curtain.

She stared at her shaking glass of wine and then back out the window. "What are you doing?" she asked, anxiety threatening to cut off her air supply when she stared at him with wide ebony eyes.

He leaned closer to her. "All you have to do is ask, Sasha. I'll give you everything." He kissed her trembling hand.

She didn't trust herself to drink the wine without sloshing it all over herself. To just fly her off to France on Christmas Eve shook her soul. How many people had he inconvenienced today because of her? She couldn't wrap her mind around his privilege. "I don't want this," she heard herself whisper.

"I'll make him go back to Geneva," Ricky said calmly.

She shook her head. "No, don't." She sucked in a breath. "What if these people had plans?" she asked, astutely aware that the attendant and pilots may have been ripped away from spending time with family and friends.

"Who do you mean?"

Or maybe the distraction was a blessing and

they had wanted to get away. Not everyone liked the holidays, herself included. She had asked for this. He was giving her what she requested and now she was throwing it in his face. She gulped her wine, not caring that the red bitter liquid dripped down her chin and splashed on her sweater. She dabbed her lips and jaw, staining the white cloth napkin the flight attendant had provided.

She shifted again so she could face him. "Okay. Let's do this. I want you to take me to a fancy restaurant where I'll embarrass you."

Ricky smiled and kissed her hand. "Embarrass me how?"

"By using the wrong fork."

He shrugged. "Then I'll use the wrong fork."

Of course he would. She couldn't stop her smile when she relaxed into the plush leather.

They touched down in Paris less than an hour later. They passed through security and got into a limo which had been waiting for them. While the limo weaved through the streets of Paris she enjoyed the view. Sasha had seen Paris from a plane, but to be in the city proper felt magical. This was the City of Love.

They approached a shop with dark windows. The owner opened the door and greeted them before locking them inside. They were taken to the back of the boutique where four people were waiting. The two women grabbed Sasha and escorted her to a private room.

She was surprised when the strange women grabbed at her clothes to undress her. She resisted. "I'm a grown ass woman. I know how to take off my clothes."

"Will go faster if we do zis," one of the women

insisted. "No time," she shrugged before yanking off Sasha's sweater.

Swallowing her anxiety, Sasha escaped into the safe corner in her mind while the women stripped her bare. She continued to fuss and complain when they waxed and plucked under her arms before they finally helped her into a dress. They didn't blink twice when they saw her naked body. As one woman sewed adjustments to lift the low back of the dress, the other applied a transparent oil-absorbing powder before finding shoes to fit her.

Before Sasha had come to terms with what was happening she had been squeezed into a tight teal satin dress with a sheer black lace overlay that sparkled with tiny black crystals. She stared at herself in the mirror. Her breasts were barely contained and damn did her ass look bootylicious. The dress went straight across her chest and had a backless V-shape that squeezed her waist and accentuated her hips. The pencil skirt ended right below her knees with a slit in the back which went up to her mid-thigh and revealed a beautifully beaded, black lace kick.

Sasha had unraveled her Bantu knots and combed her hair with her fingers. They accessorized her with a single black diamond that dangled right above her collarbone on a platinum chain. They slipped her hands into black satin gloves that went up to her elbows, and wrapped a black, faux fur stole around her shoulders.

When they did the final reveal, she didn't recognize herself. Ricky just Pretty-Womaned her like Richard Gere did to Julia Roberts in that 90s movie. One woman gave her a black studded clutch before they gathered all of her clothes she had arrived in. They kissed both of her cheeks and then left.

Was she getting her belongings back? She opened the clutch to see her phone, passport, wallet, powder and lipstick.

"You look beautiful," his voice made her turn.

He was sex in a tuxedo.

"So do you," she heard herself say, feeling nervous.

Ricky approached her with his hands in his pockets. He was wearing a white and black tux. He had a white jacket over a white dress shirt with a black bow tie. His black tuxedo pants with the silk stripe were creased over shiny black shoes.

She wished she had a stick to beat people off of him. She wasn't sure how she would be keeping herself off of him. He stood so close she had to look up.

"I like this color on you," his voice drove desire through her. He licked and bit his bottom lip. "I look forward to seeing it on my floor."

She needed a fresh pair of panties *tout suite.*

"Can I kiss you?" he asked.

She nodded.

He lifted her chin and surprised her with a soft chaste kiss. He rubbed her chin with his thumb.

She gulped her drool, thankful that the lipstick was one of those survive-a-nuclear-blast types.

"Let's go to dinner," he held out his hand.

"Where are we going?" she asked once the limo had pulled away from the curb.

"Le Cinq," he said before he kissed her gloved hand.

"I'm nervous," she admitted.

"Why?"

"I haven't had time to study French or dining etiquette."

"Ah. Just do what I do. No problem."

She trembled from the nerves, cold, and sexual tension. They arrived at the restaurant just after the sun had set. They were seated in a quiet corner and Sasha smelled the single rose which had been placed on her plate. The entire room was lit by candlelight and mostly couples occupied the tables. A man made love to the piano, his fingers coaxing the keys into a seductive melody.

Sasha asked him to order for her. The food was delicious and rich with tiny portions on decorated plates. She was glad to have the small portions because the dress wasn't meant to be eaten in.

Ricky told her about his time at Harvard. The parties were wild with even wilder women.

"I almost studied business," Sasha commented. "But I hate math. There isn't complex math in journalism."

After dinner the limo drove to the next destination. He led her into a large auditorium where there was a dance competition.

Sasha was excited to watch live dancers. They arrived just before the last waltz of the evening. She was on the edge of her seat, mesmerized by the couples of all ages floating around the floor.

"That was amazing," she whispered to Ricky when the dance ended and the participants exited the dance floor with a bow.

"You are amazing," he whispered, gazing at her.

She heated. "Maybe one day I can do that."

"They have a dance after judging if you want to join."

She glanced at him and smiled. "Really? I guess we

can do a dance or two, if that's alright."

He kissed her gloved hand. "Of course."

Within twenty minutes they were walking to the dance floor where people who stayed after the competition mingled while they waited for the free dancing to start.

"I don't have my dance shoes," she looked at the black satin heels on her feet.

"I'll take care of that." He approached one of the female dancers who was packing up her belongings. She had turned bright red while she dug into her duffel bag after Ricky spoke to her. Sasha couldn't even be mad. She'd be blushing nonstop too if a sexy lumberjack in a tuxedo acknowledged her existence.

He returned and kneeled at her feet. "May I?" He slid a hard rubber protector over each heel while she held onto his shoulder. His hand traveled up her calf to the hem of her skirt. "Better?" he asked when he looked up with a smile.

It took everything in her to refrain from ripping the tux off. "These might keep me from slipping." Too bad she wasn't in a dress for dancing. But she was going to try.

The lights dimmed and the music started. The first song was a two step that Sasha wasn't familiar with, but she left her stole and clutch on a nearby bench and tried to copy what others did.

She was having so much fun. They laughed when he spun and dipped her. Since there was no teacher, there was no pressure to be perfect. She could relax and enjoy the music and complicated steps.

Other men asked her to dance and she accepted. She wanted the chance to experience different dance partners and figured other women probably wanted to dance with Ricky and his flawless form.

An attractive man asked her to dance the waltz.

"*Je suis Jacques*," he smiled at her.

Sasha remembered he was one of the dancers who had placed in the competition. "I'm sorry. I don't understand," she felt like an ass crashing a dance party and not knowing the language.

He switched to English. "Are you American?"

She nodded after he spun her.

"Ah, I'm Jacques. And you are?"

"Sasha, nice to meet you."

"Same. Are you enjoying France?"

"It's lovely," she smiled. France had been a whirlwind so far.

While they waltzed along the dance floor, she noticed that Ricky wasn't dancing with anyone. He was leaning against the wall with his arms crossed, watching her. A couple of women standing near him were shooting furtive glances in his direction, probably hoping he'd ask them to dance.

When the waltz ended she and Jacques bowed and he held her hand while they walked off the dance floor. But then a cha-cha-cha song started and he whispered in her ear. "Shall we danz anozer?" he asked when Michael Bublé's "Sway" began to play.

Sasha agreed and Jacques pulled her back to the dance floor. He held her hand while they twisted their hips and danced back and forth. She liked his style and confidence.

"So, where are you staying?" Jacques asked her, his hand slipped from her mid-back to her hip when he guided her through a turn. A bit too confident.

Sasha tripped over him because her unease made her lose concentration.

"I've got you," Jacques said when he pulled her against him. He winked at her before pushing her into another turn.

It's just a dance. She can do this.

She found the rhythm again and fell in step with Jacques. "I'm leaving tonight," she said with half a smile.

"Ah, zat's too bad. I could show you ze ups and downz of Pari," he said with another wink.

Sasha was sure he wanted to try. She found herself studying Jacques for the first time. He was a player. She could see by the way he looked at her, winked at other women and wiggled his hips that he didn't care who he took home.

She threw her head back and laughed. Never in a million years would she let him show her his ups and downs. She decided to ignore his hand on her hip until the cha-cha-cha was over. The song ended and she bowed, thankful to move on. He walked her around the dance floor and asked if she had experienced an Eiffel Tower yet. She felt a hand slip into her free one and she glanced over her shoulder surprised.

Ricky stood there, his eyes smoldering when he said something to Jacques in French which caused the man to hesitantly release her.

"Maybe anozer time, *madame*," Jacques said before he bowed and stepped away.

Sasha stared into stormy eyes.

"Did you enjoy that?" Ricky asked through clenched teeth.

"The cha-cha-cha is okay," she said, trying to divert

his anger.

Ricky led her to the center of the floor, unbuttoning his jacket with one hand and loosening his silk bow tie. The familiar tune of a tango started. Sasha recognized "La Gloria" by Gotan Project.

When they faced each other, he dropped her hand and his whiskey eyes raked over her with feral desire. She felt the back of his knuckles slide over the racing pulse on her neck, down her shoulder, and finally to her fingertips.

She was shivering when she gazed up at him. When the violin started, he grabbed her hand and slid against her while he walked her through the complicated steps.

Her dress was too tight for him to shove a thigh between her legs and she was grateful. She wouldn't have survived if he touched her any more than he was now.

She could feel his eyes on her the entire time she looked away from him, the room spinning because she forgot to breathe and he was guiding her through steps she hadn't even learned yet. When he pushed her into a spin, there was an audible gasp around the room after Jacques grabbed her free hand and pulled her to him.

What the ever living fuck just happened?

Sasha was shook and not in a good way. But she swallowed her anger and continued to dance with Jacques when he pressed against her in a reverse walk.

If anyone else had been in this mess, Sasha would have been jealous or even applauded. Stuff like this didn't happen to women who looked like her.

Jacques was determined not to spin her. He dipped her instead, running his hand down her thigh.

She wished he was Ricky.

And then she felt him looming, the electricity of his proximity coursing through her. It was the strangest thing to feel him near her without seeing him. She took the chance to twist away from Jacques with her hand out and sweet Black Baby Jesus, Ricky pulled her into his arms. His hand grabbed her ass, pulling her against him. Ricky's teeth grazed her bare neck before he whispered, "Mine."

She almost passed out.

They danced the remainder of the song with her on the verge of hyperventilating. When the last note melted into silence the auditorium erupted into claps and whoops. Sasha bowed and glanced at Ricky who was holding her hand firmly while he walked her to fetch her stole and clutch.

Without a word, they left and climbed into the waiting limo.

The silence was deafening.

"I never vant to see a stranger touch you like that," his anger ricocheted in the limo.

The lumberjack was jealous.

"It was just a dance," she half offered.

"I hate that he put his hands all over you. Vithout permission."

He wasn't alone but she wasn't going to tell him that. There was something hot about his jealousy.

"Who's permission?" she asked with her lips pursed.

He rolled his eyes and scuffed. "Yours, of course." The tension still rolled off of him even when they drove past security and onto the tarmac at the airport almost an hour later.

They boarded the plane in silence, their clothes waiting for them in garment bags.

Once the plane had taken off and the flight attendant had taken her spot behind the curtain, Sasha turned to study her brooding lumberjack. He had his arms crossed over his chest and kept pulling at his growing stubble.

"I had a wonderful time, thank you."

He slid his gaze towards her and lowered his hand to the armrest for her to take. "I'm glad."

She could see the tension in his bunched shoulders. "What's wrong?" she asked.

He sighed before he ran his free hand through his hair and closed his eyes. "It's just been a long day."

She traced a line on his palm. "You don't need to be jealous," she said finally.

"You're a beautiful woman. I'd be stupid not to be jealous."

"No one looks at me the way people look at you," she whispered.

He gripped her hand. "They do, trust me."

"Are you angry?"

"No. I just want to protect you," he admitted.

"Protect me? It was just a dance, Ricky."

"You didn't see what I saw. You were having fun, laughing and dancing. And almost every man was watching you."

She shook her head in disbelief. "I doubt that." She sighed and looked out the small window. The view was pitch black dotted with tiny shimmering lights. They were a couple of hours from Christmas Day and she didn't want him sulking. "What are we doing tomorrow?"

He relaxed with a sigh and brought her fingers to his lips. "Whatever you want."

"Aren't you going to the charity dinner?"

He tensed again, his eyes narrowing at her. "Not without you."

Tonight had been enough high society for her. "We've been doing everything I want. Why don't you plan the day."

"If that's what you wish."

"I want to experience something you enjoy," she explained.

He studied her face for a few moments. He leaned forward slowly and she met him part way for a sensual kiss. "I can do that."

26. HIS BURDEN

December 25

When Sasha woke up on Christmas Day, big fat snow flakes were floating lazily from gray clouds. Even though she was alone in bed, she had another nightmare-free night. The only downside was that a certain lumberjack wasn't snuggling with her. She reminded herself that Ricky was a very busy man and had taken time off to be with her. She found him in gray boxer briefs, sitting at the kitchen island while talking on his phone and typing an email on his laptop. He smiled when he saw her.

She could get used to this view. Whether in her tiny kitchen or his big kitchen, the drool factor never ceased.

She kissed his shoulder when she passed him on her way to get water.

While sipping the water and watching the snow fall, she heard the buzz of her phone. She hadn't checked for messages in the past couple of days. She figured Hilda or Serena were wishing her a Merry Christmas.

When she saw the message, her heart stopped.

You made the news. Serena sent with a link.

Sasha opened the link to see a French article she didn't understand. She looked at a picture of her and Ricky dancing the tango. If she hadn't been that woman she wouldn't have recognized the gorgeous creature dancing with her lumberjack. His hand was low on her back and she was looking away while he gazed down at her. Damn, they looked sexy as fuck.

She called Serena.

"Allo?"

"Merry Christmas, Serena."

"Merry Christmas! You look so hot in that photo, no?" Serena sounded excited.

"I don't understand the article and can't find the translate-to-English option. What does it say?"

"They want to know who is the sexy mystery woman who captured Herr Bell's attention."

Her heart skidded to a stop. "Are you sure?"

"Ya, I read it twice. Where did you get that amazing dress?" Serena asked with envy.

"Can you translate the article for me?" Sasha asked. She skirted around the couch and walked briskly to her room where she closed the door. "What exactly does it say?"

"Um...hold on. Rickart Bell, the most eligible bachelors in Switzerland, made a surprise appearance at a local dance competition in Paris last night. Um.... He wowed the guests when he danced the tango with a beautiful, mysterious woman. Who is she and is the King of Glocke Industrie finally...taken?"

Sasha sat on the edge of her bed.

Serena continued, "Sounds like you had an amazing time in Paris. I'm jealous. *Un petit peu.*"

"It was nice," Sasha said, wondering if Ricky had

seen the article yet. "Thanks for translating for me. What're you and Claud up to today?"

"We're snowed in. Just dinner at town hall. Are you going to the charity ball?"

"No." How did she know about that?

"Oh. Who is Ricky taking?"

"He's not going."

Serena gasped. "Wow. That will be a first."

"What do you mean?"

"Well, he goes every year and gives a speech in honor of his mother. This will be a first for him if he doesn't attend—" There was some muffled shouting in the background, "—I've got to go. *Frohi Wiehnachte!*"

Ricky was closing his laptop when she hurried back into the living room. "Merry Christmas," he said to her when he held out a hand.

She was nervous when she hugged him. "Merry Christmas."

After they pulled apart, he studied her face. "What's wrong, Sasha?"

She showed him the text from Serena. "There was an article."

"And? There are always articles," he shrugged, rubbing her tense shoulders.

"I'm scared," she admitted.

"Why?"

"I don't want Jackson to find me."

His jaw tensed. "The one who hurt you? I'll take care of it."

"Too late for that. My picture's out there. People are going to start talking."

"Let them talk. It's no problem," he insisted.

"I don't know how to navigate your world."

A sigh escaped his lips. "That's okay. We can create our own world."

She nodded and stepped back into his open arms.

He hugged her close and kissed her crown. His phone buzzed on the counter. His jaw clenched when he looked at the name. "It's Sylvie," he sighed then answered.

Sylvie was screaming before he had spoken.

Sasha didn't know enough Swiss German to understand the angry conversation between them, but she would bet both her legs they were discussing her and his untimely absence that evening.

At some point Ricky gave up responding and just stared at his phone in disgust. Then he ended the call when Sylvie was mid-sentence.

"She's probably going to come here," Sasha panicked, watching him power off his phone.

"I changed code and deactivated her card already."

Goddayum.

Sasha bit her lip. She wasn't sure what the charity ball was for, but his absence was making waves. "Are you going?"

"No," he gave her a warning look.

"Are we still going out today?"

"Yes, let's get ready," he sighed in relief with a smile.

_ʌʌ_

He took her to see the Bell Parade where hundreds of children with bells walked the streets. He bought her a bagel from a street vendor and an espresso for himself. They watched from the sidewalk and waved to the kids. Neither of them commented on the gigantic bell-shaped float with Glocke Industrie stamped on the side.

On their way to the next place, they walked through the mall.

Sasha knew this would be her last chance to buy him a gift. Every store was crowded with last minute shoppers like herself.

"Can I just have a little time alone to buy something?" she asked him.

"Of course. I'll wait there," he pointed to one of the decorative Christmas trees.

She walked to the menswear store and went directly to the scarves. She hadn't seen him wear one because he was used to having a long beard. She felt a couple of them before she found a soft black one. Maybe next year she could learn how to knit one.

When she joined him near the tree she thrust the bag into his hand. "Merry Christmas!"

He looked down at the bag which he hesitantly accepted, his face blushing red with embarrassment. "What's this?" He reached inside and pulled out the scarf, confusion written all over his features.

"Your beard hasn't filled in yet." She grabbed the scarf and wrapped it around his neck. "Now you'll be warmer."

He swallowed when his whiskey gaze met hers. "It's nice," he said finally.

She felt deflated. "You hate it."

"No, I'm surprised. I told you, you're my gift."

She shook her head. "Okay." She knew better. She couldn't possibly buy anything for the man who can buy everything. She hugged herself. At least she had tried. "Well, let's go," she whispered before turning away.

Strong arms pulled her into his sandalwood and vanilla warmth when Ricky embraced her. In the middle of the mall, he lifted her chin for a chaste kiss that stole her breath before he gently nipped on her bottom lip. "I love it, Sasha," he whispered in her ear. "Thank you." He grabbed her hand and pulled her along, leaving her wits scattered behind them.

Their next destination was an outdoor skating rink. She had tried ice skating before but she wasn't very good. She held on to him for dear life as they skated with the throng of people.

Once Sasha had gotten steady enough, he skated beside her. Even with all of the people skating around them, she felt like they were the only ones who existed in that time and space. The way he smiled at her and securely held her hand made her feel amazing.

"Sasha Williams!" someone called her.

Hearing her name, Sasha's feet hesitated and she wobbled when she glanced over her shoulder.

Thankfully, Ricky pulled her against him until she was steady.

"Pietre?" Of all the people. Sasha gave a meek wave since it was too late to pretend she hadn't heard him.

"I can't believe it's you," he said after he skated up to them. He side-eyed Ricky and acknowledged him with a small nod, "Herr Bell."

Ricky scowled, his nostrils flared before he returned the curt nod. "Herr Furrer."

"Merry Christmas, Sasha!" Pietre exclaimed before hugging her.

She cringed and patted his shoulder. "Merry Christmas."

"I can't believe we're both here, ya? Are you in Geneva for New Years?" Pietre flashed her a smile, pointedly ignoring the man next to her.

"I think so," Sasha shrugged before she darted a glance at Ricky, trying to figure out why he was so tense and glaring daggers at Pietre. Was he that mad about the whole fondue thing?

"I'm going to a club with some friends. You and…" he narrowed his eyes but held her gaze. "Ricky should join us."

"Oh," she tried to ignore her anxiety. "I don't do well in crowds."

A group of smiling people skated up to them. "Who are your friends, Pietre?" one of the ladies asked in Swiss German after she undressed Ricky with her green eyes.

Pietre introduced everyone. Sasha didn't bother to learn their names. Names were never her forte.

"Anyway, Sasha," Pietre continued, pulling her a few feet to the side while his friends fawned over meeting the Richard Bell. "You should come. I'd love to see you again," he said when his hand patted her elbow and then stayed there.

Sasha winced and pulled away. "Yeah, well—"

Gracing her with what must have been his lady-killer smile, Pietre continued. "We can be great friends. Please come? Give me your number so I can send you the address."

"Just tell me," Ricky interrupted when he skated to her side and draped an arm around her shoulder. "If we aren't busy, maybe we'll go."

Pietre's face fell. He replaced his phone in his pocket and rattled off the venue name to Ricky even though his gaze stayed on Sasha. "Well, have a great day, Sasha," Pietre waved before he skated off with his friends.

They continued to skate until Sasha was too cold to continue. When changing back into their shoes, she inquired, "Where to next?"

"Are you hungry yet?" he asked.

"Actually, there's something I want to do today," she squeezed his hand and kissed his cheek.

_ʌʌ_

Later that evening while guests were arriving at the charity dinner, Sasha and Ricky tied on aprons and snapped on gloves to serve food.

"This is great," Ricky beamed.

They were at a homeless shelter just outside of Geneva where they were going to serve Christmas dinner together.

"I like to give back when I can," she returned his smile.

They served food for two hours. Once people stopped coming for seconds, Sasha wandered the room pouring coffee and water. Ricky helped distribute dessert and clean the tables. When service was done and the kitchen was cleaned, they made their way home.

After showering and snuggling in bed, Sasha relaxed against his chest and listened to his heart beat while he caressed her shoulder with a lazy swirl of his fingers.

"Thank you," he whispered, staring at the shadows.

"For what?"

"I haven't done that since I was a kid. My *mutter*

always volunteered since she couldn't work."

Unable to hide her shock, Sasha asked, "Sylvie volunteers?"

"I doubt that woman has ever helped anyone but herself. I mean my real *mutter*, Marie Bell."

Ebony eyes widened. He rarely spoke about his real mom. "I saw her picture on your desk," she confessed. "She was beautiful and looked so happy. Is that you with her?"

"Yes, on a beach in Italy."

Sasha ran her fingers through his chest hair. "You must miss her."

"Everyday."

"What happened?"

He answered her with silence. She heard him swallow several times.

"Never mind," she insisted. "You don't have to tell me."

"I was young. I don't remember everything."

She nodded. "That's okay, we don't have to talk about it."

He pulled her closer. "I want to. I want you to know."

She waited, their hands curled together over his heart.

"My *mutter* wasn't happy. She and Tobias fought often," he began.

"Is Tobias your dad?"

"How do you say—not by blood?"

"He's your step-father?"

"Yes."

Sasha went silent and squeezed his hand.

"I remember it was storming that night. She and

Tobias had another fight. They always had fights, but this one was bad. I could hear them hit each other, glass breaking and.... Her lip was bleeding when she came into my room. Tobias was on the ground when she dragged me out. I thought she had killed him."

Sasha's heart pounded.

"She screamed that she was leaving. She took me and my—" he stopped.

"You don't have to continue," Sasha insisted.

"I'm fine," he lied. He rubbed his eyes before holding her hand again. "I remember she was putting us all in the car—I had a sister and brother. It started raining so hard I couldn't even see the road. I remember she was crying and the car swerved. I vanted to help her see better. I took off my seatbelt and I climbed into the front seat. I still remember the look on her face vhen she turned to scream at me. And then—" his voice was thick with grief.

She couldn't hold back her own tears.

"It's my fault," he whispered.

"What is?" Sasha asked and tried to comfort him by pulling him closer.

"If I had stayed in my seat—I distracted her and she ran off road," he swallowed several times and sniffed.

Sasha propped herself up to wipe away his tears. "It was probably a freak accident. That's not your fault."

"Because I didn't have my seatbelt," he stared at the ceiling and into the past. "I got ejected. They got trapped." He dragged in a breath, tears disappearing into his sideburns.

Sasha kissed his stubbled cheek. "I'm so sorry, Ricky."

"I can still see the flames," he sniffed. "I never

told anyone but the police about that night." He looked at her. "If people knew I killed my *mutter* and...." he couldn't finish, a sob stifled behind a fist clenched so tightly his knuckles were bone white.

Sasha wiped her own tears. He was carrying around a massive burden. She wished she could take his pain away, but she was dealing with her own demons.

She kissed his cheek and pulled him to her. "Shh, it wasn't your fault, Ricky. I'm sorry I asked."

He covered his eyes with his arm. "I wanted to tell you," he whispered. "I wanted you to know that I'm not perfect."

They held each other until sleep claimed them.

27. THE ARTICLE

December 26

Sasha woke up when Ricky readjusted himself around her and his arm, which she had claimed for her pillow. Another quiet night without bad dreams.

She turned so they were facing each other. She saw sadness in his whiskey eyes so she kissed his cheek. "How are you?" she asked.

"Vorried," he admitted, his baritone deep and groggy.

"What's wrong?" She held his gaze.

"Are you leaving me?" he asked.

She backed up so she could see his body language too. "What?"

He swallowed. "I'm not sure how you feel after hearing vhat I did."

"Oh, Ricky," she pulled him close and rested on his chest. "That probably wasn't your fault."

"You believe that?"

"Yes." Memories around trauma weren't always reliable. But with his mom crying and the rain, anything was possible.

He squeezed her. "I thought you'd vant to leave."

"You get another two weeks," she teased and attempted to tickle his side.

He growled when he rolled her onto her back and tickled her ribs. "We agreed three months," his voice was gruff when he trapped her between his legs and tickled her sides again.

This playful side of him was rare. She wanted more of her playful lumberjack. His whiskey eyes were bright and his smile reminded her of the boy she had seen in the photos with unadulterated happiness.

Wrapping her arms around his neck, she pulled him close and kissed him. What started as a chaste kiss because of morning breath evolved because he invaded her mouth anyway, rubbing his body and arousal against her.

"Do you think it's safe yet?" he asked when he squeezed her breast and nipped at her neck.

Sasha's breath was shallow, her own arousal blooming. She shook her head. "My period started last night."

"I don't care about that. We can put a towel down," he said, his hand trailing down her waist to her hips before he grabbed her ass.

"Not yet," she gasped. "I'm still sore."

He nodded, his whiskers grazing her shoulder. He pushed her shirt up and pinched her nipple. "Can I show you other vays to pleasure?"

She loved when he was lost in desire and his accent thickened. "Please do."

"Did you know that a voman can orgasm vithout clit stimulation or intercourse," he said before he pulled a nipple into his mouth.

"What do you mean?" she gasped.

"You can have a psychological orgasm." He tapped above her ear. "Can I touch you anyvhere?"

Her body was already threatening to explode. She had been on edge for days due to his intoxicating presence. "Yes," she sighed.

He made her orgasm with his words and his caresses which led to her first psychological orgasm that didn't involve his curved weapon of destruction or stimulating her bundle of nerves. She was seeing stars by the time her body melted in his arms.

When her brain was working again she looked at him in wonder. "That was amazing," she admitted feeling a bit shy.

"Mmm, you are beautiful to vatch," he kissed her temple.

"What about you?" She could feel his arousal against her hip.

He hugged her close. "I don't have to."

"Do you want to?"

He kissed her neck. "Of course."

She pushed him back and told him to be still. Then she nibbled her way down his body until she reached her goal. Making him tremble and gasp with her humming and tongue made her feel powerful. Feeling and watching him release had been glorious.

When they left the bedroom for sustenance, it was almost noon. He turned on his phone and placed it on the counter before he cracked some eggs into a bowl.

"What can I do?" she offered, stretching.

"Wash fruit?"

His phone started vibrating like crazy. She opened

the fridge and took out some strawberries and the rest of the melon. Curiosity made her glance at the motorcycle on his screen and the slew of message notifications was in the double digits.

He ignored his phone and put a pat of butter into the hot pan.

Sasha rinsed the strawberries. "Should I make toast?" she asked over the constant buzzing.

"Sounds great."

When they sat down for breakfast, Ricky finally checked his phone. After a long pause, he frowned.

Unable to take the suspense anymore, she inquired, "What happened?"

He sipped his espresso and sighed. "Just the news," he answered before swiping his thumb up and down the screen several times.

She bit into a juicy strawberry. "I had a really nice time yesterday. Those kids with the bells were so adorable."

He sat his phone face down on the table where it continued to vibrate. "Do you want kids?" he asked before he lifted the espresso cup to his lips.

She coughed after inhaling a chunk of strawberry. "I can't."

The espresso cup was paused in mid-air and he gave her a questioning look. "Why not?"

She wiped her lips with her napkin. "Because I'm broken. I shouldn't be raising kids."

He looked at her confused. "You're not broken, Sasha." He sighed and set his espresso on the saucer without taking a sip.

"My therapist might say otherwise."

His eyebrows rose in surprise. "You're seeing a

therapist?"

Not knowing how he felt about therapy, anxiety crawled into her chest. "Do you have a problem with that?" she asked with a bit more sass than she intended. Whiskey eyes narrowed at the tone of her voice. "Not at all."

She relaxed a fraction. She reminded herself that Ricky was always accepting of her faults. "I've got some healing to do."

"You've been through a lot," he acknowledged before taking a bite of his eggs.

"I don't even know if I'm going to keep going," Sasha frowned.

"Why not?"

Biting her lip, and hugging herself for comfort, she tried to figure out how to put her concerns into words. "I don't think she's worked with people who have experienced domestic violence. Anyway," Sasha needed to get the focus off of herself. "Do you want kids?"

He was watching her closely. "I'd love to."

She nodded, relaxing enough to look at her hands. "You'll be an amazing father."

He shrugged. "If it happens. Life can be chaotic."

The conversation tapered off and they finished breakfast so she found her phone to plug it in. She sat on her bed in the guest room, watching TV while he checked emails in his room. Her phone buzzed.

I can't believe it! You are like modern day Cinderella! Serena sent with a link.

Sasha opened the link and her blood ran cold. This article was in German and there was a picture of her and Ricky at the soup kitchen. She didn't even remember anyone taking pictures.

She disconnected her phone from the charger and walked to his room. He was at his desk talking on his cell. She lifted her phone to his face. "What does it say?" She didn't care if she was interrupting him.

He held up a finger while he wrote something down.

She looked at the screen again and swiped up while she waited. There were pictures from the parade of them waving and smiling to the kids, him towering over her. Another picture of their kiss in the mall after she had given him the scarf. A picture of them holding hands at the skating rink. Someone had followed them. And to make the situation worse, she saw her full name in the text.

Ricky ended his call. "Don't worry, Sasha."

"Read it to me," she was shaking, she was so angry. And scared.

He sighed and took her phone. He closed his eyes and ran a hand through his hair before he looked at the tray ceiling. "It just says—"

"I want word for word."

He cleared his throat and clicked something on his computer before looking at her phone. "Yesterday, Rickart Bell spent Christmas Day with a mysterious woman. Being one of the most eligible bachelors in Europe, this is the first time Bell has been in public with a woman outside of an official Glocke Industrie event in over a year." He looked up at her. "This isn't necessary —"

"I want to hear all of it," she insisted, crossing her arms.

He cleared his throat and looked back at her phone. "The mystery woman has been identified as Sasha

Williams, the newest English teacher in Glockenvalt. Since the Bell legacy began there, we assume that is where the two love birds met. Williams is from Detroit, Michigan in the United States—this is enough," he said after glancing at her. "You're upset." He returned her phone.

"We were followed."

"Or was just cell pics," he shrugged.

"How much do they know about me?" she asked through her anger, her voice shaking.

"Not much—"

"My full name is in there!" she screamed. "They fucking mentioned where I live! Jackson can find me now!"

"No," he stood up suddenly, causing her to yelp and stumble back. Seeing her fright, he raised his hands in surrender and slowly approached her. "Listen, Sasha—"

"Just read the fucking article, Ricky!" she shoved her phone back at him with a shaking hand.

He clenched his jaw. "What fucking difference will it make?"

"I have every right to know what they're saying about me."

He closed his eyes and nodded. He accepted her phone. "No battery."

"Fuck." She had it plugged in for maybe a minute. She went to his bed and sat down with her palms pressed against her eyes.

"I won't let anyone hurt you," Ricky sat next to her. "Do you really think he'll come here?"

She looked up tears streaked down her cheek. "I don't know," she sniffed. Although Jackson had threatened her, he was an alcoholic who was barely functioning when she left. He didn't have a passport and was barely holding on to his job. What could he do to her now?

"You're safe, Sasha," he insisted when his thumb swiped away her tears.

She calmed down a bit. "I want to hear the rest of the article. Can you open it on your laptop?"

He sighed, "Of course." He sat at his computer and clicked once. He must have already had the article open because he resumed where he left off. "Williams graduated top of her class with a double major in Journalism and English in 2012.

"The couple has been spotted a couple of times. Earlier in the week they were seen at a mall in Geneva and then in Paris where they attended a dance competition on Christmas Eve.

"Last night, Bell did not attend the annual Glocke Foundation Charity event which was started by his mother, Marie Bell, in 1980. Marie Bell and her two children perished in a deadly car accident on August 15, 1991. There were a hundred of Europe's finest gathered to honor her memory. Even though Bell was not in attendance, he made an appearance at a local homeless shelter with Williams. Tobias Bell delivered the keynote speech in place of his son.

"Rickart Bell hasn't been seen in public with anyone since he was left at the altar by his former fiancée, Eva Dupris of Dupris Nationale in France, over a year ago. Everyone is wondering if love is in the air or if Bell is rebounding from a broken heart with his new fling. We shall see." He pressed his lips together and glared at the screen.

Sasha stared at him. "Is that all?"

"Yes," he sighed.

"August 15th is when I came to Switzerland," she watched him carefully, her anger deflating.

"I know," he closed his laptop with a snap before meeting her gaze.

"What were you doing out there?" She stood, her arms crossed to hide her trembling hands.

"I had just visited their graves," he admitted. "I was on my way back when I saw you," he dragged in a shaky breath.

She remembered him driving by so fast she thought maybe he hadn't seen her. The man who carried the burden of death. "Ricky," she took a step closer. She swallowed, afraid to ask. More afraid to know. "Why were you going so fast?"

He put his hands in his bourbon hair. He swallowed and looked at her with sad eyes. After clearing his throat, he said, "I vas just riding. Questioning. Then there you vere." His voice was so thick with emotion she almost couldn't understand him.

What if she hadn't been there?

Ricky stood. "You're trembling."

This was too much information at one time. Too many emotions. But there was one emotion that began to bloom in her heart.

"I think I need to go lie down," she whispered.

"Can I hug you first?"

She nodded and his arms encircled her moments later.

"I'll protect you," he murmured into her Bantu knots.

She listened to his heartbeat when she hugged him back. She looked up, her gaze tracing his tense shoulders to the slow pulse on his neck until she found his whiskey eyes. She wished she could protect him too.

The buzzing of his phone on the table made him sigh. "I have a lot of emails to answer," he whispered. "Stay here, please?"

After plugging in her phone again, she made herself comfortable on his bed. She watched him answer emails and calls through the archway until she fell asleep.

_ɅɅ_

He ordered Italian because she didn't have the energy to go out and his phone kept buzzing nonstop. They ate in silence at the table, both lost in their thoughts.

Anyone could find her now. Anyone could look into her past. She wondered if she should break her teaching contract and leave or deal with the oncoming storm.

And then what about Ricky? Every time their eyes met he would tense, making her insides tighten.

Eventually he pushed his plate away where he had mostly moved the food around. He stared at the uneaten Puttanesca with his arms crossed.

"Do you have to go back to work?" she asked him, staring at her own full plate.

In her periphery she saw him shrug. "There will always be work," he sighed.

She tried a bit of roasted tomato and happened to look up to see that his whiskey eyes were trained on her, filled with worry.

"I need to know what you're thinking," he stated, his voice laced with uncertainty. "Do you want to leave?"

Setting down her fork, she studied her hands, twisting her fingers before crossing her arms. She met his gaze again and saw him freeze, hanging on her every word. "I'm staying," she whispered. "If that's still okay."

His eyes widened in surprise. "Really?"

Biting her lip, she finally smiled at him. "I like you, and I want to give us a try."

He exhaled and relaxed. He rubbed his eyes before he looked at her again. "I like you, too, Sasha."

Not sure if there was ever a good time to discuss his ex, Sasha cleared her throat and forged into dangerous territory. "In the article, it said you had a fiancée. What happened with her?"

Ricky examined the table. "We were incompatible. She would ask me for trips and diamonds. Then she would literally throw them in my face because she wanted more. I gave her everything she wanted except for my company. Then she went to Hong Kong a week before our wedding and just…didn't come back."

Sasha raised her eyebrows. "You still love her?"

Holding her gaze, he stated, "No. Absolutely not. She was uh—how do you say—toxic. We wouldn't have lasted."

Sasha chewed her lip, watching him. "Why didn't you date anyone else?"

He sighed and ran both hands over his face before looking at her again. "I was done. I just needed a break from the lavish parties, the fights and…." he trailed off.

She hurt for him. "You deserve better."

He leaned forward. "I have found better."

Her heart skipped a beat. "I wish I could—"

"Don't push it. I'll wait." His hand reached for hers

and she accepted his touch. He rubbed a thumb across her knuckles.

She nodded and looked at their hands, at the contrast of his skin against her deep chestnut brown. "If you have time, maybe we can watch a movie or something?"

"I'd love to."

28. PENNIES

December 30

The days passed in a blur. They continued the dance lessons with Elise and then he would come home to work for a couple of hours. Sasha didn't want to go out. She just wasn't ready to face the world and he wouldn't go anywhere without her.

On Wednesday evening she was sitting on the couch watching dance competitions on the big projection screen. Her phone buzzed and she slid to answer.

"Hey Serena."

"Sasha! We're coming to Geneva. Please have dinner with us?"

She pursed her lips and asked, "Who is us?"

"Just Claud and me. I've missed our lunches," Serena whined.

She hadn't thought much about Glockenwald or what other people were doing. She was caught in the whirlwind of Richard Bell.

"I haven't been out much," Sasha admitted. "Ever since the articles."

"Oh, fuck the articles. People will talk no matter what. If it's not you, it's someone else."

Sasha shook her head. These people didn't get it. She was hiding, not trying to flaunt her juicy ass all over Europe. "Did you have a place in mind?"

"I was hoping Ricky could find something, no?"

The audacity. "Wow." Sasha bit down on her tongue so hard she tasted iron. She was bothered that someone was using her to use him. She sighed. "I'll ask if he has any ideas. But he might be busy."

"Then you come out, okay? We're stopping by Pietre's and we'll call you when we get to Geneva. See you soon!"

Sasha stared at her phone when the call ended. One thing Serena said kept echoing in her head: People will talk no matter what.

Ricky was sitting at his desk talking on his cell with a hand in his hair. He patted his lap when she walked over to him. She complied by sitting on his thigh, then listened to him talk in French. He stroked her neck absently before he twisted the office chair towards his desk and opened an email he just received. Then he ended the call.

His short beard tickled her shoulder when he kissed her jaw. "I'm sorry, I've been working."

"It's okay. I've been watching dance competitions."

"You've gotten better, ya? I enjoy the tango again." He rubbed his jaw against her neck.

She lifted her phone, "Serena called."

He ran a hand through his hair when he leaned back into the office chair. "Vhat fucking article this time?"

Sasha chuckled at his reaction, but she understood

the sentiment. "She and Claud are coming to Geneva and want to have dinner tonight."

He was visibly relieved. "If you want," he searched her face.

"It might be good for me to get out."

"There might be more articles."

"I know. You've said there are always articles. That just isn't my life," she admitted, gazing into his whiskey eyes, then admiring the dip in his chin and defined jaw. She wondered how long his beard would take to fill in like before. "I think I'm ready to enjoy Geneva."

He smiled, watching her. "Where are we meeting them?"

"Yeah, about that...."

_ _᠕ᡘ_

Later that evening they walked into the kitchen of La Petite Celeste where Chef Louis escorted them to the private dining room. Sasha was dressed in a new pair of jeans and her new white sweater.

Serena and Claud were there and stood up when they walked in.

Serena squealed and ran over to give Sasha a hug. "I've missed you!" the tall blond exclaimed when she squeezed Sasha.

Sasha hugged her back. "It's only been a couple of weeks," she said before they sat down at the table with too many plates.

After the wine was poured and orders taken, Serena looked around the empty room. "I can't believe we're here. In a private room. I didn't know this room existed," she said when she smiled at Sasha.

"It doesn't," Ricky countered before sipping his red. Everyone exchanged glances.

"I'm so jealous," Serena expressed with a pout. "We were stuck in Glockenvalt and you've been here. I bet you're doing all kinds of shopping."

"Not really," Sasha admitted. She sipped her red and noticed that Claud had tapped Ricky's shoulder and the two men were talking quietly to the side.

"But there was that romantic kiss in the mall, no?"

"We were just walking through," Sasha explained with a shrug.

Serena turned her gaze to Ricky. "Why haven't you taken her shopping? You even flew her to France and still didn't treat her?" The look of pure horror on this woman's face made Sasha laugh behind her wine glass.

Ricky straightened in his chair and raised both eyebrows at Sasha. "Do you want to go shopping in Paris?"

Sasha shook her head smiling. "Nah, I'm good. I mean, no."

He shrugged at Serena. "There you have it. She doesn't want to shop."

The fondue arrived and they talked about beautiful places to visit in Europe. Places Sasha could only dream of seeing. After dinner, she sipped water while the others enjoyed espresso.

Serena grabbed Sasha's hand. "Please, you have to come to the New Year's party with us," blue eyes begged. "I won't know anyone but Pietre."

And he was one of the reasons why Sasha wasn't going. "You know I don't like crowds."

"But we'll have a private room, so less crowds."

Sasha slid a glance to Ricky who shrugged. "I don't

have money for a dress."

Serena gestured to Ricky. "Oh for fuck sake, he won't even buy you a dress?"

Sasha had spent the last couple of New Year's in a corner of her old bedroom with a busted lip. She looked at Ricky who studied her over the rim of his espresso cup. "I'll think about it."

"I'm going to ask Pietre to put you and Ricky on the guest list, in case you change your mind," Serena tapped at her phone with her thumbs. "You may not be here next year," she said with a frown. "So I'm hoping you come. Experience life when you're living it, no?"

Sasha bit her lip. She had been hiding from life. And there was no telling where she would be next year. "You're right."

"Of course I am." Serena crossed her thin arms over her chest. "We should go shopping tomorrow. Just us girls, yeah?" she slid another glance at Ricky. "Maybe Herr Bell can spare you some francs."

He shrugged. "Whatever Sasha wants."

_⋏⋏_

When Sasha and Ricky returned to his penthouse, they collapsed onto the leather couch. He was sitting with his arm propped against the cushion and she rested her head in his lap gazing up at him.

"Thanks for dinner," she sighed and pushed her fingers up his scruffy jaw until she reached his ear and gave a gentle tug on his lobe.

He smiled at her. "It was nice sharing fondue with friends."

"I think being in a private room helped," she

reached further and tugged on his hair.

He caught her hand in his and kissed her palm. "Do you want to go to the party?" he asked.

"Do you want to go?"

"I'll go wherever you go," he kissed her finger tips.

"Do you know what kind of club it is?" she inquired, studying the contours of his handsome face.

"It's an old warehouse. Difficult to get VIP."

"Oh, that's cool. I wonder what kind of music," she said to the ceiling. She thought about the only clubbing she knew, which involved pop music and twerking. Although she had eclectic taste, she wasn't into head banging. But as long as she could find the beat she could dance.

"It's usually techno."

She didn't mind techno. "What kind of outfit should I buy?" She sat up and reached for her purse. "Actually, I need to figure out how much I can afford," she mumbled when she grabbed her phone.

"Really, Sasha?" he asked with an edge to his voice.

She glanced at him after signing into her bank account. "What?"

"Why not ask me?"

"For what? Money?"

"Yes. Why not let me buy you something?"

She sighed and leaned against the couch, hugging herself. He had opened up to her, she could do the same.

Sasha told Ricky how she had met her ex during her last year at Wayne State, and how he worked at the newspaper where she interned. At first they were friends and enjoyed going out to different restaurants. But then he asked for more and they started dating. He wined and dined her at the local hot spots, always showing her off to his friends.

When she graduated, everything changed. She got hired at the newspaper but worked in a different department, and somehow ended up earning more money than him.

"I should have broke it off when he started getting angry over stupid shit," she stated when she looked over Geneva and into her past. "But I figured all couples argue."

He would make excuses as to why she couldn't see Betty or her friends. Eventually, friends stopped calling and Betty was too busy fostering kids.

"I still remember the first time. I had teased him at work and other people joked about it, giving him shit all day. I just remember walking through the front door of our place and then blacking out because he had hit me that hard." She looked at a blurred Ricky. "I was his punching bag for three years. Then he started throwing change at me because according to him I was worth less than a penny in the hood." She shook her head. "That's how I paid to get here. I saved and hid every coin I could find."

He started to scoot closer to her but paused. "Can I hug you?"

She nodded and felt comforted in his embrace when he pulled her close.

Nuzzling against her temple, he murmured, "You didn't deserve that."

"I don't need you throwing your money at me."

He stiffened. "I'm not doing that. You know I'd never hurt you."

"I'm starting to believe that. But I didn't think Jackson would hurt me either."

His fingers caressed her shoulder. "If you ever want anything, just ask, okay?"

She perked up. "Can I have a loan?"

Pulling away, he studied her. "A loan?"

"Yeah, I'll pay you back next month after I get paid."

He stared at her, a twitch of a smile on his lips. "If that's what you want. How much?"

"Enough to buy a dress."

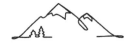

29. BEAST MODE

December 31

R ight before noon the next day Sasha exited the black Mercedes-Maybach after her chauffeur stopped in front of the mall. Ricky had to deal with issues in New York so he gave her all of the cash in his wallet and he told her the pin to his AmEx Centurion.

Serena waved to her and they hooked arms. "Ready to shop?" Serena had questions. She wanted to know everything regarding Ricky, and Sasha refused to answer. She was still figuring out their relationship and didn't want to add to the rumors.

They went to a couple of stores with clothes Sasha couldn't afford let alone fit. She had to make sure she stayed on budget. After coaxing Serena to go to cheaper stores, they finally found a place with sexy dresses in her price range.

"You have an amazing ass," Serena said with a purse of her pink lips. "You need something tight."

After trying on dresses, Sasha decided on a white, stretchy dress that hugged her curves and had circle cut outs down both sides. It was sleeveless with a leather collar around her neck, and ended just above her knees. On Serena the dress would have been mid-thigh. This was the kind of dress that wouldn't allow panties or a bra so she was glad her period had ended. She chose a pair of shiny white pumps with clear stiletto heels.

The women stood next to each other in their dresses, feeling and looking fabulous. Sasha was starting to feel excited about going out. She hadn't been to a VIP anything in many years.

Sasha allowed Serena to drag her around Geneva where they ate dinner and continued shopping. She texted Ricky every now and then so he wouldn't worry. After declining to accompany Serena to the spa, Sasha called the chauffeur, Noah, to pick her up. Going into Ricky's building without him felt weird, but the doorman nodded to her and one of the three security guards escorted her to the elevator. He touched his card and punched in the numbers to give her access to Ricky's floor.

She knocked when she arrived because just opening his front door felt intrusive. When he answered he was talking on the phone.

After returning his smile and kiss, she kicked off her shoes, then slid the leftover cash and his Black Card next to his wallet on the counter. Ricky seemed to be having a heated conversation while he paced around the kitchen and dining room. Since she didn't want to bother him, she went to get ready.

Sasha didn't have a team of French ladies helping her this time; she showered and shaved, then slathered her body in cocoa butter and added a dash of pheromones behind her ears and on her wrists. She applied the red lipstick from Paris and repinned her Bantu knots to keep her hair under control.

When she finally came out of her room Ricky was leaning against the island still talking on his cell. He must have been talking about something stressful because he was pinching the bridge of his nose with his eyes squeezed shut.

"Why did you strike intellectual property? For what I'm offering you, that includes the cost of the schematics." He looked up at the sound of her heels clicking on the marble floor. "Jeremy, I have to go." He ended the call and slid his hands into his pockets after he slipped off the chrome stool. "You look amazing. I wouldn't mind staying here and having you for dessert," he suggested, ravishing her with his eyes.

She took in his jeans and a black button down shirt with black dress shoes. "You look good too."

"I mean it," he continued to drink her in with his gaze before biting his lip. "Let's go before I change my fucking mind."

She smiled and wrapped her black stole around her shoulders. "Did you get the cash and your card?"

"Yes. You could've kept them."

"And get myself arrested for trying to use your card? No, thanks. I was able to get the dress and shoes with the francs."

While in the mirrored elevator, she could see he was mesmerized by her ass and kept running a hand through his hair. The fact that he couldn't keep his eyes off of her made her feel sexy.

They rode in the Maybach, and she wondered if Noah would've had his own plans for New Years if she hadn't decided to go to the club. The long gray warehouse had huge windows that reflected the strobe lights with shadows dancing inside. The line to get in was at least fifty people deep when the limo pulled up to the curb.

"Don't leave my side," Ricky whispered into her ear before they approached the door, skipping the line.

She could feel the bass vibrating through the walls. If this is what they were going to play all night, she was going to enjoy herself.

Once they had been scanned for weapons, one of the bouncers escorted them to the VIP lounge. Sasha took in the dark club with heavy fog and laser lights. The bass throbbed through the gyrating crowd, making her teeth rattle.

"Sasha!" Serena crashed into her. "You're a sexy bitch tonight! Let's drink!" She dragged her away from Ricky to a private bar where she asked the bartender for whiskey on the rocks.

The VIP room was full of people shouting above the bass and shuffling to the beat. It was a different scene from the crowd downstairs. The VIP lounge had three glass walls where she could see the DJ in front of the dance floor.

She saw Pietre dancing with a blond in the corner. He nodded to her but didn't approach.

Claud gave her a hug. "You guys made it!" He offered Ricky a beer, which was declined.

"Let's go dancing!" Serena shouted while gesturing to the main dance floor and the DJ.

Sasha tried to school her face. The last thing she wanted was to get lost in a crowd of two hundred plus bodies. "I don't know. I think this is enough," she gestured to the twenty or so people in the lounge.

Leaning against her, Serena wrapped a skinny arm around Sasha's shoulder. "But dancing in a crowd like that feels amazing!" she insisted. "Come on, please? Just one or two dances."

Exhaling her anxiety, Sasha swallowed the rest of the whiskey, wincing at the burn in her throat and chest. If she was about to walk through a hundred people, then she needed all the liquid courage. "Okay," she acquiesced to Serena's delight. "But I need another drink first."

"Yay!" Serena cheered. *"Allons-y mon amie!"*

After finishing her second whiskey, she allowed Serena to drag her to the door where they got a VIP stamp and then descended onto the throng of dancers.

With the whiskey courage, Sasha gave in to the beat. She and Serena joined the pit and moved their bodies to the bass that threatened to shatter their bones. They tried to keep their little bubble as they rubbed up against each other. But with the overcrowded dance floor, she was rubbing up against at least six people at once. Thankfully, no one tried to cop a feel.

There was a shift in the crowd behind her and familiar hands rested on her hips. Recognizing the heat and calluses, she looked behind her and smiled at Ricky. Somehow his scent permeated through the sweat around them. His thumb traced circles along her exposed skin while he moved against her to the beat. There wasn't much room for a lot of movement, but Sasha had to admit that the crowd moving together was intoxicating.

When Serena pulled her hand, Sasha grabbed Ricky's and they followed her upstairs.

"I need a drink!" Serena yelled after they went past

security into the VIP lounge.

Sasha felt Ricky's hand on her waist when he walked beside her. She smiled at him, enjoying being out in public for a change. "You want a drink?"

"Just water." He had been sober all night, and mostly chatted with Claud and some of the other VIP guests.

After they each downed another whiskey, they descended into the undulating pit again, this time Claud came too.

The music seemed louder than before but she didn't care. They danced until it was almost midnight and then went upstairs for champagne.

The DJ counted down to the New Year. Everyone in the club was shouting together in French. When the crowd yelled '*Trois*' she was pulled into Ricky's arms and his lips smacked against hers. He deepened the kiss, stealing her breath away. There was something feral and possessive about the way he claimed her. People started screaming around them and the music started back up with a throbbing bass that threatened to disintegrate the cement walls. They had missed the final countdown.

Serena's body crashed into them and she screamed, "Happy New Year!"

Sasha broke her kiss with Ricky and joined in the screaming. With the bass vibrating they continued dancing in the VIP lounge with champagne spilling everywhere.

"Come with me to the bathroom?" Serena begged after they had several flutes of champagne and a fourth whiskey.

Sasha told Ricky where they were going. "I'll be

here," he shouted over the bass of the music before posing to take a picture with Claud who was wearing 2017 glasses.

Serena pulled her down the back stairs to the two VIP unisex bathrooms. At least there wasn't a line. Since only one was available, Sasha let Serena go first while she leaned against the wall between the doors. Resting her head against the cool cement, she closed her eyes, hoping that the small dark hallway would stop spinning. The door to the occupied bathroom opened and Sasha squinted through the dizziness and Pietre's face snapped into focus.

"Ah, Sasha. I'm glad you came." He hugged her, but didn't let go.

"Mmm," she was drunk. Her body felt numb in the dark hallway when he kissed her neck with sloppy licks.

"Serena?" Sasha slurred her name.

"I'm almost done," Serena called from the door next to her.

Sasha felt her body floating into a dark space. She heard a door close and the distinct click of a lock. "No, Pietre," she moaned when his warm body slid against hers. She could taste and smell the alcohol on his breath when he claimed her lips.

"I've wanted you for months," he breathed against her neck, his hands exploring her curves. He squeezed her breast through the fabric of her dress and twisted her nipple so hard she winced.

Sasha's mind disconnected from her body after her attempt to push him away failed. Acidic bile filled the back of her throat along with her fear. She heard the other bathroom door open.

"Sasha?" Serena called.

Pietre covered her mouth to stifle her scream before he yanked up her dress. "Shhh," his breath against her forehead made her skin crawl. He leaned his entire weight against her, his large hand covering her mouth and nose when he tried to silence her.

Sasha closed her eyes and whimpered. Tears fell when she realized this was her life. She had a higher chance of being raped in a random bathroom than being with Richard Bell. Her eyes opened wide with panic, she struggled harder. Why did she always attract the fucking creepers? Why did she leave Ricky's side?

"Let's enjoy each other," Pietre whispered, unzipping his pants. "Herr Bell won't mind. I've seen him share his women before."

She struggled against him when he slid his leaking hardness against her thigh. Her lips ached from her teeth cutting into them because he attempted to silence her screams with brute force. When she tried to punch or scratch at him, he held her at arm's length. Another curse of being short.

She was able to move her lips enough to bite his hand.

He slapped her so hard she saw stars.

Sasha began to slip away when he turned her around and slammed her head against the wall. Her sob eased into a whimper because she teetered on the edge of consciousness. She tried to push against the wall but her arms shook. Pietre was too heavy, and she was too drunk.

"You're wet for me," Pietre's hot breath was on her temple when he slid his fingers against her.

Sasha wanted to die. She gasped when he shoved two fingers inside her.

"Do you like it in the ass?" he spread her juices to her puckered hole and she whimpered again. "I bet you like to be fucked hard." He had one arm against her face to keep her pressed against the wall. He forced her legs apart and he pushed his penis between her cheeks.

"No," Sasha found her voice. "Please stop. No—no—no—no," she begged him.

"Sasha?" Ricky called and the door handle jiggled.

Pietre wrapped his long fingers around her neck, cutting off her voice. "Shhh." He leaned his entire weight against her to shut her up.

She slapped her hands against the wall and prayed Ricky would hear her. She prayed that he didn't. If Ricky saw her like this, their relationship would be over. She knew he'd blame her just like everyone else did. Just like every time before.

There was a loud crunching bang when the bathroom door was kicked open. Ricky entered and flicked on the light. He took one look at Sasha's tear streaked face pressed against the wall, her raised dress, and Pietre's exposed penis before he lost his fucking mind. Ricky entered beast mode when he crossed the room in two steps and lifted Pietre off his feet, before slamming him into the wall next to her with a roar.

"She begged me," Pietre insisted with his hands up in surrender. "I knew you wouldn't mind sharing your whore," he said with a smirk and a complete disregard for his pathetic life.

Sasha turned to get away from them, her back pressed against the wall. She slid away until her shoulder hit the corner of the bathroom. She watched Ricky attempt to murder Pietre with detached horror.

The first right hook broke Pietre's nose. The left

hook sent teeth and blood splattering across Sasha and the wall.

Sasha's mind slid away and the edges of her vision darkened when her world began to spin and her stomach twist. With her mouth full of bile, she listened to Ricky and Pietre pound flesh and curse at each other in multiple languages.

Serena and Claud entered the small bathroom with the VIP security. Serena ran to Sasha and pulled down the blood splattered dress. She pulled Sasha into the hallway and hugged her. "What did he do to you? Are you okay?"

Sasha responded by doubling over and throwing up onto the cement floor.

It took Claud and four security guys to separate Ricky and Pietre. Ricky was dragged past her yelling in Swiss German.

"Sasha!" he yelled for her, his hand stretched toward her when two bouncers struggled to carry him up the stairs because he was fighting them to get to her. The group of men tumbled down several steps and Ricky was about to reach her but security grabbed him again. Two more joined the fray and all four were required to haul an enraged Ricky outside with him repeatedly screaming her name.

A crowd had gathered with their phones. Because her legs didn't want to work, with Serena's help Sasha followed the men carrying Ricky. She was grateful Serena tried to shield her tear streaked face from the onlookers filming the drama.

Ricky was dragged into the parking lot where he was finally released. He was pissed. He hurled words at security that she couldn't understand through her drunken haze. But when his eyes landed on her, he rushed to Sasha and cupped her face.

"Are you okay?" he asked when she flinched away from his touch, his whiskey eyes studying her features in the low light.

Sasha was in Detroit. Tears fell from her lashes when Ricky pushed her into the Maybach to get away from the cameras.

Noah pulled away so fast the tires screeched and she was thrown against the soft leather seat.

Sasha sat, hugging herself and sniffing in the silence.

"Did he—" Ricky struggled to articulate through his rage. "Are you hurt?"

Her lips felt bruised and her face still burned from Pietre's brutality. The sad part was that she had experienced much worse. She averted her eyes out the window.

Ricky inhaled a breath in an attempt to calm himself. "Did he—" he fisted his hair when he sat forward. "Did he rape you?"

She curled up on the seat. His rage terrified her. She knew that at any moment more pain would come. She buried her face between her knees, covered her head with her arms, and tried to hide herself in the bathtub.

"Sasha?" Ricky swallowed. "I know you're scared. I'm so sorry," his voice cracked. "I'm so sorry I didn't protect you." He devolved into a string of lyrical curses.

Squeezing her eyes shut and holding her ears, Sasha blocked out his anger and disappointment. She didn't need to hear anymore. This was all her fault.

When the Mercedes stopped moving, Ricky got out without her. Someone opened her door and wrapped a warm blanket around her shoulders.

"Frau Williams?" a woman's voice whispered.

Sasha looked up from her hiding place. She was staring into blue eyes she didn't recognize.

"Hi, Frau Williams. I'm Nurse Marti. I'm sorry about what happened to you. Are you able to move? Will you come with me?"

Sasha blinked at the nurse before shaking her head. After ten minutes of coaxing, she finally left the car and was ushered inside.

In the mirrored elevator they rode with the nurse standing between her and Ricky. Ricky was still beside himself with anger and he kept pulling his bourbon hair with a bloody fist.

When they entered the penthouse, there was a team of people waiting for them. Sasha didn't even recognize anyone in the sea of white faces. The rest of the night flashed by like the scenes from someone else's life. They walked her into the guest bath that no one used. Staying detached, Sasha watched as they took samples from her mouth, under her nails, and between her legs. One cop bagged her bloody dress while another took pictures of her body.

It was a blur of more violations.

Ricky kept going into fits of rage and the police had to escort him to his room. The only one able to calm him was the chauffeur, Noah. After the doctors finished taking samples, two nurses and a cop walked her into the shower where they placed a filter over the drain and asked her to rinse with water while they watched. They collected the filter for evidence and she was finally allowed to get dressed.

Two hours later, she sat on the couch in her sweats,

wrapped in several blankets.

A policewoman sat with her and asked what had happened. Years of being abused and violated bubbled over and Sasha sobbed into the blanket.

"I know this is hard," the policewoman whispered. Sasha didn't even know her name. "I need you to try and tell me what happened."

Sasha dragged in a deep breath. She gazed at Geneva under a gray lavender sky. "I was standing in the hallway, waiting for Serena," she whispered.

_ʌʌ_

After she had sobbed through her statement, the doctor gave her meds to help her sleep before bodies started leaving. Even though people were talking to Ricky the French and Swiss German words sounded harsh and she felt chastised.

After the police finally left, the chauffeur, Noah, was still there. He and Ricky spoke in hushed whispers near the door before he slipped out quietly too. Once Ricky locked up, he approached the couch where she sat wrapped in blankets.

"Sasha," he sounded exhausted and on edge.

Her eyes flicked to him. He was standing next to the window facing her, his body tense.

He took a step closer. "Can I touch you?" he whispered.

She tried to talk but her voice wouldn't come out. Her throat ached from Pietre choking her.

Ricky held up a hand. "Let me get you fresh water." He stepped out of her view towards the kitchen where she heard a glass being filled behind her.

He placed it on the side table next to her.

She gulped the water past the pain. She felt so dehydrated.

Ricky stood next to the window wall while he watched her. "Can I hold you?" he asked once she set the glass down.

Sasha shook her head.

He swallowed and shoved his bandaged hands into his pockets. "I'm so sorry, Sasha. You didn't deserve that."

Didn't she though?

Ricky shifted his stance. "What can I do for you? Can I call someone?"

Tears were flowing down her cheeks again. "I'm sorry," she croaked.

He shook his head. "For what? You have nothing to apologize for. He—" Ricky turned toward Geneva with a sneer. "I wish I had killed him," he pulled a bandaged fist from his pocket. He turned to face her. "Don't you ever be sorry, Sasha. Not for that rapist."

"It's my fault," she hugged her knees closer to herself.

"Don't say that," Ricky took a step closer to her. "Pietre raped you. That's not your fault."

"I was drunk," she explained.

Ricky shook his head. "That's no excuse for what Pietre did. Sasha, stop blaming yourself. He's a fucking monster with a history of assaulting women. Why else do you think I searched Geneva for you that day you had fondue with him? I was trying to protect you."

He didn't blame her. This was new territory. The first three times she had reported assault stateside, they had asked her what she had done to deserve it. Why did she wear skinny jeans? Why did she have two drinks? Why did she smile at him? Why didn't she fight harder? She just stopped reporting once she realized no one cared. She wiped at her tears.

"I need space," she whispered and she pushed off the couch. Her legs gave out and she stumbled to the side.

Ricky moved to help, causing her to flinch away. He dropped his hands and hovered instead while she made her way to her room. He stood in the bedroom doorway when she went into the bathroom to pee. She was sore from Pietre rubbing up against her. When she stood in front of the sink to wash her hands, she looked at her tear streaked, swollen face.

She had been assaulted.

She could still smell and feel his foul breath brush against her neck. She retched into the sink, her stomach twisted and angry when she choked on bile.

When she finally left the bathroom, Ricky was leaning against the door frame with his arms crossed over his chest. He straightened once he saw her, the sudden movement startling her frayed nerves. "I'm sorry," he raised both of his hands to calm her. "I just want to make sure you get to bed okay."

She nodded in her exhaustion. Even though she probably threw up most of the sleeping pill, she was starting to feel her mind float away. She crawled into bed with her back to the door.

"I'll be in my room. Is that okay?" Ricky asked.

Sasha nodded. He probably wanted nothing to do with her and she didn't blame him. She heard his feet whisper across the marble floor when he left.

She panicked.

Her chest tightened and she turned into her pillow and screamed through the sudden sobs. She was sick and tired of life and her fucking jokes.

The bed shifted when Ricky climbed in. "Sasha," his voice was thick. "I'll just be next to you, so you don't feel alone."

She wiped her tears and turned to look at him. She was on the edge of pure exhaustion. "I deserve to be alone," she sniffed.

"No, you don't."

"Pietre is my life."

He sighed. "Don't say shit like that. I told you, you deserve the world. You deserve better."

"I deserve nothing. I am nothing," she whispered and sniffed.

"Can I take you away from here?" he asked with red-rimmed eyes, watching her.

She was falling to sleep. "What?"

"Let me show what you deserve," he reached and rubbed the tears from her cheeks.

"I don't deserve you," she whispered when exhaustion closed her eyes.

"Please let me show you?" he begged. "Can I take you away?"

"Yeah," she murmured before her world went dark.

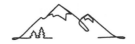

30. MALDIVES

January 1

Ricky gave her a gentle shake. "Wake up, Sasha." Her eyes were crusted shut and she could have sworn she had just fallen asleep. "What time is it?" Her throat felt like sandpaper. She gently rubbed some of the crust off her swollen eyelids so she could see.

His hand caressed her temple. "We have to get to the airport."

Sasha attempted to blink. A blue sky with fluffy clouds greeted her from the wall of windows. "Okay." She decided not to argue. She remembered he wanted to show her what she deserved. "How much time do I have?"

"About an hour."

"Where are we going?"

"To the beach. Let's get out of Switzerland. Is that okay?"

She turned to squint at him. She would love to get out of Switzerland and away from it all. "Yes. I don't have anything for the beach though."

"You don't need clothes where we're going."

_ʌʌ_

An hour and a half later, Sasha boarded the same private jet as before with 'GLOCKE' stamped on the side. She sat across from Ricky and next to the window where she leaned against the wall. Her head throbbed, but the meds had kept the swelling and the worst of the pain at bay. Besides a swollen top lip and puffy eyes, she looked mostly normal. She used his scarf to hide a couple of bruises on her neck.

Ricky kept his arms crossed and his eyes closed while they flew to Dubai where the plane had to refuel before their final destination to the Maldives.

Sasha couldn't believe he had flown her half-way across the world. The weather was warm and breezy with breathtaking views of a turquoise lagoon and a sapphire ocean. Since it was morning when they landed, he took her shopping for clothes. She tried not to feel awkward about him buying her dresses and three bathing suits. She would have been fine with one bathing suit, but he insisted she get a bikini which prompted her to buy a cover up, a hat, some silk scarves to cover her neck, and large white sunglasses. Then she needed flip flops and sandals so she wasn't walking around in hiking boots.

After they shopped, they took a boat ride to get to the Four Seasons Resort on Kuda Huraa. He had managed to book a villa with a private beach.

When they arrived, Ricky ordered breakfast.

"This is crazy," Sasha croaked while staring at the

turquoise water lapping at white sand.

"Good crazy?" he asked when he opened the glass sliding doors. They were both overdressed for the warm weather and she couldn't wait to change.

She stood next to him on the deck. "I've never seen the ocean this close before. I can throw a rock at it."

He laughed. "Or we can go for a swim," he offered.

She cleared her sore throat. "I don't know how to swim," she admitted, looking at her hiking boots with embarrassment.

"Ah, that's too bad. I can teach you," he offered.

She shook her head. "It's not that important."

He stretched and yawned. "We can do whatever you want. They have snorkeling, sailing, dolphins—"

"Dolphins?"

"Yes." He stepped closer to her. "Can I touch you?"

After the fiasco with Pietre, he had reverted to asking for permission. Besides the caress to wake her up, he had been careful not to touch her.

She sighed. She missed his touch. "I appreciate you asking," she whispered before nodding. "I'm sorry."

"Never be sorry," he ran a hand up her arm. "You have to work through the trauma when you're ready. I'll never force you."

Her breath hitched. He hadn't asked to kiss her either. He was being so careful with her she wondered if he was even attracted to her anymore. "Okay, thanks. I should call my therapist and set up an appointment for when I get back."

"That's a good idea. Do you want to take a shower before breakfast gets here? I always prefer washing off plane travel right away," he said and he walked toward the bedroom with the king bed.

She nodded and picked up the carry-on he let her borrow and walked to the second suite on the other side. The bedroom was large with two twin beds, a couch, and a wall-mounted TV. There was a wall of windows and sliding doors so she could walk to the private beach from her room. The bathroom had a turquoise glass-tiled shower and double sinks. She noticed a door that exited to a beautiful outdoor garden with a shower for rinsing off sand. There was a tall privacy wall covered with lush greenery and bright flowers.

During their separate showers breakfast arrived. They sat and ate at the dining table, the ocean breeze blowing through the room.

Ricky was dressed in a pair of navy chino shorts with pink flamingos and a white polo.

Sasha made a face when she took in his muscled legs and arms. She can't take him no where. Even when pasty he looked like a snack.

"What's wrong?" he asked, sipping his espresso. He always found a way to have that bitter liquid.

She shook her head.

"You're making faces at my clothes," he looked down and smoothed his shirt. "Did I get espresso on my shirt?"

She pursed her lips and looked at her eggs and toast. "No. Just self-sabotage."

"What do you mean?" He set down his cup.

She shoved a strawberry into her mouth and bit off a gigantic piece so she didn't have to talk. She just smiled and shook her head and pointed her gaze to the blue ocean.

"Is your room okay?" he asked, changing the

subject.

"Yeah. It's got two twins."

"We can switch," he offered.

"No. You barely fit my bed in Glockenwald."

They finished breakfast and walked outside to relax on the lounge chairs. They enjoyed the view in silence with tension between them. Before lunch she put on the white hat and sunglasses to hide her swollen eyes, and gently tied a pink scarf around her neck before they went for a walk to see the island.

The resort was a family place and there were lots of kids. Nearby was the Reef Club and a public beach with plenty of sand where people were sunbathing and kids were running in the waves.

They made their way to the recreation center because she wanted to see the dolphins. The private yachts were all booked for the weekend, so Ricky reserved one for Monday afternoon.

They walked along the beach back to the Reef Club. Sasha felt weird since he walked with his hands in his pockets. She didn't know what to do with hers since she didn't have any pockets. She ended up just folding them in front of her.

They had cocktails at the Serenity Pool while they relaxed on a daybed. The space between them felt like a crater.

"Do people actually live in places like this?" she asked him to distract herself from her anxiety. Kuda Huraa was breathtaking but she felt like there was a boulder compressing her chest.

Ricky had one hand behind his head while he sipped on his rum and coke. "Well, some live to work here. But sure. Do you like it?"

"It's nice here. Thank you. I probably would've never visited this part of the world if you hadn't whisked me away."

"You're welcome. I hope you enjoy yourself."

"And you?"

"What?" he peered at her, confused.

"You seem tense," she pointed out.

He sighed, but didn't say anything.

Knowing that his blue mood was her fault, Sasha tried to press on. "Are your hands okay?" she asked.

He moved his hand from under his head and flexed his fingers. Even with the gauze and bandages, they looked bruised and bloody. How hard had he hit Pietre? "Sore."

She could see the scabs forming on his knuckles. "You didn't break anything, did you?"

"*Nai*. No problem," he placed his fist back under his head. His eyes followed some kids running around the pool squealing. "What do you want to do tonight?" he asked when he finished his rum and set the empty glass on the table next to the daybed.

"What about you, Ricky? Let's do stuff you want to do too," she insisted.

Whiskey eyes tinted with sadness side-eyed her. "Okay. I'd like to go swimming. With you."

"Alright. I can put my legs in the water."

A smile hinted at his lips but didn't reach his eyes. "That's fine."

After she finished her cocktail they walked back to the villa where they changed into bathing suits. She watched him slip into their private pool which was framed by the patio that connected their rooms and the living room. He swam around the pool while she sat on the edge and kicked her feet, and gazed at the ocean. The water felt warm and she wished she knew how to swim. "It's not deep. Come in," he urged her, floating on his back.

"I'm kind of scared," she admitted.

He swam toward her and then stood. "Look, it's not even four feet." He pulled off the wet bandages and flexed his left fist. His knuckles didn't look as bad with the bandages off and she breathed a sigh of relief. He pushed away from the wall and her ovaries attempted to push her in.

Sighing, she slipped into the warm water which went to her armpits. There was a long built-in bench where she could rest and float. She walked toward it while he swam next to her. "This isn't too bad," she said to him. She propped herself up on her elbows and let her legs float behind her.

"If you get scared, just stand up," he said, watching her legs float. "And I'm here."

"Thank you, Ricky," she stared at the ocean that was beyond the deck and a short walk away.

"For?"

She pushed up and twisted so she could sit on the pool bench, the warm pool water caressing her waist. "Thank you for saving me. For stopping Pietre."

Ricky gasped and he stood. "Did he—" he averted his eyes before meeting her pained gaze again. "Never mind. You shouldn't talk about it."

Sasha stared at the water. "He—" she swallowed her anxiety. "He fingered me."

His jaw clenched and a wave of emotion crashed over his features after he closed his eyes.

"He didn't get further than that," she explained

because his face was so pale she wasn't sure he was breathing.

Ricky shook his head. He looked like he was going to throw up. "I'm so sorry I didn't get there sooner." He stepped towards her. "I wish I could take the pain away." He stopped a foot away from her, the pool water rippling between them.

Sasha swallowed. "I appreciate you bringing me here. But, we can stop this," she gestured between them, feeling like she might cry again.

"What do you mean?" he asked, confused.

"I understand if you don't want to be with me anymore."

He struggled to find the words. He ran a hand through his wet hair. "Sasha, I don't blame you for what happened. You're still a beautiful, intelligent woman."

"I'm damaged," she whispered, her voice cracking.

He drifted so close his waist almost bumped her knees. "No. The world around you is damaged."

She looked down at her hands. She shook her head. "Okay. I'm sorry I said anything."

"Never be sorry," he said before stepping back.

"Let's just enjoy the trip," she suggested.

"Okay," he lifted his hands. "Whatever you want." He lunged back into the water and away from her.

She watched him swim lazy laps around the pool until her stomach growled. She rinsed off the chlorine in the garden shower and pulled on a swimsuit cover and wedges. They walked back to the Reef Club where they shared a pizza and bottle of wine for dinner. The restaurant was busy with lots of guests enjoying the view while the sun slipped below the horizon.

"I can't get over how beautiful it is here," Sasha

commented. She finished her slice of margherita pizza.

"I'm glad you like the Maldives. I used to come here often. Since this was so last minute, I only got the villa due to a cancellation. We got lucky."

Sasha wondered if he funded said cancellation. "I would have been fine eventually," she insisted, finishing the last of her wine.

He checked his watch. "It's only two in Geneva, yet I feel tired after traveling. Do you want to stay and watch the sunset? Or are you ready?" He motioned for the check.

"Looks like you're ready." She was disappointed. She was upset that he was standoffish because of what happened to her. She wanted Ricky and he couldn't even look at her right now.

He gazed at the table, tapping his credit card. "I'm just paying. We can stay as long as you like."

She gave a curt shake of her head and slid her gaze to the sky again. The sun had edged below the horizon, but the golden to purple glow was still breathtaking.

After he paid he shoved his hands into his pockets and they walked back to the villa. There were many people milling about, enjoying the cool ocean breeze. Sasha even thought she had glimpsed his chauffeur, Noah. But she convinced herself that she had imagined him due to mixing meds and alcohol because she doubted anyone would be able to enjoy the Maldives in a suit and tie. After locking and bolting the door behind them, Ricky excused himself to the bathroom so she went to her room.

She freshened up and wandered to the beach. The villa faced east and the sky was full of stars already. The sand felt warm under her feet when she made her way to the ocean. There was a fence on both sides surrounded by trees to give them privacy. She tried to see through to the neighboring villa from where she stood and couldn't.

"How's the water?" Ricky asked when he joined her.

"Warm," she replied when she glanced at him. She wiggled her toes in the soft sand.

He nodded and smiled, his eyes darting to her lips. Ricky cleared his throat and he looked away, shoving his bruised hands into his pockets.

"I should go to bed," she heard herself say. She was exhausted after everything that had happened. "Sleep well," she whispered before she walked to her room.

"You, too," he called after her.

Sasha showered and climbed into one of the twin beds. She missed Ricky's heat. She missed her lumberjack and the way he held her every night. Fucking Pietre raised her walls again. Besides, Ricky deserved better than her. She wiped at her tears and turned on the TV. She stared through the screen until she cried herself to sleep.

31. WÖLFINLI

January 3

B reakfast was awkward and they ate in silence. He turned on the TV to watch the news while they finished eating. Then they walked around the island so she could enjoy the nice weather. She couldn't stop stealing glances at Ricky, couldn't stop wondering what he was thinking.

They took a speed boat to another island. He went surfing and she sat on the beach and watched him navigate the waves. After they returned to the villa they watched the blue sky deepen into black velvet while nibbling on delicious Indian food. Ricky had been quiet through most of the meal. He would start to say something then guzzle down wine instead.

Once she was full, Sasha walked to the edge of the private beach and stared at the dark ocean. She loved the whooshing sound of the waves. She was feeling better, the desire to push what Pietre did to her was urged on by the loneliness she felt standing next to her lumberjack. Physically, she was mostly recovered. Hopefully she could push forward her appointment with the therapist because she wanted to move forward with her life. She wanted to be worthy of the man who dropped everything to bring her here.

While the gentle waves licked at her ankles, Sasha felt a surge of gratitude.

He cleared his throat when he joined her. "Would you like to watch a movie or something?" he asked, gazing at the dark waves.

She glanced at his tense body, his hands shoved in his pockets. Sasha realized that he was waiting for her. She felt so stupid. She had been traumatized. Then she was moping over Ricky giving her what she had asked for: space.

"I'm okay, Ricky," she turned to face him.

His whiskey eyes studied her. "That's good."

"I've had enough time to process things. I need you. I need you to touch me, to kiss me, to fuck me, to—"

His whiskered lips collided into hers with a heady groan.

Sasha's body vibrated with appreciation and the boulder of anxiety lifted. Her soul exhaled when his tongue glided against hers. They became frantic, deepening the much needed kiss. He reached down and pulled her onto his hips and her legs wrapped around his waist. She enjoyed the lingering kiss and heated closeness. He carried her up the stairs to the villa, and through the open sliding doors into his room.

They fell onto the bed with a grunt, his body crushing hers. God he felt good. His weight, his hardness, the roughness of his short beard against her neck sent her nerves into a chorus of need.

He pulled her head to the side and bit her shoulder. She writhed under him, her heels digging into his ass when she pulled up his shirt so she could feel his skin.

"I need you, Sasha," he panted against her chin, his hand rubbing her inner thigh.

"Please," she begged. "Please just fuck me." Her body and mind needed a reset. She needed him to remind her that she was alive.

He yanked her bikini bottoms down to her knees, forcing her legs together. He reached into his shorts and took out his wallet, tossing it aside after he slipped out the foil packet. "I've been vanting to fuck you all day, *Wölfinli*," he growled.

Her eyes rolled and she panted. "Oh god, please." She gulped, watching him shove down his shorts and kick them off. She licked her lips when she saw his hard flesh spring free. She had missed that glorious curve.

He growled when he saw her reaction. "Fuck, voman. Your mouth is sexy," his baritone vibrated through her when he rolled on the condom.

With her legs against his chest he pressed into her. Her bikini bottoms were still around her knees and she didn't care.

He bent her in half while he fucked her ragged. This was pure carnal need that transcended the desire to pleasure. He got rougher when he grabbed the headboard to anchor himself. His head was back, his eyes closed as he used her.

Her channel was on fire. Watching his primal need to fuck snapped the fragile threads of her sanity. Since he had bent her to his will, every stroke in and out rammed against her G-spot.

Then he looked down at her, his whiskey gaze a storm of need. "Sasha," he grunted, her name rough on his slack lips.

The final thread snapped, causing her body to arch and her muscles to tighten when her mind exploded. The orgasm thrummed through her so hard she couldn't breathe, the edges of her vision darkening.

Ricky reached climax but sounded like he was in pain. "Argh, Sasha," he groaned. After two slow pumps he rolled to the side.

They were both panting from the fast and hard encounter.

"Are you okay?" he asked between gasps.

Her body was aching, pulsating, and twitching. "I think so," she panted. "You?"

"Ugh. I thought you vere going to rip my dick off."

"Stop lyin'," she chuckled.

"You vere so tight," he exhaled. "I need to rest," he inhaled, attempting to catch his breath. He rested a hand on her thigh.

After his breathing had normalized, Ricky sat up. "I think you squirted on me," he said, looking down at his shirt and stomach.

"What? I did not pee on you!" she exclaimed, horrified.

"Not pee. Squirt. Women can ejaculate too. No wonder you squeezed me so tight. That's fucking sexy."

She stared at him dumbfounded. "I cannot ejaculate."

He patted her thigh and pushed off the bed. "Yes, you can," he said with a smug smile. He went to the bathroom to wash off.

After he wiped her clean, he went through the villa and made sure all the doors were closed and locked while she used the bathroom. "Will you sleep here?" he asked when she stepped back into the room. He was shirtless and pulling on his boxer briefs.

"Is that okay with you?" she asked him. She pulled off her swimsuit cover and top.

"Of course."

She got under the sheets and waited for him. She was tired after being thoroughly fucked.

He finally slid into bed next to her, he pulled her onto his chest where he kissed her temple. "You're amazing," he whispered into her hair.

She hummed and closed her eyes. "What does vul-fin-ly mean?"

Mirroring her hum, he squeezed her shoulders. "My little wolf."

32. SANDCASTLES

January 4

The feel of his whiskers against her shoulder when he kissed her, made Sasha open her eyes. Why can't this be her life?

"Come watch the sunrise with me?" he whispered against her neck.

Sasha stretched against him and nodded. "I'd love to."

He grabbed her hand and helped her out of bed. He pulled back the curtains, then opened the sliding door and they stepped outside.

"Should I put on clothes?" she asked with hesitant steps.

"No one will see us. This is a private beach and quite early," said the man in boxer briefs.

She refused to move so he got her a robe and then they walked into the dawn. The sky was a heather gray in the east that stretched into lavender which blended into navy.

The sand felt cool and damp where the ocean waves rolled over the shore. They walked out onto the little pier to the sitting area that stretched into the water. They sat on the round couch and he pulled her close.

Sasha exhaled. She closed her eyes and leaned against his side, his arm around her shoulder. She imagined they were the only ones left in the entire world. There was no Detroit, no Geneva, no one else existed in their little bubble. Just the two of them on this beach being blessed by Mother dawn.

Ricky kissed her temple. "I hope I didn't hurt you last night," he whispered before he pulled the robe down her shoulder so he could rub his nose and lips against her bare skin.

"I'm sore," she admitted, before inhaling sharply because his whiskers felt like heaven. "You were kind of rough."

He stilled. "I'm sorry. It had been so hard not to touch you for days. Especially after what happened. I didn't want to push you, but I needed you, too. Giving you space was torture."

She looked up at him. She hadn't considered that he would need comfort. She had made him suffer in silence. "I'm sorry."

"Take this off," he begged and he tugged on her robe. "I want to feel your smooth skin against mine."

She scooted forward and he pulled the soft terry cloth down her shoulders.

He tapped his inner thigh and she readjusted so she sat between his legs with his warm chest against her back.

Sasha covered herself with the robe. "I needed you too. I missed us," she whispered.

His warm hands slipped under the robe and he

filled them with her breasts. "I should have brought condom."

"We're both clean."

Ricky tensed and his fingers stopped stroking her nipples.

She looked over her shoulder, catching his whiskey gaze. "What?"

"I've never gone bare," he admitted after he cleared his throat.

"Oh," Sasha stared at the changing sky with confusion. "Not even with your fiancée?"

"Especially not with Eva," his hands dropped to his thighs. "She liked to have multiple partners at once. Which I don't mind, I just never knew who she had been with. But I'm always careful. I just never know if there are other motives."

She hugged herself. "It's fine. I'm kind of sore anyway." She brought her knees closer to her chest and leaned forward. Did he think she had ulterior motives?

The sky was becoming a brilliant goldenrod and warm rays kissed her skin.

He ran his knuckles over the delicate ridges of her spine. "You'd be my first," his baritone whispered.

She rested her head on her knees and looked back at him. "Condoms are fine."

He sighed, "Okay."

They watched the sunrise while he drew lazy lines on her back.

_ʌʌ_

After eating a light breakfast at the Reef Club, they relaxed at the Serenity pool with cocktails.

She watched Ricky swim in the pool while relaxing

in a lounge chair, decked out in her white hat, sunglasses, and white tankini.

There was something mesmerizing about a wet Richard Bell. Shower wet was different from pool wet. In the pool he was flexing muscles while he glided through the water like Superman. Dear lordt! Sasha was drooling from both sets of lips.

When Ricky stepped out of the pool dripping wet, several mouths dropped open. Maybe she should keep him in their private pool.

He ran his hands through his hair as he approached, glittering water dripping off his rippled muscles like he was filming a body wash commercial.

Sasha lowered her glasses to make sure her view was unobstructed.

He lifted her hat and kissed her lips. "I really wish you'd come in with me," he said before he relaxed onto the lounge next to her.

"You need a towel?" she asked. He sparkled like Edward Cullen from Twilight. Maybe she wasn't that sore after all.

His biceps flexed when he put both arms behind his head. "I'll air dry," he closed his eyes.

Sasha pushed her glasses up and her gaze darted around them. He wasn't even trying but he had a captivated audience.

After he had air dried they went for a walk around the small island. This time, he held her hand. They walked knee deep in the clear ocean water since that was as far as she was willing to go.

They sat on the wet sand while the waves kissed their legs. Sasha dug her fingers into the sand, enjoying the soft grit exfoliating her skin. "Can we live here?" she asked, watching the waves and yachts in the distance.

He was making a sand volcano between his legs. He looked at her surprised. "You want to live with me?"

"Um, well, I do enjoy spending time with you. But that's not what I meant. I just really love being here. The beach life is relaxing. And you haven't checked a single email."

He leaned back onto his elbows. "I did when you were in the shower."

She shook her head and smiled. "Sneaky."

"It's hard to get away completely. There's so much happening all over the world." He leaned forward and rinsed his hands in the gentle waves before relaxing onto his back.

She could already see he had tanned since they arrived. "We should put sunblock on you before you start to burn."

He nodded, his eyes squinting against the sun as he held her gaze. "We can come back here whenever you want."

"We don't even have a week left," she sighed and rinsed her hands. She leaned back onto her elbows, the ocean waves licking up her thighs.

"What do you mean?"

"Our three weeks are almost done," she looked out at the deep sapphire ocean with white foam waves, wishing she could make time stand still.

He rolled onto his side and propped up on his elbow, studying her face. "I thought we had three months?" his jaw tensed.

Sasha inhaled and she looked at him. "Well, I wasn't sure how you felt after Pietre."

"I told you, that wasn't your fault. If anything, I

need to do a better job protecting you."

She sighed. "Okay. I guess we're down to almost two months."

He growled and his sandy hand rubbed across the peak of her bare stomach. "Three months start after three weeks," he insisted.

She smiled, "You're a tough negotiator."

His kiss surprised her. It wasn't the usual chaste kiss he gave her in public. This was borderline starvation when he rolled on top of her, pressing her into the wet sand, the waves licking around them. His arm had even saved her hair from the grit.

She pushed him away, breathless. "There are kids out here," she reminded him, searching his hooded gaze.

His growl vibrated through her and she hissed her own arousal. If they had been on their own private beach, she would have requested he rearrange her insides. He rolled off of her and rested his head on his arm. He sighed, "Thanks for reminding me."

A pair of young boys flew past them. Sasha watched with apprehension when they jumped into the ocean to fill their buckets with warm water. Thankfully the lagoon didn't have huge waves. A mom with a baby on her hip ran by chastising the kids for entering the water without her. The two boys were already running back splashing water out of their buckets in excitement. The youngest boy tripped next to Ricky, his bucket landing on Ricky's chest and dousing them both with warm water.

"Whoa," Ricky sat up. "Are you okay?" he asked the boy who couldn't be more than five.

The little boy nodded with a grave face. He grabbed

for his bucket, kneeing Ricky between the ribs in the process, and then ran off to refill it.

"I'm so sorry," his mom ran up. The baby girl on her hip looked cute in her pink and yellow hat. "Are you okay?"

"It's just water," Ricky insisted, massaging his side. "No problem."

"Oh god. Still," she shook her head and swallowed her frustration. "Their dad is surfing and I thought I could handle them. Timmy! Come apologize!" she screamed, trying to keep her eyes on both kids who were running in opposite directions.

Ricky put up both hands. "It's no problem really."

Timmy ran up with his fresh bucket of water. His eyes told Sasha he didn't have time for this, but he shot a worried glance at his mom. "Sawwy," Timmy said. "Jus' buildin' sancasows," he smiled and ran off.

His mom released an exasperated sigh. "Again, I'm sorry," she said with an embarrassed smile.

"I'm an expert at sandcastles," Ricky said. "I can help keep them entertained, if you want?"

The frazzled mom looked at Ricky surprised. Then she eyed Sasha and Ricky with suspicion. "It's okay. No one wants to be bothered with my monsters."

The older of the two brothers ran toward the water with two empty buckets.

Ricky pushed to a stand. "I love kids. Really, it's no problem." He rubbed some sand off his back.

The mom's eyes went wide when she stared at him. "Okay."

Ricky reached down and pulled Sasha to a stand and they walked with the mom to a group of beach towels and chairs.

The older kid ran past them with two filled buckets sloshing with water.

"Hey guys, I'm Ricky," he introduced himself to the boys after he kneeled. "Can I help you build a sandcastle?"

"We can't speak to strangers," the older one answered with a proud smile.

"Strangers are bad," Ricky smiled and glanced at the mom.

"It's okay, Mikey. He can help you this one time. I'm Tonya by the way," Tonya extended a hand towards Sasha and they introduced themselves. "This is Mia," she tickled the baby's ribs. "That's Mikey and Timmy."

"We're gonna build the biggest sandcastle ever," Mikey stated when he packed wet sand into his bucket.

"Biggest evur," Timmy echoed.

Sasha sat next to Ricky and the boys, and Tonya sat behind the group so she could watch them.

"Your mom said it's okay, can I help?" Ricky asked.

"Do you even know what you're doing?" Mikey eyed him with suspicion.

"Yes, I've built sandcastles bigger than you," Ricky answered.

"Reewy?" Timmy asked.

"Yeah, right." Mikey said before he patted the wet sand. "I'm pretty big."

Sasha smiled, this kid was something else.

When the boys ran to get more water, Ricky went as well to watch over them. Sasha readjusted so she could watch the ocean with Tonya.

"Do you guys have kids?" Tonya asked, trying to keep Mia from eating sand with a chubby fist.

Sasha shook her head. "No, we don't."

"Ugh, you're lucky. I remember the pre-kid days," Tonya sighed and shook her head. "They were so relaxing."

"They can be," Sasha smiled and watched Mia wiggle her fat little toes.

Ricky returned with the boys and he helped them mix wet sand.

"This sandcastle is for boys," Mikey stated when Sasha tried to help.

"My bad," Sasha lifted her hands off the sand.

"That's not nice, Mikey," Tonya chastised.

"Sandcastles are for everyone," Ricky winked at Sasha. "Especially for girls."

"I guess," Mikey said, giving Sasha a side-eye.

Sasha scooted away. She preferred to watch anyway. They had already built a solid rectangular foundation.

"Time for more water, guys," Ricky said when he gathered the buckets and reached for Timmy's hand.

Sasha's heart thundered while she watched Ricky walk toward the ocean. He looked good with kids.

Tonya leaned towards her. "He's amazing with the boys. How long have you been married?"

"Oh, we're not married," Sasha corrected with a shake of her head.

"Oh? How long have you been dating?" Tonya pried.

Sasha distracted herself by brushing the sand off her thighs. "Um, we're not exactly dating."

Tonya lifted an eyebrow. "That was a dating kiss I saw earlier. Shit, I'd date him if I wasn't married," Tonya's brown eyes followed Ricky who was walking back with the boys. She watched them mix sand and water.

Sasha bit her bottom lip. "Yeah, well. We're just..." she shrugged, unable to finish the sentence. What were they?

"I get it," Tonya said. "Enjoy him," she smiled.

Sasha smiled at the sand. She was enjoying him.

Tonya and Sasha talked while Ricky and the boys kept adding layers to the sandcastle. The more she watched him interact with the kids, the more she wanted this. She wanted children for the first time in her life. She wanted his kids. She never disliked children, she just didn't think she was good for them. But she had decided that when she was living a life full of abuse and fear.

Ricky had been patching her cracks and making her feel whole.

The sandcastle ended up being almost four feet high. How Ricky managed to stack the sand, she had no idea. The boys squealed after Timmy placed a cocktail umbrella on the highest turret, then they began running around their creation with their arms flapping.

"It's the biggest ever!" Mikey yelled before he high-fived Ricky.

"Evur!" Timmy jumped up and down and gave Ricky a high five with a high pitched squeal that made Sasha wince.

"Good job, guys," Ricky stood with his hands on his hips appreciating the castle.

Tonya leaned towards Sasha. "Is it me or does Ricky look like Superman?"

Sasha chuckled, "Girl, you should see him when he shaves."

"Mmm," Tonya slid Sasha a look. "If you don't lock

that down, someone else will. He's a keeper."

"Daddy!" Timmy squealed before he took off past her and Tonya at break-neck kid speed. He tumbled over a mound of sand, but hopped up as if nothing happened.

"Daddy!" Mikey was not to be outdone and ran as fast as he could to the dark haired man approaching.

Tonya twisted to look over her shoulder. "Oh, thank fuck."

Ricky walked around the sandcastle and offered Sasha his hand. He pulled her into a stand. Timmy and Mikey came running back with their dad jogging behind them.

"Look, daddy! Look!" Timmy pulled his dad's hand while pointing at the massive sandcastle.

"Hey, babe," he greeted Tonya before he bent to pick up Mia and pressed a kiss against the baby girl's chubby cheek.

"This nice couple here kept me company," Tonya said. She stood to kiss his lips. "This is Sasha and Ricky. This is my husband Andrew."

They shook hands while the boys ran around them.

Ricky rested his hand on the small of Sasha's back and looked at his watch. "Well, we should probably go," he glanced at her with a smile that made her heart flutter.

"It's time to feed the spawns," Tonya said. "Thanks for helping with the boys."

"Yeah, that's a pretty impressive castle," Andrew said, taking a picture of the boys posing in front of the sand structure.

"Thanks. Mikey and Timmy were excellent sand engineers. Take care." Ricky fist bumped the brothers before a final salute.

Ricky guided her down the beach, his hand slipping into hers. "I'm sorry about that," he apologized.

"I'm not. Looked like you had fun," Sasha smiled up at him and he leaned down to kiss her temple.

"It's been a while," he sighed, and put his arm around her shoulders. "Last time I built a sandcastle was with my mother," he explained when he stared down at her as if searching. He stopped and tipped her chin up so he could kiss her lips. After he inhaled her scent he deepened the kiss making her moan.

She pulled away and wrapped her arm around his waist. "What was that for?"

"Hmm," he continued walking, pulling her close. "We have an hour before the dolphins. Do you want to go see some turtles?"

ⁿᴬᴸ

At the Marine Discovery Center Ricky took pictures of Sasha holding a turtle and they observed the exotic fish at the aquarium. Then they boarded the private yacht and sailed towards the dolphins.

Sasha was flat on her stomach, looking over the side of the yacht. She squealed when she saw the first dolphin swimming below. "Look, Ricky! They're so beautiful."

He leaned next to her, his hand on her hip. "They are intelligent, majestic creatures," he noted, watching them swim around.

Soon they were surrounded by ten dolphins that kept circling the yacht.

"I'm going to ask them to take a picture," Ricky

said, taking out his phone.

Sasha turned to face, then scooted against Ricky's side. He put his arm around her shoulder and pulled her close while they both smiled for the picture.

She enjoyed watching the dolphins jump around them, splashing water and talking to each other.

When they got back to shore, Sasha couldn't stop talking about her new obsession while they walked to the Baraabaru Restaurant for dinner.

Ricky squeezed her hand. "I didn't know you liked dolphins."

"Same. It's different seeing them in person," she skipped and swung their arms. "They swim so fast and they're always smiling."

"I love it when you smile," he sighed, watching her. "I've missed it."

She exhaled and met his whiskey gaze. "You give me plenty to smile about. Do you—"

He pulled her to him and he kissed her. "I can't get enough of you," he whispered against her lips before he released her.

Sasha had to remember to breathe after she slid down his chest. She hadn't expected the quick taste of him or the passion that made her toes curl. She gulped and they continued to walk in silence. She kept darting glances in his direction, trying to figure him out.

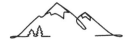

33. THE FIRST

Once they got back to the villa after the delicious dinner of tandoori lobster, they showered and then settled onto the daybed next to the pool.

"Is it legal to own a dolphin?" she asked, watching the sky darken. She was resting between his legs, his bare chest against her back.

"Hmmm," his hand caressed up her bare stomach and he stroked the bottom curve of her breast. "I might be able to make that happen. I'd have to call in a lot of favors," he smiled against her shoulder.

"I wish. They might be my new fave."

"We'll come back. Or go somewhere else. There are dolphins all over the world."

She turned so she could face him, her breasts against his furry inferno. "Thank you. I feel better. I'm even enjoying myself," she stretched to kiss his whiskered chin.

"I'm having a good time, too," he looked down his crooked nose at her, his fingers stroking her naked back.

"The view is amazing," she said, holding his gaze.

"Beautiful," his eyelids dropped and she could feel him harden against her hip.

She hissed her desire and he closed his eyes.

"Are you still sore?" he inquired, his voice a low whisper. He opened his eyes and watched her.

Sasha bit her lip. "Can you be gentle?"

He grabbed her ass, his eyes full of lust. "I will try." He pulled her up so he could kiss her. His tongue flicked against the roof of her mouth. He flipped them so she was on her back and he hovered above her, his eyes appreciating her soft curves.

She ran a hand over his tight chest, following the hard pecs to rippled abs. "You're unreal," she whispered.

"What do you mean?" he asked, lowering his heat to cover her.

She shook her head and swallowed her desire. "You're a fantasy. Handsome, kind, a body like Superman and you're with me. I just—"

"I can be your fantasy," he offered with a smile before he kissed her jaw. "And I'm glad you find me handsome. Can I touch you?" he asked.

She nodded. "I'm okay, you don't have to ask."

His fingers explored her silk folds. "You're beautiful," he whispered against her lips.

She closed her eyes when he rubbed gently against her bundle of nerves.

"Is this okay?" he asked.

Sasha nodded, he knew how to work her body. A cool, salted breeze blew around them, the sound of soft waves obscured their sighs and moans when he lowered his body so he could lick her core.

With her head back, she looked at the stars above them while he coaxed her towards ecstasy.

Since they were outside, they tried to keep quiet, their whispers dissolving in the gentle ocean breeze.

When she came down from her orgasm, he faced her again, his whiskey eyes searching her ebony depths.

She reached for him and pumped his curved length. "Your turn," she whispered.

"Your hand feels good," he sighed. He positioned between her legs. "I want to feel you," he whispered against her ear. "I want you to be my first," he sighed, studying her face.

"Are you sure? I don't mind the condoms." Her hands rubbed up to his arms and shoulders. She arched her hips against his.

"I'm positive," he growled, rubbing his throbbing head against her entrance.

She gasped when he pushed his muscle against her sinew.

Ricky's lips were soft and sensual against hers, slow and deep. His hard thickness penetrated her soft heat with a gasp of disbelief. He closed his eyes and sighed. He felt hard and smooth when he filled her. *"Mon Dieu,"* he whispered. "Sasha, you feel so soft and varm." He rocked against her, holding his breath.

She wrapped her arms and legs around him as they joined in nirvana. "Ricky," she moaned. "Don't stop," she encouraged him when a tremor ran through the length of him.

"I'm not going to last," his voice was strained and his arms tightened around her. "Fuck, your pussy is heaven." He kissed her with desperation, his hips pumping faster.

She squeezed him with her core. She could feel the ridge of his thick head rubbing deep inside of her. She moaned, "Come for me, Rickart."

He pushed up his eyes trailing down her body until

he watched himself slide into her. He started speaking his mother tongue, his eyes rolling to the back of his head. He grabbed a breast and squeezed her nipple, causing Sasha to moan. His hands moved to grab her hips and he started to thrust harder, making her nerves sing and her channel clench his shaft.

"Fuck, I can't—Sasha, I'm—Sa—ahhh." With his head pressed against her shoulder, his fingers digging into her hips, he released deep inside of her. A strangled gasp brushed across her neck and chest before he readjusted so his hands were on either side of her shoulders. Eyes wide with shock, he tried to catch his breath. "I can't believe I just came," he gasped. "I don't think I lasted a minute." He lowered onto her. "Fuck. You can have my dick vhenever you vant," he whispered before kissing the sensitive skin right below her ear.

She laughed, "I wish."

"You didn't come," he said with chagrin.

"I came already," she stroked his shoulder and relaxed. She could feel him shrinking inside of her.

"This is embarrassing," he swallowed.

"It's not. I get to be your first." She hugged him close.

He groaned and rolled them so she was against his side, her head resting on his shoulder. "I don't want any man near that amazing pussy of yours without my consent," he rumbled.

"Um, I thought we weren't dating other people."

"We're not. You're mine now," he growled.

She smiled and stared at the expanse of inky ocean and twinkling stars. Then her heart pounded when she realized she was falling hard for him. Then it stopped when she wondered if she could get pregnant.

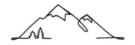

34. BACK TO REALITY

January 5

Bearded kisses on her neck woke Sasha from a dreamless sleep. She hummed her happiness when he pulled her close.

"Shower with me?" he asked.

She could smell the sex from last night. She stretched against him. "I'm surprised you aren't answering emails."

"I'll check during breakfast," he said into her bonnet.

She hummed again. Her body was already responding to him. "A shower would be nice."

He pushed out of bed taking his heat with him and she stretched again, listening to the shower start. He returned for her and held out his hand. She appraised his body. His naked form was worthy of carved marble. Timeless. It was time to resurrect Michelangelo, he had important work to do.

The shower was warm when they entered. He insisted on washing her, massaging her muscles with hands that memorized her. Worshiped her. There was something stimulating about seeing a naked man on his knees washing her feet and massaging her calves. "It's my turn," she insisted, washing his shoulders. He picked her up, her legs wrapping around his waist. "Better?" he asked, his tongue massaging a circle on her neck.

She laughed and washed his shoulders, neck, and hair. "You're handsome," she told him.

Ricky lifted his head so he could gaze into her eyes. "You're kind, intelligent, and sexy as fuck." She tapped his arm and he let her down. She washed his stomach and hips. She got on her knees and washed his short pubic hair, being gentle with soft orbs and semi-erect flesh. She looked up into his whiskey eyes watching her move down his thighs. "You're generous." She scrubbed his muscular calves and each foot. Then she stood and asked him to face the frosted glass wall. She washed his back. "You deserve happiness. You deserve love. You deserve the world." She scrubbed his butt, enjoying the firm muscles under her hands.

"So do you, *Wöfinli*," he said over his shoulder. "Let me give it to you."

"Shhh, this is about you right now." She slid her arms around him, pressing her luscious breasts against his back. Her hands rubbed up and down the bumpy muscles on his stomach when she held him. The tip of his throbbing head bumped her arm. "I'm going to pleasure you like this," she whispered and she hung the wash cloth on the safety bar and then stroked him, leaning against his back.

Ricky braced himself against the wall and groaned. "That feels good."

She tightened her grip and pumped him with one

hand while fondling the soft flesh below. "I want to feel you come," she whispered, resting her cheek against his firm back muscles.

"So hot. Don't stop."

She could hear every gasp with her ear against his back and that turned her on. "You're so sexy, Rickart Bell," she gasped, making sure to pronounce his name in Swiss German.

"Faster, Sasha," he moaned.

"You felt so good last night." She stroked hard with one hand while gripping the base of his dick with her thumb and forefinger and putting pressure on his heavy balls with the other.

His body tightened in her arms. "Sa...sha," was all he could say before he threw his head back with a grunt when she milked every drop.

She could feel his legs shaking against her when he turned to face her, searching her eyes. "You're incredible."

"So are you," she responded.

_ᴧᴧ_

While they ate a simple breakfast in the villa of toast and fresh fruit, Sasha was lost in thought about her life. Even including Pietre, what she was dealing with was still better than Detroit. She was beginning to love Glockenwald. The people there treated her like she belonged. And then there was Ricky, her lumberjack, sitting next to her with his hand on her thigh while he gazed at the ocean, sipping his espresso.

If she hadn't gotten stranded on that road, would she even be in the Maldives? If she hadn't juiced his motorcycle would he have looked at her twice?

Whiskey eyes turned to her. "What do you want to do today?"

"I'm not sure. The days are flying by."

He nodded. "We could go to the spa or ride jet skis."

"Don't I have to know how to swim to ride a jet ski?"

"Not at all. Plus, I'll be there."

"What do you want to do?" she asked.

"Honestly, I want to hear more about you," he admitted. "My life is public, but you're a mystery and I want to know everything."

"There isn't much to tell," she said sadly. "And for the record, I haven't searched for you online."

"Really?" he lifted an eyebrow and set his espresso next to his phone. His phone vibrated and a message appeared on top of the motorcycle on the lock screen.

"Honest to god truth. I'd rather find out from you."

"So you haven't seen my Instagram, Twitter or Facebook?"

"I'm not on social media anymore," she shrugged.

He lifted an eyebrow, "Why not?"

"Easier for me to hide," she admitted.

Ricky tensed and leaned forward. "I won't let him or anyone else harm you, Sasha. You don't have to hide anymore." He reached for her hand, gazing at her fingers in his.

"I guess the world knows I'm in Switzerland," she shook her head in disbelief. She didn't even last six months. "But it's for the best. The less time I'm on social media the better."

He brought her fingers to his lips, his beard tickling her. "Whatever you want." Ricky stood up and stretched. "Come, let's talk."

They moved to the daybed by the pool where they watched the turquoise waves lap the beach.

Sasha didn't know where to start. Her beginning was a mystery because she was abandoned at a church. She didn't know anything about her parents.

"When I was a kid, I used to make up these wild stories about my mom finding me. This beautiful woman with deep brown skin like my own would show up at the park one day. Sometimes she would be a princess, other times she would be a ballerina. But as I got older, I knew better. I knew I wasn't meant to be loved."

"That's not true. You deserve love," he whispered before he kissed her shoulder.

She shrugged. "No one gave it to me." She took in a deep breath and continued. She recounted the many foster homes and how awful they were for little Black girls. Some of the caretakers just wanted a check and she had to scrounge for food. Others would find any reason to abuse her. Then there were the ones who molested her.

She became a violent child. The neglect, the loneliness, and the fear had her lashing out at others before they could get her. She went to juvie twice due to fighting with other kids.

"I bounced around until I was sixteen, that's when I met Betty. She was a nice enough woman who treated me well. She told me if I helped take care of the younger foster kids, she would adopt me. It's weird because most kids that age don't get adopted. We just age out of the system."

"Where is she now?"

"In Detroit, doing her thing. Even though she's the closest person I have to a parent, Jackson drove us apart. He alienated me from everyone." She sniffed because her heart ached. "It's another reason why I haven't bothered with social media, what's the point when there's no real connection to anyone anymore."

Ricky kissed her temple. "You should reach out to her."

"Maybe. I'm sure she's busy. At least I have lots of shit to discuss with my therapist," she chuckled despite the serious subject. "Actually. I've been meaning to call her. Do you mind?"

"Not at all. Would you like privacy?"

She reached for her phone and pushed the home button to unlock it. "Nah. Shouldn't take long." She found the number in her contacts and pressed the phone icon. The phone rang twice before someone answered.

Feeling nervous about using her Swiss German, Sasha spoke in English. "Hi, this is Sasha Williams and I'm calling to see if I can change my appointment with Dr. Meier."

"Frau Villiams, please hold," the secretary said before the line went silent.

Sasha lifted her eyebrows when she glanced at Ricky who was busy checking emails on his phone.

There was a click followed by some rustling. "Frau Villiams," Dr. Meier said. "I've only got a minute, but I'm glad you called."

"I was hoping to move my—"

"I have to cancel our sessions," Meier interrupted, her voice clipped.

"What do you mean?" Sasha asked, confused.

Static crinkled over the phone when Dr. Meier heaved a sigh. "I'm afraid ve have—vhat do you say? A conflict of interest."

Feeling anxiety grip her, Sasha tried to stay calm. "I don't understand."

"Pietre Furrer is my nephew by marriage. I don't feel comfortable treating a patient who claims one of my family members hurt her."

Eyes wide in disbelief, Sasha stared straight ahead. She tasted bile in the back of her throat when she kept opening and closing her mouth, unsure of how to respond.

Dr. Meier didn't need to hear a response apparently because she stated with a cold detachment, "I vill email you referrals tomorrow. Thank you for understanding," before the call ended with a double beep.

"What?" Ricky asked when her hand flopped down to her lap and her phone fell onto his hand that was resting on her thigh.

"I guess I need to find a new therapist," she shrugged.

"Why?"

"Pietre is her nephew."

Whiskey eyes got so wide she wondered if they'd pop out of his head. "I'm sure there are others." He gave her thigh a reassuring squeeze.

"Yeah."

His phone vibrated and he checked the caller ID scrolling across the motorcycle. Ricky frowned when he answered. His responses were curt and short, mostly he just listened. At one point he looked at his phone as if he was trying to make sure he was hearing correctly, fury contorted his face.

Sasha scooted away from him. She didn't deal well with rage.

He said a few words in French before he ended the call.

She decided to stay silent. Better not to bring attention to herself.

With fists clenched he cursed. "I'm sorry." He rubbed his eyes with his palms before pushing off the daybed. "I need to think," he said, his eyes looking wild when they darted around the patio. He stalked into the villa, leaving her to gaze at the ocean.

Besides Pietre, what could send him into a rage like that? The part of her in Detroit wanted to hide. But the healed part of her wanted to comfort him. She found herself standing by the sliding door to his bedroom where he was doing push-ups on the rug at the foot of the bed. "Is everything okay?" she asked.

"I'm sorry," he said before he pushed up, his form impressive.

"Don't apologize. What happened?"

He shook his head. "It's just bad business."

"With New York?"

"No," he lowered his body closer to the floor.

She wasn't going to push him. "I'm sorry you're upset. I'll be outside."

"Don't go," he said between push-ups. "Just give me a damn minute."

"But you look hot doing that," she heard herself say.

He stopped mid push-up and glanced at her. "You're welcome to join me," he smiled, his anger deflating. He pushed off the floor and sat on the bed where she joined him. "I apologize for getting so angry. Back in July one of my junior accountants noticed some strange money transfers and we've been secretly investigating. He just confirmed someone has been stealing from Glocke."

"Shit. What're you gonna do?" She stroked his shoulder.

"Gather more information and then turn him or her in," he gazed at the ocean. "This is bad for the company."

"I'm sorry." She reached for his hand. "Do we have to go back early?"

When he looked at her, his eyes were sad. "No." Ricky exhaled and he relaxed back onto the bed. "I'm going to get busy, Sasha. Let's enjoy our time together."

_ʌʌ_

With warm weather and even hotter sex, the remaining days in the Maldives flew by at supersonic speed. Before Sasha knew what was happening, they had flown back, and were sitting in his black F-250, driving through the snow covered mountains.

Sasha's hands were shaking when she attempted to unlock her door.

Ricky put a hand on her back. "Let me." After unlocking the door, he carried her heavy luggage inside and kicked off his shoes.

She closed the door behind her, looking around her tiny place. No view of Geneva here. No turquoise waves with smiling dolphins. And soon there would be no Ricky. She sat on her couch in shock.

"It's fucking cold," he said, rubbing his hands together. "I'll start a fire, ya?" He opened her goblin and placed a couple of logs inside.

Once the fire was started he checked her fridge and cabinets. "I should've bought food," he said to himself.

"It's fine."

"I have to get going," he approached her.

She stood to hug him. "I know."

He searched her ebony eyes. "You're upset."

A lot happened in three weeks. They had arguments, became a scandal, he almost killed Pietre, and they traveled the world. "I'm going to miss you."

"I'll be back soon," he promised. "I would stay, but Glocke is getting fucked. I have to protect my company."

She nodded, tears flooding her eyesight. "Of course. Maybe I'll see you in a couple of weeks?"

"You will. But if I don't leave now, I'll get snowed in."

"Yes, you should go. Thanks for letting me stay with you. I had an amazing time."

Ricky pulled her into a deep kiss. "I'm going to miss you every night, but especially every morning."

"You should go."

His lips burned her forehead before he saluted her, tapped his chest twice, and was out the door.

Sasha sat on her cold leather couch and stared at her tiny kitchen. Back to reality.

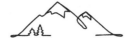

35.
#BEAUTYANDTHEBELL

January 12

To distract from her cold bed, Sasha immersed herself in ballroom dancing and learning Swiss German. She continued to go to town hall every evening. There were many inquiries into her relationship with Ricky and she kept her lips sealed. Everyone had questions about the pictures and videos from New Year's. She couldn't even look at them, she didn't want to be reminded of what Pietre did to her.

Yes, she spent three weeks with Ricky. But she didn't know if there was a relationship to talk about. They enjoyed each other, but did that mean they were dating or just experiencing orgasmic bliss? She decided to be realistic.

No one had ever loved her and no one ever would.

So she would enjoy his company and try to ignore the way her heart ached without him.

Ricky texted her every morning. He usually sent a picture. The first one was of the Christmas tree and he asked if he should keep it up until her visit in February. In the evenings he would call to talk after his shower.

Sasha would practice French and Swiss German and he would help her with her pronunciation. People always said the fastest way to learn a foreign language was to get a foreign lover.

Serena begged for a lunch date the day before a small town party. Sasha had avoided Serena and Claud out of embarrassment and anxiety. She ignored all of their texts and if they happened to be in the same place, Sasha excused herself. But after a week, she decided to hear Serena out. They sat in the café because the view was nice and Sasha didn't have to walk far to get there. Most of the tourists were on the slopes, so it was just the two of them and some guy on his phone.

"I'm sorry about Pietre," Serena gazed at her espresso, shame glittering in her blue eyes. "I didn't know he was like that," she trailed off.

Sasha sighed. "Shit happens. Hopefully I'll never see him again."

"Never," Serena agreed. She took a sip of her espresso. "Can I ask how you and Ricky are?"

Sasha shrugged. "I told you in Geneva there's nothing to tell."

Serena picked up her phone and opened an app. "That kiss on New Year's was not nothing. And the pics from the Maldives."

"What pics?"

Serena gave her a weird look. "Are you not on Twitter?" She handed Sasha her phone.

Apparently they had a hashtag. There was a picture of them kissing in the club with people screaming and shouting behind them. The caption said: The only way to bring in the New Year. #BellAndSasha #BlackCinderella #BeautyAndTheBell

The next picture was in the Maldives. They were on the public beach making out while the waves lapped at their entwined legs.

Sasha shook her head feeling sick to her stomach. They were a hashtag? She handed Serena her cell. "I'm not going to talk about Ricky."

Serena crossed her arms, put out. "I guess I'll just get my updates from Twitter then. Do you want to come to dinner tonight? Claud bought some board games."

"Maybe. I have dance tonight. I'll text you if I feel up to walking over."

"Great," Serena smiled. "We can pick you up. I've got to get home. I really just wanted to apologize in person about Pietre." She pulled on her coat and picked up her purse. "Hopefully, I'll see you later."

Sasha smiled and watched her leave. She wrapped up half of her sandwich then checked the clock on the wall behind the register. Her lunch was almost over.

"Excuse me."

Sasha looked up to see the tourist who was on his phone approach her. He had a thick, deep accent that wasn't local.

"Yes?" She felt anxious that a random stranger was talking to her.

"Are you a toureest too?" he asked. He stopped next to Serena's empty chair.

She tried to keep her face pleasant. But something about this guy put her on edge. He appeared to be normal dressed in his jeans and thick sweater. He even looked clean with black hair cropped close to his head and stubble on his jaw. But his black eyes were narrow and piercing when he looked at her. This man was from the streets.

Clearing her throat, Sasha tried to decide what to do. "No. I work here."

"Oh, that's nice," he smiled. "Then you know all the hotspots." His obsidian eyes darted to the mountain view.

"Ah, no, I don't. Actually, I don't ski." She packed the remaining half of her sandwich into her bag. "I can't help you. But I hope you enjoy your stay."

He nodded and backed away from her with his hands up. "Thanks." He returned to his seat and went back to his phone. He waved and smiled at her when she left the café.

Sasha scolded herself for being skittish when she glanced over her shoulder. Glockenwald was crawling with death-sticks enthusiasts.

_ᴧᴧ_

After Sasha got home from dinner and games, she called Ricky.

"I just got done with my shower," he said when he answered.

"Did you know we have a hashtag?" she asked, making a face that he couldn't see.

"A hashtag?"

"Beauty and the Bell is all over Twitter." She still couldn't believe people cared.

"Ah. That."

She gasped, "You knew?" She felt betrayed.

Ricky sighed, "Of course I know. I get tagged all day. It's no problem."

She adjusted in bed so she could lie on her back and stare at the ceiling. "You looked so hot in the Maldives," she smiled. She couldn't do anything about the tweets. But damn did he look amazing in every photo.

"Mmmm, you just made me hard."

She bit her lip. "I'll take care of that tomorrow."

He moaned his frustration. "I might have to skip work, yeah?"

She smiled. She would like as much time with him as she could get. "You work a full day tomorrow?"

"Unfortunately. Don't worry about Twitter. They are just admiring you."

She heard the rustle of him getting into bed and she became hyper aware that he might still be naked. "I'm sure not all of them like me."

"True. Some Swiss are upset you are American," he yawned. "Tomorrow is a long day. I need to sleep. I'll see you at dinner."

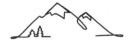

36. THE SECRET

January 13

Even though the ski season kept the locals busy, they still had events to unwind and catch up. Town hall was the spot to be during these events where the kirsch flowed and the food was plentiful. Sasha was looking forward to dinner and a weekend with Ricky. To prepare she cleaned her apartment and started her laundry at town hall. Since only Hilda was in the office, Sasha asked if she could see the old albums again.

Hilda studied her. "Why see those old pictures?"

Sasha twisted her fingers before crossing her arms. "I'm an orphan," she said, dropping her gaze to the ground. "I've never seen so much history before." She looked into Hilda's ocean blue eyes. "I want to learn more about this town and Ricky's family."

Hilda nodded before she grabbed her keys to unlock the storage closet. They had to move the stashed Christmas decorations before they could dig out the photos. Thankfully, Hilda didn't rush through the albums this time. They went through each picture, starting with Leon Glocke and the building of town hall in 1851.

Hilda talked through the history, reading each caption that was written in a delicate cursive script. Richard Glocke started the first Glocke Company in 1880. Each generation grew the company until it became an international conglomerate. Richard Bell II only had one child, Marie Bell.

"She was so clever and intelligent, brilliant in business. But Glocke Industrie was not ready to have a woman at the helm, so Tobias took her name."

"Why did he change his name?"

"There has always been a Bell running Glocke. We Swiss are a bit weird when it comes to money, power, and lineage."

Sasha switched her clothes to the dryer then they proceeded to peruse the album with Marie and the kids.

"You said she had changed," Sasha mentioned, looking at a gaunt Marie Bell kissing the chubby cheek of a toddler Ricky.

"Marie had always wanted to marry for love. In order to keep her shares of the company, she was forced to marry Tobias. They fought all the time over money and his mistresses. I don't think he ever wanted to marry her. I'm positive he only wanted the prestige that came with the Bell name." Hilda shook her head then turned to another page. Her hands started to shake. "This was the last photo taken of her."

The photo on Ricky's desk. Sasha swallowed back her emotions. "She looks happy."

"Of course. Before the trip, she told me she was leaving Tobias. She had made arrangements and this was supposed to be their last trip together." Hilda wiped at her tears then turned the page.

A newspaper clipping of the crash was folded into the album.

Hilda started shaking. She dropped the album into Sasha's lap before standing so suddenly, that the force of air dislodged the newspaper, causing it to float to the hardwood floor. "I need a break." She walked briskly to a back office and closed the door behind her.

After retrieving the article, Sasha struggled to keep her composure when she looked at black and white photos of the deadly crash. The charred remains of a car smashed around a scarred trunk of a large tree took up half the page under a headline she didn't understand. The next article showed the single survivor, Richard Bell III, his head wrapped and his nose bandaged while he rested in a hospital bed.

There was another article about the funeral. Three caskets and the boy who survived surrounded by a throng of people dressed in black. Sasha recognized the younger versions of Hilda and Eric, standing off to the right. An angry looking man who reminded her of a young Robert Redford stood with his stiff hand on boy Richard's shoulder, white strips over his left eye.

Sasha turned the page of the album to see a somber boy Ricky standing with that same man in front of town hall. The script read 'Tobias Bell with his son Richard Bell III'.

Hilda came back, blowing her nose. "Sorry, I get emotional, ya."

"It's okay. She was important to you. But I have a question. Who is Ricky's father? He told me Tobias isn't his real dad."

Hilda sniffed and shook her head. "That's a well

guarded secret. It would have been a scandal." Hilda regarded her with narrowed eyes before she dug into the box and pulled out a large sealed envelope. "I don't think Ricky has seen these," she admitted. "You have to promise not to tell anyone."

Sasha nodded, her heart pounding when Hilda ripped the envelope open.

"Everyone has secrets. And Marie had hers." She pulled out official paperwork written in Cyrillic. And then she pulled out the photos.

Sasha gasped when she stared at Marie in a long lace wedding gown, beaming up at a tall handsome man that reminded her of Ricky in a tuxedo. "Wait, who's that?"

"Ricky's father. Marie was secretly married. Maximilian Popov owned a small logging business outside of Zurich."

His dad was a lumberjack. Maximilian Popov was a beast of a man with impressive broad shoulders who dwarfed his bride. He had short bourbon hair and a wild beard, his eyes were the color of whiskey when he smiled at the camera, holding Marie Bell's hand. "Why was it a scandal?" Sasha couldn't look away from him.

"He wasn't Swiss. He was a Russian man who had built a small logging business, but relations with Russia were tense during the Cold War. Their marriage would have caused havoc with Glocke Industrie expanding internationally. No one trusted Russians back then. Her father was beside himself. He tried to break them up. But Max died in a tragic logging accident anyway. Marie was a widow before Ricky was even born."

Sasha shook her head in disbelief. "And the twins?"

"The twins were Tobias' children," Hilda explained,

before closing the album on the tragic legacy.

_ᴧᴧ_

An hour later, Sasha was walking back with her laundry, her mind in overdrive. Ricky knew Tobias wasn't his real father. He was also the last living Bell which made her nervous. No wonder the claws were coming out ever since he started prancing them around. Lineage and prestige were at stake.

With the laundry basket on her hip, she tried to be careful when she walked down the snow and ice covered road to her apartment. She was concentrating so hard that she didn't notice someone approaching her.

"Do you need help?" the tourist's thick accent startled her.

"No," she stopped in her tracks and darted a glance at the many from the café. "I'm fine. Thank you." She took a step and her foot started to slide.

He grabbed Sasha to steady her which caused terror to seize her lungs.

"Please don't—"

He held her because her legs attempted to do the splits. Thanks to his strong arms, she didn't fall.

"—don't touch me," she whispered after her feet stopped sliding.

"I've got you," the stranger said around his lit cigarette when he lifted her with a grunt and plopped her next to him in the snow.

Sasha sank down to the top of her boots. "Thanks," she murmured when he let go of her.

"Sorry. I deedn't mean to scare you," his obsidian eyes looked down at her while he pulled on his cigarette.

Sasha didn't know what to do. She didn't want him to know where she lived. After what happened with Pietre, she wasn't going to be naive about being safe in Switzerland anymore. "Okay. I'll be fine. Thanks." She waited for him to walk away.

"My close friends call me Sasha," he offered one hand while he held the cigarette to his lips with the other.

Eyes wide with fear she wondered if he was fucking with her. "What?"

"Sasha. My neeckname."

They stared at each other, freezing in the uncomfortable silence.

Sasha hesitated. "But, I'm Sasha," she whispered, feeling as if she had been struck dumb.

He laughed, his features softening which eased some of her anxiety. "Ah. Okay, then you can call me Aleks."

A nervous chuckle escaped her lips. "Nice to meet you, Aleks."

He exhaled and the smoke wafted around her when he nodded. He dropped the butt of the cigarette in the snow before he gestured to her apartment. "Are you going to make eet okay?"

Her stomach clenched. He knew where she lived. "Yeah, thank you. Have a nice day." There was no point in waiting. She turned and walked away from him, snow filling her boots as she trudged through the snow banks to avoid falling on the main road. She was shaking and not from the cold. She glanced behind her and he was sauntering towards the café.

The dread in the pit of her stomach made her want to throw up. She got into her apartment and dropped her laundry on the couch. She stared at her shaking hands after she sat next to her laundry and attempted to push the stranger from her mind. She was overreacting. He hadn't done anything and she was hypersensitive after Pietre.

She rested her head against the couch and gazed through the ceiling. The Bell history kept nagging at her. She had known from the beginning that Ricky was too good for her and a crater separated their worlds.

The image of Marie Bell with her secret husband kept swimming before her eyes. Her happiness flowed through the picture. For the first time in years, Sasha wanted that for herself. She had been pushing Ricky away and holding him at arm's length. Now, she wanted to fight for him, if he would have her.

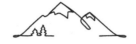

37. STATUS

Sasha sat with Serena and Claud in the crowded town hall. They were squeezed onto the wooden benches while everyone talked and ate sweets and drank kirsch or espresso. Ricky was late and Sasha couldn't keep her eyes away from the stairs.

"He's okay," Serena placed a hand on hers. "You should come to France with us."

"What's in France?" Sasha asked, distracted.

Claud leaned forward. "We're going skiing."

Sasha scrunched her face. "I'd rather not."

"You don't have to ski, but it's so beautiful there. You can always bring Ricky and spend the day in a hot tub," Serena winked.

Sasha shook her head and smiled down at her slice of butter rum cake. A shiver of electricity ran through her body and she looked up to see Ricky cresting the top of the stairs in his snow coat, jeans, and snow boots. There was a raising of glasses and greetings when he reached the top. Everyone had a soft spot for Ricky.

His whiskey gaze zeroed in on her before he crossed the room with a determination that made her quiver. She climbed off the bench to give him a hug but he claimed her lips instead, pulling her close and rubbing his tongue along the top of her mouth causing her to moan into him.

There were a couple of whistles after the shock subsided.

"I missed you," he said against her lips before easing her back to the floor. They made room for him on the bench and he squeezed in next to her.

Eric approached and gave Ricky a hug and asked about the supplies.

Sasha's head was still swimming. She was having issues concentrating on anyone but her lumberjack. His presence consumed her with desire and nervousness.

After dessert was done, Sasha and Ricky helped clean up before they left.

He drove his truck and parked it next to her apartment. He unloaded a couple of boxes while she got the fire started in the goblin.

"What's all of that?" she asked after he slid a long box into her tiny apartment and then locked the door.

"This," he pointed to a big square box with 'La Spaziale' stamped on the side, "is my espresso."

She chuckled. This man and his espresso. He slid the box against her bare wall, and shrugged out of his shoes and coat. "How long will that take to set up?" She was happy to see the scarf she had given him for Christmas hanging around his neck.

"We will find out tomorrow." He held out his hand for her. "Come."

Ricky was slow and meticulous when he undressed her, his hands appreciating her curves and hips.

Something was different. His kisses were longer and softer, sometimes his caress quivered.

"What's wrong?" Sasha asked him.

"Nothing and everything," he whispered.

He hadn't done anything besides touch and kiss her. She was aching for him. Her heart skipped a beat.

"You must be exhausted...."

"*Nai.*"

"Okay."

He nuzzled her neck. "I want more."

Her eyes widened and she stared at the ceiling. "More?"

Using his thumb, he nudged her chin so he could search her eyes. "I want more of you."

She stared back at him. "There isn't much more I can give," she said, the dread of not being enough settling in her gut.

"I want the world to know we're together," he stated before he nuzzled her shoulder.

"According to Twitter, they already know," she teased.

"Those are from other people. I want it to come from me, that we're a couple."

She gulped. "You want to change your relationship status." She stared at the wall behind him. This was big. He wanted to make them official.

Heads were about to roll.

"I'm not on social media," she reminded him.

"I know," he pulled her close.

"I'm not reactivating any accounts," she stated.

"That's fine. I still wanted to ask you," he searched her eyes again.

"It's your socials, do what you want."

"That's not vhat I mean, *Wölfinli.* I vant us to be more. Vill you be my girlfriend?"

Her heartbeat quickened even though some of the stress faded. "Yes," she smiled. "I can try dating you for a couple more months," she joked.

He growled before he kissed her. "I need at least a year." He kissed her with slow, sensual strokes of his velvety tongue before guiding them both into the abyss.

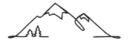

38. THE ALBUMS

January 14

T he buzzing of her phone scared her awake the next morning. She had had a nightmare about Jackson. He hadn't invaded her dreams in a while. She pushed the intrusive memories from her thoughts and inhaled the scent of espresso when she checked who was calling her.

"Serena?" Sasha asked through the cloud of sleep.

"I've been asking for veeks," Serena sounded pissed. "It's all over the news that Rickart Bell has declared himself in a relationship on Facebook. Vhy didn't you tell me?"

Sasha groaned. She was not awake enough for this. "He asked me last night."

Serena's anger melted away, "That's so exciting! Is he coming to France with us?"

"I haven't even decided if I'm going yet," she reminded her overeager friend.

"I hope you come. We're getting a group of friends together. By the way, you are all over Twitter today. Everyone is talking about Rickart Bell and his

Cinderella."

"Ugh, I gotta go. I'm still waking up."

"Come by for dinner and games?" Serena asked.

"Maybe." Sasha ended the call and stared at her ceiling. Why would a relationship status make the news? People needed to get a life.

Ricky had taken it upon himself to rearrange her furniture to fit his espresso machine. If this was his biggest vice, she was okay with it. He had moved the couch in front of the sliding door and had hung up a heavy cream colored curtain. He got rid of her coffee table and replaced it with a tall wooden table that held a black and chrome LUCCA espresso machine and a couple of espresso cups. Above the espresso machine he had hung her poster.

Her living room looked bigger somehow. "You should teach me how to use that contraption," she suggested when she stood next to his chair.

He looked up from his cup. "You want me to make you one?"

"No, I want to be able to make you espresso."

He stared in surprise before smiling. "Of course." He pulled her down onto his lap and kissed her temple.

⁓⋀⋏⋄

Ricky had brought work with him. He plugged into her router and had a couple of video conferences while she sat on the couch wearing her earbuds and listening to a tango mix. The electronics company in New York was finally a part of Glocke Industrie and he listened in on meetings while the board discussed new acquisitions and where to open factories. Although

Sasha wasn't interested in his work, she couldn't ignore the heated discussions around cutting costs versus humane labor practices.

After his last meeting, they sat in silence while he decompressed. He readjusted so his head was in her lap, and because he was tall, he propped his legs against the wall.

His fingers caressed her chin, tracing her jaw and the contours of her neck. "Did you find a new therapist?" he asked.

Licking her lips while she searched for an answer, she looked down at him. "No," she admitted. "To be honest, I'm kind of hesitant."

"Why?"

Sighing, she wondered how to explain her concerns about being one of the few people of color in the area and how that added to her anxiety. "I just don't think therapists here will get what I'm going through."

Whiskey eyes studied her. "I'm sorry to hear that."

"It's okay. Maybe I'll search for one online who specializes in domestic abuse trauma, anxiety and the other shit I'm battling." She laughed to conceal her nerves and pain. "Maybe." Her phone buzzed and a text from Serena scrolled across her screen. "Ready to eat?"

They joined Serena and Claud for dinner and played some board games while Serena tried to convince Ricky to go to France. He declined and said he had important meetings he couldn't skip.

They were walking back to her apartment when thick snowflakes started falling from dark gray clouds.

"Will you be able to drive in this?" she asked him.

"It will be better tomorrow." He put an arm around her shoulder and pulled her closer. "Let's take a picture," he raised his phone.

She threw up her hands. "Please don't."

"It's just for me. I want more pictures of us, ya? For memories."

"Okay," she exhaled when he lifted his phone and she looked up and smiled, her gaze slipping to his handsome face right before he took the picture.

_ᴧᴧ_

Sunday morning, Ricky was preparing to leave when there was a knock on her door. Sasha answered and Hilda rushed in holding the box of old albums.

"I can't keep these anymore," Hilda said in English. "It would be selfish." She handed the box to Ricky and watched him pull out the newest of the albums.

"*Mutter.*" He collapsed onto the kitchen chair, his hand over his mouth while he gazed at his mother holding his baby sister. "Where did you find these?" he asked in his mother tongue.

Sasha rubbed his shoulder in a poor attempt to comfort him. She could feel him shaking.

"I hid them," Hilda admitted. "Tobias wanted them destroyed. Only Sasha has seen them."

He looked up at Sasha then back to Hilda. "Thank you," he placed the album back inside the box. "I'll look at them once I get to Geneva." He looked at the box of ghosts and shook his head when he stood.

He hugged Hilda and thanked her again before she left.

"Are you okay?" Sasha asked when they were alone.

"Tobias told me there were no pictures," he dragged in a shaky breath. "Can you make me espresso? I need a quick walk." He shrugged into his snow coat and wrapped the black scarf under his beard before stepping outside.

Sasha prepped his espresso and set it on the table. She sat and waited, staring at the box and remembering the secret wedding. Ignoring the urge to search for the pictures, she drummed her fingers on the table while she watched a waltz instruction video on her phone.

When he returned, his eyes were red. He kicked off his boots and sat across from her. He sipped on the warm, bitter liquid. "I'll come get you in a few weeks," he said to the cup before meeting her gaze.

The weeks that felt like years when she wasn't with him. She had her follow-up appointment with the doctor. "I can't wait."

"Me too. My place feels empty without you." He frowned at his cup.

Once his espresso was gone, she walked him to his truck. He stowed the box of pictures behind his seat before pulling her into a lingering goodbye kiss.

"Be careful," she begged. She had no idea how the roads were.

"Always safety," he kissed her forehead and then climbed behind the wheel.

He took his time maneuvering the truck through the town, the chains chomping into the snow and ice. Sasha walked beside his truck along with others who came to see him off. He honked and saluted before he disappeared around the curvy bend into the mountains.

"Who was that?"

Sasha turned to see the tourist, Aleks, holding a hot drink in a paper to-go cup. He must have just stepped out of the café.

"That was my boyfriend," Sasha said carefully, wrapping her arms around herself.

Obsidian eyes studied her while he sipped the fragrant liquid. "Ah. He doesn't leeve here?"

Sasha glanced around, a bunch of tourists were milling about, but no one she knew. She swallowed. "Did you find a nice ski spot?"

"Yes. Eet was too easy. I like them hard and weeth curves," his eyes dropped to her hips.

Her stomach bottomed out and she took a step back. Why did she always attract the fucking creepers?

"Maybe you should try France."

He nodded and lifted his cup. "Good idea. More challenges een France. But I'm here for a couple of weeks first."

"Well, enjoy your trip, Aleks."

"Have a great week, Sasha." He smiled and she saw a flash of metal in his mouth and wondered what it was. With a wave, he turned around and entered the café.

Sasha walked back to her apartment even though she kept glancing behind her. Her apartment was visible from the café due to the lower elevation. She locked the door behind her and inhaled deeply. The aroma of espresso, sandalwood, and vanilla soothed her.

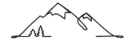

39. A DRAWER

February 14

S ince her February appointment was on a Wednesday, she took the entire week off. Ricky rolled into town Sunday afternoon, the truck full of boxes. Sasha had been sitting with Serena at the café when they saw his F-250 creep by. They ran out to greet him.

He felt like heaven. Almost a month of no physical contact had been torture. While the truck was being unloaded they went to her place to get her stuff. She made him an espresso while he stretched his neck and relaxed.

"The roads are bad," he explained. "It will be slow going back."

"Should we leave tomorrow instead?"

"No, it will storm tonight. Might get snowed in." He sipped his espresso while whiskey eyes watched her. "We just go slow."

He had explained before that the empty bed of the truck made it difficult to drive the mountains. "Can we put wood or something in the back?"

"It's okay."

It wasn't okay. The snow started when they were halfway through the mountains.

His claim that he knew the mountain roads didn't matter when they weren't even visible. Sasha couldn't see the trees as he navigated down the mountain in first gear through snow so thick all she could see was a wall of white fluff.

She was so scared she didn't utter a single word because she didn't want to distract him. Instead she listened to him encourage the purring truck along, keeping an eye on his phone for their GPS location.

Almost five hours after leaving Glockenwald, they pulled into the underground garage.

"That was terrifying," Sasha admitted when he put the truck into park and cut the engine. She patted the dashboard, "Well done." She wanted to write Ford a letter of thanks.

Ricky got out and stretched. "I'm starving. Let's have takeout." He grabbed her luggage and they went upstairs.

The Christmas tree and garlands were gone, but the red pillows and throw were still on the couch. He called in an order for food while he took her luggage to his room. The assumption made her smile when she followed him.

He ended the call and pulled open an empty drawer in his dresser. "Is this enough for you?"

She stared at the drawer. "Sure. I'm just here for one week."

"Not one week. Just leave stuff here, ya? For next time."

He placed her luggage next to the dresser and went

into his bathroom to start the shower.

Ricky had cleared out a drawer for her.

What does that mean? Asking for a friend.

When going into his bathroom, there was another doorway that led to his walk-in closet. He was in there undressing when Sasha found him.

"Thanks for the drawer," she was still wrapping her head around the meaning.

He nodded to some empty shelves and a rack with unused hangers. "For your shoes and dresses, ya?" He had emptied a third of his closet.

Her mouth fell open, "Okay." She didn't even own enough clothes to fill the space he had made for her. She slid her gaze to his nakedness when he approached.

He kissed her forehead. "Can I shower you?"

She nodded, eager for the contact. Once in the steaming shower, she watched the water bounce off him like diamonds.

"I'm lucky I found you," he whispered while he pumped soap onto the huge loofah. He moved the soft sponge up her arm and across her shoulders then down her other arm.

"I'm the lucky one," she countered. "I was stranded. And the wolves would have eaten me."

He chuckled. "Ah, right. *Wölfinli* and her wolves." He lowered to his knees, his whiskey gaze following every peak and valley of her curves. "You've been through so much, and yet you gave me a chance."

"You gave me a chance too."

His hands with the sponge traveled up her leg to her thigh. "I admire your perseverance. I'm eager to grow with you."

"Grow with me?" She hated that her voice was

breathy and hesitant, but his hands were working their way around her body and making her knees so weak she had to lean against the cool slate wall. Thankfully the shower cap kept her hair protected.

"Yes. Whatever this is between us, I'm eager to see our evolution."

_ʌʌ_

After their shower, they went into the kitchen to find several bags of takeout on the counter.

"Who came in here?" Sasha asked, her skin crawling.

"Security. No worries."

"We were in the shower, that's creepy."

He took out a couple of styrofoam containers. "I'm sorry. It won't happen again."

She rubbed her arms feeling violated. Who else had the code and could just walk into his place?

Ricky must have been starving because he ordered a four-course meal. They shared a delicious niçoise salad, a garlic soup, roasted chicken with root vegetables, and a tarte tatin for dessert while watching the snow blanket the city in front of them.

"I have some important meetings this week," he said when he cut into his chicken.

"That's okay. I can amuse myself," Sasha sipped on white wine.

"Would you like dance lessons with Elise?" He glanced at his phone when it buzzed.

"Without you?" Sasha saw that his wallpaper had changed. Was that her feeding a dolphin?

"She will provide a partner."

She preferred dancing with Ricky. "I guess."

"Then you can teach me later, no? A private lesson."

Sasha nodded and looked down at her food. She knew he had things to do: intelligent lumberjack, conglomerate things.

"What?" he asked, after setting down his knife and fork, he sat back in his chair.

"It's Valentine's Day," she looked at her hands in her lap.

He groaned and he rubbed both hands down his face. He looked exhausted, "I'm sorry. We don't celebrate that here." He shook his head, running a hand through his bourbon hair. "I didn't even consider that you'd want something special."

She inhaled sharply. "Forget I said anything. It's not a big deal." She picked up her fork and tapped it against her chicken.

"Is celebrating important to you?" he asked, studying her.

She shook her head. "Nope, it doesn't matter. If the Swiss don't celebrate, then I don't care anymore."

Ricky sighed and picked up his knife and fork. "No, we do not celebrate. And I've got such a busy week."

"It's fine," she forced a smile. "The chicken's good," she said before she ate a piece, trying to change the topic.

He seemed to have second thoughts and put down his knife and fork again. Picking up his espresso instead, he took a sip before clearing his throat. "I did some research and found a therapist for you."

Looking up from her plate with wide eyes, she stared at him in disbelief. "You did what now?"

"I know it's important to you and I wanted to help

however I could."

She put her fork down, unsure how she should feel. "So you found me a therapist?"

"I did."

Unable to school her face, Sasha grimaced with the discomfort of having to navigate the situation. "I don't want to see another Swiss therapist," she said, finally hugging herself. "I don't think they can ever understand the nuances of—"

"She's American." Whiskey eyes studied her body language.

Sitting back in the suede chair, Sasha stared at him for a hot minute. "Okay. I didn't think there'd be an American therapist here."

Clearing his throat again, Ricky fidgeted with his espresso cup. "She's available tomorrow. And anytime you want to go. You can see her after your dance lessons with Elise. If you want."

"Wow. Thank you." Part of her wanted to turn down his offer, but Sasha knew she had trauma to work through. "I'm up for meeting her tomorrow after dance. Before I have lunch with you."

"I'll text her." Ricky confirmed.

_◠◡◠_

When Sasha opened her eyes, the room was shrouded in darkness. Needing to chase away the nightmares of Pietre and Jackson she ran her fingers through Ricky's chest hair and shimmied against him. Then she pulled on his short beard.

Ricky rumbled in his sleep and readjusted, inhaling deeply.

"I need you," she whispered in his ear.

"Mmm, Sasha," he whispered and turned onto his side, but his eyes were still closed. His hands found her face and he lifted her chin and kissed her in his sleep.

Sasha fisted his hair, pulling him in closer. "Fuck me, Rickart," she begged. Her body pulsed with desire. "Please, take me."

He groaned when she gyrated against him. He rolled them until he was on top, crushing her.

She didn't care if she couldn't breathe as long as he made her forget. She wiggled against his weight and pushed down his boxer briefs. "Ricky? Please," she begged. She fisted his curve and he groaned. "Ricky, fuck me," she was so desperate to have him, she guided him to her core and pushed against him.

His eyes finally opened and he looked down at her surprised. "Ugh, Sasha. I thought I was dreaming," he penetrated deeper before he kissed her. He sighed against her lips. "Did you ask me to fuck you? Or vas that a dream?" his voice was full of gravel when he braced himself above her.

A sound escaped her lips that she had never heard before. "Please, Ricky," she begged. "Make me forget." She was prepared to beg him for the rest of her life.

Confusion crossed his sleepy face and he stopped moving. "Forget what?"

She gulped. She hadn't told him about the nightmares. "All the bad," she whispered.

"Just give it to me," he whispered. He found her hand and weaved his fingers between hers.

She wrapped her legs around him and squeezed. She pulled him down for another kiss with her free hand and he seized that one too.

"You're mine," he grunted. He claimed her with each tantalizing stroke.

Her breath hitched. She wanted everything with him. "Rickart," she gasped.

He hummed against her lips and released her hand before he ran his callouses down to her ass where he squeezed her delicious curves. "Mine," his voice was husky and low, vibrating through her.

The coils inside her snapped and her walls vice-gripped him when she came.

"Fuck, Sasha," he grunted into the pillow, his beard tickling her ear while her body milked him. He relaxed on top of her while he caught his breath. "No more bad."

She attempted to breathe and wipe away tears when she sniffed.

"Vhat happened?" he braced himself and searched her face in the low light. "Did I hurt you?"

She shook her head. She felt emotions for him she never knew could exist for her. "I'm just...." her voice was too thick to articulate what she was feeling.

He kissed her cheek and forehead and pulled her closer. "I've got you," he whispered against her temple.

Sasha wiped at her tears and pulled him into another kiss, hoping he felt what she felt.

40. HE DID WHAT NOW?

February 15

W atching Ricky get dressed for work was difficult because his suit begged to be ripped off. The fabric felt soft when she ran a hand over his shoulder while he buttoned his jacket.

"Damn, you look good in this suit," she drooled. This man dripped swag and she was here for every delicious drop.

He smiled at her and fixed his maroon tie. His beard was filling in nice and thick. He smoothed the whiskers with beard balm and ran a comb through it before using a lint roller over the front of his blue suit.

Her hand followed the muscles of his back to his hip causing him to pull her into a hug. "Keep doing that, ve vill both be late," he threatened. Her wicked thoughts must have shown on her features because he groaned before checking his watch. "I can't be late."

She nodded and pulled away. She grabbed her dance shoes off the shelf in his closet and let him escort her down to the Mercedes-Maybach waiting for her. He re-introduced her to Noah, her chauffeur dressed in a black suit and tie, who ushered her into the car and then she was off to see Elise.

Noah didn't just drop her off like he had when she went shopping with Serena in December. He stood by the door and watched her dance with his arms folded over his chest.

Elise chastised Sasha's poor American posture. "You need to valk vith book on your head!" Elise tapped the top of Sasha's crown and then used both hands to push her shoulders down and back. "Elongate," Elise pulled Sasha's chin up. *"Jetzt, eins, zwei, drei!"* Elise clapped, counting the beat in German while Luca walked Sasha through the waltz.

After being excused from Elise's sight, Sasha followed Noah to the black Mercedes parked outside.

Once he slid into the driver's seat and started the car, he glanced at his watch. "You have a meeting vith Frau Miller before lunch vith Herr Bell."

"Why did you stay for my dance lesson?"

He turned to look at her over his shoulder. "I'm just here for your safety, Frau Villiams."

She crossed her arms. "My safety? They teach combat at chauffeur school?"

He faced the steering wheel and checked the traffic on the road. "Vould you like to make any stops before meeting vith Frau Miller?"

"No. I'm good." She looked out the window and watched the cars pass them. "I remember you from December. How long have you worked for Ricky—Herr Bell?"

His green sea glass eyes studied her from the rear-view mirror. "Many years," he answered after he pulled away from the curb, his tone ending the conversation.

Sasha didn't know what she expected, but a hotel wasn't it. She figured the therapist would have an office. Instead Noah pulled up to The Woodrow where he passed the Maybach to a valet attendant and escorted her through the lux lobby.

When the door opened, Sasha was shocked that ebony eyes greeted her.

The two women smiled at each other and Sasha exhaled in relief.

"Sasha?" Ms. Miller asked. She was a tall Black woman with thick locs that were pulled over one shoulder. She was dressed in a coral pantsuit and a crisp white blouse. "I've been waiting to meet you."

After throwing a glance at Noah, Sasha entered the suite. "Yes, I'm Sasha."

"I'm Imani Miller," she introduced herself before shaking her hand. "Please call me Imani."

"Nice to meet you. Is it too much that I ask for a hug?"

Raven eyes studied her for a second. "Get in here," Imani opened her arms and hugged Sasha with a squeeze.

Feeling her body relax, Sasha tried not to be overcome with emotion. She hadn't realized how much she missed seeing folks who looked like her until that moment. After taking another deep breath of Imani's peaches and mint perfume, she finally ended the hug with a smile. "Sorry about that, thank you."

Nodding, Imani gestured further into the room. "Have you been missing your people?"

"Girl, yes."

"I vill stay in the hallvay," Noah announced, making both women stop short and dart glances between each other and him.

Imani waved to the living room and kitchen. "It's a two bedroom suite. You can sit anywhere you like, Mr. Kerr. We can use the second bedroom or the balcony."

Nodding, Sasha agreed. "You should relax."

A grimace crossed Noah's face before his features snapped back to neutral. "That's fine."

Imani led Sasha to one of the bedrooms that had two armchairs next to a small table. After closing the door for privacy, they sat across from each other.

"You don't have an office?" Sasha asked.

Imani laughed. "I do. In New York."

Eyes narrowed in confusion, Sasha looked outside the window. "New York? But not here?"

Shrewd raven eyes studied Sasha. "I'm guessing Mr. Bell didn't tell you much about me?"

"He mentioned your last name," Sasha offered.

"Wow. I thought.... Okay, let me take a step back." Imani's raven eyes glanced out the window before meeting Sasha's gaze. "First let me tell you that I'm on your side. Even though Mr. Bell is paying for your sessions, I take doctor-patient confidentiality seriously. Are you following me?"

Nodding, Sasha tried not to let the anxiety eat her alive.

"I'm telling you this because you have a right to know. I got a call about a week ago and I honestly thought it was a prank. This man with an accent offers me a job here in Geneva for an indefinite amount of time." Imani crossed her long legs and unconsciously played with one of her locs.

"He did what now?" Sasha asked through her shock.

Chuckling, Imani shook her head in disbelief. "Oh, he did that. But it gets better." She uncrossed her legs and leaned forward, causing Sasha to lean forward too because she was absorbing every word. "I told him I have clients and don't have time for games. But he told me to name my price. So I did and girl...." Imani shook her head. "Let's just say he made a counteroffer that caused me to hang up."

"What did he offer you?"

"Double!"

Sasha didn't even know how to respond. "That's crazy."

"No. What's crazy is that he called me back immediately after I hung up. Offered to fly me over here on a private jet, to pay for all of my living expenses and everything."

Sasha gulped her anxiety. "I can't believe this."

"You can't believe this? When I tell you I've never googled someone so fast in my life," she recounted with a shake of her head, one of her hoop earrings getting caught on her collar. "Anyway, he had one caveat to me accepting his offer," Imani continued, her voice suddenly getting quiet when she leveled Sasha with an inquiring gaze.

Clearing her throat, Sasha leaned back into her chair. "And that was?"

"You."

"Me?"

"I have to make myself available to you twenty-four-seven. Whether you want to see me in person, call or text. You are my priority."

Feeling overwhelmed, Sasha dragged in a shaky breath. She was rendered utterly speechless and the silence between them dragged on for so long she started to feel uncomfortable.

Imani folded her hands together and rested them on top of her knee. "So, Ms. Sasha Williams. Tell me why I'm here."

Not knowing where to begin, Sasha flicked her gaze to the window where she stared at Lake Geneva. Ricky went through great lengths to find someone who could help her. She wasn't about to squander this opportunity to heal. She returned her gaze to the beautiful woman waiting patiently. She cleared her throat before she began. "The first time I was molested, I was eleven."

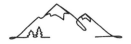

41. THIS BITCH

After a tearful session, Sasha asked Noah to take her to the mall so she could buy a thank you gift for Ricky. Having Noah for a shadow reminded her of shopping in the States. She felt like he was security waiting for her to steal some shit. He walked just behind her right shoulder from store to store. But once she entered a store he backed off and gave her a bit more space.

She went into a menswear store and purchased a black silk tie. She bought herself another pair of snow boots so she could alternate between pairs. When they passed a lingerie boutique she paused. She didn't have lingerie, but maybe Ricky would appreciate her in sexy lace.

"Can you wait out here?" she asked Noah, embarrassed.

He flushed a dark pink when his eyes darted to the display window. "Of course. I'll take your bags."

She perused the lace and silk garments, trying to imagine which one Ricky would like. There was a sexy red and black corset, but when she saw the price her heart fell. Why was everything so expensive? She still owed him for the bloodied white dress.

She walked out with nothing.

"Vhere's your bag?" Noah inquired.

She shook her head. "It's too expensive."

"Herr Bell has instructed me to pay for the rest of your purchases." He gestured toward the boutique.

Sasha grimaced. She would never be able to pay him back for the therapist. "No, I don't want him spending any more money on me." She started to walk away but Noah surprised her by stepping in front of her. Her involuntary flinch made him take a step back.

"He's been happy vith you. Please," with his intense sea glass eyes he guided her back toward the shop.

Well, this was weird. But Noah wouldn't let her leave without something so she tried on the red and black excuse for sex. She had to strap herself into it, which was a challenge with her curves, but she liked what she saw in the mirror. After changing back to her clothes, she took the items to the register where Noah had placed a garter belt, thigh-high lace stockings, and black fuck-me platform shoes.

After Noah paid, he grabbed her bags. "Herr Bell vill meet you vhen you are ready."

"I'm ready." She followed him out of the store and tried to ignore the fact that he just paid for her lingerie.

"Sasha Villiams!" someone shouted her name.

Turning toward the voice, she was blinded seconds later by a flash. Instinct made her raise her hand to shield her eyes so she almost didn't catch Noah moving in front of her.

If she had blinked, she would have missed everything.

Noah yanked the camera so hard that the

photographer made a choking noise when the strap bit into his neck. With a quick flick of his wrist, Noah had taken out the memory card and removed the lens which clattered to the floor.

The photographer yelled something Sasha didn't understand, but his stance said he wanted to fight.

Noah released the camera which knocked against the man's chest with a thump, then he pocketed the memory card. He bent to pick up the lens which he shoved at the photographer causing the man to stumble back several steps. In one swift move, he scooped up the bags he had apparently dropped, grabbed her arm and ushered her toward the exit.

"Who the hell was that?" Sasha asked, still trying to wrap her head around what just happened.

"Paparazzi."

"Yeah, right."

"You're dating Herr Bell. It's to be expected."

Eyes wide with disbelief, she allowed Noah to guide her to the valet where the Maybach was waiting.

_ᴧᴧ_

Twenty minutes later, Sasha couldn't hide her curiosity anymore. "I didn't know they taught moves like that at chauffeur school," she said, trying to keep her voice casual.

Their gazes met via the rear-view mirror and his eyes crinkled with amusement. "Ve're here, Frau Villiams."

Sasha's mouth had dropped into her lap when Noah pulled up to Glocke Industrie. The impressive building had to be at least twenty floors with floor-to-ceiling windows between slabs of charcoal slate.

After handing the keys to the valet, Noah escorted her through the four-story atrium. Sasha didn't know where to look. The floor was the same slate as the exterior and her eyes moved up to follow the glass and chrome guard rails.

They had to go through security where she was given a visitor's badge before Noah escorted her up to the thirtieth floor.

When they exited the elevator, Sasha could feel the eyes throwing daggers at her.

This felt like a perp walk.

She was in jeans, a black sweater, and hiking boots. She felt drastically underdressed compared to everyone in their posh European business attire.

Noah walked her past a secretary who acknowledged them with a nod. He knocked on one of two massive double doors before escorting her into a large office.

She didn't notice Ricky, she noticed the long-legged blond standing next to his desk. What the fuck was Bernabitch doing here?

They both looked up from paperwork they were studying.

Sasha's jaw must have been on the floor because Bernatwat smiled with smug satisfaction.

This bitch.

Ricky checked his watch. "I'll call you when I'm done with lunch," he said to Bernwhatever when he took the paperwork.

"Of course, Herr Bell," Bitch-might-die-before-leaving-this-fucking-office said when she sashayed her way past Sasha in a skirt that barely covered her tiny

European ass.

"I'll be back in an hour, Frau Villiams," Noah whispered before he excused himself.

Ricky approached her with a smile. "I'm so glad you're here, Sasha. How was dance?"

She glared at him.

He faltered, "What's wrong?"

She couldn't keep the anger out of her voice. "You work with her?"

He had the cockacity to look confused. "Who? Who are you talking about?"

She gestured to the closed door behind her with a shaking hand. "You work with Bernabitch?"

Ricky closed his eyes and sighed. His jaw clenched before he looked at her again. "Bernadette is an executive at Glocke Industrie."

Sasha felt sick to her stomach. "Why am I here?" She looked around his office with slate floors and an impressive view of the city and Lake Geneva. He had a bookcase behind his L-shaped desk lined with business volumes, a black globe, and business awards. Her mind decided to fuck with her and imagine Bernatwat bent over his desk.

"Sasha," he stood in front of her so her eyes stopped roaming, forcing her to gaze up into whiskey depths. "I've never ever touched her. She's not my type."

"Oh really? Tall and sexy isn't your type? She's my type and I'm not even into women." Sasha shook her head, the anxiety ate at her. She couldn't get the image of the two of them standing shoulder-to-shoulder looking like a proper Swiss couple.

He dragged in a deep breath. "I have no interest in her. Only you."

"Yeah, for now," Sasha was pissed. She skirted around him and sat in one of the white leather arm chairs and squeezed her legs together while she hugged herself. The tightness in her chest made it difficult to breathe and she couldn't swallow around her sadness.

"You have nothing to worry about. Okay?"

She wasn't okay. How was she supposed to compete with women like that who got to see him every single fucking day? She was a shrek compared to these modelesque women. She swallowed and blinked away her frustration.

He leaned against his desk, standing in front of her. "Sasha," he rubbed a hand through his hair. "Don't you trust me? I feel like I've made my intentions clear. I only want you."

There was a knock to the right and Sasha glanced over and saw a conference room through a glass door that she hadn't even noticed. Someone rolled in a cart and placed food on the conference table before leaving through glass doors that led to the hallway.

"She wants you," Sasha said when she stared at the shine of his black glass desk next to his hip.

"Bernadette? I don't want her."

Sasha shook her head. "I'm sure she'll make a move on you."

He shook his head. "She's an executive, nothing more to me."

Sasha bounced her leg and wondered if Noah was still around.

"I've ordered lunch. I hope that's okay," he said, attempting to change the subject. His fist tapped lightly on his desk while he waited for her to say something.

"I've lost my appetite," Sasha murmured while she

studied her hiking boots.

Releasing an exasperated sigh, he sat partially on the desk. "I'm sorry to hear that. How was therapy?"

Attempting to keep her cool was almost impossible. Bringing up her therapy at that moment felt like a low blow. But she didn't have the privilege to act like a damn fool. Releasing a shaking breath, she reminded herself that he went through a lot of trouble to find someone for her. She shrugged. "It was fine. I made an appointment for tomorrow."

"That's great. If you want someone else, just let me know."

"Umhm."

Silence reigned for several moments.

Eventually, Ricky heaved another sigh. "If you're not hungry, do you want to dance?"

She looked up, surprised. "Wait, what?"

"I don't care what we do, but I have—" he looked at his watch, "—fifty minutes." He stood up and slid out of his suit jacket. "Show me what you learned today."

She kissed her teeth. "Fine. I could use the practice." She pushed out of the chair and stood inches from him.

He took out his phone and thumbed in his password.

Sasha's heart pounded when she saw their faces in the evening snow as his wallpaper. He was smiling at the camera and she was gazing up at him. She remembered their conversation from December while she watched his whiskey eyes search for a song. He had explained that his wallpaper was always something he wanted.

He wanted her.

That revelation almost knocked her back into the armchair.

Violins filled the room from speakers in the ceiling. Sasha was positive the entire floor could hear the string quartet.

They danced the waltz across the slate floor. After every dip he pulled her in for a kiss. The dancing helped to distract her from her inadequacies.

After she had calmed down from the shock of Bernadette, they sat in the conference room to eat. With a push of a button, the glass walls frosted, giving them privacy.

"I see your flex," she said to him before biting into an apple slice.

"What do you mean, flex? Like this?" He flexed his arms as if he was posing for a bodybuilding competition.

She laughed. "No, I mean this," she gestured around them. "You're showing me who you are, your wealth, your power. It's a flex."

He looked down at his espresso and shook his head. "No, that's not it. My flex is you."

She coughed on the apple chunk. "What?"

"I'm flexing you. You're mine and I want everyone to know it."

Her heart beat staccato. "I'm not much to flex," she admitted, looking down at her jeans and hiking boots.

"Of course you are. You're beautiful, intelligent, and mine."

"I look a mess. I don't even have clothes for a place like this."

"Clothes are easy. Go buy clothes. Noah will take you."

"You're throwing money at me," she warned.

"No, I'll never throw money at you," he insisted. He leaned forward and caressed her knee while gazing into her eyes. "But I will provide for you. If you want clothes, go buy clothes. Whatever you want, please, let me give it to you."

She watched him bite into his sandwich while shaking her head. "Just about everything I buy here has to be altered. There won't be much that fits me."

"Then get them altered."

She watched him sit back, his sleeves were rolled up and he crossed an ankle over his knee. "I'll think about it." She looked behind him to the frosted glass. "How much can they see from out there?"

He glanced over his shoulder, then shrugged, "Not much. Maybe a shadow. Why?"

She got up and sat in his lap. "Last night felt good," she bit his bottom lip.

He bit her back and nuzzled her neck. "Wear a skirt tomorrow?"

The idea of him taking her on the conference table had her pulsating. She was sure they wouldn't be the only ones to use the room for adult activities.

She slid off his lap, making sure that he felt the friction from her luscious booty.

"Fuck, Sasha," he examined his tight pants. He took a breath and gazed up at the ceiling before he started counting.

After the food was gone they only had a couple of minutes left. Sasha straightened his tie and smoothed his jacket. When she looked up he was watching her with a hooded gaze.

"I'll be home after seven." He caressed her chin

before kissing her.

Sasha nodded once he pulled away. "Okay," she smiled with a sigh on her lips.

"I'll bring dinner tonight, yeah?" He kissed her forehead before bringing her into a hug. "Noah will take you wherever you want to go from now on."

"Why?"

"We're official now. He texted me about the paparazzi. I can't risk you traveling the city alone anymore." He rubbed his hands up both her arms and kissed her temple.

"Okay. Has anyone ever threatened you?"

He shook his head. "No. But after the club, I won't take any more chances. Noah will protect you with his life."

"Asking him to risk his life is a bit much for a chauffeur."

Ricky tilted his head. "Noah," he said carefully, "isn't a chauffeur."

There was a knock before Noah entered, interrupting the conversation. He stood next to the door and he waited with his hands clasped in front of him.

Ricky took her hand. "Come. I have a meeting in five minutes."

They walked to the elevator holding hands, Noah leading the way. Several people stopped what they were doing to stare at them.

At the elevator he pulled her into another kiss before she stepped in. She watched Ricky watch her as the elevator doors closed between them.

"Vhere to, Frau Villiams?" Noah asked when the mirrored elevator descended.

"I need to go shopping again," Sasha said, crossing her arms. It was time for her to flex back.

42. ARE YOU READY?

After Noah escorted her into the penthouse hours later, she thanked him for his help and started her preparations. She only had about an hour before Ricky would be home and she had a lot to do.

She scattered rose petals from the door to his bedroom. Then she showered, and rubbed herself down with cocoa butter. When her alarm went off at a quarter to seven, she filled the jacuzzi tub and lit candles in the bathroom and on the kitchen island.

She found champagne flutes and filled a bucket with ice and took a bottle of champagne from his wine fridge. She placed them on the island with a note: *I'm waiting*. She had just enough time to squeeze into his gift.

Ricky arrived just when she was clipping the garter belt to the thigh-high stockings. She stuffed the tags into the bag and hid them in the closet when he called her name.

She panicked because she hadn't decided where she wanted him to find her. She was just coming out of the closet when he walked into the bedroom holding the flutes and champagne bottle.

Whiskey eyes widened in surprise before they became hooded with lust. "Wow, Sasha," his Adam's apple moved when he swallowed. He set the flutes and champagne on the dresser.

"Welcome home, Rickart," she bit her lip and leaned her hip against the door frame.

"Please let me touch you," he started to approach her.

"Not yet," she said, holding up the black tie she had purchased earlier that day. "I have some business to attend to first."

She undressed him down to his navy boxer briefs, tied him to one of the dining chairs in the dining room, then found "Drop it Low" by Ester Dean on his iTunes.

When the beat dropped, so did she. She gave him a lap dance that had him begging for her. She swirled her hips and twerked for him, making him watch her bootylicious bounce.

"Fuck, Sasha," he growled when she climbed onto his chair, stretched her leg up and rested a platform on his shoulder. He groaned when his gaze found her bare core. He leaned forward and nipped at the skin just above the black lace stockings. His beard made her tremble. He captured her ebony depths with his whiskey eyes when she grabbed the hair on his head to steady herself.

She screamed when he lifted her into the air. He had untied himself at some point.

He licked at the moisture between her thick thighs while he carried her to his room, his hands holding her waist because she straddled his shoulders. He lowered her to his hips so she wouldn't hit her head on the doorframe. He stood her next to the bed, his eyes hooded while he stared down at her. "Take this off," he growled, tugging on the red and black lace.

She undid the hooks while he watched, stroking himself through the thin fabric of his boxer briefs. She could hear the bass of the music on repeat in the living room. She dropped the corset to the floor and was left wearing the garter, stockings, and four-inch stiletto platforms.

"Better. Let me assist you." He got down on one knee in front of her.

Sasha felt light headed when she stared down at him. Electricity jolted through her when he ran a hand up her calf, another hand caressing her hip.

He lifted her leg and slipped off her shoe which caused her to grip his shoulder for balance. He rested her foot on his bent knee. "That vas a sexy dance," he whispered, releasing the two clips attached to her stockings. His hand rubbed up the back of her thigh until he grabbed her thick ass. He sighed when he gazed up into her eyes and then he rolled the stocking down her calf while he kissed her bare knee.

Sasha's entire body vibrated with need. He was so sexy in his boxer briefs with his curved print.

Once the stocking was off he put her foot back on the carpet and raised her other foot to his knee, but this time he pulled off the stocking with his teeth. His beard and lips tracing a line from her thigh to her knees, then he slowly rolled the thin nylon down and tossed it to the side. He pulled down the garter belt and she stepped out of the lacy contraption.

He looked up at her, fisting himself again. "How do you vant me?"

Sasha swallowed. "Hard. And deep."

He pushed down his boxer briefs after he stood, towering over her with a sigh. His whiskers brushed her neck with feathered kisses. "Get on your hands and knees," his voice was so low she barely heard him over the desire ringing in her ears.

With quivering legs she climbed onto the bed. He positioned behind her, grabbing her ass and growling his appreciation for the view.

"How hard do you vant it?"

"Just don't hit me," she looked behind her, the soft glow from the evening life of Geneva illuminating his hard planes and curves.

He leaned forward and snaked an arm across her shoulders and pulled Sasha up so her back was against his chest. "I'll never hurt you," he whispered, his breath warm against her neck. "Ve can stop. Just say the vord."

She exhaled, "I trust you."

His hands caressed her heavy mounds while he kissed her neck. "Close your legs and bend over," he ordered. His hand squeezed her hip while he stroked himself.

She did as he requested, squeezing her legs together so he could place his on either side of hers.

"I'll go slow." He penetrated her with a groan. Her knees being together had tightened her slick channel. "Fuck. I can barely get in," he whispered and readjusted behind her, his hands squeezing her hips.

Each thrust caused her to moan, igniting a blaze that licked through her body. His curve touched her in all the right places when he claimed her from behind.

He leaned forward so he could cup and massage her dangling breasts. "Are you ready for me to fuck you?" he asked.

"What?" She thought that's what he was doing. "Make me come," she gasped.

"Put your head down," he pushed gently between her shoulder blades until her cheek was against the comforter.

His next thrust sent electricity coursing through her entire body, her thighs twitching uncontrollably.

"Oh god," she panted when her nerves tingled the second coming.

"I'm going to fuck you now," Ricky promised and he slid against her G-spot again.

She felt him readjust so she watched his shadow on the wall squat behind her, giving him a higher angle than if he stayed on his knees.

The next thrust dragged her soul out of her body.

She moaned so deep and throaty she didn't recognize her own voice. She dragged in a breath and grabbed onto the comforter.

His dick was killing her and she didn't care if he was sending her to heaven or hell.

Callused fingers dug into her thick hips as he drilled her fast and hard, igniting her body with each punishing stroke. He fucked them both into insanity. "I'm going to come," his voice was strained and higher than usual.

Sasha saw stars from his universe when they chorused in paradise.

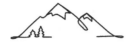

43. LEVEL UP

February 16

The next morning while she and Ricky got dressed, she asked, "Are you coming to my therapy session today?"

His eyes found hers in the mirror's reflection. "Did you want me to?"

"No. I just wondered if you wanted to do a couple's session."

"Not today. I have a conference call with New York that I can't skip," he explained while he brushed his beard.

"That's okay. Imani suggested I ask why you're dating me even though I don't have money or family." Sasha almost felt bad for throwing her therapist under the bus.

The statement must have surprised Ricky because he tilted his head and turned to face her. "I have enough money for both of us," he said finally.

"I've been poor my entire life. Money is nice and all, but I just want to be safe."

He stepped closer and rubbed his hands up and

down her shoulders. "Do you feel safe with me?"

"I do." She didn't even have to think about it.

His hands went still for a moment before he continued. "As for family. You've said you don't have one and mine is... toxic," he said carefully. "We can create our own family."

Her heart skipped several beats. "You mean kids?"

A bourbon eyebrow lifted. "Hopefully. But you and I can be a family. Just the two of us."

Her chest grew warm and threatened to explode. She stepped closer and leaned against his soft suit. "I've been rethinking kids."

"Oh?"

"Maybe after a couple of years of therapy, I might want to try. If we're still together that is."

His arms tightened around her. "Hmm, I'd love little Bells," he murmured before kissing her forehead.

_ᴧᴧ_

After another severe dance class with Elise, Noah took her to therapy.

Imani had a hot espresso and some delicious looking pastries waiting for Noah when they arrived. Although Sasha doubted the man ever relaxed, she thought the gesture was nice.

"So, how are you feeling today?" Imani asked once they were situated in the bedroom.

"I'm actually feeling alright."

"Any anxiety attacks?"

"Well," Sasha explained the fiasco of finding out that Bernadette worked at Glocke.

"How did that make you feel?"

"Pretty insignificant. I was in this fancy ass building in my jeans and this woman's skirt was so short it looked like her skinny ass got hungry and ate it."

Imani tried to stifle a laugh.

"I almost threw hands at that bitch."

Nodding and tapping her pen against the notepad, Imani asked, "How do you feel about what happened now?"

Frowning, Sasha examined her jeans. "I guess I feel better. He told me I have nothing to worry about."

"And you believe him?"

"Yeah. I also went shopping so I won't be poppin' over there in jeans no more."

"Good idea." Imani looked down at her notepad. "Before you left yesterday, I asked you to think about your current goals and what you want to achieve through our sessions."

Forcing her gaze from the window, Sasha met Imani's raven stare. "I don't want to be broken anymore. I want to become worthy of a man like Rickart Bell."

MML

"Ready?" Noah asked, after he picked Sasha up from her spa treatment right before lunch. His wide sea-glass eyes kept darting to her luscious cleavage.

She was in a tailored navy dress with silver buttons down the front. The V-neck top barely held her breasts and the black lace of her bra peeked along the edges. Although the pencil skirt went just past her knees, the curve of her hips and booty were accentuated. The only piece of jewelry she wore was the black diamond he had gifted her in France.

"Yes."

When she rode the elevator to the top floor of Glocke Industrie a little while later, Sasha reminded herself she had an ass some women paid money for. It was time to flex what the good lord gave her. "Stay behind me," she instructed Noah.

"Of course, Frau Villiams."

She could hear Elise telling her to fix her posture. She straightened her back and lowered her shoulders to elongate her neck. The elevator doors opened and Noah held the door while she walked out.

Time to level up.

When Sasha power walked down the hall to Ricky's office, heads turned and jaws dropped. Conversations hung in silence as she passed desks, and a few people stepped into the hallway to watch her.

She walked into Ricky's office without knocking.

He was on his phone and typing on his computer. He ended the call with two words and set his phone on the glass desk.

"Sasha," he stood and approached her. *"Merci,"* he said to Noah who nodded before disappearing into the hall.

Ricky stood in front of her with storming eyes, his jaw clenching. He side-stepped through the door behind her. "Hold all calls. Absolutely no interruptions," he ordered in Swiss German.

Then he closed the door and slid the deadbolt into place while holding her gaze.

44. BROKEN

February 17

The next morning Sasha stared at the gynecologist. After another ultrasound and examination he sat her down and began explaining his diagnosis.

She swallowed back her tears. "What did you just say?"

"The human body is amazing, you may be able to have children, but it will be difficult due to the extensive scarring along the uterine wall. Any viable pregnancy will be high risk with an increased chance to miscarry."

Her heart broke for the final time. She could not be with Richard Bell.

The doctor handed her a tissue box.

"Does Herr Bell know?" she asked, sniffling.

The doctor shook his head, his hands folded in front of him.

She nodded, the tears continuing to fall. "I have to go." She pushed up from the chair and walked out of the office as fast as she could in three-inch heels.

Noah caught up with her. "Frau Villiams?"

"Get me out of here," she whispered, a sob threatening to escape.

He placed a hand on the small of her back and escorted her out of the building. For once she didn't flinch away from Noah's touch and even found herself leaning into him.

"You have lunch vith Herr Bell next, Frau Villiams," he stated when he pulled the Mercedes into traffic.

"Can you take me to Glockenvalt?" she asked with tears flowing down her cheeks.

"There's a storm. It's not safe."

She stared at the thick snow flakes falling against the window. "Can you find me a hotel?" she asked Noah. "Something cheap."

He eyed her via the rear-view mirror. "Should I call Herr Bell?"

She shook her head. "I need to pack. Please cancel lunch with Herr Bell." She was shaking too much to message him herself.

His eyes narrowed before he picked up his phone. "Of course, Frau Villiams." They were at a red light so he quickly thumbed a message before making a U-turn and taking her directly to Ricky's condo.

Instead of dropping her off, Noah pulled into the garage and escorted her to the mirrored elevator. After seeing her own hopeless reflection, she couldn't hold in the sobs any longer. Noah swallowed his apprehension but didn't touch her.

"I'll vait for you here," he said after he let her into the penthouse.

Sasha was already running to the room where she jumped onto the bed with her tight pink dress and heels. She released the scream that had been building in her chest into Ricky's pillow. She held the pillow and inhaled his scent while she mourned the future she was never meant to have.

Eventually she dragged herself to his closet and opened her suitcase. She cried while she packed, emptying her drawer. She left all the clothes he had ever bought her. Maybe he could sell them to a thrift store.

A door slamming somewhere made her jump. She rushed to close her suitcase.

"Sasha?" Ricky called, his voice tinged with panic. His footsteps sounded in the hallway when he ran towards the bedroom. "Sasha? Vhat happened?" his eyes were wild when they darted between her and her belongings. "Vhat's this?" he gestured to the suitcase.

"We can't be together."

He stared at her speechless. Then he shook his head and said, "Please, talk to me. Vhat did the doctor say?"

She looked up into his whiskey eyes. "I can't have kids," she cried fresh tears.

His face dropped. "I'm sorry, Sasha." He took a step toward her. "Can I hold you?"

She stepped back and shook her head. "We can't do this."

"Vhy the fuck not?" he shoved his hands into his pockets. "I don't care that you can't have kids."

"You're the last fucking Bell!" she heard herself scream. "What about your legacy?"

He shook his head. "There are options."

"And they don't involve me."

His breath hitched. "Don't leave me, Sasha. Ve can vork this."

"You deserve a life I can't give you. I literally can't give you anything."

"Ve can adopt," he offered. "Or not have kids. Vhatever you vant."

"I'm broken, Ricky. My mind. My body. I'm sorry. It's over."

He stepped towards her. "No, Sasha. Please, no." He cupped her cheeks, rubbing a tear away with his thumb.

She sniffed and looked up into his red rimmed eyes. "You still want a broken woman?" she asked him.

"You're not broken. Stop saying that."

She sniffed again, leaning into his hand. "But I can't give you little Bells."

He kissed her forehead. "That's okay."

Sasha shook her head when she remembered him holding Timmy's hand on the beach. "You deserve a family. What if I can't even give you that after years of therapy?"

"You've shown me I can love, and that's enough."

"What?" she looked up, confused.

"I love you, Sasha."

Her heart palpitated. Her breath wavered. She was speechless and just stared at him.

Ricky watched her, his thumb caressing her soft chin. "That night, in August," he inhaled and exhaled. "I had visited my mother's grave. I asked her to help me." His bottom lip quivered. "Being the last Bell is lonely. Being rich is lonely. Most people only want me for my money or connections. I was so guarded after Eva, I shut everyone out. Frankly, I'd given up on life."

Sasha's eyes were wide. "You were going to kill yourself."

He shrugged. "Maybe just run off road and take the chance." He sniffed. "I had closed my eyes and my head was up," he paused, fighting for composure. "Then

I heard my mother's laughter." A tear slipped into his beard.

She gasped. She had heard laughter too.

"It scared me. I opened my eyes and I saw yellow."

Thank you sweet Black Baby Jesus for that bright ass yellow Vespa.

"The car ve crashed vas yellow. It vas my *mutter's* favorite color." He shook his head. "I thought I had seen a ghost."

She didn't want to think about what would have happened if she hadn't been stranded on that road.

"I vent back, because I thought I had gone crazy. But there you vere, crying."

She remembered the way he had stared at her like she was a ghost.

"I took you to Glockenvalt, remember?"

Sasha nodded, remembering the orgasms she had on his Harley. The way he had caressed her thigh when she squeezed him.

"Then I vent back to get your stuff and...." he trailed off and dropped his gaze to her lips.

"What?" she asked.

"I swear I heard her laugh again. I knew it vas because of you. My *mutter* sent me you." His thumb caressed her cheek and his whiskey eyes watched her reaction.

Sasha swallowed.

"I've loved you since December, Sasha. And I don't care that you're an orphan. Or that you aren't rich. You're all I need," he whispered when he wiped away another tear with his thumb. "I love you."

She stared at him in shock. She had been falling for him since he first climbed off his Harley on the side of the mountain. Her eyes trailed down his beard to his peach tie with avocados.

His hand fell and he slipped it back into his pocket.

"What did you say?" she asked in a whisper. Sasha wanted to make sure she had heard right. The only other person to tell her that he loved her, had beat her for three years.

"I love you, Sasha." His whiskey eyes captured her ebony depths. "It's okay if you don't love me. I just wanted you to know."

She saw the fear in his eyes. "I flew halfway around the world to escape, to find myself." Her eyes dropped to his tie again. "Instead I found a lumberjack who saved me." A lumberjack who loved her.

Ricky attempted a half smile. "I'll always be your lumberjack," he said with a twinge of sadness before he took another step back.

The Swiss and their matchmaking. Even beyond the grave they meddled. She had been seeing random streaks of yellow and hearing eerie laughter for months.

She stared at his handsome face. "I don't know when I started to love you," she whispered. "But I—"

His lips collided with hers when he embraced her with a sigh.

She felt lightheaded when he deepened the kiss, his whiskers tickling her nose and chin. She moaned against him and her soul soared.

He loved her.

Even with her random freakouts and anxiety, or her lack of prestige and lineage, he loved her. Even after Pietre in the club, he loved her.

Ricky sat on the bed and pulled her between his legs. After she sat on his lap he relaxed back onto the comforter, his lips never losing contact with hers in the slow scintillating kiss.

She pulled away for air because she felt like she was going to pass out. She panted and stared at him. A smile crossed her lips when she searched his whiskey eyes, her fingers in his bourbon beard. "I love you, Rickart. I'm sorry I freaked out."

He rubbed the tip of his nose against hers. "Never be sorry, *Wölfinli*. I'm just glad you're still here. And that you love me."

She scrunched her face as if she was thinking about it. "Yeah, I suppose I do."

He growled when he lifted her further onto the bed. "You owe me lunch." He yanked up her skirt before rubbing his face in her cleavage.

Sasha squealed before laughing. "Are you about to eat me?"

"Mhmm."

"You got time for that? And I think you're vibrating."

"Mmm," he rested his head on the comforter and shimmied his phone out of his pocket. "It's probably work. I left in the middle of a meeting."

They both stared as 'Sylvie Bell' scrolled across their faces on his lock screen.

(To be continued...)

ACKNOWLEDGEMENT

I'd like to thank my family and friends, especially my husband for not complaining when I stayed up all night writing or editing. We wouldn't be here without Natasha. Girl, you're my first fan and without your unyielding support I might have given up in 2019. Thank you Garry Michael who held my hand through the self-publishing process. His patience is unreal and he believed in me even when I didn't. I'd like to thank my creative half, Matt. His keen artistic eye fueled my creativity. I'd like to thank my Patrons for sticking by me for so long. You deserve this as much as I do. I'm thankful for my Wattpad readers who kept me real and for my ARC Team who has kept me positive as we charge forward.

And finally, I want to thank you, Reader. Without your support, I wouldn't even be here. Thank you for your time, for your patience, and for asking me to get the next book out already.

I look forward to hearing from you.

ABOUT THE AUTHOR

E. B. Slayer

E. B. Slayer lives in California with her husband and daughter. After getting a degree in business, she taught English in Japan for two years. Now she enjoys cooking with her family, and reading or gaming during her free time. When it comes to writing, she creates stories that feature Black women that are usually based on her dreams.

You can find her on social media. Visit her website to connect with her:
https://ebslayer.com